Praise for Patricia Harman and the Hope River Novels

Once a Midwife

"Patricia Harman . . . brings [...] Second World Wars upon the p[...] [...]ural America. . . . True love, family, friendsh[...] [...] [...]ture, culture, and babies. What more could a reader possibly w[...]."

—Alicia Bay Laurel, *New York Times* bestselling author of *Living on the Earth*

"Long after I turned the last page, the character of midwife Patience Hester stayed with me. She is with me still. For we all need role models like Patience—fiercely loyal, brave, and forgiving. *Once a Midwife* is a remarkable read, full of individuals to love and birth stories to inspire."

—Amy Wright Glenn, author of *Holding Space: On Loving, Dying and Letting Go*

The Midwife of Hope River

"Memoirist Harman (*Arms Wide Open*; *The Blue Cotton Gown*), herself a certified nurse-midwife, takes readers back to hardscrabble times and adds plenty of medical drama and a dash of romance to offer an uncommonly good piece of American historical fiction."

—*Library Journal*

"The moments of joy between new parents and their baby, between the mothers and the midwife, and between the midwife and her young assistant light up the pages. Amen, baby!"

—Penny Armstrong, CNM, author of *A Midwife's Story* and *A Wise Birth*

"*The Midwife of Hope River* . . . is still on my mind days after finishing. This is one I'll read again, more slowly next time."

—Johanna Moran, author of *The Wives of Henry Oades*

"A luminous novel of new beginnings, loss, love . . . and, yes, hope! Patricia Harman's all-too-human stories of birth mingle with the harsh realities of rural life in the 1930s. . . . A thoroughly satisfying read by a talented storyteller."

—Gay Courter, author of the *New York Times* bestsellers
The Midwife and *The Midwife's Advice*

"Harman has created such a striking and original heroine that pregnant women everywhere will be wanting Patience Murphy to deliver *their* babies, while the rest of us would consider ourselves lucky to call her friend."

—Theresa Brown, author of *Critical Care:
A New Nurse Faces Death, Life and Everything in Between*
and *New York Times* opinion columnist

The Reluctant Midwife

"This title is sure to appeal to fans of American historical fiction or anyone else looking for a story with plenty of emotion, spunk, and community spirit."

—*Library Journal*

"This poignant, powerful novel does not shy away from the gruesome facts of life and death. Fans of the BBC's *Call the Midwife* . . . will enjoy Harman's inspirational and introspective story."

—*Booklist*

"Laced with drama, accurate detail, and imagination, *The Reluctant Midwife* will educate and engage readers eager to further explore Hope River."

—Penny Armstrong, author of *The Midwife's Story*

"An entrancing saga of birth and rebirth, of people you come to love as they confront loss and guilt, poverty and fear, silence and doubt."

— Pamela Schoenewaldt, author of *Swimming in the Moon*

"A very enjoyable sequel to Patsy Harman's first novel, *The Midwife of Hope River*, this new book reconnects us with beloved characters from that story while introducing an appealing new midwife, Becky Myers."

— Teresa Brown, RN, author and
New York Times columnist

The Runaway Midwife

"*The Runaway Midwife* takes us on a journey from loss, grief, and guilt to love, forgiveness, and redemption."

— Mary McNear, *New York Times* bestselling author

"In the vein of *Where'd You Go, Bernadette* by Maria Semple and *Falling Uphill* by Wendy Nelson Tokunaga. . . . Full of hope and heart, this will appeal to anyone tempted by the thought of complete reinvention."

— *Booklist*

"A fast-paced, engrossing tale of a woman on the run from a bad marriage and an estranged daughter. . . . The characters are convincing, the plot tight and the conclusion convincing."

— Roberta Rich, author of *The Midwife of Venice*

"Fans of Maria Semple's *Where'd You Go, Bernadette* will enjoy this story of a woman's courageous reinvention."

— *Library Journal*

Once a Midwife

A Hope River Novel

Patricia Harman

WILLIAM MORROW
An Imprint of HarperCollins*Publishers*

P.S.™ is a trademark of HarperCollins Publishers.

ONCE A MIDWIFE. Copyright © 2018 by Patricia Harman. All rights
reserved. Printed in the United States of America. No part of this book
may be used or reproduced in any manner whatsoever without written
permission except in the case of brief quotations embodied in critical
articles and reviews. For information, address HarperCollins Publishers,
195 Broadway, New York, NY 10007.

HarperCollins books may be purchased for educational, business, or sales
promotional use. For information, please email the Special Markets
Department at SPsales@harpercollins.com.

FIRST EDITION

Designed by Diahann Sturge

Library of Congress Cataloging-in-Publication Data has been applied for.

ISBN 978-0-06-282557-5
ISBN 978-0-06-286933-3 (library edition)

19 20 21 22   LSC   10 9 8 7 6 5 4

Dedicated to the individuals of conscience and courage around the world. Stand tall.

Acknowledgments

I'd like to thank my husband, Tom Harman, and my friends and family for supporting and encouraging my writing.

A book is not a solitary effort and I appreciate all who have helped me. Foremost would be Lucia Macro, my editor at William Morrow (and her wonderful staff), and my wise agent, Elisabeth Weed.

And now a note to my readers. Life is not easy. I've said this before, but every day, I get a note from someone telling me how much they like my books, and this keeps me going.

I hope I encourage you too.

This is our purpose, to love, to lift up, to inspire each other.

*I have been lost before and come into these woods
to lay my body down.*

*And you have taken me in arms of light and sang to me,
rocked me gentle in the limbs of trees.*

*You have taken me in arms of light and sang to me
and wiped away my tears with new green leaves.*

From the private journal of Patience Hester
Liberty, West Virginia, U.S.A.
1941–1943

Winter

1

November 22, 1941

The Ties that Bind

"Mama, what's that?" my son, Danny, asks as a vehicle roars over the stone bridge that spans the Hope River, just outside of Liberty, West Virginia.

I look away from the newspapers in the rack set out on the sidewalk in front of Gold's Dry Goods and shake my head, swallowing fear. NAZIS TAKE SEVASTOPOL IN RELENTLESS ADVANCE TOWARD MOSCOW, the headlines read. I try to keep it from the children, but I'm worried about Europe's war spreading like a virus around the world. It's happened before. It could happen again.

In the last few weeks, the Germans have taken Kiev, Odessa, and Kharkov, places my veterinarian husband, Dr. Hester, has obsessively marked on the National Geographic Map taped inside our bedroom closet.

The roar gets louder as a bolt of lightning streaks down Main. Mira, my littlest, clings to my skirt. Sunny and Sue, the twins, stand hugging each other. "I don't know," I answer, catching our reflections in the store's shiny window, a Norman Rockwell painting, *Farm Woman and Children Go to Town*.

There she stands in her blue wool coat, small but strong. She wears wire-rim glasses that keep falling off her short nose and her straight shoulder-length brown hair is tied back with a ribbon, a pleasant rosy-cheeked woman, with her shoulders back, but not what you'd call a real looker.

Her brood of four is healthy and handsome too. The dark-haired boy wears a wool cap and clean overalls. Twin towheaded girls in red dresses with plaid jackets turn from the displays in the store window, and a smaller girl, with freckles, has a worn brown teddy bear tucked under her arm.

The vehicle spins around in front of the Saved by Jesus Baptist Church at the other end of Main and I can just make out a bright-red motorcycle with a sidecar of the same color. The driver, dressed in black leather with a scarlet scarf around his neck, races his motor and heads back this way. He stands on the seat like a circus performer and salutes as he passes.

"Wow!" Danny yells.

The motorcyclist stops again on the bridge over the Hope, revs the motor, and shoots back into town. He screeches to a stop in front of Gold's Dry Goods, then cuts the motor, slowly pulls off his helmet and goggles, then shakes his black curls.

"Ma," Mira whispers, squeezing my arm. "That's a woman!"

The female rider, with large brown eyes and skin the color of a newborn fawn, stands with one hand on her hip, swinging her leather helmet by its strap. A thin blond boy, with pale blue eyes, sits hunched and unsmiling in the sidecar.

"Bitsy!" I yell, jumping off the high curb and almost falling on my hands and knees in the street. "You're home!"

HAVE YOU EVER noticed that when you're reunited with an old friend, someone you've been through hard times with, it's like you've never been apart? That's how it is with Bitsy and me.

I turn the page in my journal. It's a beautiful book that I've had for years, but it won't last much longer. Even with my cramped cursive, it's almost full.

When I saw the bouquet of tulips embossed on the cover in Stenger's Pharmacy years ago, I had to have it, so I spent my last dollar and bought three! This was before Wall Street collapsed in '29 and I still had a dollar.

Inside the brown leather, in the top corner of each lined page is a small colored print of a poppy or a rose, a toad or snail, some living thing. There's a lock and a key that I keep on a long ribbon around my neck, along with my gold watch . . . the gold pocket watch Mrs. Kelly, my midwife teacher and friend, left me when she passed on.

My life has been difficult at times and the delicacy of the empty pages in the journal is what charmed me. The diary is like a friend I can talk to, some gentle, sensible woman . . . someone who would laugh at the things I laugh at and understand when I cried.

TONIGHT, AFTER MY husband, Daniel, and the children are in bed, Bitsy and I sit curled on the sofa in front of the fireplace with my old beagle, Sasha.

"Nice place," Bitsy says, looking around. I adjust my glasses to see what she sees: a fireplace with a large framed mirror on the mantel, an upright piano, a worn blue davenport, two rocking chairs, and a new electric floor lamp with an amber glass shade.

There's an oil painting of me as a girl hanging over the sofa and my husband's framed photographs of racehorses, farm horses, and hunting horses all over the walls. A braided red rug gives warmth to the room and there's a wood heater stove near the stairway.

"The stained-glass lamp is the first new thing that Dan and I have bought since the Great Depression," I tell my friend. "That's what they call it now, the *Great Depression*."

"It was *depressing* all right!" Bitsy laughs.

"So where the hell have you been?" I ask. "No phone calls. Not even a postcard."

"You really want to know?"

"Well, yes! And who's the boy?"

"The whole story?"

"Maybe the short version. It's been almost ten years." I start to laugh, but stop when I see my friend's face.

"What?" I ask, touching her on the knee. "*What?*"

My friend wipes her eyes. "I'm so ashamed."

"Tell me. Start at the beginning." I scoot over and put my arm around her. "You left West Virginia with Byrd Bowlin, your sweetheart, the night the KKK came to our farm. After what happened, I couldn't blame you."

Bitsy's brown eyes focus on the flames. "Byrd and I were married by a justice of the peace a week after we got to Philly," she recalls. "I know you thought we were already shacking up, but you were wrong. There was nothing but kissing going on, and not much of that.

"We lived with my brother, Thomas, at first, and he got Byrd a job as an electric-trolley-car driver, but it turned out because of the economy people didn't have the money to ride trolleys. Since Byrd was new and a Negro, he was transferred to shoveling coal at the power plant.

"All day long Byrd shoveled coal for the electric cars, but within a month he quit. It was as bad as being a miner, he told me. At first, he went out every day looking for work, walked the streets, stood in line at the unemployment office, but no one was hiring. Fifty percent of the colored men in Philadelphia were unemployed, thirty percent of the whites. I guess it was the same all over.

"Thomas was supporting us, but it was hard on Byrd's pride. Finally, I got a job in a colored woman's beauty shop called Sweet Pea's Salon and we rented a studio apartment for just $12 a month.

"Mostly I just washed hair, oiled it, and swept up. Miss Evelyn, the owner, was from Harlem. I'm not sure she was even trained as a beautician, but she sure knew what she was doing.

"Byrd didn't like it. He said a woman's place was in the home, and since *he* was the man, *he* should be working. That's when things started going downhill. Whenever I got paid, he'd take the money. He said he'd buy groceries, but he gambled and drank.

"I tried to hide the cash in my brassiere or my loafers, but he knew how much I made and he'd . . ." She glances at me and wipes her eyes again. "He'd make me strip until he found the cash. Then to punish me he'd force me to kneel naked on the cold floor all night." Here she stops and rubs her knees as if she still feels the pain.

"Oh, Bitsy!" I say. "I'm so sorry. Why didn't you come home to me?"

"I wanted to, but Byrd wouldn't think of it. Also we had no money. Finally, I quit the salon; thinking if we were broke, maybe Byrd would start looking for work again, but this was the thirties, remember. Most young colored fellows were just sitting around on their front porches drinking beer or shooting craps.

"Then one day he hopped a freight train for the West Coast like the other hoboes. I never heard from him again . . . my heart was broken." She puts her hand on her chest and looks in my eyes for a long time. "My heart . . ." she says again, as if trying to hold the shattered pieces together.

For a moment I say nothing . . . then, "That's enough for tonight. You must be tired. You can sleep here on the sofa. You can sleep here forever. You are home now, Bitsy. You are home."

2

November 23, 1941

Baby Cabin

Because I stayed up late talking with Bitsy and then wrote in my journal, I'm tired this morning. It was after midnight when we went to bed and I didn't get to ask where she picked up the boy. All I learned is his name, Willie, and that he's her ward.

Outside, Sasha barks up a storm and the children call, "Ma. Ma. There's a car in the drive!"

I lift myself out of the kitchen chair too fast and a moan comes out. Sometimes I can rise with little pain if I do so carefully, but not today. My left knee has never been right since I was kicked when helping my veterinarian husband do tuberculin testing on Mr. Dresher's cows. That was four years ago, and we were dead broke, so I didn't go to the hospital in Torrington. What would they have done anyway?

When I look out the front window I see a new burgundy Cadillac crossing the wooden bridge over Salt Creek. The vehicle is unfamiliar, but as Union County's midwife, these interruptions are not unexpected. What shocks me is the gleaming luxury of the new auto.

"Bitsy," I yell to my friend who's upstairs making beds.

"We got company, probably someone coming for the midwives." I say it like this, as if we've been doing deliveries together for the last decade, but in reality she was only my assistant for ten or twelve months. This was back in '29, the year of the crash.

"What can we do with the children?" she asks. "We can't take them with us."

"No, we don't have to *go* anywhere. Didn't you see the little log cabin behind the farmhouse? The cabin is a place where women come to have their babies. Daniel and Dr. Blum built it for me when our family expanded and we adopted the twins. We'd better get a move on."

"Kids," I announce as we come out on the porch, "Aunt Bitsy and I are going to be in the Baby Cabin. You know what that means. Don't interrupt us unless someone is bleeding or the house is on fire."

"Do we need Mrs. Kelly's birth satchel?" Bitsy asks.

"It's already out there." I smile, realizing that more than a decade ago, when we did deliveries together, we always carried the medical bag. "I only use it now when I go to home births. If the women come to me, the cabin is equipped with everything we need, except hot water . . . I still have to carry that from the kitchen."

"Sir, do you need assistance?" I ask as **we** approach the Caddy. A man wearing a natty brown **tweed** suit and a brown fedora gets out, slams the door, and wipes his very pink brow. The woman inside wears a green floppy hat that covers her face.

"Oh, thank God. Are you the midwives? I'm Mr. Faye. We just drove down from Pittsburgh for a Sunday ride in the country and now my lady friend, Opal, has gone into labor. We stopped in Liberty, but there's no hospital. Someone at the Mountain Top Diner told us about you. The thing is; she's too early. Her physician at West Penn Hospital says she's due near the end of January."

Bitsy stares at the man, then looks at me as we both calculate how premature the baby will be: almost two months . . . unless the doctor is wrong.

"Well, you've come to the right place. We have a little lying-in home on the farm that we call the Baby Cabin. Would you like to see it? Why don't you bring Opal inside and I can at least examine her and tell you what I think. Maybe there's time to get her to Boone Memorial in Torrington."

Bitsy is way ahead of me. She's already assisting Opal, who's of African descent, out of the auto and guiding her along the stone path toward the cabin. The expectant mother is a look-alike for a young Marian Anderson, the famous colored opera singer.

I catch up with them at the porch just as Opal has a contraction.

"Oh, baby doll. I'm so sorry," Mr. Faye says, the leather suitcase banging against his legs as he runs to get the door. From the look of his heavy tweed suit, his shiny shoes, and his fancy auto, he's a city slicker for sure.

Just as we get Opal inside, she gives a great grunt and

her water bag breaks, but having set up the Baby Cabin for just such eventualities, I grab a handful of folded rags and wipe up the mess. The fluid is clear and that's a good thing.

"Oh my God!" Opal waves one hand in a frantic way as if trying to bat the pain away, and then leans down with both hands on her knees. "*Something's coming!*"

Single Footling Breech

*B*itsy, who's as sharp as a briar, pulls back the covers on the double bed, throws a towel on the sheet, and helps the woman pull down her wet bloomers.

"Aghhhhhhh!" Opal bellows, and bears down. I reach for a packet of sterile rubber gloves, intending to do a vaginal exam, but catch my breath when I see a tiny foot at the opening.

"I think I'm going to be ill," the man says, and backs out of the door.

"It's a single footling," Bitsy whispers, gently pinching the infant's blue foot to see if it still has circulation. The baby kicks her hand away, a good sign.

"We have to break up the breech," I say. "I've seen it done twice by Mrs. Kelly."

Quickly, I go to the cupboard and get out the birth pack, sterilized in the oven a week ago. Then, while my friend gets Opal more comfortable, I pull over the wooden table on wheels that our friend, Dr. Blum, made for me. I wash my hands and untie the pack. Inside is a simple collection of things we'll need for the birth (and a few we hope we don't need).

Bitsy, as if she does this every day, quickly lays out our supplies; scissors, a rubber suction syringe, cotton tape to tie off the cord, and a bowl for the placenta. There's also a container of oil that I use to help the baby slide out and equipment for stitching if we need it.

With rubber gloves on, I work one finger in and release the second leg. Then, as quick as a wink the rest of the body slides out as far as the umbilical cord.

"It's a boy, Opal," Bitsy says. "We can tell the sex already. You're doing great!"

Before I even ask her, Bitsy has the patient's buttocks on the edge of the bed and we allow the weight of the baby to help with the delivery. My assistant supports the tiny body while I keep one hand on the patient's lower abdomen. With a breech, as with any delivery, we must keep the head flexed. My friend smiles and I smile too. We're working as a team, as we used to do. "Once a midwife, always a midwife!" I whisper.

"Left arm. Right arm," I say to myself as I gently turn the baby, and then lift him up until the chin comes out and he's free. "You did it, Opal!" I tell her. Bitsy quickly wraps the tiny wailing boy and lays him on his mother's chest.

"Oh blessed God," she whispers. "Is he okay?"

"Yes, hear him cry!" Bitsy says. "He's fit as a fiddle."

"The baby is beautiful, honey," I say, ten minutes later, as I take him back from his mom, weigh him on my hanging scale, and give him a quick exam. He's scrawny and brown like Opal, has all his fingers and toes and regular facial features. I check his palate, which is intact, and I smile when he sucks on my finger. If I'd had to guess I'd have said he's a few weeks early, but not two whole months.

While I'm doing the newborn assessment, Bitsy helps the new mom take off the rest of her clothes and re-dress in one of the flowered nightgowns I keep on hand for such occasions. Then we place the crying infant on the breast and cover both mother and baby with a quilt.

The new mother softly touches his cheek. He turns his head toward her, rooting for milk. "Oh!" says Opal, startled. "Does he want food already?"

"Yes. All warm-blooded animals are ready to eat as soon as they're born. A healthy human baby is no different from a colt or a lamb and even though you don't have much milk yet, the sucking will bring it on."

Outside, the burgundy Cadillac roars into life. My partner and I look at each other and step to the window. *Now, where is the man going?* I ask myself. *Doesn't he want to see his new baby?*

Two hours later, the baby's father still hasn't come back. "Where could he be?" I wonder under my breath.

"Maybe he went back into Liberty to get some smokes or to celebrate with a beer?" Bitsy guesses.

I run back over to the farmhouse and find the children listening to *The Lone Ranger* on the radio. *"From out of the past come the thundering hoofbeats of the great horse, Silver! The Lone Ranger rides again!"*

Willie, who appears to be only a few years older than the girls, has found three cans of Campbell's chicken soup in the pantry and laid them on the counter, ready for dinner. He's a resourceful little man and since my husband, Daniel, is out on a vet call, the lad has apparently taken charge.

"Hi, kids," I call from the kitchen. "Were you good?"

"Yes, Mom!" they all cry, then go back to their program.

"Thank you for getting the soup out, Willie. I keep it around for just this sort of day. I can also open a quart jar of home-canned tomatoes and there's some fresh-baked bread and butter in the pantry. We just had a baby boy in the Baby Cabin, only five pounds but he's healthy. Did you see where the father went, the man in the fancy car? Did he say anything?"

Willie, responsibly hands me a folded piece of paper, and I open it, feeling puzzled.

All the note says is "Thank you for delivering the baby and please take care of Opal. Tell her I love her." There are five twenty-dollar bills folded inside, more money than I've ever seen at one time.

"Is the man coming back?" I ask.

Willie shakes his head no and his blond hair falls over his forehead.

"Maybe he was going into town to get the baby some clothes and blankets."

"I doubt it."

"Why?"

"Because," Willie says sadly, "he didn't look me in the eye."

November 23, 1941

*Male infant born to a young colored girl, Opal
Johnson of Pittsburgh, brought to our Baby
Cabin by her companion, a white man named
Sonny Faye. The baby was thought to be several
months premature and was a single footling
breech, but Bitsy Proudfoot and I delivered it
without difficulty.*

*The infant weighed 5 pounds, 8 ounces and
breathed right away. I would guess that he's close
to 36 weeks. Placenta delivered spontaneously.
Blood loss average. No vaginal tears.*

*Mr. Faye left one hundred dollars with a
note and drove away in his sparkling dark red
convertible. Opal has not yet given the baby a
name, but he's nursing just fine.*

Hush-a-Bye

"Come on, kids, do you want to see the new baby? The
mama says it's okay."

After our noon meal, I take the children over to the
Baby Cabin. This is something special that my young
ones enjoy and it makes me smile. They are so tender and
respectful. Willie says he's never seen a newborn before

and his pale blue eyes, in his very white face, are round and shining.

"Touch him," Mira, my six-year-old, says, pulling the big boy over to the cradle by the sleeve. He holds back, but she insists. Opal is patient and proud. She still hasn't asked about her mister and this strikes me as odd, but maybe she assumes that because he's a man, he doesn't want to be around childbirth.

The Hope River Valley has changed that way since I've been the midwife. Not often, but sometimes, the father will at least stay in the room and hold his laboring wife's hand. When I began attending births fifteen years ago, that *never* happened, and I'll admit, the first father I ever allowed at a delivery fainted and fell on the floor. That was Mr. Macintosh, the owner of the now defunct Macintosh Coal Company.

"See," Mira says to Willie. "See how soft he is. Touch his little hand."

Finally the boy reaches out with one finger. He strokes the baby's palm and the infant's tiny fingers hold on. Willie's mouth is half-open, but he doesn't say a word.

"Any sign of the father?" Bitsy whispers when the children are gone and we're standing out on the steps of the Baby Cabin.

"Nope." I shake my head and hand her the note.

"*Thank you for delivering the baby and please take care of Opal. Tell her I love her,*" she reads out loud, and frowns. Then I reach in my apron pocket and hand her the pile of twenties.

"Lordy!" says Bitsy.

"The money was wrapped in the note."

"Lordy!" she exclaims again. "I've haven't seen such a pile of green since I left Bricktop's, but that was on the gambling table and didn't belong to any one person."

"I'll get the kids fed and in bed. Willie told me you allow him to stay up to listen to *The Grand Ole Opry*."

"Only until nine."

I don't even ask about the gambling table because I'm picking up a dim hum of a motorcar coming this way.

"Do you hear that? A vehicle. Maybe Mr. Faye's coming back." An auto bumps into the drive, but it's not Mr. Faye, it's my husband, Daniel Hester, veterinarian surgeon, in his old Model T. I watch as he gets out of the vehicle. He's a tall, thin man, over six feet, with a straight back, and I always feel warm when I see him.

"Who is it?" Opal calls. "Is it Sonny?"

"No, honey, it's Mr. Hester, Patience's husband," Bitsy tells her, reentering the cabin. "We don't know where your man went, but he did leave a note," she explains.

"Is the note for me?" Opal asks.

"Actually, I think it's for all of us. Maybe mostly for you." I go to the bedside, but my hand is cemented into my pocket. I don't want to give the callous message to the new mother. It seems so cold, the rich white man leaving his colored woman and mulatto baby behind.

Bitsy takes charge and sits on the edge of the bed. "Mr. Faye left you a note and some money. One hundred dollars. Miss Patience should keep ten for the delivery. Do you have somewhere to go? Do you have family in Pittsburgh?"

Opal reads the words and finally understands. She was so strong for the birth, so calm and determined, but now she crumbles like a piece of cornbread.

"That's all? A thank you and a hundred dollars!" she says with tears running down her face.

"Do you have kin? Someone we could call?" I ask. "I have a phone in the house."

Here Bitsy looks impressed. Twelve years ago, when we lived together in the house with the blue door at the end of Wild Rose Road, we didn't have a telephone. No electricity either.

"Hush. Hush," I say to Opal. "I know you're hurt, but you need to stay calm for your baby. If you don't have friends or family, we'll figure something out. You're safe here and with the cows and chickens and our canned vegetables in the cellar we always have enough to eat."

Bitsy brings the infant to feed again. "*Hush-a-bye, don't you cry,*" Bitsy sings, stroking the young mother's hair. "*Go to sleep, little baby.*" I look around at the pleasant space, the golden logs and the red and white quilt on the bed, the rocking chair, the cot in the corner, the cradle, all hand built by Daniel and our friend Dr. Blum and I come in on the next line. "*When you wake, you shall have, all the pretty little horses. Blacks and bays, dapples and grays, all the pretty little horses . . .*"

Back at the house, I warm up what's left of the soup on the cast-iron cookstove and tell Daniel the news. Willie has fallen asleep on the sofa curled around our dog, Sasha.

"The bastard just left his sweetheart and his new baby?" Dan exclaims under his breath, his eyes flashing. "What's she going to do? Does she have family? I guess we'll have to drive her home to Pittsburgh, assuming she has a home." He's concerned about our patient, but happy too that Bitsy's back, because he knows how close we were.

I cover Willie with the blue-and-white quilt in the flying-goose pattern that I made myself when I first moved to West Virginia, and move to turn off the news, but Dan raises his hand signaling me to wait.

On the radio, Edward R. Murrow summarizes in his deep voice the latest developments in Europe, "Adolf Hitler, Chancellor of Germany, announced today that all Jewish establishments are ordered to display a Jewish star on the doors and windows . . ." Dan shakes his head . . . "Go ahead," he says sadly, and I turn off the radio.

"You okay?" I ask Daniel. "You've had a long day. Up at seven in the morning, home after nine. And then to return to all this! I didn't tell you the rest . . . Mr. Faye left a hundred dollars and a thank-you note. Bitsy says most of it is for the mother, and I guess that's right." I lay the five twenties on the table.

"Holy cow!" He touches the crisp green bills with his big work-roughened hands. He glances at me and gives me his crooked smile. "We could do a lot with this . . ."

I put my hand over his. "I know, but it's for Opal."

After I clean up the kitchen, I go back to check the Baby Cabin one more time. "She's doing well," Bitsy tells me in a hushed voice. "Her uterus is three finger-breaths below the belly button and the bleeding is minimal. She nursed one more time by herself. I'm going to go over to wash up and kiss Willie good night, then I'll sleep here on the cot.

Is Dr. Hester okay with us staying for a few days? I don't know what to do about Opal."

"He's fine about it. He was off making rounds all day and is exhausted, but he suggested we could drive Opal to Pittsburgh in my old Oldsmobile tomorrow if she has family there."

"That would be good." Bitsy grins, showing her white teeth. "I'd hate to take her in the sidecar on the motorcycle."

3

Buffalo Girls

*A*t ten we hit the sack, Bitsy in the Baby Cabin and me back in the farmhouse, but I don't sleep well. I toss and turn, pulling the covers off Daniel, reliving in half dreams the last time Bitsy and I were together at the house on Wild Rose Road.

It was eleven years ago, the fall of 1930. We'd returned late from a delivery and were just going to bed when three vehicles drove up. Eight men got out wearing white pointed hoods, and surrounded our house.

"Buffalo girls won't you come out tonight. Come out tonight. Come out tonight," the men warble. Bitsy and I cower behind the curtains, shushing the dogs. Bitsy is crying. "I'm so sorry, Patience," she says . . . as if it were her fault that the racists are after us.

Then there's a blazing cross on the lawn and the picket fence burns. The drunken bastards throw torches at the house, threatening, in rough voices, to rape us or burn us out.

"*Buffalo girls won't you come out tonight,*" the guys sing, wild with drink. The laughter crescendos, the fire flares, and more flaming pickets twirl toward our roof.

"Come on, Bitsy, we have to get out of here. Bring your rifle," I whisper.

Scuttling like crabs in the dark, we crawl out the back door and make it to the barn, but when we're mounted on our horse, Star, I see two white feed sacks hanging on a nail and I change the plan. We tear holes in the sack for our eyes and put them over our heads. "I'm tired of running," I hiss. "I've been running my whole life."

If there were music to this scene, it would be something from a John Wayne movie. "Hold on," I growl, filled with rage, and I nudge our horse into a canter and out the barn door. I have no idea what I'm doing. I just don't feel like sneaking away, coming back in the morning to find the KKK has turned our sweet little home into a pile of ashes.

"You fucking Pillow Heads!" I yell the worst words I can think of as we gallop into the firelight, right up to the knot of men, anger and fear coming out of me in a low roar.

"You fucking Pillow Heads!" my friend echoes, and fires her gun in the air.

The singing comes to an abrupt halt. The men are confused. Who are these new masked riders? Bitsy and I, on top of the wild-eyed beast, tower over them.

"You have business here?" I snarl in the lowest, gruffest voice I can work up, nudging Star farther into the crowd.

Bitsy reaches down and strips off one man's hood. He's too startled to speak, covers his face, and jumps into his truck.

"Coward!" I yell through my dusty feed sack. Bitsy gets into the spirit of things and fires into the air twice more. Flames, I am sure, are shooting out of the top of my head and I'm reckless with fury.

I dance Star around as I pull off three more hoods. The other men duck down where I can't reach them and bump into one another as they scuttle like crabs toward their cars.

"That's right, *run*! Put your coward tails between your legs and hit the road."

I sit up in bed, laughing at the vision of Bitsy and me chasing the Klan off. Daniel still sleeps, snoring softly.

There's a shadow in our open bedroom door. Susie, my anxious adopted daughter, stands there in her white nightgown. "I'm sorry, Mama. I peed the bed."

4

November 26, 1941

A Plan

If I had to choose one electric appliance, the Maytag would be it. I could do without electric lights. Kerosene lamps work fine if you keep the globes clean and trim the wicks daily. I could do without the Frigidaire. The spring-house at my little farm on Wild Rose Road kept things quite cold, but the washer is a godsend. Without it, I would spend all day pumping and hauling water, scrubbing on the washboard and hanging clothes on the line.

When the Maytag is loaded and agitating, I add the Borax and my special ingredient, lye, then I leave Daniel serving breakfast to a tableful of kids and take a tray of coffee and porridge over to the Baby Cabin.

"Everything okay?" I whisper as I put the tray on the rolling table. Bitsy is up and dressed, but Opal still sleeps. The poor thing is exhausted or just doesn't want to wake up and remember that the man she loved has abandoned her.

Bitsy waves me to the door and we step out on the stoop. "She has no one. Her family disowned her. Her father said she'd come to no good when she moved to Pittsburgh to get a job. After that she was afraid to tell her parents she was pregnant with a white man's baby."

"I'm not surprised," I answer. "Even in Pittsburgh, where it's against the law to segregate hotels and restaurants, not everyone accepts mixed races."

"Yeah, her parents are from Connellsville, a small industrial town outside of Pittsburgh, and they're very closed-minded. She can't go back."

I tighten my mouth. "How did she get involved with this Sonny Faye anyway?"

"She was a maid at the William Penn Hotel. Sonny is one of the managers. He told her he loved her, but because of his position, they can't wed. She's been living in a room in the basement of the William Penn for the last five months."

"Well, what was the plan? What were they going to do with the baby?"

"He was going to rent her an apartment. She'd already looked in the paper and made a list of places she wanted to see, then they went on this country ride and . . . well, you know the rest."

We sit down on the cabin steps. There's a chill wind but we rest on each other and I can hear the children laughing in the house when the kitchen door opens and my nine-year-old, Danny, comes out to feed the chickens.

"Do you want to use the outhouse and go in and wash up?" I ask Bitsy. "Willie seems to be doing fine. He's reading my Hans Christian Andersen book. What's his story anyway? Who is he?"

"You don't know? I thought you'd know right away. He looks just like Katherine. Katherine MacIntosh."

"I see it now. But where's his mother . . . Katherine?"

"Dead," Bitsy tells me, not sugarcoating it.

"Oh, no! She was the first patient you and I delivered together. Willie was the baby I thought would be stillborn. What happened to his beautiful mom?"

"Another long story. I'll tell you later. It's been a couple of years. Right now I'm going for a ride on my motorcycle, and stop to see the Millers out at Hazel Patch," she says.

"Oh, Bitsy, those folks are all gone. During the deepest part of the Depression everyone left, going north and west looking for work. It's a ghost town now."

"Well, I have to find *somewhere* to live."

"Why don't you just stay with us? We'll work something out. We always do."

"No," Bitsy says. "I came home to the Hope River and to you because you're all the family I have, but I'm not going to mooch off you and Daniel forever. I have to find my own place. I've got to ride. . . . It will help me think."

Two hours later, I'm battling wet sheets at the clothesline when Bitsy roars into the drive. She hops off her motorcycle and removes her helmet. "I have a plan," she says, full of energy, "but I'll need a horse and cart."

Daniel strolls over, along with Willie, who carries a basket. "Look," he says to Bitsy. "I've been helping Dr. Hester gather eggs." He's so proud you'd think he'd laid them himself.

"I have a Model T and a tractor with a hay wagon," Dan says. "What do you have in mind, Miss Bitsy?"

"I found us a place to live!" she says. "Willie, Opal, the baby and I are moving to Hazel Patch!"

"Oh, Bitsy. You don't have to do that. Those houses have been abandoned for years and the hooligans from town have thrown rocks through the windows. Opal can stay here too, as long as she needs to."

I glance at Daniel, knowing he already feels the house is too crowded and knowing we don't have the money to take care of everyone. He raises his eyebrows in response, as if to say, *Really?*

"I appreciate your hospitality, but I've thought it all out," Bitsy declares. "We'll split the $100 that Mr. Faye left. That will give Opal and I a nest egg to get started.

"I'll need some help getting one of the houses in Hazel Patch fixed up," Bitsy goes on. "The old Bowlin place is in the best shape. There's still a cookstove in the kitchen and only one broken window."

5

The Drums of War

Yesterday, Bitsy and I were in Liberty picking up supplies for her new home and as we crossed Main, we heard male voices in heated discussion. There were six men arguing under the bare trees in the courthouse park, smoking cigarettes and talking politics.

"That bastard Roosevelt! The U.S.S. *Ruben James* should have never been there in the first place!" says one tall, lean fellow I've never seen before. "Two dozen American sailors dead and another hundred injured when the ship was attacked by a damned German U-boat; even one boy from West Virginia got it. FDR has been *pushing* this war since he rammed the Lend Lease Act through Congress."

"Charles Lindbergh says getting us involved in Europe's war is a conspiracy to keep the president in the White House for another four years," adds a young man with red hair, who I recognize as one of the clerks from the feed store. "No other president has stayed for three terms. Does he want to be king?" A ripple of laughter follows.

"What about that little runt Hitler? He's nuttier than a bed bug in June. You want him running the world?" a fellow wearing a black wool coat and a crisp wool fedora puts in quietly and I realize it is Joseph Gold, the owner of Gold's Dry Goods.

"Well, he wants to keep the white race pure. You don't want a bunch of mongrels, do you?" another man growls. I recognize him too, one of the Bishop brothers, always trouble.

My grip through my friend's arm tightens. I feel protective of Bitsy when talk comes to racial matters.

"Well, what are we going to do?" a thin razorback, with a patch over one eye, asks. "Wait until the Krauts land on our shores and then wake up and say, *By golly!*"

"Hitler's already taken over most of Europe. If England and France fall, do you think he'll stop there?" the redhead argues.

"Let's get out of here," Bitsy whispers. "Those good ol' boys don't even know Germany already captured France."

When I get home, I find Daniel reading the *Torrington Times* in the kitchen. He glares at the headlines with disgust. NO NEW SURVIVORS ON THE U.S.S. RUBEN JAMES. "It's a follow-up to the article a few weeks ago," he says, "when the Nazi submarine destroyed our ship."

"Bitsy and I heard men arguing about it on the courthouse lawn today. Some blamed Hitler. Some blamed the president. They said FDR has been goading the Germans by sending our ships across the Atlantic with supplies for the Brits."

"I have to say, I agree," Dan says. "Roosevelt is spouting rhetoric about staying out of the war, but if he hadn't set up the Lend Lease Act, our destroyer, the *Ruben James*, wouldn't have been with the British convoy in the first place.

"*What did he think was going to happen?* Hitler was just going to let munitions and supplies be shipped from the U.S. across the Atlantic into the hands of his enemies?" He wads the paper into a ball and throws it across the room, then stands and stares out the window, tightening his jaw, as if he sees Judgment Day coming.

National Savior

I pull a kitchen chair out, sit down, and put my arm around my husband. Daniel was a cavalry soldier in the Great War. He was fresh off the farm and put in charge of the horses.

The first day I met him he described how he saw thousands of the animals slaughtered. "It was hell for them," he told me with tears in his eyes. "They stumbled through mud and rain to bring us supplies. I watched them die of exhaustion, broken bones, bloody wounds, and tetanus.

There was nothing I could do. They should never have been there in the first place. Modern weapons made them sitting ducks."

"So, I know war has been brewing for years," I go on. "The Germans were beaten back in the Great War. What's made them so aggressive?"

Daniel, a bit of a history buff, leans back in his chair. "Well, Germany lost all of their colonies in Africa and thirteen percent of their territory in Europe with the Treaty of Versailles, and then they were hit hard by the Great Depression. Millions of people were out of work, just like here, and the mood was grim. Their humiliating defeat was still fresh in their minds. Germans are a proud people." Here he smiles. "I know that from living with my grandparents. . . .

"During the Depression, ordinary Germans lost confidence in their government. They called their representatives the 'Do Nothings.' The conditions were perfect for the rise of a new party, the National Socialist German Workers Party."

"Sounds like something I'd join in my younger days in Pittsburgh," I admit, and Dan smiles his lopsided smile.

"Yeah, probably!" he agrees. "More coffee?" He pours us both another cup. "NAZI is the abbreviation for their party, innocent enough in German, *Nationalsozialist.* Adolf Hitler, as head of the party, rose to power because he stood for the workingman. He was former military and a spellbinding speaker.

"Remember, this is during the deepest part of the Depression. Hitler attracted a following of people desperate for change. He promised a better life for everyone. He'd make Germany great again, a superpower like it once was. There'd be jobs for all. They'd throw non-Germans out. Limit immigration."

"So Hitler was elected by democratic vote?"

"Not exactly, but his party was. Hitler was appointed chancellor, which is like the prime minister in Britain, and most of the people believed they'd found their national savior."

"He seems like a madman to me!" I exclaim. "Do you think the German people realize he's trying to conquer the world? That's not the same as making Germany great again."

My husband shrugs, but I swallow hard. "I don't like it, Dan. People are saying it's inevitable that the U.S. will get involved."

"I don't like it either, Patience. These are dangerous times and people think the solution is easy. Just battle it out until the Germans capitulate. But don't worry about me, Patience. I told myself after the Great War, I'd never fight again." He stands and walks to the sink, and then he says it again: "I won't go, Patience. If they call me up, I won't go!"

December 7, 1941

America First

As I walk across the white frosted grass to the chicken house, the sun rises orange in the clear blue sky and despite the cold I think how glad I am to live with such beauty. . . . When I first came to the Hope River Valley from Pittsburgh, Mrs. Kelly and I were on the lam and I thought of West Virginia as the Siberia of America, a good place to hide, somewhere so poor and backward no one would ever want to live here. Now the comfort of these green mountains wraps around me like a quilt.

Across the yard, I can hear Daniel in the barn talking to the cows as he throws hay down from the loft.

"Here chick, chick, chickies," I call as I fill my bucket with cracked corn from the metal bin. I open the door to let the chickens out of the henhouse.

"Cluck. Cluckity-cluck-cluck," the reds answer in their soft, soothing voices. Though there are fifty of them, they are like pets or maybe friends. Only one worries me. She's the runt and is often picked on until her yellow feet bleed. If the bullying continues, I'll have to put her in a cage by herself where the others can't get to her.

By noon, Dan has dropped the kids off at the little house Bitsy has fixed up in Hazel Patch and I've changed into a gray skirt and blue sweater. It's Sunday, but we're not going to church. We're on our way to a meeting of the American First Committee in Liberty.

"Hurry, up Patience," Dan calls to me as he puts out our beagle, Sasha, and banks the stove. "We don't want to be late or miss the speech. B.K. Bittman has gone to a lot of trouble to get this event set up. America First is a coalition of pacifists, progressives, and conservatives that oppose the U.S. getting in the war. It's right up our line. There are close to a million members."

Once at the schoolhouse, we find seats near the back and I'm surprised to see about thirty people present. I glance around the room to see who's here. Sitting up front are our good friends Becky and Isaac Blum, a handsome couple in their forties, both with dark curly hair. Becky's a registered nurse and her husband's a physician.

Years ago, we all lived together when I was pregnant with Mira and bleeding. Becky, in fact, took over the home births in the county, since I was on bed rest. Dr. Blum was off his rocker for a while, but he's fine now.

Then five years ago, Becky and Isaac, Daniel and I, along with our neighbors, the Maddocks, adopted the four little Hucknell sisters, Sonya, Sally, Sunny, and Sue, after their parents and little baby brother were killed in the forest fire of '35.

I wave at Becky, and when she smiles I remember how much I miss her. We're all so busy lately, working, taking care of our families. . . . Becky and Isaac run the infirmary at White Rock Civilian Conservation Camp on the other side of the county.

B.K. Bittman, the grocer, is here with his wife, Lilly, along with Ida May, the town hairdresser. Mr. Stenger, the balding pharmacist, and his wife, Mrs. Stenger, are sitting next to Mr. Linkous, the young lawyer. Even One-Arm Wetsel is present, standing in back next to Sheriff Hardman, who looks the crowd over, rubbing the scar on his chin, the thin red line that came from a knife fight.

The guest speaker, Senator Holt of Weston, West Virginia (tall, shock of white hair, very pink face), begins his speech as if he's standing before Congress.

"Shall the United States become a merchant of death?" Holt asks rhetorically in a booming voice. Daniel leans forward. "My fellow Americans," the speaker continues, adjusting his spectacles, "We're being *bamboozled*! No nation threatens us! President Roosevelt and his cronies are trying to convince people that if we don't enter the war in Europe, the U.S. will be Germany's next target, but that's not the case and has never been. This is a slippery slope, folks.

"Whether or not we do enter the war," the senator goes on, looking in the eyes of his audience, "rests upon the shoulders of you in this meeting and upon meetings like this all across the country. By the latest polls, only one in four Americans favors the U.S. going to war. *We must not let big business and big government push us into this*. We can only lose."

B.K. stands up. "Thank you so much, sir. We're honored that you came out of your way to give this presentation. I'd like now to open the floor to questions and comments."

Mr. Linkous stands first. "I think the whole affair should be Europe's problem. Germany wasn't treated fairly after the last war. A lot of their territory was taken away. Now they just want it back." Several in the audience echo his sentiments by calling out. "Hear, hear!" and then Lucille Stenger, the pharmacist's wife, rises.

"I agree that war is not the best solution, but when you have a madman like Adolf Hitler on the rise, we can't afford to sit idle. America is a powerful country and if we assist Great Britain and France, we can turn the tide. . . . I'll tell you something else. My family comes from Poland; some

of them still live there. Have you heard about the extermi-
nation camps where they kill the Jews? This war isn't just
about Britain or France and losing their empires; it's about
humanity. Do we want a maniac like Hitler running the
world?" She plunks her heavy bottom down on the chair

"Oh, that's just Roosevelt's propaganda and reporters
trying to sell papers," responds a voice in back. "It's horse
manure. Nothin' like that ever happened. If Jews in Poland
were being slaughtered I think the hell we would know
about it."

I whip around to see Aran Bishop in his coveralls and
flannel shirt. He ran against Sheriff Hardman in the elec-
tion last year and lost by only a few hundred votes. His
meek blond wife, Cora, twenty years his junior, gives him
the elbow, warning him to watch his language.

"Hear! Hear!" a few fellows cheer, and then more people
speak up. "Yeah, half the things you hear in the paper, or
on the radio, are outright lies."

"We should mind our own business!"

"We've got to take care of our own, not spend our hard-
earned cash on some European squabble."

Finally, we break for coffee and cake served by the
Methodist Women.

Then at three, B.K. gets everyone to sit down again and
Senator Holt comes to the front.

"Again, thank you all for coming," he says. "Americans
must show courage! If you believe in an independent des-
tiny for our country, if you believe that we should *not* enter
Europe's war, we ask you to sign this petition and join
America First!"

Just then the oak doors of the school slam open and we all turn around. It's Loonie Tinkshell from the Texaco Station almost running down the aisle. Dan and I look at each other. Loonie hands the speaker a piece of paper and the speaker's face goes white.

Senator Holt turns to B.K., whispers something, and then returns to the podium.

"Ladies and gentlemen, this meeting is over," the senator states abruptly. "I ask that you leave in an orderly fashion and drive straight home with great care. . . . I have just been handed a telegram from Washington that says that this morning at seven forty-eight A.M., Hawaii Time, the Japanese Air Force bombed the U.S. naval base at Pearl Harbor. The attack is still going on. Thousands of sailors and officers are dead, as well as civilians. What we say here is no longer of consequence. *God be with you all. God bless America.*"

6

War

One minute the war was theoretical, the next it was real. As Dan and I walked silently hand in hand out to our auto it started to snow, and the ride home was as somber as if we'd just been to a funeral. When I looked over at Dan, his knuckles were white on the steering wheel and his face was a mask; what was under the mask, I did not know.

When we got to Hazel Patch, we learned that Bitsy, Opal, and the children had already heard about the attack. Everyone was glued to the old console radio that Mr. Gold of Gold's Dry Goods had given Bitsy. Mira and Susie ran into my arms.

"*Who's Pearl Harbor, Mommy?* Do we know her?" Mira asks, her freckles standing out in her very white face.

"No, baby doll, it's a place, not a person—a place far away."

"The radio said Pearl got *bombed* and a whole bunch of other people too. Thousands, maybe." Susie cries. She knows about death, both the twins do. Their parents and baby brother are buried in the Hope River Cemetery on our Wild Rose Farm.

"Find your coats, kids," Daniel orders, "and get in the car."

"You okay, Bitsy?" I can see that she isn't.

"Wait," Willie says. "Can we say a prayer first? You say it, Ma." This appellation of "Ma" surprises me. When did that start? Bitsy has always referred to him as her ward.

Bitsy takes his hand and he takes mine and I take Danny's and Danny takes Opal's . . . until we make a circle in the middle of the living room, now nicely outfitted with sofa and chairs and even an old rag rug that neighbors have provided.

"Okay . . . ." my friend begins. "Dear Lord, we know that war is scary, but there are bad people in the world and someone has to stop them. Now our country must do its part. Please help our soldiers. Help our sailors. Make them brave and strong. Bless their families because they will have to sacrifice. We will all have to be brave and strong and we will all have to sacrifice, because we must win. . . . Amen."

Family Meeting

Everyone sit down," Dan commands when we get home. I'm surprised at this, because I know there's nothing we both want more than to listen to the radio.

"You heard about the attack on Pearl Harbor," he starts out. "The United States has a naval base, where we keep our ships and airplanes, on an island in the Pacific Ocean, which is way on the other side of the world. The Japanese who live even farther away bombed our base. This is a terrible development, and now our country will have to go to war and fight the Japanese, but life won't change for us here in Union County.

"We'll still have our farm work to do and new babies to deliver. I'll continue to take care of people's animals. You'll go to school. Every night we'll pray for the soldiers, but *we will not be in any danger.* Do you understand?" Our four children nod, but I don't think they believe him.

"The reporters like to tell exciting stories, and this is very exciting, but it does *not* affect us. Now, who wants some gingersnaps?"

Later, Dan and I go out to the barn to do the chores. The snowfall is heavier now and comes down like sand, little hard pellets that sting my face and hands. For a second it stops and I glance around the barnyard, at the stone farmhouse, the golden light streaming out the windows, the snow and Spruce Mountain leaning over us, a peaceful Christmas scene. Too peaceful.

When I get back to the house, I discover that the twins, Sunny and Sue, all by themselves, have made ham sandwiches on the last of the homemade bread. They've also put out a pitcher of milk and a quart jar of canned peaches. Mira has set the table. "We'll wait for, Pa," I say. "He's still feeding the horses."

From the living room I can hear *The Chase and Sanborn*

Hour on the radio with the sassy dummy, Charley McCarthy, and his sidekick, the ventriloquist, Edgar Bergen. It's one of our Sunday favorites, but every ten minutes it's interrupted with an update on the bloodshed and destruction in Hawaii. The Japanese have also attacked our base in the Philippines . . . Manila is on fire.

Once the children are tucked in and Dan and I are ready for bed, I get out my journal.

The news of war in Europe and the Far East has swirled around us for years, the voices getting louder, but still the impact of the unprovoked raid on our *own* base, our *own* people is shocking. I turn over expecting Dan to be asleep, but he's staring at the ceiling and I slide closer, resting one leg over his.

"The world's going crazy isn't it, Dan? The only place I feel safe is lying in your arms." I nestle in, but he doesn't answer and his body is rigid and as cold as ice. "You okay, honey?"

"I won't go, Patience. I told you before, I won't go!"

7

December 9, 1941

War

*I*t's official. The United States of America is at war.

Today, Dan was called out to attend to a horse with bad colic on the other side of the Hope River and he didn't get home until bedtime. While passing through town he bought a fresh copy of the *Liberty Times* and when he opened it on the kitchen table, we read it together.

U.S. CONGRESS DECLARES WAR—THREE THOUSAND CASU-ALTIES IN HAWAII—HUNDREDS DEAD IN THE PHILIPPINES—GREAT BRITAIN JOINS OUR FIGHT the front page screams.

"Part of what's upsetting the politicians so much," my husband explains, "is that there was a delegation of Japanese diplomats in Washington last week, supposedly meeting with the president trying to find ways to *avoid* war while their aircraft were secretly on their way across the ocean to Pearl Harbor."

I point to the side column about Great Britain. "So England's coming to our defense with the Japanese, but

we won't help them fight the Nazis? That's neighborly
of us."

"Oh, we will! FDR has been waiting for something like
this. Remember his speech about the sinking of the *Reuben
James* by German submarines? '*There are those who say
that our great good fortune has betrayed us—that we are
now no match for the regimented masses who have been
trained in the Spartan ways of ruthless brutality.*'"

Dan perfectly imitates the president's New England
accent. "'*They say that we have grown fat, and flabby,
and lazy—and that we are doomed. But those who say
that know nothing of America or of American life!*'"

"It's only a matter of time until we declare war on Germany and Italy too, or they on us." He folds his arms in
despair and puts his head down on the table, something
I've never seen him do.

"The children are in bed, Dan, and the house is quiet.
Why don't you go to sleep? I can do the chores."

"You're right. I'm exhausted. I'll just take the paper upstairs and read it in bed."

"No, hon. Leave it here. It will only upset you."

"Right again. I'm sorry, Patience. I saw Sheriff Hardman
and Judge Wade in town and they asked me to be on the
Draft Board and the Civil Defense Committee. God, the
attack on Pearl Harbor only happened two days ago and
they're already talking about having blackout drills."

"What did you say?"

"I'd have to think about it. This war hysteria is out of
control. I just told the kids that what happened in Hawaii

wouldn't affect us, that we're safe and out of harm's way. Next week we'll probably have to tell them we're hanging blankets over the window and using candles, because the Japanese or Germans might bomb us. People get whipped into a patriotic fever and start thinking the other side is pure evil; now look where that's gotten us. The whole damn world is ablaze with hate and fear."

"Come on, honey . . . bedtime. You're really wound up." I lead him upstairs, rub his back, and cover him up. Then I go back down to the kitchen thinking about Dan. Something is festering in him, something that smells rotten, like meat that's gone bad.

I stare at the headlines again. U.S. CONGRESS DECLARES WAR!

December 11, 1941

Family

*D*o you think Opal will go home to her family?" my friend Becky Blum wonders as we motor toward Hazel Patch to convey the message that Opal's family has tracked her down and wants her to come home.

All along the gravel road into the once prosperous community are abandoned one- and two-story houses, some made of logs, others of peeling painted wood. Once the village contained dwellings for about 100 colored people, subsistence farmers who thrived and supported one another, a beacon of harmony led by the Reverend Miller. One by one everyone moved away during the depths of the Great Depression.

"Why shouldn't she go back?" I challenge. "At least she *has* a family. Her father's a porter on the B&O Railroad and, thanks to the union, the porters make good money. Mr. Johnson said on the phone they'll take care of Opal and baby Joey too."

"Maybe she'll have too much pride," Becky says, winding a lock of her short dark hair around her finger. "Maybe she likes her independence."

"She's *not* independent," I remind her. "Bitsy's taking care of her."

A few minutes later we bump over the ruts in the rough road and pull up at the old Bowlin place. Bitsy's outside splitting wood, her slim arms as strong as maple limbs.

"Everything okay?" she asks. "Anything new about Pearl Harbor?"

"Just more of the same. You heard they attacked the Philippines too, and things aren't going so well for us there?"

Opal comes out on the porch and I introduce her to Becky. "I've been so scared," Opal says, "listening for bombs all the time, though I know it's foolish. Why would the Japanese bomb Hazel Patch?"

I remind myself that this young woman is only eighteen, a year older than Sally Blum, Becky's adopted daughter, who seems like a kid.

"You probably know that Congress officially declared war. No surprise. I brought you a copy of the paper. The battleship *Oklahoma* was sunk in Pearl Harbor and the battleship *West Virginia* was all but destroyed. Some of the sailors were trapped inside the ships and couldn't get out. The navy's trying to drill through the metal."

"Come on in," Bitsy says, swinging her ax so it sticks in the stump. "It sounds terrible. Can you imagine?" I'm a little tense, because Becky and Bitsy don't know each other very well and since they're both my good friends, I want them to like each other.

"Nice place," Becky says. "You've really done a lot with it."

"Every time I turn around, someone from town who remembers me from their birth gives me something," Bitsy says. "Prudy Ott brought me the sideboard under the window. She said it was just in her attic gathering dust." I look around the room at the white curtains Opal made out of worn sheets, the old sofa with a red patchwork quilt spread over it, and the rocking chair in the corner. Luckily, the abandoned home still had a wood heater stove.

"I had a phone call this morning, Opal." I begin my mission.

The girl jerks her head up. "Was it Sonny?" Her eyes are big and shiny.

"No. It was your father. He wants you to come home."

"Does he know I have a baby?"

"Yes. I told him."

"Does he know it's half-white and I'm not married?"

"Yes."

Bitsy goes over and sits on the arm of the sofa next to her. "How'd he find Opal?" she asks.

"They've been looking all over since Pearl Harbor was bombed. First they went to the hotel. One of the maids sent them to Sonny Faye and Sonny told them a yarn that he didn't know whose baby it was, but he'd heard Opal was dating a white man. He made himself out to be the *hero*, that he took Opal under his wing and found a place for her to stay with some midwives that were friends of his mother."

"Oh, for God's sake, Patience. I hope you told Mr. Johnson the truth, that the SOB Sonny Faye abandoned her." Bitsy groans.

"She can tell that part if she wants to, but none of it really matters now. . . . Opal, your father and mother are coming to see you and the baby at my house in a few days, so you need to think what you want to do."

"Don't go if you don't feel like it," Becky says. "They can't force you and they can't take your baby either. He's yours."

"Thank you," Opal says. "I don't want to be my parents' little girl forever, but I do miss them, especially now. . . ." She looks at the baby lying in a cradle that I lent them and then at the headlines on the front page of the paper. It's printed two inches high. U.S. DECLARES WAR.

Another World

So do you miss Opal?" I ask Bitsy a few days later as I sort through a box of old pans and dishes, things I got down from the loft of the barn that I thought she could use at her new house. The kids are out in the yard playing war.

"Die, you dirty Jap!" I hear Danny yell.

"I do miss her a little, but Willie misses the baby *a lot*. He's never had a brother or sister."

"So what's Willie's story? Don't you think you should fill me in?"

"He's my ward. You delivered him on Black Sunday, back in '29. Remember? The day Wall Street crashed."

In a flash it comes back to me. I'd listened for an hour for the infant's heartbeat, running my wooden fetoscope up and down Katherine's belly, and when I told her that her baby would be stillborn, she screamed. Even if you were outside on a warm summer evening and heard that sound through an open window, you would know what it meant; a mother had just lost a child. It doesn't matter if it was an unborn baby, a toddler, or a twenty-year-old soldier, the sound is the same.

Amazingly, Willie survived. He was the first infant I had to resuscitate, and it still seems miraculous . . .

I slide back to the present, still pawing through the carton. "How about this blue pitcher? I think Mrs. Kelly got it from someone she delivered. . . . Are you lonely out in Hazel Patch?"

"It's not so bad, I'm used to being with just Willie."

"Want some more tea? I dried the peppermint myself." I return from the kitchen with two cups, determined to get her story out of her. "So where the heck have you been for the last eleven years? Last time I heard, Byrd had just left you in Philly. . . ."

"Well, let's see . . . It will take a while." Bitsy picks up her cup. "I guess our marriage was doomed from the start.

I learned later that the whole time Byrd was courting me, he was playing around with some girl from Delmont. After he left me, I went back to live with my brother, Thomas, but then he lost his job driving trolley and wanted to try his luck in Chicago. Looking back, it was a mistake. He was killed on the way north."

"Oh, Bitsy. Was he riding the rails? Did he fall off of a boxcar?"

"No, it was murder. Someone, in one of the hobo camps, slit his throat in the night for his pocket watch. The fellow was never found." She pauses. "All for a lousy pocket watch that wasn't even gold. After that, I had no one, so I looked up Katherine MacIntosh, in Baltimore." Here, she stands and squints out the window into the past. "Do you really want to hear all this, Patience?"

I nod, my eyes not leaving her face.

"Well, Katherine asked me to stay with her and be Willie's nanny in 1935. He was only six then, so I did. Then, because she still had a little of her parents' money and was getting restless, we all went to Paris."

I'm still waiting to hear how Katherine dies, but this stops me in my tracks. "You went to Paris? Paris, France? Really?"

Bitsy laughs. "Yes, the *actual* Paris, *in France*. What did you think I meant, Paris, Indiana? That's where I met Bricktop."

"Who is this *Bricktop*? A man or a woman?"

"You've never heard of her?" Bitsy is shocked. "She's a redheaded colored woman from Alderson, West Virginia, and she owned the most famous nightclub in Europe. When

Katherine and Willie went back to the States, I stayed on as Bricktop's personal assistant.

"It was wonderful. Every night at the club there would be all kinds of celebrities. Bricktop knew everyone. I met Paul Robeson, Ernest Hemingway, Duke Ellington, Cole Porter, and the duke and duchess of Windsor."

"Oh, come on! The duke of Windsor."

"For sure! Bricktop taught him to do the Black Bottom. At first, I thought Miss Bricktop was taking me on as a charity case, but after a while I realized she just liked someone from the mountains around. Sometimes, I'd cook for her. You know, cook like Mama did, making baked beans, collard greens, biscuits, and fried green tomatoes. She loved my biscuits. Sometimes I'd do her hair.

"In Paris, the negro is treated with respect. It's a whole different world. There are thousands of brown-skinned people, musicians, dancers, artists, intellectuals, and businessmen from the U.S. and the Caribbean."

"Well, why did you come back?"

"You know, *the war.* If Hitler was determined to eliminate Jews, what do you think he'd do with Negroes?"

I make a bad face, realizing how little I know what it's like to be Bitsy.

"If it wasn't for the Nazis, I probably would have stayed. I loved it there. You could be colored and no one cared. You could walk down the street and hold your head high."

"How about the war? You saw things firsthand that we only read about."

"Well, I wasn't on the front line. Denmark and Norway fell in April of '40. Then Hitler invaded Belgium and the

Netherlands. The noose was tightening. It was worse for the Jews. There was nowhere they could go.

"Roosevelt called a meeting about it in France in '38. There were delegates from thirty-two countries, including Great Britain, France, Canada, and Australia, but only the Dominican Republic agreed to accept additional Jews. Then the U.S. Congress limited Jewish refugees to *only ten percent of the quota*! They even refused to admit twenty thousand Jewish children fleeing the Nazis."

I shake my head sadly. "Little kids! We couldn't even take the little kids?"

Just then *our kids* rattle in. "Can we have a snack, Mom?" Sunny wants to know.

"Pleeease!" begs Mira. "We are *so* hungry battling the Japanese."

"To be continued." Bitsy laughs.

8

December 14, 1941

Billy Blaze

"Did I tell you Bitsy got a job at the woolen mill and Willie is going to go to school with our kids on the school bus?" I tell my husband as he and I and the kids drive toward Liberty on Saturday. She applied for a position about a month ago and just got the letter.

"Right after the declaration of war, an order came in to the mill, from the army, for one million woolen blankets. Now they run day and night and they're hiring anyone, coloreds, teenagers, women, and even old people. Sixty cents an hour. Isn't that great? I thought of trying to get a job there myself . . ."

"Forget it, Patience," Dan says. "You already work too hard on the farm and the money isn't worth it if you lose your health. Anyway, you can help Bitsy by taking care of Willie before and after school. How's he doing anyway? The other boys treating him okay?"

"He's holding his own."

"Look!" Danny announces from the backseat as we drive down Main Street in Liberty. "The town already has a draft board in the old dress shop. There's a line of men waiting outside. I wish I could join up. I'd be a pilot and lick those Japs!"

The windows of the shop have been decorated with red, white, and blue streamers and political posters. ARE YOU DOING ALL YOU CAN? one says. WE'RE BEHIND YOU SOLIDER: KEEP AMERICA FREE, says another. JOIN THE ARMY NOW! says a third.

"I'm already tired of the whole thing," I complain. "There's nothing on the radio but war, war, war: '*Sources at the White House say gasoline will have to be rationed. . . . Americans on the home front are asked to sacrifice. . . . Hong Kong falls to the Japanese!*'" I imitate a radio announcer. "It goes on and on . . ." Daniel doesn't think I'm humorous, but the girls and I have a good laugh.

After a few trips up and down Main, we're fortunate to find a good place to park right between Stenger's Pharmacy and the movie house.

Our first stop is Stenger's, where we buy a tin of Bag Balm for Daniel's poor chapped hands. I glance at the *Torrington Times* in the rack. HITLER DECLARES WAR ON UNCLE SAM! the headlines shout.

"No surprise," Dan says, and hands a dime to the plump Mrs. Stenger.

"I agree," says a tall dark-haired man as he approaches the counter. He's wearing round tortoiseshell glasses and a red bow tie. "That's my article, by the way. I'm the new editor of the *Liberty Times*. Billy Blaze." He sticks out his hand to my husband, but ignores me.

"Daniel Hester," Dan says, shaking it. "Town vet. This is my wife, Patience, town midwife."

A glance at the front page confirms the fellow's claim: BY WILLIAM J. BLAZE it says in bold letters under the headlines. I look at the timepiece around my neck and before the men can get into a political discussion, I cut in. "Got to go," I tell Daniel. "Nice to see you, Mrs. Stenger, and you too, Mr. Blaze."

Dan comes out with *three* newspapers, the *Liberty Times*, the *Charleston Gazette*, and the *Torrington Times*. I roll my eyes. They probably all say the same thing, but I guess we can afford the thirty cents.

I was flabbergasted when I found that Mr. and Mrs. Johnson, Opal's parents, had left two twenties on the mantelpiece when they came to get their daughter. A note with the cash said, *Thank you, and God bless you for helping our daughter and beautiful grandbaby.* I thought the money should go to Bitsy, but now that she has a job, she said I should keep it.

"Look at all the flags, Mama," says Susie, pulling on my coat. Susie, the smaller of the twins, is my most sensitive child, but she's always the most observant. There are American flags everywhere, hanging on doors, stuck in women's hats, and waving at half-staff on flagpoles at the school and the courthouse.

Last night I tried to talk to Daniel about Christmas. I wanted us to make a decision about what presents we should buy and how much we should spend, but he said he couldn't get in the mood.

"Well, what are we going to do, then?" I asked, a little peeved. "There's only eleven more days to get ready." He just shrugged and went back to the newspapers. He hates the war, but devours every speck of information on it. This is not like Daniel. Usually, he gets as excited as the kids during the holidays.

As we stroll pass the Eagle Theater, Mr. Flanders taps on the glass of the ticket window and waves us over.

"Hello, Lloyd," Daniel says. "How are things?"

"Are we going to the movies?" the kids ask in excited whispers, pulling on my coat sleeves.

"No, baby dolls. Christmas is coming and we need to save money," I answer, forgetting that we actually have the cash.

"That's what I wanted to tell you," Mr. Lloyd says. "There's no charge." He points toward the lighted marquee above us. FREE TODAY. SPENCER TRACY IN BOY'S TOWN AND DONALD DUCK IN THE WISE LITTLE HEN.

"Luella and I wanted to give the community a lift after what's happened." He rips off six tickets and hands them to Dan.

"Thanks, Lloyd," Daniel says. "That's real neighborly!" The kids jump up and down.

"Now we have to hurry and get our errands done." I try to get us organized. "Let's split up. I'll go to Bittman's Grocery, sell our eggs, and get the coffee and sugar, and you go to the farmers' supply to buy chicken food," I say to Dan. "I'll meet you and the children there."

"Sure," Dan says. "Let's go, kids, and don't beg in the store." The prospect of the free motion picture seems to cheer him.

When I get to Bittman's, I'm surprised to see more red-white-and-blue bunting draped around the glass door. "Do you like our decorations?" Lilly asks me, her pale, sightless eyes staring at nothing. She's been blind since she had a fever her first year of life.

"They're really nice," I compliment her, and put my basket of eggs on the counter. Though Lilly can't see, she still helps tend the store, knows where everything is by feel and has all the prices memorized. "All I need is a five-pound bag of white sugar and a pound of coffee. There are four dozen eggs."

B.K., whose short dark hair sticks up like he forgot to comb it, measures out a pound of coffee. "People are saying because of the war, the government will probably start rationing sugar like England did last time."

I frown. "Oh, yeah. I didn't think of that. I'd better take another five pounds, then."

"I have some peppermint candy canes in the back," Lilly says. "Do you want me to lay some aside for the children's stockings? A penny apiece."

"No, I'll buy them now. Can I get a dozen? With all the worry about the war, I haven't done a thing to get ready for Christmas."

My next stop is the dry goods store, where Mr. Gold is standing behind the counter, wearing his trademark red suspenders and wire-rim glasses, the same kind as my specs.

"Mrs. Hester," he greets me. "Would you like a free flag?"

"Really? Sure." He gives me a miniature stars-and-stripes, like the one hanging on the store's door.

"Gosh, thanks. I noticed in your window display you have some balsa-wood airplanes. Can you tell me how much?"

"You mean the models? They're a dollar for the whole set, a good deal. There are two American Mustangs, two Hellcat Bombers, and a British Spitfire. That would be enough for your whole brood, wouldn't it?"

"That's what I was thinking, with one to spare. I also want some colorful felt to make some stuffed animals. Can you sell me several different colors off the bolt? I don't need very much."

"I can give you a half yard for twenty cents each and throw in one extra if you buy three colors." Joseph Gold frequently offers a bargain and always gives me a good deal.

"Sure," I say, not in the mood to haggle. My intention is to make stuffed Peter Rabbits for the girls, similar to the design I saw in one of Becky's issues of *Ladies' Home Journal*, so I choose pink, yellow, red, and blue. A glance at my pocket watch reminds me that I need to get going.

Mr. Gold observes me and quickly wraps up my package. "Going to the picture show?" he asks.

"Yes, I'm meeting my husband and children at the feed store and then we're off to the movies. Did you hear the tickets are free? I imagine the house will be packed."

"We saw *Boys Town* when we lived in Pittsburgh with my brother during the hard times. It's nice to be back in Liberty, where we know everyone."

I take my basket and hurry out the door just as the schoolteacher, Marion Archer, comes in. She's a talker and there's no getting past her.

"Oh, Patience. How nice to see you! I wanted to talk to you about the school holiday program."

"I'm sorry, but I have to run. We should talk later."

"Yes," she says. "Maybe next week. Susie seems to be having a some difficulties."

Difficulties! What could she mean? I stop at the Olds to put my packages in the trunk and then hurry on to the Farmers' Lumber and Supply, where I find Dan chatting with one of the feed store workers, the red-haired young man I saw in the park and later at the America First meeting.

"Yep, I'm going to enlist as soon as we get through spring planting," he says. "My mother's alone on the farm since Pop died, with just my sister and younger brother. I'll enlist in June, unless the draft gets me sooner."

"Isn't there some sort of deferment for a man whose mother depends on him, Patrick?" Dan asks.

"To be honest, I don't know. See, I *want* to get into it, Dr. Hester. I'd go right now if it weren't for Ma." He flashes a big grin. "I can't wait. If the war's over before June, I'll actually regret it."

"Me too," Danny says, looking at Patrick as if he were already a hero. "I hope it lasts a long time. Then I can join."

IT TAKES THE usher some time, in the nearly full theater, to find seats where we can all sit together, but after a few minutes of shining his flashlight up and down the rows he locates six in the middle of the front section.

Struggling over legs and feet we finally sit down, with Daniel and me in the middle, the girls next to me, and Little Dan next to his pa. Then Susie whines that she doesn't want to sit next to a stranger, so Sunny agrees to a switch. I touch Mira's leg to get her to stop kicking the seat in front of her and return in my mind to what Mrs. Archer said.

Great way to end a conversation . . . with the teacher informing me Susie has problems. What could she mean? Am I not helping her enough with her homework? Am I not giving her enough love? I break two of the candy canes in half, give one piece to each child, and then break the third in half to share with my husband.

Dan gives me one of his crooked grins and takes my hand. It's so nice to see him smiling. Since the war started, there hasn't been much of that lately. The ushers go up each aisle seating latecomers, then the lights in the theater go down and the blue velvet curtains open. A squadron of Japanese bombers roars across the screen to great fanfare and a newsreel begins.

"Mommy!" Susie squeals as she reaches out for me with both arms.

"Come here, honey," I whisper, and pull her into my lap.

The movie camera in Hawaii pans to a housing development of one-story stucco houses. One bungalow is intact, the next one destroyed, the third is on fire. It's clear that the bombing was random.

The narrator, in a clipped, excited voice, tells us how *orderly* the citizens reacted, as ambulances wail on the big screen. Nowhere is there panic. Nowhere do we see wounded. Nowhere do we see parents running through the streets with their bleeding children. Nowhere do we see all eight U.S. Navy battleships sunk in the water or the damaged destroyers or the shattered airfield, and I realize this film is a piece of propaganda.

The scene shifts to American planes battling the Japanese in the air, a real dogfight, with patriotic music in the background that gives the viewer the impression that, even though it was a surprise attack by the enemy, we were the victors. I shake my head in disbelief. Everyone must know that 2,400 Americans died and another 1,700 Americans were wounded. I look at Daniel and he stares back. Everyone in the theater must know it's a lie.

9

December 18, 1941

Telegram

A sad thing happened yesterday, but I was so tired I didn't write about it. With all the talk about the attack on Pearl Harbor, and after seeing the bombs and fighter planes in the newsreel, I was looking forward to a quiet, normal evening meal with my husband and children . . . but that's not what happened.

Just before dinner, Daniel was called out to the Pettigrew farm, for a horse that tore its leg on a barbed-wire fence, and when he returned I could tell something was wrong.

"Can you talk about it?" I asked, thinking maybe he had to put the animal down.

"While Isaac Blum and I were at the Pettigrews', Sheriff Hardman brought them a telegram," he tells me while we're in the kitchen and the kids are still bunched around the radio.

"Was it some kind of summons for back taxes or something? The Pettigrews are pretty well off; if they didn't pay, I'm sure it was an oversight."

"No, nothing like that. Blum and I were on the porch, saying goodbye, when the sheriff showed up. His face was grim. You know what he's like. Even if you told a good joke, he wouldn't smile.

"Mrs. Pettigrew opened the yellow envelope and fainted right there. Her husband, Walt, caught her before she hit the floor, and Blum cradled her head. I picked up the piece of paper and I couldn't help reading it.

"It was one of those letters they used to send during the Great War. 'The Navy Department deeply regrets to inform you that your son, James Edward Pettigrew, Seaman First Class, U.S. Navy, was lost in action in the performance of his duty and in service to his country . . .'"

"Oh no! Was he at Pearl Harbor?"

Daniel nods, his face as still as the air before a storm. "The first casualty of Union County. He was on the U.S.S. *West Virginia*. They'll start listing the dead and wounded in the paper now, like in the last war."

"Did the parents know he was stationed in Honolulu?" I asked.

"No, the last letter they got was from San Diego at the big naval base. God, it was so sad. Think if it was Danny?"

My husband goes out to wash up on the back porch and I bring him warm water from the wood stove. I'd like to hold him and let him hold me, but he's already scrubbing the horse blood off his neck.

By the time I get the fire in the heater stove banked, Sasha outside to do his duty, and the lights turned off, Dan is already asleep.

I think of the long day and all the children's talk of war. It's becoming an obsession. Dan said not to tell the kids about the Pettigrew boy, but maybe we should, just to bring a little reality to the situation. I don't know Mrs. Pettigrew, but I would like to hold her in my arms tonight, absorb with my body some of her pain. I have said this before, but I'll say it again. You bring children into this world. You care for them. You love them and sometimes they die. *Life is too hard.*

Orphan

Sleep comes in fits and pieces and as I lie in bed watching the midnight moon cross the sky, I think of all those *I've* lost. I was born Elizabeth Snyder, in Deerfield, a small town north of Chicago and a few miles inland from Lake Michigan. My mother was a teacher, my father a first mate on a freighter hauling iron ore across the Great Lakes from Wisconsin.

As a little girl, I attended the Congregational church, where Mama played organ and Papa sang in the choir when his ship was in port. I sang and played the piano too. I was an avid reader, a treasured only child, and then, when I was fourteen, everything changed.

My father's ship, the *Appomattox*, on its last run of the season across Lake Michigan, foundered in a November fog. The freighter, the longest wooden ship on the Great Lakes, carrying a load of iron ore, was grounded on a sand bar in the mist. Papa was the only crewmember who died, swept overboard by a ten-foot wave.

When the representative from the shipping company brought the news, Mama looked at me and said, "At any minute your life can change. Remember this. Between one breath and another, the song can stop." She was right.

In our first months of grief, things went from bad to worse. Mama was shocked to learn that we were destitute. Our savings were gone, gambled away by my father in high-stakes card games out on his freighter. Because of his debts, the bank foreclosed on our home and we moved to a rooming house in Deerfield. Those were hard times.

Fortunately, Mother was able to retain her teaching position, but our quarters in the rooming house were cramped and her pay minimal. I was taken out of school in the eighth grade and sent to work with Mrs. Gross, the seamstress.

Only two years later, Mama developed a cough and came down with consumption. She was spitting up blood when she died. Because I had no family left, I was shipped to Chicago to stay with Mrs. Ayers, the widowed sister of our solicitor, and worked as a laundress in her small inn. A year later, Mrs. Ayers found a new husband and shipped me off to St. Mary's House of Mercy, an orphan asylum for the impoverished. Mrs. Ayers cried a little when I left, but I wasn't her responsibility, not even kin. I understood that.

Now here I am, two or three lives later . . . having been an orphan, a wet nurse, a nanny, a suffragette, a union radical, a widow, a midwife, and now a mother of four. One thing I've learned . . . strength grows when you feel you can't go on, *but you keep going on.* Sometimes you don't have a choice.

December 20, 1941

Morning Interrupted

"Want some help?" I ask Dan as I finish my coffee at the kitchen table. He's sterilizing the milk buckets. First he washes the metal receptacles with soap and water, then he rinses with cold and finally pours boiling water in them again and swishes it around.

"No, I'm almost finished."

"Can we talk about Christmas?"

"Sure," Daniel says. "More coffee?" This is a pleasant ritual, a break that we take whenever we can, after the stock are fed and watered, the milking done, and the children on their way to school on the bus. It doesn't happen often, but both of us are happy when it does.

"What's there to talk about?" my husband asks.

"Well, we have what's left of the sixty dollars from Opal's birth and the seventy buried in the tin box under the willow. What do you think we can spend on presents this year and what should we buy?"

"I don't need to buy anything. I already have it covered," Daniel tells me.

"Okay . . . I didn't know that. I bought a few things in town. What are you making?"

"You think I'd tell you? Have you been a good girl this year?" He smiles his old lopsided grin.

"Mostly," I say, realizing he's flirting. (We haven't made love since Pearl Harbor. That's how we think now. There was before the attack and after the attack. The bombs changed everything. . . .)

"Maybe we should go upstairs and talk about it."

"Talk about Christmas?"

"Talk about if you have been a *really good* girl," Dan says, rising from the kitchen chair and taking my hand. He stops in the pantry, reaches up on the top shelf, and grabs a small bottle of rum.

Patting my butt the whole way, he scoots me up the stairs and we fall into bed together. For an hour we are no longer Ma and Pa. We are no longer midwife and vet. There is no war looming over us like a dark cloud. We are just Daniel and Patience celebrating our love, only the two of us, warm and strong and beautiful.

10

O Tannenbaum

*Y*esterday afternoon, while I was upstairs working on my presents, Daniel went up the mountain and chopped down a seven-foot spruce. Most people in the Hope River Valley don't put up their tree until Christmas Eve, but I feel if we are going to take a live tree down, we might as well enjoy it for a few days.

After a simple supper of pancakes and buttermilk, Dan brought in the box of lights and glass balls and we all took turns putting ornaments on and then we had the lighting ceremony.

First we turn off the electric lights, then everyone sits on the sofa, and we pretend to roll the drums. Rrrrrrrrrrrrrrrrrrr!

"Ready?" Dan says.

"Ready!" we all yell.

When he puts in the plug, everyone's as silent as if we'd just seen the northern lights.

"The colors make my heart warm," whispers Mira.

There are now only three more days until Christmas and I'm frantically knitting new socks for Dan. I've also made cookies for the Blums and the Mattocks. A few years ago, Christmas got to be so much work, we collectively decided to stop exchanging gifts between the three families. There's one more thing though. I want to get something really special for Bitsy, and that involves a trip to town.

Just after I return from the henhouse, I get a call from Becky Blum. "I have to go to Stenger's Pharmacy to get a few things for the infirmary at the CCC camp, do you want to come?" she asks.

"That's perfect. I was just thinking I need one more present."

"OK. I'll pick you up in thirty minutes."

"Gosh," I say to Sasha, our beagle. "I'd better hurry!"

As WE ENTER Liberty I'm surprised to see a new billboard, just before the bridge over the Hope River. It's a picture of a smiling farm family, a little towheaded boy, a man in overalls, and a pleasant-looking young woman in a simple pink housedress. AMERICANS ON THE HOME FRONT, DO YOUR PART! it says along the bottom.

"What's our part?" I ask Becky. "I put the flag Mr. Gold gave me on the kitchen door and the children and I say our prayers for the soldiers every night."

"Haven't you heard? The mayor says we're supposed to start saving scrap metal and rubber to be reused by the military. They're desperate for the raw materials to make tanks and bombers."

"Oh," I say. "Maybe I'd better start reading the paper again. It gets me so down. I don't want to hear about each battleship lost or how many men die. Things aren't going so well for us."

We pull into a spot right in front of Stenger's Pharmacy. "I'm going over to Gold's Dry Goods," I tell Becky.

"Okay. I'll meet you back here," she responds.

When I enter Gold's, the owner is engaged with the fellow Dan and I met in town last time, Billy Blaze the newspaperman, and while I stroll around, I listen to their conversation.

"You know, I'd enlist right now. It's what every patriotic fellow should do," the man of about thirty explains. "But I have asthma and bad knees. Anyway," he says, "who else in this little backwater town would run the paper?" Today he wears a sweater vest and a tweed sport coat as if he's a hot-shot reporter in some city like Pittsburgh.

Mr. Gold polishes the counter and finally asks, "So, is there anything else you need, Bill? Just the smokes?"

"No, that's it, unless you can tell me if you've heard anything about a pack of wild dogs roaming the area. I'd like to get a line on that story."

"Sorry," Mr. Gold answers, still polishing the counter. "Can't say I've heard about it."

When Billy Blaze leaves, Joseph Gold approaches me with glee. "That gentleman really loves to talk. He stops here about this time every day . . . What can I do for you, Mrs. Hester?"

"Well, I need a special present for a woman friend. The trouble is, I don't know what I'm looking for."

"Take your time. There are racks of store-bought clothes for women—blouses, sweaters, and skirts. There's a table full of silk and nylon undergarments and stockings, but that won't last long and I doubt I can get more.

"There's a bookshelf lined with books some new, but some used. There's even a bargain counter in back."

"Thanks," I say, heading toward the rear of the store. "I'll just look at the bargains first." That's when I see it, a beautiful little clock made of dark walnut with roman numerals on the face and shiny golden pillars on the sides. Three dollars, it says on the label, and I'm so excited I tuck it under my arm and carry it around the store as if I'm afraid some other customer might snatch it. Finally, I stroll back to the counter.

"Well, hello again, Mrs. Hester. I see that lovely old timepiece caught your eye? Three dollars is a bargain."

"Does it work?" I ask, setting it on the counter.

"Well, sure. I can vouch for it." He winds it up. "It was my wife's, but we got a new one."

"I'll take it!" I say, and open my pocketbook.

"Nothing else today, Mrs. Hester? I just got in a dozen sets of wooden dominos . . . very popular with the young people this year. Only one dollar."

"That would be fine. I'll take one." I decide on the spot to get a set for Daniel. He loves games and can share it with the whole family.

Mr. Gold seems disappointed he made the sale so easily, because he wanted to haggle, but he puts the clock in a carton and slips the dominos along the side. "Save the cardboard," he says. "We're starting a paper and cardboard drive at the courthouse. Scrap metal too."

"I will. And Merry Christmas. . . ."

I CLOSE MY journal, take off my glasses and rub my eyes. Daniel sleeps next to me snoring softly, the poor dear. He works so hard. I pull the covers up around his neck and I try to imagine what he would write if he kept a journal. Becky keeps one. She calls it her Nurse's Notes, and for a while, back when he couldn't talk, even Dr. Blum kept one.

Tomorrow night is the school Christmas program, and I wonder if Mrs. Archer will bring up Susie's problems again. I've been watching my daughter and I know she's shy, but she doesn't get in fights and she always gets good grades. I hope the teacher and I have time to talk.

Thinking about the Christmas program I remind myself that I must make cookies and get the family's best clothes ready. It's nice that Dan got me an electric iron for my birthday last year. It's a luxury, I'll admit, but a few more work-saving machines wouldn't hurt me.

Mrs. Wade, for example, has an electric sweeper that cleans the floor, the carpet, even furniture, by suction. I've never seen it, but Becky told me about it. Many wives and mothers are getting jobs now and buying their own Hoovers. Sometimes, I'm tempted to join them and then I remember that if I worked out of the home, I'd still have to do the washing, the chickens, the garden, the housework, the cooking, *and* take care of the kids, including Willie, until Bitsy gets off work at the woolen mill.

No, I shall just go on in the old-fashioned way. Daniel is right and he takes good care of me.

December 23, 1942

Deck the Halls

This evening, after eating a quick supper of fried ham, home-canned applesauce, and cold milk from the springhouse, we quickly dressed for the school Christmas program. The girls buttoned one another's back buttons and Daniel tied his son's tie. I put on a red wool sweater and a long green skirt.

"Radio says a storm's coming in," Daniel tells us as we get on our coats. "Dress warm. I put chains on the tires so we won't have any trouble."

At the schoolhouse, the side parking lot is already full and we have to park in the playground, but at least we aren't late. A few men still stand on the porch steps smoking. Lights blaze out the windows of the four-room white clapboard building and each pane is decorated with snowflakes and snowmen.

The children run off to their classrooms to prepare and Daniel and I find seats in the community room next to Becky and Dr. Blum. I'm sad that Bitsy and Willie didn't come, but she said she'd rather stay at home than cause a big fuss because of her being the only colored person in an all-white school.

Dan relaxes back in his folding wooden chair, but I lean forward, looking around. I've been in the homes of many of these families and delivered some of their children.

There's Addie and Norton Hummingbird of Dark Hollow. I delivered Carlin without difficulty. He was ten pounds, one of my biggest. There's Lilly and B.K. Bittman. Becky delivered their daughter, Velvet.

I notice the red-haired kid from the feed store, Patrick, and that must be his mother, a worn-looking fifty-year-old also with red hair. He makes a joke and she looks up at him laughing. His younger brother and sister are both students here, and if they have red hair too, they'll be easy to spot.

There's Mr. and Mrs. Linkous. The lawyer, like me, is surveying the crowd and our eyes meet in recognition.

A buzz runs through the audience as Mrs. Archer, the head teacher, takes the stage. She's wearing a long red dress that just barely fits over her ample bosom. "Shall we stand for the Pledge of Allegiance?" she says. Daniel and I look at each other. This is unusual. I don't remember saying the pledge at other Christmas programs, but the words have more meaning in times of war. A tall boy walks out carrying the flag like a soldier in a Fourth of July parade, and we all put our hands over our hearts.

"I pledge allegiance to the flag of the United States of America . . ." It's not the flag that we pledge to, I think, but what it stands for.

Give me your tired, your poor. Your huddled masses yearning to breathe free. The wretched refuse of your teeming shore. Send these, the homeless, tempest-tost to me. I had to learn that poem from the Statue of Liberty in seventh grade.

When we sit back down, the curtains open on the stage and all the younger children parade out in front of a spectacular twelve-foot lighted Christmas tree. Our two white-haired twins are in the back row, next to their sister Sonya Maddock, who's one year younger. Mira, being only in the second grade, stands up front pulling at her red plaid pleated skirt, a hand-me-down and a little too short. She looks around for us and I stand and wave.

Then Mrs. Archer taps her baton and Mrs. Goody, the Saved by Faith preacher's wife, plays a few chords on the piano and the program begins. "*Dashing through the snow, in a one-horse open sleigh. O'er the fields we go . . .*" The children all sway back and forth as the teacher leads them.

Mira is still twisting her skirt and now she's put a little swing in her sway. I nudge Daniel and look up at him. He grins and gives me a wink as if he thinks it's funny. It's hard not to notice Mira, and I hear giggles in the audience. A man with a huge camera and a flash the size of a saucer is taking photos. It's the newspaperman, Mr. Blaze, who wears a red Christmas sweater and his brown fedora with a little tag in the hatband that says PRESS.

Our daughter sees him and begins to sing louder. Louder and louder she sings and I don't know whether to be embarrassed or laugh, but soon there's no choice. It's so funny, my gurgle turns into a honk and tears run down my face. "*Jingle bells. Jingle bells . . .*" the children sing. Mr. Blaze snaps more pictures. "*Jingle bells. Jingle bells . . .*" Mira warbles.

The room isn't big, and I'm afraid my youngest can hear us cackling. Daniel puts his arm around my shoulders to steady me, but he's laughing too. When the choir gets to the chorus, Mira turns her volume up even louder and I can't tell if she's hamming it up or just enjoying herself so much she doesn't know she's drowning out the rest of the singers.

"*Oh, jingle bells jingle bells, jingle all the way! Oh what fun it is to ride in a one-horse . . . open . . . sleigh . . . Hey!*" Mira shouts and throws her arms in the air.

America the Beautiful

After the comedy routine by our daughter, there's the usual portrayal of the nativity story with Danny as one of the shepherds. Sonya Maddock and Sally Blum, the other adopted Hucknell sisters, are dressed as angels.

I'm surprised when, near the end of the program, a man in uniform from the National Guard in Delmont, comes up onstage and clears his throat for attention. "My fellow West Virginians," he starts out. "I'm so grateful to be here tonight for this festive celebration. Even in these dark times, we need to remember that there is joy in family and friends. . . ." He pauses.

"On the other hand, we must not forget that we are fighting a war now, a war against tyranny, a war to protect our liberty, our democracy, and our way of life. It's not just our brave servicemen that are fighting. It is all of us on the home front, even here in Union County.

"In time there may be rationing as there was in the Great War in England. We'll need volunteers for the Red Cross to roll bandages and knit socks for the soldiers. Some of you may be asked to be part of your local defense council, but I want to tell you about something you can do today.

"Uncle Sam is asking us all to buy war bonds. The bonds are an investment in democracy. You can buy them at your local bank for $18.75, and when the war is over you'll get back $25.00. That's an investment that will help protect your family and also be a savings you can count on when we're victorious. . . ."

He lifts his head with pride and goes on. "In a few minutes, some of the boys are going to hand out a savings card for every family. The card has slots for seventy-five quarters. When it's full, you'll have enough for a bond."

Young men in khaki uniforms and smart military hats begin to move down the aisles and I notice that nearly everyone takes a card. For a second I think Dan's going to wave them on, but when I nudge him he puts one in his pocket. What's wrong with him, for God's sake? Even if he doesn't approve of the war, he should at least be patriotic.

Then Peaches Goody comes onstage. Becky attended Peaches in labor when I was on bed rest for Mira. The young lady was only twelve and didn't even know she was pregnant. She must be eighteen now and she wears a lovely long dark green velvet dress and has her hair up in curls like the singer Kate Smith.

Mrs. Goody, her mother, plays a few chords and Peaches begins an Irving Berlin song: "*God bless America, land that I love! Stand beside her and guide her through the night with the light from above.*"

Everyone in the audience stands and comes in on the chorus, those who can sing and those who can only croak. "*From the mountains, to the prairies—to the oceans white with foam . . .*" I wipe my eyes and look at Dan, wondering if he's as moved as I am, but his face is as lifeless as an image on Mount Rushmore. . . . "*God bless America—my home sweet home!*"

AN HOUR LATER we're all packed in the cold car and on our way home through the snow. I wasn't sure whether to scold Mira for her antics or not. She was certainly disruptive . . . but we were all having such a good time enjoying the Christmas party that I didn't have the heart.

I'd also thought of chewing Dan out about his lack of enthusiasm for our country, but then Mrs. Archer pulled me into a corner and started going on about poor Susie's *problems.*

"I don't know what to do with her," the buxom lady said. "I'm at my wits' end. . . . She does a fine job on her homework, so I know she's capable, but she won't respond to any questions in class. When I ask her to recite, she just stares at her desktop.

"Now, Sunny, her twin, is just the opposite. She waves her hand like a flag and wants to answer *every* question. And today was the final straw. Susie refused to get up and go to the blackboard to do a math problem and I made her stand in the corner and then she urinated! An eleven-year-old emptied herself right on the floor like a toddler!"

"She does that sometimes when she's scared. . . . It was just an accident . . ." I started to explain, but Mrs. Archer cut me off.

"I don't know what to do, Mrs. Hester! I just can't have it. I'm sure the other children tease her. Maybe she needs to go to a special school or something. The Children's Home Society has a place for slow children near Elkins."

"Mrs. Archer! You just said she's bright. There is no way . . ."

Accident

You're awfully quiet," Dan whispers. Mira, stuffed between Daniel and me on the front seat, is already asleep. "You okay?" I shake my head and he frowns, but I can't tell him here, with the kids in the car, about Susie peeing on the floor and Mrs. Archer's suggestion that she needs to be in a special school. I'm surprised that none of the other kids told me about what happened in class. Maybe they didn't want to spoil the evening because they know how furious I get when one of my children, or any child, is mistreated.

The snow blows in sideways and the wind jolts us so hard, my husband has to swing the Olds back into the road. Ahead, it's all white, but I've always been confident in Daniel's driving and I just stare passively at the feathery flakes as they sweep through the headlights.

"What's that?" Dan shouts, and slams on the brakes. There's a single red taillight in the ditch and someone is waving. I start to get out, but he motions me to stay. "I'll go," he says. "Someone's had an accident."

I wipe the steam from the passenger window and try to see out. "What's happening?" Danny asks from the backseat. "Why'd we stop?"

"I don't know. Your pa's checking. Someone ran off the road. I can't see because the snow is so heavy."

White. White. Whirling white and the windshield wipers flip back and forth. "Should I get out to help?" Danny asks.

"No, they're coming . . . two people with your father." As the dark shapes move toward us, I realize it's someone we know and one of them is limping.

"Bitsy! Willie! Are you okay?" Bitsy stumbles through the snow toward the car wearing her leather helmet and an old army trench coat, probably from the Great War. She's crying and Willie has his arm around her. "Are you hurt, Willie?" I call.

"It's just my knee. I banged it," he answers.

"Just a little. Bruised. Nothing's broken but my motorcycle. It's just that I can't get to work without it and I'll lose my job. Negro women are always the last to be hired and the first to be fired."

"What the hell were doing out like this at night?" I start to scold her, then think better of it. "How long have you been out in the cold?" I change my tone. "You must be freezing."

"There's an old lady on the colored side of the tracks in Liberty, someone my mother, Big Mary, used to know. We took her some Christmas cookies and stayed later than we meant to. It wasn't snowing when we started for home."

"We've been trying to pull the motorcycle out," Willie adds, "but we weren't getting anywhere. We were hoping you would come along after the school thing."

"Come on, now. Get in the car. Get warm." I open the back door and have Willie scoot in with the kids.

"It's my job!" Bitsy says again. "I have to get to work in the morning. If I don't, I'll get fired. They won't give me any slack." There are tears in her eyes and I brush the snow off her face, then I push her into the front seat and go back to the motorcycle that's resting on its side. "How bad is it?" I ask Daniel. He's squatting down in the snow.

"Looks like she slid into the ditch and was thrown off. Will was strapped into the sidecar. I can't tell in the dark if the fender's bent of it's something worse. They just need to come home with us and bed down for the night. I'll come back in the morning with the tractor."

"Bitsy's worried about losing her job if she misses work," I explain.

"Who's the foreman?" Dan asks. "They can't expect her to get to the woolen mill in weather like this."

"She thinks because she's a woman and colored, she'll be canned."

"What time is it?" Dan asks as we walk back to the car.

"It must be almost ten. Why."

"I'll call her foreman when we get to the house."

"Bitsy won't want you to."

"Why?" Daniel looks surprised.

"Well . . . she's very independent. It's not like you're her husband or father."

He shakes his head as if he still doesn't get it. "Well, I'll drive her to work then. She can't argue with that."

11

December 24, 1942

Visitor

*D*aniel has spent most of the day working on Bitsy's motorcycle while I finished wrapping my presents, and at four, just as he's getting ready to go get Bitsy at the woolen mill, the phone rings.

"Daniel Hester," he answers. "Who?" He looks over at me and raises his eyebrows. "Sure. . . . Well, thank you. . . . It was nothing. Bitsy is our neighbor and friend. . . . We'd appreciate that. . . . You positive it won't be out of his way? . . . That's fine then. . . . Thanks again. Bye."

"Who was that?" Willie asks when he hears Bitsy's name.

"It was Mr. Vipperman of the Vipperman Woolen Mill!"

"Is Bitsy okay?" Willie asks anxiously. "We flew into the ditch pretty hard."

"Yeah, she's fine. Vipperman even gave her high praise. They appreciated her making it to work this morning. With the snowstorm, about half the employees didn't show up. He thanked me for driving her and said his foreman will drive her home.

"Let's go, boys. I pulled Bitsy's cycle out of the ditch and I think I can finish fixing it before she gets home. You can help me."

"I want to help too," says Sunny.

"Well, come on then!" That's Dan.

Two hours later there's a dark-green Plymouth in the drive and the children are tumbling down the stairs to see who's here. I watch from the kitchen window as a man in a black tweed jacket and black beret gets out of the vehicle and courteously opens the passenger side for Bitsy.

He walks her to the front porch and we all run through the living room to see. "Shhhhhh!" I say to the children as I open the door.

"Hi, Patience. This is Mr. Louis Cross, my foreman at the mill. He was kind enough to bring me home," Bitsy says, her light-brown face flushed rose.

"Won't you come in, Mr. Cross?" I say just to be hospitable, expecting him, since it's Christmas Eve, to respond that he needs to get going.

"Well, thank you, ma'am." The foreman steps into the living room and takes off his beret. He has thick brown hair, a cleft in his chin, and wide brown eyes. "I believe we have a mutual acquaintance, Becky Meyers. *Nurse Becky* we call her at the CCC camp."

I look at Bitsy, unsure what to do next, but Daniel walks in just then and makes the decision. "Sit down, Mr. Cross," he says. "We've met before, at the memorial service for the victims of the fire." (There is no need to say which fire. In Union County, everyone knows he means the wildfire of '35 that destroyed 10,000 acres of forest and took nine lives, including Sunny and Sue's mother, father, and baby brother.)

The foreman removes his tweed jacket, revealing clean gray coveralls over a white shirt and a red, white, and blue tie. He chooses a seat on the davenport, scratches Sasha behind the ears, and smiles at the girls, especially Mira, who sits down beside him as if they're old friends.

"Are you the little girl that was in the paper?" he asks.

"Me? I was?"

"Yeah, there was even a photo. I've got a copy in the car. I'll give it to you later. Nice home," he says to me as he takes in the blaze in the fireplace, the stockings hung for Santa, the lighted Christmas tree, and the upright piano against the wall. He stretches out his long legs. "Who plays?"

"Both Patience and I," Dan informs him. "How long have you worked at the woolen mill, Mr. Cross?"

"Since I got back from the Spanish Civil War in '39." Daniel takes a seat and leans forward, interested in what the veteran has to say about that earlier war against fascism.

"Why don't you stay for supper, Mr. Cross?" my husband asks. "We have plenty, don't we, hon?"

"Aaaah . . . sure," I say, wondering what Bitsy thinks. I imagine she wants to be off duty and get rid of the man. *Too late for that now.* "It's just simple fare, Mr. Cross, but you're welcome."

"Call me Lou," the man says.

"I'm Dan. Dan Hester." My husband rises and shakes the fellow's hand and that's when I notice the scars up his arm.

"Injured in combat?" Daniel asks, holding the man's right hand for a moment as a doctor would.

"Yeah. That's partly why Old Man Vipperman hired me. With a major war on the horizon, he knew if the U.S.A. got involved, I'd be 4-F and wouldn't be called."

"What happened?" Danny asks in his forthright way.

"Well, I made it through the Union County wildfire without losing a hair and then came the Battle of Jarama. . . . Have you kids heard about that?" The children move in, ready for a story, and Lou Cross is a natural storyteller. This is better than the *Lone Ranger* on the radio.

"You know about the Spanish Civil War and the Lincoln Battalion volunteers?" Mr. Cross asks us.

"We learned a little about it in school," Sunny says.

"Yeah, well this good old boy from Union County, along with another four thousand Americans and Canadians volunteered to go. We had big ideas. Gonna help the Spaniards fight General Franco, the fascist."

"Did you fly a plane?" Danny wants to know.

"No, I drove a tank. That's how I got blown up. I was just coming out of the hatch when one of Franco's devils threw a grenade. I tried to chuck it away, but it exploded. I'm lucky I didn't lose my hand." He stares at his scars, which are like the bark on an elm tree. Mira reaches over and touches them with one finger.

"Honey!" I say, thinking she's being too forward, but Lou holds out his arm so all the children can see.

"You know the song about the Jarama River? It's to the tune of 'The Red River Valley.' Can you play it, Dan?" The man is so relaxed, he acts like one of the family.

"I've got it here somewhere," Dan says, looking in the piano bench and pulling out a little yellow songbook, *American Favorites*. He sits down and plays a few bars of the familiar tune and Lou begins to sing just like Roy Rogers.

"There's a valley in Spain called Jarama. It's a place that we all know so well. It is there that we gave of our manhood. And so many of our brave comrades fell.

"Now let's all sing together," Lou leads us. *"There's a valley in Spain called Jarama . . ."*

December 25, 1941

Silent Night

This afternoon, we had our community Christmas party at the Blums', which was nice because Dan and I didn't have much to clean up afterward. Everyone was there, including two new friends of Becky's who have no family: an elderly lady, Mrs. Stone, and her neighbor, Mr. Roote, whom I recognized as one of the old vets who marches in the Fourth of July parade every year.

We had dinner and dessert and then sang carols. Before Bitsy left, I took her outside and gave her a wooden fighter plane wrapped in tissue for Willie, and the little mantel clock. She said it was the loveliest thing she'd ever owned and before she drove away with Willie, she handed me a copy of the newspaper Mr. Cross mentioned the previous evening.

"You won't like the story," she said. "The picture is cute, but the reporter made it sound like Mira ruined the whole Christmas program. He called her a six-year-old exhibitionist. Don't let it get under your skin. Cut out the picture, but burn the article." (I did what she said, determined not to let my irritation ruin the holiday.)

Now Christmas is over. The children are all tucked in bed, the girls with their stuffed felt bunnies under their pillows and their wooden planes on their dressers and Danny, with his fighter plane and a basketball under the covers. Daniel came through, after all, with a new brown-and-white pony, a trade for work he'd done for Mr. Dresher, his German farmer friend and client.

"Did you hear Sally Blum got a job in Torrington at the munitions plant?" he says as we sit together in the dark looking at the Christmas tree lights. "The Blums are upset she dropped out of high school. Isaac wanted her to go to college."

"Almost all of the boys over eighteen have dropped out and enlisted. No surprise that some of the girls are dropping out too," I comment. "Becky's usually so conservative, I was shocked that they let her go, but she confided to me that it was either let her work in the munitions plant in Torrington or let her work at the Westinghouse plant in Pittsburgh. At least she has a roommate in the Torrington Boarding House for Women, someone she knows from school." I look up at Dan. "I'd hate for one of our kids to work making bombs, wouldn't you? So dangerous."

"Life is dangerous, Patience. Want a rum toddy?" Dan asks.

"Sure." I smile, catching his eye.

While he's in the kitchen I survey our parlor. The room is dim except for the colored lights on the tree. It's been tidied of all the wrapping paper, and a fire crackles in the fireplace. I take a big breath and let it out slowly. The holidays are always so hectic for me. I never get ready ahead of time, like Becky.

"What did you think of Churchill's speech on the radio?" Dan asks, coming back with two mugs of the sweet warm drink. "He's spending the holidays in the White House with the Roosevelts."

"I guess it gave me comfort. I liked what he said . . . *'Here in the midst of war, raging and roaring over all the lands and seas . . . we have tonight the peace of the spirit in each cottage home and in every generous heart.'*

"It does seem like a world of storm, doesn't it?" I rest into my husband's warm body.

"Like a fierce blizzard, and it will only get worse," Dan interjects. "With a blizzard, you know in a few days it will end and you can dig yourself out, but this madness . . . we don't know where it will stop."

"What if the Japs and the Germans win, Dan? They can't win, can they? They can't take over the whole world."

"I'd like to say, no, Patience, but the U.S. is starting from a disadvantage. We're a rich and resourceful country, but our army is the same size as Sweden's. Our factories are just starting to produce bombers and tanks instead of Maytags and Fords."

"But if every man and woman in the U.S. made the grand effort, we could triumph, couldn't we?"

"Not every man, Patience."

"What do you mean?"

"I told you before. I won't go."

"Well, you won't have to. You fought for the country once already."

"I don't know if it will be that simple. . . . Shh . . ." He kisses my palm before I get on my soapbox.

Daniel and I never used to talk politics. Our children, our work, our animals, and the farm have defined our lives. He knew I'd been a socialist, went to radical meetings, marched for women's rights, and once had union ties. And I knew, in a general way, that he was against killing and greed. Now the shadow of the war hangs over us.

"Let's sing," he says.

The rum toddy is having a pleasant effect. "The kids are asleep!" I giggle.

"We'll be quiet, I promise." And so we sit down on the piano bench together and I begin to play softly . . .

"*Silent night. Holy night* . . ." Outside it's snowing again and the flakes swirl like white embers.

12

January 7, 1942

The Good Cause

CITIZENS OF UNION COUNTY ASKED TO SAVE TIN CANS, reads the headline of the *Liberty Times*. And underneath there's an impassioned plea, penned by the newspaperman, Billy Blaze.

"Many an unsuspecting West Virginia housewife helps Hitler and the Japs every day," he writes. "One look at the city dump demonstrates why. There, in the melting snow, lay thousands of cans that could be reclaimed for the U.S. war effort.

"Two tin cans contain enough tin for a syrette, which is used to administer morphine to wounded soldiers on the battlefield. Tin is used on airplane instrument panels, and since tin is the only metal that isn't harmed by saltwater, it's used to ship food overseas . . . *Save your cans, citizens, and win the war.*"

Even the school's gotten involved. The first day back from winter break, the kids were told they would be required to bring something that can be reused for the war effort every week. The first collection was rubber. Since the Japanese have cut off U.S.A. supplies from Asia, we have no choice but to reuse rubber products while scientists are developing a substitute.

It was an effort, but yesterday the children and I finally found one old tire in back of the barn that Daniel said was past the point of repair, and all four of them carried it in to Mrs. Archer together. Willie, however, went to *all* the abandoned houses in Hazel Patch and found *four tires*—a gold mine!

Now the assignment is copper, and I tell you, I'm at a total loss. Where do you get a piece of spare copper? Susie was so worked up about not having any to take to school that she peed herself again. Apparently, if you don't bring something for the drive, you get a bad mark.

The one good thing in her having another "accident" was it gave me an opportunity to address her urinary problems.

I TAKE SUSIE into to my bedroom to change her underpants. "Honey, I'm not mad at you. Here are some clean bloomers. Do you know what's causing you to pee when you get scared?"

"No," she says, sniffling.

"Does it happen often, like at school or anywhere?"

"A few times it happened when I was called to speak in class, but only a little bit and no one knew, but then one other time it was awful. Mrs. Archer got mad at me and made me stand in front of the class for a long time. I was so scared a whole bunch of pee came out and I ran away.

She chased me down the hall and slapped me. She thought I did it on purpose. Now she never calls on me at all, but I'm glad."

I wince. *Lordy, what are we going to do?* "I'll talk to Mrs. Archer, Susie. She must not understand how shy you are."

The fact is, I don't know what else to say to Mrs. Archer. If I make a big issue out of it and reprimand her for slapping Susie, she may go to the school board and try to get Susie kicked out.

"Do you think it would help if you wore a pad?"

"Like a diaper? That's for babies!"

"No, I meant just a little pad. Like ladies wear."

"Ladies wear pads?"

"Ladies and older girls like your big sister, Sally."

"I guess. If Sally wears them."

I don't tell her I'm thinking of cutting down a Kotex napkin. It's an expense, but if it will help her stay in school, I don't mind.

"Did the other kids say anything to you about what happened? Did they tease you?"

"Only one boy. He called me Wetty Pants!" Here she starts crying again. "But Willie punched him and then he stopped."

"Willie punched him?" I wipe the smile from my face before she can see. *Good for him!* I think. Bitsy was worried he might be too backward, but when push comes to shove, the kid has guts.

"Yep! And he told the boy that if they ever laughed at me again, he would punch him harder." Now Susie smiles.

"Okay," I say. "Fighting at school isn't allowed, but it was for a good cause." I pull Susie into my arms and give her a hug. Her white-blond hair smells like flowers.

"Like having a war is bad because of killing?" she says. "Unless it's for a good cause."

January 24, 1942

Mourning

Today, when we got up at six A.M., everything was covered in frost. White on the fence rail. White on every branch and twig. White on the grass so thick it looked like snow. I was cooking oatmeal when Daniel reminded me that today the Pettigrews were having a service for their son who died during the attack on Pearl Harbor.

"Did they finally get his body back?" I ask.

"No. The army sent an American flag and a letter that said their son's remains will be returned after the war is over . . . if they can find him."

"What do you mean *if they can find him*?"

"Well, they're doing their best to bury everyone close to where they died, but war is chaotic and sometimes when men die far from home bodies get mislaid. I saw it first-hand, Patience. Sometimes we just had to dig a trench and lay ten or twenty men in, but the chaplain would always say a prayer and we made sure everyone had their dog tags on. Anyway, do you think we should take the children?"

"Yes," I answer without hesitation. "They need to know the consequences of war, especially Danny. He thinks it's all battles in the sky with fighter planes and actors like John Wayne. He forgets that the soldier who dies is a real person with people who love him."

AFTER BREAKFAST, DAN gathers the children around him. "This afternoon we're going to a memorial service in Liberty for one of the men killed in the attack on Pearl Harbor. Thousands of soldiers and civilians died that day, and they were someone's brother or someone's son.

"This is just one sailor who happens to come from Union County. His name was Jimmy Pettigrew and I've known him since he was a boy your age, Danny. He was only nineteen when he died, just a little older than your sister Sally, girls. Now he's dead and we're going to the Saved by Jesus Baptist Church to support his mom and dad and to say prayers for the other servicemen who have died."

"It was the Japs that murdered him!" Danny exclaims. "We should kill as many of their boys as they kill of ours. An eye for an eye, it says in the Bible."

"It isn't that simple, son," Daniel says. "The Japanese and German soldiers have mothers and fathers and sisters and brothers too. If we go on with 'an eye for an eye' each time someone dies, wars will never end."

LATER IN THE afternoon, following our usual trip to Bittman's Grocery and the Farmers' Lumber and Supply Store, we all file into the church. Isaac and Becky arrive soon after us and are seated about three rows ahead.

I'm surprised when Bitsy and Willie come in. Willie is still limping and they are escorted up the stairs to the colored balcony. They're the only ones up there, as far as I can see, and no one makes a fuss that Willie is white.

When I turn around and catch Bitsy's eye, she gives me a nod, then I remember that the Pettigrews' older daughter, Maggie, works with Bitsy at the woolen mill. Bitsy told me they often have their noon meal together.

Up front, there's a carved oak cross on the wall behind the white pulpit and an American flag on a stand to one side. In the center of the dais is a wooden table with a photo of Jimmy in his uniform, a photo of him on his prize horse on the farm, and another American flag folded and placed in a triangular wooden case.

Just when the children start squirming, Preacher Goody in a long black gown, followed by a contingent of the National Guard from Delmont, marches in and an organist plays a few bars of "America the Beautiful."

"All rise," the pastor intones. The Reverend Goody, tall and balding, with eyes so dark they seem almost black, is familiar to me. He's of the fire-and-brimstone variety.

The assembly stands and sings along with the choir. Even the children sing, and this time Mira behaves and doesn't try to steal the show. "*America! America! God shed his grace on thee . . . And crown thy good with brotherhood from sea to shining sea.*"

When the song ends, I can hear someone crying and I know who it is: Jimmy's mother.

The trip home is a solemn one. Daniel doesn't say a word.

During the sermon and following hymns, I'd looked over twice to see him wiping his eyes. I cried too, though I didn't know Jimmy. I was crying for *all* the people who died at Pearl Harbor, for *all* the sailors and soldiers and their mothers and fathers. That's how I think of the war now, from the mother and father's point of view.

I remember the loon I saw once in a bay on Lake Michigan when I was a girl. The waterfowl swam with its chick on its back. We humans are like that. We carry our children on our backs until their flesh becomes part of our bodies. When a child dies, it's like a piece of us is torn out and that chunk won't grow back.

By the time we get home it's almost dark, and it's snowing again. I hustle the children into the house to change out of their good clothes and get their chores done. Daniel goes into the pantry for clean buckets and hurries out to the barn.

He's out there a long time and when he returns we're just getting ready to eat, but he says he's too tired and goes right to bed.

"Is Pa okay?" Susie asks me.

I look into her blue eyes, wishing sometimes she weren't so observant. The other kids are already sitting at the table, as hungry as little pigs.

"Yes, honey. He just feels sad about his friend Jimmy Pettigrew. He'll be okay in the morning." The truth is, I am not sure he will be okay. It's like something is breaking inside him.

When supper is over we go through our nightly rituals, clear the table, wash and dry the dishes. No singing while we work. No spit-baths tonight because we all bathed before going to town. The kids get their nightclothes on and we sit around the radio to listen to our Saturday-night shows.

"Can't you turn that damn radio down?" Daniel yells from upstairs. His words are slurred and I realize now that what kept him out in the barn for so long was not just the cows and feeding the stock, but nursing the little bottle of rum he grabbed from the pantry.

The kids roll their eyes and giggle. They aren't afraid of their father. Unlike most parents in Union County, he's never whipped his children, has never needed to. They listen to their pa, love him, and obey.

"Is Papa a little cranky?" Mira asks.

"Yes, honey. He's had a hard day."

"More than just *cranky*," Danny says under his breath. "He's been hitting the hooch." I slash my eyes at him to be quiet. Our only boy frequently goes out with Daniel and Dr. Blum on their vet calls and has seen men inebriated.

We turn down the volume on the radio and when the show's over, head for the outhouse and then up to the girls' room for storytime. It's different tonight, going through our nightly rituals without Daniel, and I think of the families whose fathers have gone to war.

When the children are tucked into bed, I creep into our room, undress, and put on my long flannel nightgown. I take out my journal and, sitting in the rocking chair, begin to record the last few days' events. Daniel snores in his sleep. Not the little delicate snore that I'm used to, but the big honking snore of a drunk. An empty fifth of rum lies on the floor.

After a while, I pull the covers back and try to slip into our bed, but Daniel is smack in the middle and when I gently nudge him, he won't move. Drool wets his pillow and he smells like a brewery.

Ruben, my husband before Dan, the union organizer who died in the Battle of Blair Mountain, drank beer on occasion, but I never saw him drunk. Now, for the first time in years, I miss him. Ruben was a fighter.

Daniel is against the war and sometimes, like now, he seems weak, self-indulgent, and even unpatriotic. I shut that thought down and look around the dark room. I need to sleep somewhere. . . .

In the end, I pull the covers up over my husband's shoulder again, take my pillow, and creep downstairs. Lying on the sofa in the dark, I stare out the window. I wish I could listen to the radio. If I could get away from the news about the war, I'd turn on some jazz and pretend I was young again. I'd be at a union meeting, flirting with Ruben. Then I remember how Ruben died.

13

Fear and Rage

It was during the dog days of August, muggy and hot, that our little Pittsburgh coalition, my roommates, Mrs. Kelly, Nora, and I, climbed out of the passenger train in Marmet, a village on the banks of the Kanawha River, and right away I saw trouble. Close to ten thousand miners had already gathered and they were armed with rifles and revolvers. I'd never been in such a crowd and the mood of the men was ugly.

RUBEN AND THE other men from our group rush off to try to talk to the leaders, but no one will listen. Urging them on is Bill Blizzard, the fiery southern West Virginia organizer. He pushes Ruben aside. Deep in the mob, our friend Mother Jones stands on a dynamite box, but her back is turned and she doesn't see us.

"Tell your husbands and fathers . . . tell them there's no need for bloodshed," she cries. "Bring them to their senses!" The women, mothers and sisters, daughters and lovers, *try* . . . but it's no good; the union men's anger has already been ignited.

They begin marching south like soldiers, wearing red bandannas around their necks, toward Logan and Mingo, the last of the non-unionized counties. They're going for the mine owners, the bosses, anyone who opposes them, and woe to those who get in their way. Like an army of ants, the mass moves south, thirteen thousand of them, over mountains and through valleys, high on their own rage and moonshine.

We should have just gone home when Ruben saw how it was going, but he still thought he could do some good. For one brief moment my husband and I hold each other. He wears a red bandanna, like all the others, and I kiss it for luck. "Love you," I say with my hand on his cheek. He picks me up, laughing, swings me around, and then my friends from Pittsburgh and I lose track of him and travel along with the medics.

It's on the third day, at the edge of Logan County, that all hell breaks loose. The coal company forces, wearing white armbands, have built fortified positions at the top of Blair Mountain, their weapons, machine guns and carbines, pointed straight downhill. Within minutes, we're surrounded by men in hand-to-hand combat, guns going off and the smell of liquid courage on half the fellows' breath. Through the crowd, I catch sight of two men down on my lover. One has his hands around Ruben's throat.

It isn't a bullet that kills my husband. The truth is much worse. I held the murder weapon, a rifle still wet with blood that I'd lifted from a dead miner's hands. One slashing blow, from the butt of the gun, used as a club and meant for the two men straddling Ruben's chest, crushed my lover's skull. Rage is contagious and I meant to kill someone, just not my husband.

Ruben's brown eyes go wide and snap shut as his life's blood flows out of him and I collapse as if the blow had hit me. Nora drags me away and throws the gun in a ditch. Within hours, she, Mrs. Kelly, and I were hidden in the back of a preacher's wagon heading north toward Pittsburgh. Two hundred men died that day. Some say three hundred . . . I never saw Ruben again and no one can say where he's buried.

Upstairs, Dan's snoring starts up again.

Oh Ruben, I miss you. We were warriors together.

January 25, 1942

Absolution

Sorry about last night," Daniel says as he's straining the morning's milk at the sink. He awoke before I did, built up the fire, and went to the barn, so I ran upstairs and dressed in our bedroom to make the children think this was an ordinary morning.

Now the kids are on the school bus and it's just us at home. I chew on my lower lip, unsure what to say. In a way, I'm mad, but he's trying to apologize, so I should meet him halfway.

"Sorry about last night," he says again.

"Well, you were pretty out of it. What was going on, anyway?"

"Did I do anything stupid?"

"Not too bad. You went to bed and then you yelled that we were playing the radio too loud. You didn't dance around with a lampshade on your head, if that's what you mean. Danny knew what was up. I don't think the girls did, though Susie said you were *cranky*."

As I stand to pour myself a cup of coffee, Daniel takes my wrist and kisses it, an act of contrition. I start to pull away, but how can you refuse to forgive a man who kisses your wrist?

"So what was going on?" I ask, waiting.

Daniel sits down at the table. "I don't know, Patience. I was just so sad. Jimmy Pettigrew was a nice kid. Hell, they're probably all nice kids . . . on both sides."

"Not the Nazis," I say. "Not the actual soldiers, the SS and the Nazi Youth. Not Hitler and his pals. They're brutal killers."

"The German people have been brainwashed like the rest of us," Dan responds, tossing back the rest of his coffee. "It's hard to imagine how or why they think all Jews are evil, but it's easy to convince any group they're superior. Hell, look at us. Whites think they're better than Negroes and Asians.

"Given the right circumstances, don't you think some charismatic leader could convince Americans that we're the superior people? Look at what we did to the American Indians, for God's sake! Treated them like animals. Almost wiped them out. Look what we did to the slaves.

"Anyway," he goes on, "last night I just wanted to forget for a while. I took a few swigs from the bottle when I was out in the barn and talked to the cows. They agree with me, by the way." Here he gives me a little of his crooked smile. "War is a waste of life. You don't see herds of Jerseys battling herds of Holsteins. They settle it bull to bull, man to man, and leave the cows and calves out of it."

"But there have always been wars," I argue. "It must be human nature. Maybe you have your head in the clouds."

"So, does that make it right?" He pushes back his chair and paces around the kitchen. "Does that make it smart? Does it need to go on forever?"

"Take a deep breath, Dr. Hester. You're getting yourself worked up again."

"Thanks." He breathes in and out. "Want to go on a walk?"

"Now? I have housework to do."

"Come on. It will be fun."

Bundling up in our work clothes, heavy jackets and knit caps, with our tall black mud boots on, we climb up Spruce Mountain. There's new snow, but it's only a few inches deep and even with my bum knee if we keep to the trail it's easy hiking. When we get near the top, we can see the Hope River, a piece of blue yarn winding through the white. A bare, flat rock beckons and we perch like two lions surveying our kingdom.

"All I want to do is live with my family, do good work, and laugh with a few friends, Patience. *That's all I want . . .* to live in harmony with my neighbors and my land."

I blow out my air. "That would be nice, Dan, but life isn't a fairy tale. There's good and evil in this world and sometimes we have to make choices."

14

February 7, 1942

Winter Blues

The Vipperman Woolen Mill is closed for repairs. There was a fire in the main engine room, but the owner swears they'll be running tomorrow. Meanwhile, Bitsy has a day off and has come with Willie for a visit.

"I was surprised to see you at Jimmy Pettigrew's service," I say to my friend as we settle ourselves on the sofa and turn the radio low. Another two inches of snow came down in the night and Daniel has taken the girls sledding while the boys build a snow fort. Our old dog, Sasha, prefers it inside by the fire.

"I thought I should go for Maggie Pettigrew's sake. She's a nice kid. She came back to work a week after they got the telegram about Jimmy. Said it was because she was afraid she would lose her job, but Mr. Cross told her to take as much time as she needed. I think the real reason she returned so soon was to help her forget. Her mother is shattered, as you'd expect, and Maggie said she just couldn't stand so much sorrow."

"Do you still like working at the mill?"

"It's kind of rough lately. Maggie Pettigrew is the only one who will eat lunch with me, and sometimes the other workers give me a hard time."

"Like what?"

"Call me a nigger." Bitsy stares out the window. "I'm not used to it. My skin isn't as thick as it used to be . . . Mr. Cross refuses to put up with it though. There was this one gal, every time she passed me on the loom, she would spit on the floor. I just ignored it until she started spitting *on me*. Then I had to tell Mr. Cross. . . . I wasn't going to let myself be treated that way.

"He fired her at the end of the shift and told the other workers he wasn't going to go looking at the color of a person's skin when he needed competent employees. We were all there to do a good job and the U.S. military was depending on us."

"Oh, Bitsy! Who was she? Anyone I know?"

"Probably not. Her first name is Cora. She's married to one of the Bishop brothers, from over by Burnt Town, one of the KKK that came to the house on Wild Rose Road."

"I *know* Cora. Becky brought her to meet me at the Baby Cabin. She was so excited to be pregnant; unfortunately, she miscarried. I never dreamed she'd be so prejudiced, but they're a hard bunch, the Bishops, ex-bootleggers. Dan's had trouble with them too. They beat him up once and he and Dr. Blum got into it with them on the Fourth of July a few years ago."

"Daniel? He seems such a peaceful guy."

"He is . . . most of the time, but he's a fighter too when he gets angry." Then I change the subject. "I felt bad at the service when the ushers put you and Willie in the balcony."

"Better view up there." Bitsy laughs.

"Seriously, doesn't it get to you?"

"You can't fight every battle, Patience. I'm Willie's mom and I don't want trouble."

"You think of him like that now, do you? As if you are his ma? At first you called him your *ward*."

"I've taken care of him for half his life. Do you think because he's white with blue eyes it makes any difference? I just called him my 'ward' because it's easier for people to accept, like I'm his nanny or something. Colored women have been taking care of white children in the U.S. since it was formed. It's only in front of people like you and Dan that I declare I'm his *mom*."

I twist my mouth, not knowing what to say, so I change the subject. "Did I tell you Judge Wade asked Daniel to be an air-raid warden? They wanted him to be on the draft board too."

"What did he say?"

"He said no. He thinks it's silly . . . No Japanese airplanes are going to target Union County, West Virginia. And no to the draft board too. He doesn't believe in it."

"Part of the function of the air-raid drills is to make people feel like they're doing something," Bitsy argues. "And as for the draft board . . . how are they going to raise an army in a hurry if they wait for people to volunteer?"

"I know. I'm with you. I went to my first Red Cross meeting last week. It's the same thing. We rolled bandages. Makes you feel like you're helping. It was kind of like a quilting bee.

"Ida May was there with her sister-in-law, Annie Arnold, from Beckley, who's come with her two girls to stay in Liberty while her husband, Ida's brother, is in the air force. I asked Annie where he was stationed, but she wouldn't say. Maybe she doesn't know.

"We all wore white aprons and I was given a large red felt cross to sew on the front. In addition, Mrs. Wade took a small gold pin with a red cross and attached it to my collar in a little ceremony. We gossiped and had refreshments. Meanwhile, men are getting killed on the other side of the globe."

A familiar tune comes on the radio and Bitsy taps and sways to the music. "Let's dance."

"Oh, for heaven's sake, Bitsy! Right here in the middle of the day? Right now?"

"Why not. I miss dancing. I'll show you how to do the Black Bottom."

When Bitsy left, I bundled up and went out on the porch. I let my friend teach me the Black Bottom, and it was fun while it lasted, but the truth is that dancing and the Red Cross meetings aren't helping me much.

At first I thought I was feeling low because of the war, but then I remembered that *every* February, I experience a slump, as if winter will last forever. To remedy this fit of sadness, I got out my old seed catalogue from last year and began thumbing through it.

The 1942 catalogues won't come until March, but just looking at the colorful pictures of purple-topped turnips, shiny green lettuce, and bread-and-butter corn made me happy. I also made note of the flowers I want to plant: zinnias, sunflowers, and marigolds.

To cheer myself more, I played the piano and sang the old spirituals as loud as I could . . . *"I'll fly away, oh Glory. I'll fly away . . ."* and then, before the children got home from school, I went out to walk Sasha.

There was something about the day that was different. A strong wind pushed high, white clouds through the sky. I lifted my head and sniffed like a dog, and then I knew what it was . . . the earth was coming alive.

Spring

15

March 1, 1942

Fisticuffs

At eight this morning Dan got a call from one of his clients. Mr. Dresher's prize workhorse had fallen through the ice on his pond. All day I waited to hear what had happened, but it wasn't until three A.M. that the tired man crawled into bed.

"Ooh, you're stiff with cold and shaking. Let me curl around you. You'll settle sooner if I warm you. How was it? Is the horse okay?"

"Yeah, it took a tractor and six men, but we finally got him out of the pond. The ice was still six inches deep in some places but weak from the thaw in others. I had to creep out on it on my stomach to spread my weight out and give the animal an injection to calm him. He was thrashing around so much, he'd worked himself into a frenzy.

"By the time we got him out of there, his legs were pretty torn up by the ice and he was hypothermic, but I stitched him up and we got him warm by covering him with blankets from the house . . . I got in a fistfight though . . ."

This wakes me up. "*Oh, Dan, what happened?*"

"It was the Bishop brothers again. Before I got there, Mr. Dresher called in all his neighbors to help, and the Bishop farm is right next door. The three brothers came, but they'd been drinking."

"I thought the one they called Beef was the mean one, the one that died in the wildfire."

"Oh, Beef was half-crazy. Remember he was the one beating his dead horse, all the while blaming me for its death. He was part of the KKK too, but apparently the rest of them are just as nuts, especially when they're liquored up. They used to be bootleggers, and I think moonshine must have rotted their brains."

"So what started the fight?"

"Apparently, word is out that I refused to be on the draft board. Aran Bishop is a big-shot air warden now and he got in my face and asked me if I'm some kind of traitor. He knows I speak German, because I occasionally converse with Mr. Dresher in German.

"Then his brother, George Bishop, came in saying I must be a coward. None of it made any sense, and before you get all riled up, Patience, let it go. They only punched me three or four times before I got in a few licks, then Mrs. Dresher went into her house and got a shotgun and blasted it up in the air in the yard, and everyone went home."

"Oh, Daniel! It will be all over Union County!"

"It's okay. I expected something like this would eventually happen. Sooner or later, I'll have to defend my beliefs, I just didn't think it would be so soon."

"I guess I hadn't thought about it. Generally, you're so respected. Is this going to be like in the Great War, where vigilantes accuse people of being enemy sympathizers and then drive them out of town?"

Daniel gives me a hug. "Nah. The Bishop men are just nuts. I probably shouldn't have even told you about the fight, but I thought I might have a black eye in the morning. If anyone asks, I'm going to tell them the horse kicked me."

"Are you warm enough now?"

"Mmmmmm," Daniel moans. "Deliciously warm." He pulls me closer. Within minutes he sleeps, but my eyes are wide open.

March 2, 1942

Raggedy Ann

Today, there was another problem and they had to close the woolen mill, so when I received a call from Earl Spraggs that his wife, Daisy, was in labor, I asked Bitsy if she'd like to go with me.

"Dan will watch the kids, and Mr. Spraggs is back working in the coal mines and is usually generous," I told her. "We might get paid five or ten dollars, or maybe not. You never can tell. Midwives are sometimes considered to be less than medical professionals, just nice ladies who like to deliver babies for fun."

"The trouble is," she responded with a wide grin as she pulled on her jacket, "most of the time it *is* fun. Still, especially in hard times, it's nice to get something . . . a few dollars, a ham, or a wagonload of split firewood."

Now the two of us are sitting in the Spraggses' tidy kitchen drinking tea while Daisy naps upstairs. I've been dying to have a little time alone with Bitsy to talk. (It's Daisy's fourth baby, and though she's in early labor, I like to arrive in plenty of time just in case she goes fast.)

"So let's get back to your story. Tell me more about Paris and Katherine and Willie. I checked on Daisy a few minutes ago; she's sound asleep and her kids are all down the road with their father and grandfather at the old man's farm. So, dish it out. What happened next? Last I heard, it was 1940, the Germans were marching toward Paris, and you were on your way back to the U.S.A."

"Well, let's see . . ." Bitsy takes a sip of tea.

There's a noise from the woman upstairs. "Daisy, you okay?" I call. Bitsy stands and takes the stairs to the bedroom two at a time. I limp along behind, but our patient appears to only moan in her sleep.

"Is everything ready for the delivery? Maybe she'll sleep through the whole thing," I joke. "She seems awfully tired."

"Everything we need is laid out on the dresser. I'll heat up some water and bring it up." My assistant trots back down the steps. Before the Dreshers' cow kicked me, I took the stairs like she does, two at a time. Now I move slowly.

Across the hall from the mother and father's bedroom is

a second room for the older kids, a boy and two girls. The two double beds are made up neatly with colorful quilts, and I decide it won't hurt to rest for a while.

"Come on, Bitsy. Let's lie down. I always tell new mothers, 'When the baby sleeps, the mama must sleep.' It should be the same for midwives: If the patient sleeps, the midwife should sleep." Bitsy agrees and takes the other bed. Within minutes I'm dreaming.

It's summer and I rest on the bank of the Hope River, looking up at the big puffy white clouds. There are wild roses and daisies. Somewhere downstream I can hear children playing.

When I open my eyes a few minutes later, I remember that I'm at the Spraggses' home. Holy cow! I'm supposed to be attending a woman in labor! When I look at my pocket watch, I'm shocked to see I've been out for over an hour. My assistant is still sawing logs on the other bed.

"Bitsy," I whisper. "Bitsy!" I stand and give her shoulder a shake. "Wake up. Look outside, it's already getting dark and Daisy needs to have a baby. I'm going to see if I can get her moving."

Across the hall in Daisy's room, I find the patient still snoring. Her blond bob is matted against her face and one hand droops over the side of the bed. Below on the floor is a large brown bottle. PAREGORIC: OPIUM CAMPHORATED TINCTURE, it says on the label in small print. The bottle is half empty.

"What in Sam Hill!" I say out loud. "Daisy Spraggs!" I try to get her up but she's as heavy as a sack of sand. Her eyelids flutter like a butterfly's wings and close again over her green eyes. "Bitsy, come help! Daisy's in some sort of stupor. I think she's been tipping back some medicine."

Bitsy wanders through the bedroom door smoothing her dress and yawning. "That was a nice nap." Then she sees the bottle and frowns. "What's Paregoric?"

"It's a medicinal remedy for pain or diarrhea and it's available in any pharmacy without a physician's note. People give it to fretful children or babies with colic. They use it for bad coughs. Some doctors recommend it for arthritis or severe menstrual pain, but its main ingredients are opium and alcohol."

Bitsy picks up the bottle and stares at it. "I know about opium, and heroin too. The high-flyers in Paris were crazy about it. It was the rage at Bricktop's . . . I tried it once. It wasn't for me." (I'm shocked but I try not to show it. I thought heroin was just for gangsters and hoods in the Bowery of New York or the slums of Chicago.)

"I'll get some cold water," Bitsy says. "Maybe if we wash her face, she'll come around."

Sitting down on the edge of the bed, I study our patient. It's hard to imagine she's had three children. She's only twenty-five, but her once-pretty face is slack and worn. I wonder why she's been taking the patent medicine; painful false labor, perhaps, or maybe diarrhea?

"Come on, Daisy. Come on. Time to wake up!" Her pulse is regular, but very slow at sixty beats per minute. I roll her over. She weighs only as much as one of Daniel's newborn calves and she's nine months pregnant! *Way too skinny.*

The unborn baby's heartbeat is 120. That's slow too, but

still in the normal range. Finally, I get her blood pressure. Also low, 100/50.

Thinking back, I remember that Daisy came only two times for her pregnancy visits at the Baby Cabin and never participated in the Pregnant Ladies Society. This was not what I prefer, but she'd delivered her other three babies at home without difficulty and I didn't make a fuss about it.

Now here she lies, out cold.

Rise and Shine

*B*itsy reenters the room carrying warm water in a pot and a cool washrag in the other hand. She pulls up a wooden stool and cups Daisy's head.

"Time to *rise and shine*," she says, and I smile, remembering how my mother used to call me with those words on cold, dark winter mornings back in Deerfield, my mother who died of consumption when I was twelve. When I think of it, it makes my heart sad; there's *still* no cure for TB.

"Come on. Come on!" Bitsy washes the woman's face a little less gently and then drops her head on the pillow. "She's really blotto!"

"What shall we do?" I wonder out loud. "She might not even be in labor. Maybe I better do a vaginal exam."

"You know, it's *illegal* under the West Virginia Midwife Statute of 1925," Bitsy teases as she hands me my sterilized red rubber gloves.

"I know, smarty," I return. "But Daisy won't tell."

Gently, I touch my patient's inner thigh, speaking to her as if she could hear me. "Okay, now, Daisy, I'm going to check you to see how your labor is advancing."

I insert two fingers in her vagina and am surprised to feel a hard round ball, low in the pelvis. Feeling for the cervix, I discover it's gone. "She's completely dilated!" I look over at Bitsy with surprise.

"We have to get her up to walk," Bitsy decides.

"How can we? She's a Raggedy Ann doll."

"Come on. Let's try. She can't weigh very much."

"Okay, okay," I agree.

Together, we drag the woman's legs over the side of the bed and let them hang down. Daisy moans. "Hoist her up," says my assistant. Though Bitsy is half my size, she's as strong as a cougar. I shake my head to get ready for the effort, as we each sling one of Daisy's arms over our shoulders and begin to march back and forth across the room . . . only Daisy's not marching . . . She stumbles. She moans again and tries to lie down.

"Daisy, wake up. You're about to have a baby!" Bitsy yells in her ear, but Daisy slides to the floor like a drunk.

"Hello!" comes a man's voice from downstairs. "It's Mr. Spraggs! How's my woman coming? Is anything wrong? The other little ones only took a few hours."

"One minute, Mr. Spraggs. I'll be right down," I holler.

"Can you hold her?" I whisper to Bitsy.

Downstairs, I find the parlor empty. Mr. Spraggs is out on the porch lighting a cigarette. He's a big man, over six feet with wide shoulders and a thick neck. His eyes shift back and forth with worry and he blows out the smoke. "Is everything okay? Should I get her in the truck and head for the hospital in Torrington? I know this pregnancy hasn't been easy on her, not with her back trouble and all."

"Her back trouble? I didn't know. Right now she's sleeping, but the thing is, Mr. Spraggs, we can't get her to wake up. Has she been taking the Paregoric for pain?"

"Oh, quite regular. She gets it in Delmont. I doubt she could manage the house, the garden, and our kids without it. I'd help her more, but I have the sheep and cattle and I work every day in the coal mine."

"Well, the thing is, the opium in the medication has impeded the labor and made her too sleepy. We're walking her around now and if she could just push, the baby would be out in a jiffy."

"Opium!" He looks toward the house. "She never said it had opium in it. That's bad stuff, right?"

"Well, it's strong stuff and it can be addicting if you take it often. Our problem now is just getting her to *come to* and get the baby out."

"Is there something I can do? I know this is women's business."

"Maybe you could just sit in your truck and we'll call you if we can think of anything." Upstairs I hear footsteps.

"Mmmmmmmmmgh." There's a groan.

I take the steps as fast as I can. "Bitsy?" The patient is down on her hands and knees with the side of her face resting on the bed. This time her eyes are open.

"Something's coming," she says like a happy drunk. "Can I have some more of my tonic?"

"No, Daisy, not now. Your baby needs to be born. It *wants* to be born."

"Okay." She smiles again. "That's fine. What should I do?"

"Well, for heaven's sake, can you push?" Bitsy exclaims.

"Do I have to?"

"*Yes!*" we both say together.

"Okay." The woman gathers herself and makes one mighty lunge, head down like a bull charging a red flag. "Ugggggggggggh!"

"One push. That's all it took," Bitsy crows. "One push. Nice work!"

The cord is still attached and pulsing. Daisy smiles in contentment, but the baby's not crying. I give him a rub and blow on his belly to make him gasp. *The breath of life*, Mrs. Kelly called it. He opens his eyes, but as the moments go by, instead of turning pink, he turns gray. Now the cord is thin and flat, no oxygen coming from the mother to the infant. "Come on, kid, time to rise and shine!"

Bitsy is already reaching for the sterile scissors. "Shall I cut the limp cord? It's not doing anything to help now, is it?"

"Yes, cut. We've got to get this kid breathing. I know he's in there. He opened his eyes and looked right at me, but now he's gone back to sleep." *That must be it,* I think. *The Paregoric. The opiate.* As soon as the cord is cut, I lay the baby on the bed and begin to breathe for it.

Mrs. Kelly was the first person I saw do this. Three very gentle puffs in the infant's mouth usually gets the baby going. I wait a few seconds. When he doesn't gasp or cry, I repeat the procedure. Puff. Puff. Puff.

"Wake up, Daisy! Wake up. Your baby needs you," Bitsy yells. "Wake up and talk to your baby."

We hear heavy footsteps on the stairs and the bedroom door flies back. Bitsy is holding the mother's head and shouting in her face and I'm kneeling like a druid priestess over his newborn son breathing into his mouth.

"What the hell!" he shouts.

"It's the Paregoric," I say between puffs and Bitsy finishes the explanation.

"Your wife took too much medicine and now the baby's sleepy and won't breathe. He has a heartbeat, but Patience is trying to give him some air."

"Won't breathe, will he!" The man grabs his infant and turns toward the door.

"No! Mr. Spraggs!" I rush after him, but he's way ahead of me, running down the stairs. What's he going to do! The miner heads for the kitchen sink where a pan of cold dishwater sits ready for dishes and he dips the child in. Dip one. Dip two.

"Sir! You mustn't. You're chilling the infant."

Dip three. Up and down the baby goes in the father's big hands. Dip four . . . and the infant lets out a wail and not just a little one. He's mad! *Who woke me up from my nice sleep?* he says. Mad. Mad. Mad!

March 2, 1942

Called to the home of Daisy and Earl Spraggs for Daisy's fourth delivery. The labor was very unusual. The mother slept through most of it.

After five hours, we finally got her to wake up and the baby was born with one push. It turned out the patient had been taking large amounts of Paregoric and was extremely sedated.

The baby was sedated too. He didn't breathe. I gave him several puffs of air and blew on his stomach to get him to gasp, but nothing worked until the father grabbed him and dunked him in cold water. Then the child howled right off. (Daniel told me later that farmers sometimes do this when a newborn lamb doesn't breathe. They just dunk the lamb in the livestock water trough and it usually works.)

Franklin Delano Spraggs, named after President Roosevelt, was born at 6:34 P.M.

6 pounds, 4 ounces. Bitsy and I were given ten greenback dollars, which we shared.

16

March 4, 1942

Opium Eater

"Hello?" I answer the phone, waving to Mira to turn the radio down. "War Time Blues" by Sonny Boy Williamson is playing and she sings along. "*Now, it ain't no use you worryin'. That ain't goin' to help you none. If you can't fly no airplane, maybe you'll carry a gun!*"

Since I can't think of a woman due at this time, I imagine this will be a vet call.

"This the midwife?" a man's voice asks.

"Yes . . ."

"Earl Spraggs here. Our baby is poorly. I wonder if you'd come."

"How do you mean, poorly?"

"Jittery, like he's got a Mexican jumping bean in his diaper and also he cries all the time. He cried so hard last night, none of us got any sleep. It might be a bellyache."

"Is he passing stool?"

"It's watery like." *This doesn't sound good. Maybe I can get Becky to come with me if she isn't at the CCC camp.*

"Well, I guess I could drive over this afternoon. Anything else wrong?"

"Daisy is poorly too. I took away the Paregoric and now she says her womb hurts."

I suck in a deep breath. "Okay, I'll be coming, but not until after the midday meal."

Daniel comes in with two buckets of milk. "What's up?"

"Daisy and Earl Spraggs's baby boy is ill. She's bottle feeding formula, so it might be a reaction to that."

"Mother's milk is best." He pours himself a cup of coffee and warms his hands on the mug.

"You saying that to impress me?"

"No. Every farmer and vet knows that if a piglet is deprived of its mother's colostrum for the first eight hours of life, it's almost guaranteed to become sick and die. It's the same with newborn horses, cats, and dogs.

"Most mammals are born without any antibodies, or only the tiniest amounts in their blood. Without the antibodies, they can't fight infection. No reason human babies would be different."

"Well, I tried to convince her with the last two babies and she refused, so I guess she doesn't care, or just doesn't understand it, but I love it when you talk all scientific. Did you know that? You're so smart. It's like Casanova whispering words of love in Italian."

Daniel raises one eyebrow. "I could tell you about the new DDT that's just been invented. It's going to save lives. We could discuss the discovery upstairs. . . ."

"Sorry, bud. Duty calls. I'm going to see if Becky can go out with me to check the baby."

An hour later, Becky and I turn onto the Spraggses' road. When we step on the porch we can hear a radio turned up high and a baby wailing almost as loud. "*We interrupt this program*," the announcer says, as we knock at the door, "*to bring you an update on the fighting in Port Moresby, New Guinea, the last defensive post held by the Allies to protect Australia. The Japanese have landed. I repeat, the Japanese have landed and have apparently taken over the island. More to come on the evening news.*"

I'm surprised when Daisy answers the door still wearing her red-and-blue bathrobe. "Thank God you're here! I'm at my wit's end." She has the baby on her shoulder, wrapped in a blanket, and she's patting him frantically. Before I can get my coat off, she plunks the screaming infant in my arms and runs upstairs. Her three other children sit on the sofa, pale and afraid.

"Is the baby okay?" the boy asks. He has a slight lisp.

"I don't know yet. Where's your father? He's the one that called us."

"Pap had to go down in the mines. He works second shift. Won't be home until dawn," a sister answers.

"Is there somewhere Nurse Becky could examine the baby? Somewhere quiet?"

The children look at one another. "In our bedroom, I guess."

The baby's still bawling and kicking his little feet against my chest, so I quickly motion Becky upstairs. I brought my hanging scale, so the first thing we do is weigh him. "Five pounds eight," I say out loud so that Becky can write it in her notes. "He's lost ten ounces. Not good."

Then we lay him down on the bed and watch while he kicks and screams some more. He vomits once, and then I can't stand it any longer and have to pick him up again.

"We better ask Daisy what's going on," Becky says. I cross the hall and tap on the mother's bedroom door. "Daisy?" No answer. I tap again louder, getting irritated. Still nothing. "Daisy!"

Finally, I push the door open and find a familiar scene. Daisy's sleeping and there's only one way anyone could sleep through this racket. She's hitting the Paregoric again. "It's the opium," I tell Becky. "I asked Mr. Spraggs to get rid of the stuff, but apparently Daisy got some more. Here, you take the baby. I'll go downstairs and warm up a baby bottle." Becky takes the inconsolable infant back to the kids' room and sits on the bed. Outside, it's snowing again.

Little Franklin cries and cries. I've never seen anything like it. Maybe there's something wrong with him from loss of oxygen when he was born. How long did it take for him to breathe? One minute? Two? Three?

I go back to the mother's bedroom and shake her awake. "You've been asleep a long time again, Daisy, and the baby and the children have been unattended."

"I just lay down for a short nap," the woman murmurs.

"No, you've been asleep since right after we got here at two. It's now four thirty." Daisy looks at her hands, which are trembling. When she sees me watching, she hides them between the folds of her robe.

"Your husband called me because he's worried about the baby."

"Sometimes Franklin throws up and he has diarrhea. He's stiff like and won't settle. That's why I'm tired. He cries and cries and I can't sleep at night."

"Well, I think it's more than that. I think you're using the Paregoric again. We shook you and called to you and you didn't wake up. That's not normal. . . . Becky, can you come in here with the baby?" I call.

"It's the cramps. I have to have something. They're real bad, Miss Patience." She glances toward the bureau, where I observe the familiar brown bottle of the tincture of opium.

"Are your bowels working?"

"Not very well, but they never do." I perform a quick exam and find nothing wrong, temperature normal, uterus soft and non-tender. Becky stands at the door, holding the screaming infant. "I think you're just constipated, Daisy, and the opium in the Paregoric is making it worse. Now, about Franklin . . ."

"I know what's wrong," says Becky. "The infant is going through withdrawal. Both you and your child are addicted to opium."

"How could that be? He's only a few days old," Daisy argues.

"Did you take Paregoric all through your pregnancy," I ask, indicating the bottle on the bureau.

Daisy looks down. "Maybe. Is my baby going to be okay?"

"Well, he is and he isn't," Becky answers. "Physically he's smaller than average. He has diarrhea. He's jittery and having small seizures. He's going to need round-the-clock care as he goes through withdrawal from the opium."

"I'm no opium eater!" Daisy protests.

"Opium is the active ingredient in the pain medicine you've been taking. Opium is *in* the Paregoric. Didn't you read the label?" Becky asks.

"I don't read so good," Daisy says.

"Well, be that as it may," I interrupt, "you have to stop using it. I asked your husband to get rid of the bottle, but before we leave this time, we'll search the house."

"You can't do that! Earl won't let you."

"There's no shame in this, Mrs. Spraggs." Becky comes in. "Many people become habituated to patent medications or even ones prescribed by their physician. You will have to go through withdrawal too. It will take a few weeks. The baby is going through withdrawal already. It will be hard."

"Where do you get the medicine, anyway?" I ask.

"Doc Burch, on Rock Forge near Delmont," she answers, lifting her chin as if to dare us to say anything bad about the old healer.

"Well, you just have to stop taking it. In addition, I think I should take the baby home and care for him until he gets well."

Daisy's eyes widen. "No!"

17

March 18, 1942

Substitute Mom

The children were delighted when I brought Franklin home. They love babies. Sunny and Sue lost their infant brother in the wildfire of '35. (He drowned when their mother dropped him as she slid into the creek to hide from the flames, a tragic event.)

Now here I am, a substitute mom, sleeping with the Spraggses' infant in the Baby Cabin while his mother and he go through withdrawal. I give him drops of laudanum on a graduated schedule that Dr. Blum prescribed. The mother is going it alone with just her sister to help her.

Daniel was furious when I first brought the little one home, but when I described the scene with the inconsolable screaming baby, the drugged mom, and the terrified older children he got over it. Daisy and Earl visit on Sundays and it's nice to see the mother acting halfway normal. At least she's not nodding off.

With caring for Baby Franklin and the rest of our brood, my house is a wreck and March is almost gone. The girls are helping me wash the eggs, but we couldn't get into town to sell them last week and they're starting to mount up. Not only that, I'm only sleeping about five hours a night.

On Sunday, Bitsy comes over to help me so I can get some housework done, but we end up sitting in the Baby Cabin together while she rocks Doodlebug. That's what we call the baby now, *Franklin Delano* just seemed too grand.

"How's Willie?" I ask. "Does he like school? Does he like his teacher?"

"He's doing okay, but he's so quiet and shy. I wish he could be around more fellows."

"Oh, I doubt they think he's so quiet and shy. Did you hear about him punching some big boy who was making fun of Susie at Christmas?" (I tell her the story and she smiles.)

"Maybe not so backward and shy, then? It's good to protect someone who's getting bullied, but he still needs some male friends," Bitsy thinks out loud.

"He has Danny, though he's two years younger. I'll speak to Dan. Maybe he and Dr. Blum could get him involved in the vet work. How did you end up taking Willie away with you anyway?"

Bitsy laughs, because I'm always digging to hear her story. "Well, remember, I just made it out of Paris as the German army advanced. The first place I went when I returned to the States was to Katherine's. I was shocked when I got there. Katherine had died just a month before.

Miss Jones, the new nanny, was leaving. *Someone* needed to take care of the boy."

"What about Katherine's family? They were wealthy, why couldn't they take care of him?"

"They'd passed before we went to Paris. Her father died of a heart attack and her mother died of breast cancer a few years before."

"What happened to Katherine, was it cancer like her mom?"

"No, she drowned in the bathtub."

"Drowned in the tub. Oh, Bitsy! Suicide?"

"No, the coroner determined she had a brain tumor. He thought she'd had a fit from pressure on her brain and slid into the water."

"A brain tumor! I'm so sorry." We sit for a minute paying silent homage to the beautiful blond woman who, though she grew up wealthy, had such a hard life. Money doesn't protect us from suffering. Death and loss come to everyone.

Outside the children play army on the greening lawn and their laughter comes through the open window. Too bad real war isn't as much fun. "Do you mind holding Doodlebug, while I feed the kids and do some laundry. I'll send Willie back with a sandwich for you."

Two hours later, I'm back in the Baby Cabin, only now Willie is rocking the baby. He's singing a song by Roy Rogers and Dale Evans, low and sweet, and the baby and Bitsy have both fallen asleep. "*Happy trails to you, until we meet again. Happy trails to you. Keep smilin' until then.*"

"That's beautiful, Willie." He smiles and keeps singing and I join in.

"*Some trails are happy ones. Others are blue. It's the way you ride the trail that counts. Here's a happy one for you.*"

18

March 21, 1942

Peepers

*W*hen spring comes to the Appalachian Mountains it comes with a rush. One week the daffodils are poised half-frozen at your doorstep and the next they're a graceful battalion of yellow. One week the buds on the apple trees are carved at the end of what looks like dead branches, and then the whole tree turns pink.

Doodlebug is gone. In the middle of the week, Mr. and Mrs. Spraggs came over and demanded their infant. What could I say? The baby was doing well and only had a few days left of his laudanum.

Daisy acted quite normal. She was off the Paregoric, promised to never to take it again, and mostly I believed her. One thing Mrs. Kelly taught me is . . . you can't do a woman's labor for her. That's her work. And you can't live her life for her, either. I just hope the baby and the other little kids do okay.

Now at last we can get our normal lives back, what's left of normal since our country's at war. The first thing I do is get out the new Burpee's seed catalogue and try to decide what to plant. I've dried and saved tomato and bean seeds, but my squash seeds all rotted. We have leftover potatoes sprouting in the root cellar that I can cut up and use for seeds, but I have a craving for some collards and lettuce, sweet peas and kale, fresh healthy things!

This morning, Dan took the tractor over to Wild Rose Road to turn over Becky and Isaac's garden. It's on a slope and better drained than our farm. We have to wait for our soil to dry before he can plow our bottomland. Hungry for greens, I decide, while he's gone, to go out and find some. There must be dandelions growing somewhere. I've seen a few flowers.

Carrying a clean bucket, I carefully cross the wet field. Only a few years ago, I walked this land without thinking about tripping, but now, because of my knee, I must be careful and I don't like it. I'd rather be looking up at the swift-moving clouds tumbling over Spruce Mountain. I'd rather be gazing at the new red buds on the maple trees or looking for birds.

Yesterday at the bird feeder, I saw a purple finch, a nuthatch, a redbird, and a chickadee. These are names I have learned from Mrs. Kelly's worn copy of *Birds of Village and Field* published in 1898. I know there are newer guides, because Becky has one called *The Field Guide to Birds*, but they cost a small fortune. Anyway, my old book has served me just fine.

As I follow the stream, my eyes become sharper and I

find dandelion leaves everywhere. Then I catch sight of a tiny blue bird high in the treetops. "*Zee zee zee zizizizi eeet!*" it calls with a trill. You know it is spring when you hear the first cerulean warbler.

For dinner I made the dandelion greens and the family gobbled them up. I had no idea how hungry we are for fresh food. After Dan and I put the kids to bed, we sat on the porch in the mild evening air.

"Listen!" Dan whispered.

"What?"

He put his warm hand on the back of my neck and turned my ear toward the creek. That's when I heard it, the ringing of a thousand tiny silver bells. The peepers are back, little frogs that live in wet places and peep at night, another sign of spring.

I have thought this before about the four seasons. A year is just long enough to forget some sign of nature. Then all of a sudden, it's there; the sound of thunder before an afternoon storm, the smell of a rose, the vision of yellow leaves against the blue sky, the tickle of the first snow on your nose or the peepers of spring.

March 21, 1942

Equinox

Sunday evening, to celebrate spring, we asked everyone over to our house to play Charades.

From youngest to oldest, we all took turns, with Mira acting out *Little Orphan Annie* to Mr. Roote doing *Stars and Stripes Forever*. The talk, when we took a break for refreshments was all about the war.

"We've been checking the records of the boys at the CCC camp and making sure they're all registered for the draft," Isaac Blum says. "We had to drive a few of them over to the draft board in Liberty and help them fill out the forms.

"The whole camp would volunteer in a minute if they weren't already enrolled in the Civilian Conservation Corps. Washington is trying to get that straightened out. These kids can read now and they're in top physical shape and used to army discipline. They'd make darn good soldiers."

"I'd go in a minute if I were old enough," Danny says.

I look over at Daniel as he stares at his hands. He hasn't taken a bite of cake and I notice his little flask of rum is right by his side. Isaac takes a nip and the men all pass it around. When it comes to Daniel, he tips it back hard.

"The whole county is in a panic," Dan growls. "Everyone's wondering what will happen next. Will the Japanese bomb Los Angeles or San Francisco? Or will the Germans come from the other direction and go for Washington, D.C., or New York? One thing, it's not going to be Union County."

"Can you say that for sure, sir?" Willie asks. "West Virginia has coal; the nation needs coal to make steel and we need steel to make guns, tanks, and airplanes. Also, there's the munitions plant in Torrington."

Daniel looks at him fondly. "I'm pretty sure we're safe, Will. There are a lot bigger targets less than a hundred miles from here. That's the trouble when people panic. They're like a deer in the headlights. Their brains shut off."

"What are you saying, Daniel? That you think the war is a mistake?" Mr. Maddock asks. "We have to fight now. The Japanese attacked us, and Hitler is a madman. He'll stop at nothing."

"Let's play some more Charades." Becky changes the subject before the men get in an argument. "Come on, now. Who wants to be next?"

I volunteer, hoping to get us back in the party mood, but just as I begin to act out the book *The Secret Garden*, the phone rings.

Luella

"*I*s this the midwife?" a soft voice asks when I answer, and I can't tell if it's male or female.

"Yes. It's Patience Hester. Can I help you?"

"My mom said to call."

"And who is your mom?"

"Luella Bonnet of Burnt Town. She's expecting a baby and she's awful sick. She says come quick."

"Is there someone with her, a woman or your father?"

"No, just my little brother. I have to go now."

Lord, I think. *That wasn't much of a report.* I know Luella, but she's way over on the other side of the county and she didn't even tell me she was pregnant or come for a visit this time. I delivered her last baby four or five years ago and you'd think she would at least call.

Everyone looks up when I come back in the room. "I guess I have to go to Burnt Town for a delivery. Anyone want to come with me?"

"I'll come!" says Willie.

"Oh, ech!" says Little Dan. "I'd rather watch a sheep give birth than a lady."

"Dr. Hester and I will take you with us during lambing season, Willie," Isaac Blum says.

I turn to Bitsy. "How about you?"

"I could do it. The plant is closed while they bring in new equipment tomorrow."

Dan walks me to the door and looks out. "The sky's clear. No sign of a storm and the roads should be good. Take the Model T, the tires are better." He pulls my knit cap down over my ears.

"Keep a lid on the booze, okay?" I whisper.

"Right, boss," he says, and he kisses my nose.

On the way through Liberty we stop at the Texaco station for gas. This is one of our big expenses. With Daniel's job he often travels at least ten miles a day, and with fuel at twelve cents a gallon it mounts up. Sometimes, I've had to drive twenty miles to a birth.

"Hi, Loonie, Give me five" I say when the attendant runs out of the gas station wearing a Texaco uniform, complete with the hat. (Loonie isn't really Loonie. That's just his nickname. His real name if Louis Tinkshell.)

"*Five greenback dollars* of gas," he kids.

"No! Five *gallons of gas* and not a drop more, sixty cents' worth."

"You know, gas will probably be rationed soon," he informs me.

"I guess we'll face that if it happens."

Just as we're leaving, a blue Ford sedan drives up, pulling a small travel van. A colored man gets out and asks where they might camp. He's wearing clean new coveralls and is almost as big as Mr. Hummingbird. The woman who gets out with him is pregnant. Two children watch from the backseat.

"People used to camp under the Hope River Bridge," Bitsy tells them through the open passenger window. "It's safe there, the water is good and you can fish."

"Do you know them?" I ask as we pull away.

Bitsy shakes her head no. "They were probably just traveling through the area," she says. "Do you think I know every colored person in West Virginia?"

"Just about."

March 22, 1942

Arrived at the home of Luella Bonnet of Burnt Town at 4:05 and shortly afterward, at 5:37 P.M., Baby Boy Bonnet (no name yet) 7 pounds, 3 ounces was born to the widow Luella Bonnet, with a hand presentation. No complications. Present at delivery, Bitsy Proudfoot and myself.

Luella was as silent as Time through the whole labor, rocking in her chair and then, like Daisy, she refused to push, even though, in this case, she was conscious and wide-awake. It was like she didn't want the infant to come out.

Finally, when I saw the baby's hand along the side of his ear, I took Luella's index finger, put it near her vagina, and the unborn infant grasped it, as if he knew it was his ma's. The feeling of his tiny grip must have brought the woman out of her trance, because with four mighty grunts she soon delivered him.

Later, we learned that Bo Bonnet, the father, was another victim of the attack on Pearl Harbor. A medic in the navy, he went down trying to save other sailors. Now I know why she didn't call or come visit me. She was grieving. How hard must that be to let go of one love and give birth to a new love at the same time!

Luella seemed pleased with her baby and put him to the breast right away. The two other children were as good as gold and waited in the living room until the baby was born and then they crawled in bed with their mother.

Sometimes life is just too sad, I think, but I must remember that tiny hand coming out, reaching . . . reaching for the light . . . and then taking hold.

19

March 30, 1942

Cave-In

On my way to Luella's, making a postpartum visit to the grieving woman, yesterday, I felt a jolt. A huge blast shook my Olds and at the same time I saw smoke billowing up over the mountain.

Instantly, a forlorn siren began to wail. I'd heard that sound before, and an iron spike stabbed through my middle. It was the emergency siren at a nearby coal mine, and it meant trouble, big trouble—an explosion, a fire, or a cave-in.

Remembering the cave-in at the Wild Cat Mine ten years ago, when Dan and I together tended the injured, I follow the sound of the siren into the camp. Here, small identical wooden houses line the road on both sides. On every porch, a woman stands listening, wondering what's happened.

When I get to the source of the warning signal, I find myself in an industrial compound of five brick buildings.

An enormous structure called a tipple, which is used to load the coal into hopper cars, looms four stories above the buildings.

At the farthest end of the brick-paved lot where the rails thread into the mountain, smoke pours from the mouth of the mine. Men rush toward the hole, but a foreman blocks the way. "Stand back!" I hear him say through a megaphone, but the siren obscures most of his words. All I can make out when I jump from my car is . . . "Unsafe . . . one hundred and five men still in the tunnel . . . levels of methane too high and it's burning . . ."

The faces of the miners, blackened by coal dust, show evidence of their concern. These men must have been on their way home from the previous shift, but they've rushed back to try to save their comrades.

At the door to the toolshed, five men with "Rescue Team" written on their yellow jackets are putting on firefighting equipment and gas masks, preparing to enter the inferno. Since I'm apparently the first medical person to respond, I stand back and watch as scores of silent women, some carrying babies and toddlers, stream into the area.

This is a much bigger operation than the Wild Cat Mine over by Hazel Patch. Here I don't know anyone and have no idea how to offer my services. I'm thinking of retreating when a pickup truck pulls in behind my vehicle and cuts me off. Three men jump out of the cab and another four out of the truck bed. They have clean faces, some brown and some white, but all wear the familiar hard hat with a lamp on the front and I imagine they're miners from the graveyard shift here to help.

"Hey fellas!" I call. "I was just passing when I heard the explosion and a siren went off. I'm a nurse and thought I might be able to help. Is there a clinic around here or someone in charge?" (This is not strictly true. I'm not a *registered* nurse, like Becky, but I have nursed many ill people and I do know first aid.)

"Follow me, ma'am," a short, swarthy fellow wearing blue coveralls, yells. "Name's Frank."

The office we enter is in chaos, and since there are no injured to help yet, I shrink into a corner and look around. All over the wall are patriotic posters. "MINE AMERICAN COAL . . . WE'LL MAKE IT HOT FOR THE ENEMY," one says.

"Rescue teams of five men will be readied at the tool shop every fifteen minutes. Anyone who wants to can sign up to volunteer . . . and men . . . I don't need to tell you this, but I will; say your prayers for those trapped, and if you go back in, be as careful as hell."

The man I take to be a supervisor collapses in a wood chair as the miners hurry out. "Frank," he whispers to the man in the blue coveralls. "Can you shut and lock the door before a new crowd comes in? I have to think." He pulls out a roll of paper and studies a map of the mine.

"Right, Chief," Frank says, complying with his orders.

"I'm sorry," the boss says, sensing my presence in the corner and looking over. "Are you someone's wife or sister? As you can see, we're working on a rescue plan and I can't give you any more information."

"She's a volunteer nurse with the Red Cross," Frank informs him, embroidering the facts to fit his imagination.

"I told her to come in here to find out where she can set up a treatment station." (There's no need to correct the fellow at this time, and I *do* wrap bandages for the local Red Cross.)

"Oh, thanks. I didn't mean to be rude." The supervisor runs his fingers through his silver hair. "We don't have a physician in the camp. He joined the army a few weeks ago and we haven't found a new one. You can use the clerk's office for a hospital. Get some of the women to run home for blankets and bandages. It will give them something to do."

Frank leads me out to the cobbled yard and points to a tall, olive-skinned woman with a red bandanna over her hair. "Ask Felicia Ricci. Her husband is trapped in the mine. She'll help you." Then he runs toward the tool shed.

"Mrs. Ricci!" The dark-haired beauty whips around and I introduce myself. "A miner named Frank said you were a woman who could get things done. I'm Patience Hester, a nurse, and I've volunteered to set up a makeshift infirmary."

There's another explosion farther up the mountain and a new hole opens on the face of the slope. Felicia's face turns white and she makes the sign of the cross. More smoke billows out of the main entrance. "My Martino is in there," she explains with tears in her eyes.

Finally, someone thinks to turn off the siren. A hundred silent women stand peering into the black hole, hoping to catch a sight of a loved one limping into the light.

Rescue

Felicia and I quickly organize the makeshift hospital. Women bring blankets and pillows and we put them on the desks and tables to make beds. We bring in more water, rip up old sheets for bandages, and then go back outside to await the news. Every few minutes my assistant puts her hand on her belly as if she has a stomachache. Every few minutes she makes the sign of the cross.

One by one the rescue teams enter the shaft with picks and shovels. There must be twenty-five men in there by now. Exhausted, the first crew comes out, but the news isn't good.

The rockslide about half a mile from the entrance is blocking the way, and there are several uncontrolled fires.

Finally, help begins to arrive from outside. First on the scene is a truck full of volunteer firemen from Delmont. Then from Liberty comes the hearse, followed by Sheriff Hardman and my husband in the squad car. The hearse, I think, is premature, until I remember that the long black van doubles as an ambulance. Dr. Blum and Becky must be at the CCC camp, miles away.

"Dan! Dan! Up here!" I call from the porch of the makeshift infirmary, relieved to have a more experienced medical person at hand, but he and Hardman head for the toolshed, where men are volunteering. Dan's carrying his vet bag and he and Hardman approach the supervisor.

Suddenly, there's action at the mouth of the mine and two rescue workers stumble out, carrying the first victim on a stretcher. The man's face is covered with his bloodied shirt and one of his arms droops over the side of the pallet like a piece of rope. The boss, on the steps of the head-quarters, waves that I should step forward.

Stethoscope, from my birth kit, around my neck, I hurry through the crowd, trying to look like I know something useful, but the results of my exam are not good. The man's head is crushed and he has no pulse. I look at the boss and shake my head sadly.

A young woman falls to the ground and is surrounded by other women. The dead man must be her husband, and since I was careful to hide his shattered face she has recognized him by the wedding ring on his limp hand.

Next, a low coal cart arrives pulled by three burly fellows. It's full of dead men, and the wailing of mothers and sisters, wives and lovers continues. Frank follows me with a clipboard writing down the names of the deceased.

Finally, there's some good news, forty-two dust covered miners, some limping, some half dragging comrades, appear from behind us, straggling down the road from the coal company village, singing, "*Over hill, over dale. As we hit the dusty trail. And those Caissons go rolling along.*"

They have burst through a barricade in an unused shaft and marched around the mountain. Martino Ricci, Felicia's husband, leads the crew, and I will admit I cried for joy when she ran to him.

"Don Stoddard is still alive down there," Ricci says to the boss. "His left arm is shattered and trapped under a two-ton slab of sandstone. Another explosion and he's a goner. If we had a doctor, he could amputate . . . and we could get Don out in thirty minutes."

The supervisor wipes his face and looks around wildly. *Not me*, I think. *Maybe Nurse Becky could amputate an arm, but not me.*

Sheriff Hardman steps forward and nods toward Daniel. "We have a doctor of veterinary medicine here!"

The next thing I see is Dan putting on rescue gear. He will not fight Hitler or the Japanese, but without a thought for his own life, he's going a mile underground in a hole filled with methane gas to do the emergency surgery. He looks up at me, standing on the porch of the makeshift clinic, smiles, and salutes like a soldier.

March 28, 1942

Heroes Underground

The Saturday *Liberty Times*, for a change, was not all about war.

SIXTEEN MEN BURIED ALIVE! EIGHT MORE RECOVERED DEAD the headlines say. And underneath, the article begins, "In the blink of an eye, women were widowed and children became orphans."

According to Mr. Blaze, the Delmont Coal Company isn't unionized, and though the mines are supposed to be inspected, inspections are rare. The reporter celebrated the fallen miners as heroes, the same as soldiers who take up arms to protect our liberty. There was no mention of Dan.

When we went to the coal miners' memorial service a few days later, we left the children with Becky.

In front, on the dais of the First Presbyterian Church in Delmont, there were two American flags on poles and a table lined with framed photographs of the men who died. The preacher spoke of the miners as heroes underground who should be praised the same as soldiers who die in battle. I look around at the widows and children, some crying, some dry-eyed staring forward. The lives of these family members are forever changed.

"Grief takes about a year," Mrs. Kelly once told me. "It's different for everyone, but one thing I can tell you. You'll suffer with the first daffodil, the first red leaves of the fall, the first snow. . . . On each occasion you'll think of the person you love and it will rip your heart out, then when there's nothing left you'll get better." She was right, but she knew from experience.

WHEN THE SERVICE is over, we all march down to the church basement for lunch, and at the bottom of the stairs we stop to shake hands with a representative of each grieving family.

Standing in line for food are about twenty people, dressed in their Sunday clothes, including Felicia Ricci, the woman who helped me set up the medical triage area, and her husband, Martino. We wave to each other across the big room and I can now see a little round belly under her navy blue dress with red, white, and blue buttons. Funny I didn't notice it before, but my mind was on other things.

A few CCC men in uniform are already sitting at the tables, mostly officers. One is Lou Cross, and I'm glad when he comes over to greet us. "Nice to see you, Mr. and Mrs. Hester," Lou says in a friendly way. "Though it's a sad occasion . . ." Like the other CCC men he's dressed in uniform, but he wears his with style, his pants low on his hips and his brown tie tucked neatly between the second and third button of his khaki shirt.

"Yes, a terrible time," Dan says. "The disaster must have devastated the mining community. Patience was passing by, pulled in to help with the injured, and saw the whole thing firsthand. I came at the end and was able to help a little." He shrugs, minimizing his own heroic actions.

Mr. Cross steps so close, I can smell his shaving soap. "It shouldn't have happened, you know. The federal government gives the mine operators wartime quotas to meet, but when men are tired they get sloppy; they make mistakes."

"That's why we need unions. This wouldn't have happened if the United Mine Workers had been here," I start to get on my soapbox, but Dan gently squeezes my arm.

"Let's get a cup of coffee," he says.

"That's all I want," I answer, moving up in line. "It always seemed strange to me to have a big feast after a funeral. I was surprised to see you wearing the CCC uniform, Mr. Cross. I didn't know you still worked at the White Rock camp."

"Oh, it's only to give the brass some time off, occasionally, and it won't be for long," he answers, looking around as if he's passing on secret information.

"I heard the gossip," Dan says.

"Not gossip!" Lou counters. "You can take it from me, the CCC camp's closing. It's just a matter of time. . . ."

Soon, we are on our way home, passing through Liberty. "You're awfully, quiet. Something wrong?" Dan asks. "I mean, other than feeling sad for the miners and their families."

"No . . . I mean, it *is* sad. All of it . . . the war . . . the death of the miners, but I was thinking about the CCC camp."

"You mean, what Lou said . . . about the camp closing? There's been talk before."

"If it's true, Isaac and Becky will be out of their jobs."

"You know that old expression: *I've had a lot of worries in my life, most of which never happened.*"

I can't help but laugh, and below us, as we cross the stone bridge, the Hope River laughs too, sparkling golden in the low setting sun.

20

April 2, 1942

The Pregnant Ladies Society

*T*oday is my day for spring prenatal visits. I used to have patients schedule appointments every month, but it took most of the afternoon and half the people didn't show up. Now I put an announcement in the *Liberty Times* about four times a year that says something like "The Pregnant Ladies Society will meet with midwife Patience Hester at her home on Salt Lick Road from 10:00 to 12:00 on Wednesday. All mothers welcome." I call the group a *society* because it sounds more like a social club.

As expected, the group today is small. Only Ada Mullins, a blonde, who's eighteen and just a few months pregnant showed up, and later a new woman, Ruby Martin, who's seven months along. Ruby, a red-headed cook from the Mountain Top Diner, who wears scarlet lipstick and nail polish to match, said she's trying to decide if she wants to deliver at home or in the hospital. Both women are expecting their first child.

After I did their examinations, we talked about the advantages and disadvantages of both places. "Home is more private," I told them. "You're cared for by those who know and love you. Mothers can walk around inside their houses during labor or even out in their yards. They can eat light nourishment. They can deliver in any position they want and hold their baby right away. The father can be at their side . . . the disadvantage of home delivery is that in an emergency a Cesarean is not immediately available, and neither is pain medicine."

Ada had no doubt that homebirth was for her; home or the Baby Cabin, but after she saw the cabin, I think she found it appealing. Ruby wasn't so sure.

"But what if something happens?" she asked, her red lips tight with worry. "What if the mother bleeds too much or the baby's too big? What if he doesn't breathe?"

Finally, I had to ask. "Ruby, what makes you even consider a homebirth or birth in the Baby Cabin? You seem to be focused on all the bad things that can happen. The fact is that with a healthy mother and an experienced midwife, those things rarely occur at a home delivery or can be dealt with at the time. Note, I don't claim they *never* happen."

"My granny says I'm made for birthing babies!" Ada interjects in her squeaky Minnie Mouse voice, her smooth, narrow face as innocent as Mira's. Ruby just stares at her, amazed at the young woman's confidence.

Finally, Ruby opens up. "It's the strangers in the hospital," she says. "I hate being around people I don't know. Even now, see how my hands shake. Every time I go to the doctors in Torrington, my blood pressure goes up. They keep talking about toxemia, whatever that is, and it makes me more nervous." (When I did Ruby's exam, her blood pressure was 154/90. Hoping she'd settle down, I planned to repeat it after we ate refreshments.) Soon, I have to decide what to tell her.

"Is it high?" Ruby asks as I take off the blood-pressure cuff again. "I like you a lot. I don't think it's high."

"Actually, Ruby, it's 170 over 90. I don't usually deliver women at home with high blood pressure. I think your body's telling you something. You need to be in the safest possible environment. You'll probably be fine, but just in case, it would be better to be where there are doctors and medicines."

Ruby's gray eyes fill with tears. "Now I'm really scared," she whispers.

Ada, clearly uncomfortable with the other woman's emotions, stands and pulls on her sweater. "I better get going," she says in her high-pitched voice. "See you next time, Mrs. Hester. Good luck," she says to Ruby, and bounces out of the cabin.

"I'm sorry," I tell Ruby. "I don't want you to be afraid. I just want you to be safe. Homebirth isn't for everyone. Just find the nicest doctor they have at Boone Memorial and ask him if he would come when you go into labor. Tell him how scared you are and maybe you can also find a comfortable, experienced, woman to be with you. Fib to the nurses in the Obstetrics Ward, if you have to. Say she's your sister. It's not a real lie. We are all sisters."

April 5, 1942

He Is Risen

On Easter Sunday, the girls all look so pretty in their Sunday best with their new hair ribbons, and my two men look handsome in white short-sleeved shirts and ties. I just wore my spring church dress, the yellow one with the tiny white flowers, and a white hat and white gloves.

As I always do, I scan the pews in the Methodist Chapel in Liberty to see who's here. The place is packed with the Christmas and Easter crowd. When we stand for "Onward, Christian Soldiers," I notice Lou Cross singing to beat the band. *"Onward, Christian soldiers! Marching as to war. With the cross of Jesus going on before."*

The pastor's patriotic sermon surprised me and it bothered Daniel, I could tell. He squirmed in the pew, let out long sighs, and at one time I feared he might stand up and leave.

"In these days of war," the pastor proclaimed, "it is our *duty as Christians* to throw back our shoulders, double up our fists, and fight for our country. This will take sacrifice, but let us remember that our savior sacrificed for us."

The preacher went on and on and finally concluded. "Christian patriotism will fuel the fight for freedom. America has many privileges, but it also has great responsibilities. Our first responsibility is to God, but we are duty-bound to our beloved country too. Let us pray."

The prayer was almost as long as the sermon, but I did learn that already twenty-three soldiers from Union County have lost their lives. West Virginians are very patriotic, and in every war they volunteer for military service with the highest number per capita of any state. A Mountaineer will defend his family at all costs and by extension he will defend his motherland.

I look around, wondering if any of the women sitting in the pews this Easter are the mothers, sisters, wives, or lovers of those twenty-three dead. In this war, women will sacrifice too.

On the way home from church, the children are bursting with excitement. "Can we have the Easter-egg hunt before Sunday dinner, Pa?" Danny wants to know.

"Please!" Susie and Sunny beg together.

"It's fine," Dan says without expression.

We don't go in for the Easter Bunny myth. Even Mira wouldn't buy a story that a magic rabbit could personally dye millions of eggs and distribute them around the country-side overnight, but Dan's lack of enthusiasm surprises me. The patriotic sermon must still be getting to him.

After we change out of our church clothes, we take turns hiding the beautiful eggs out in the yard. First Daniel and I hide them for the kids. Then the kids hide them for us. Afterward, we usually have a Sunday meal at home, but this year we're going to Hazel Patch for a picnic, where Bitsy and Willie have opened the abandoned chapel for the occasion. I don't know what it will be like, but there used to be plenty of picnic tables out on the lawn, and apparently Bitsy and Willie are working like bees to get it cleaned up.

As we pull into the churchyard, I see the Maddocks' truck, the Blums' Pontiac, Lou Cross's Plymouth, and Bitsy's motorcycle, but there's another vehicle too . . . an old yellow open-sided hack that used to transport our children when they went to the Hazel Patch school five years ago. Reverend Miller and Mrs. Mildred Miller are here!

The kids jump out of the back of the Model T as soon as we park and Danny runs over to Will, who's playing horseshoes with Lou and Bitsy. Reverend Miller is raking dead leaves from the daffodils along the side of the chapel and Mrs. Miller is holding court at a picnic table. Dan starts raking leaves too, but I head straight for Mildred Miller.

"Well, look who's here?" I call. "A sight for sore eyes. Are you here for good or just visiting?"

"For good, we hope. Our daughter Cassie and her family moved to California, so we had no reason to stay in Pittsburgh. We thought we'd see what's left of the community. I'm surprised there isn't more damage from storms or vandals. The chapel is still in good shape." She stands to embrace me against her big, soft chest.

Reverend Miller, except for the gray in his hair, looks about the same as he always did, though I see, as he talks to Daniel, that his face is lined with care. The Great Depression has been hard on him, hard on all of us, really.

"How about your log house? Can you live in it or will it need a lot of work? Daniel is so busy with the rush of lambing season, but I can come over and give you a hand."

Without a pause in the conversation, Mrs. Miller scoops my girls into her arms and holds them there, as familiar as if they were her own.

"Most of the furniture we left in the house is gone. But we still have bookcases, bedsteads, and the stoves. A few of the windows are broken, but Bitsy says we can move in with her until we fix things up. That Willie is a nice boy. It's so good for Bitsy to have a family."

"She's doing well at the woolen mill too," I chime in.

"Yes. She told us she got another raise and promotion and we met her boss for the first time last night, Mr. Cross. He brought her home. Quite a fellow."

An hour later, sheets have been spread over three rough picnic tables that are situated under the cottonwood trees. Our potluck meal will be a feast, with deviled eggs, ginger carrots, fried chicken, and corn bread.

I call for the children and find them in the overgrown field behind the chapel, now playing army with Willie and Lou, and by the time we get back to the tables, everyone is holding hands, waiting patiently for Reverend Miller to say grace. After the impassioned homily about patriotism at the Methodist church this morning, I'm expecting more of the same, but I'm pleasantly surprised.

"O Lord," Pastor Miller begins. "We thank you for the trees that shelter us from rain, for the birds that sing, and for the river that sustains us. We thank you for our friends and for their love. On this Easter Day, let us not forget those who have no friends, those who are hungry or cold. Blessed Savior, watch over the soldiers who battle for freedom.

"We know there have always been wars, but help us find a way to peace so that all wars end. As Jesus died for our sins, let us rejoice, for he still lives and we are resurrected

with him. In the name of the Father, the Son, and the Holy
Spirit, Amen."

"Amen," we all murmur.

"Hallelujah." Lou Cross laughs. "Let's eat!"

WHEN WE'VE ALL filled our stomachs, everyone cleans up
while Bitsy and I carry baskets of dirty plates back to her
house. "Hey, there's something I've been wanting to ask
you about. In the newspaper photos, I always see the colored soldiers making not just the right-handed V sign for
victory but a V with both the left and the right. What's
that about?"

"I read about it in the *Pittsburgh Courier*, the Negro
paper, a few months ago. You know the V sign with one
hand means victory over tyranny right?" I nod. "Well, the
second V represents victory for Negroes fighting for freedom *here in the U.S.A.*

"When the war is over, there will be a new struggle for
equality at home. Not just for whites, but for coloreds and
for women too, so that's why we do the double V. Get it?"

"I'm going to do it too and I'll teach the children about
it. . . . There they are now."

Again, the kids are busy playing war and we stop for a
minute to watch them. Danny and Willie roll on the ground
and start crawling forward on their elbows, like soldiers,
through the new green grass. My son takes a clod of dirt,
pretends to pull a plug, and throws it like a grenade.

"Take that, you yellow devils!" he shouts, but the girls
don't give up. They come roaring straight at Danny and
Willie with arms outstretched like dive-bombers.

"You are all dead!" they yell, throwing themselves on their brother and Willie with a noise like a bomb. "Now we're all dead!"

Friendly as anything, the five children lay in the grass laughing and looking up at the sky. If only real war were like this. No blood. No lifeless bodies carried away on stretchers. No mothers' cries of grief.

April 9, 1942

*B*efore dawn Dan is called to a lambing. April is the busiest time for a vet in West Virginia, and for weeks we see him only a few hours a day.

"*Mary had a little lamb*," the song goes (or two or three little lambs!). Most ewes can give birth without assistance, but during this busy time, it's recommended that ewes be vaccinated for clostridium and tetanus. By vaccinating the pregnant ewe, the lambs will acquire immunity when they drink their mother's first milk. That's why, even before the lambs come, Dan is running around giving vaccinations all over Union County.

The real challenge, he tells me, is helping deliver multiple lambs that are all tangled up in the uterus. This, he says, is also the most satisfying part of the job. Imagine the potential difficulty with triplets! Sometimes Dan finds a hoof while doing an internal exam, and he has to figure out which lamb it belongs to.

When I hear his Model T come in the drive in the middle of the night, I rise on one elbow, switch on the lamp, and look at the Big Ben alarm clock. It's one A.M. Soon Dan is clomping up the stairs, too tired to try to be quiet. As usual, he's left his dirty coveralls on the back porch and stands before me in red long johns wet from the ankle to the knee.

"Hard day?" I ask. I know that it has been. He left at dawn.

"Yeah. I wish to hell these farmers would round their sheep up before I get there. I swear the Bishop brothers actually chase their flock to the most remote spot on their farm on purpose. I had to cross a good-size stream and found one ewe already delivering triplets on the other side of the bank."

"Did the lambs live?"

He smiles. "Yep, every one of 'em. . . . I'll tell you more about it tomorrow."

I get out of bed in my white flannel gown and unbutton his long underwear, then kick it under the bed. "Get in," I instruct as I turn off the lamp.

"Naked? No nightclothes?" he asks, and I hear him smile in the dark.

"You know what we midwives say, skin-to-skin is the best warmer," I answer, pulling my gown over my head, crawling under the quilts naked, and curling around him.

"Ahhhh!" Daniel says, and then he's asleep.

In the morning he's gone before I get up and after the kids are off to school, I go out to tend my thirty-six tiny tomato plants in paper cups under our makeshift greenhouse, an old window leaning against the bottom of the porch. The glass captures the sunlight and tricks the seeds into thinking it's summer, when in reality, in the mountains, we could have a frost until June.

When I stick my head under the glass to water my babies, the smell of earth and growing things makes me smile. Sometimes, I think all I need to be happy is sunlight, earth, and water.

And it's not just me. Bitsy and Mrs. Miller are putting in their gardens soon and at the last Red Cross meeting, I learned that people in town are hopping on the bandwagon. It's called Food for Victory because the more produce people grow in their backyards, the more real farmers can grow to feed the military.

I felt like an expert, telling Mrs. Wade, Ida May, and Marion Archer which seeds they can plant early in spring (peas, spinach, radishes, and lettuce and cabbage, because they're frost-hardy) and which they had to wait on (beans, corn, tomatoes, peppers, and squash).

This evening, after chores, Dan and I sat on the porch, listening to the spring frogs. "I'm so content here," I say to Dan, leaning up against him. "It's hard to believe that we live in such grave times and that much of the rest of the world is suffering.

"At the Red Cross meeting, Mrs. Stenger told us the Nazis in Poland are arresting all the Jews and putting them in barracks. Whole families are separated, the men from the women and children. Wouldn't that be awful, to stare at each other through a barbed-wire fence? So helpless."

"You know the U.S. has its own concentration camps," my husband tells me.

"Where'd you hear that? I don't believe it."

"Yeah. The feds are rounding up all people of Japanese heritage—men, women, and children—on the Pacific coast. Whole families, even those born in the U.S.A., on the off chance that they might be spies or saboteurs. They're taken by bus to enclosures in remote inland places like Colorado and Arkansas. The buildings are little more than chicken coops with windows. Basically they're prisons, with barbed wire, guards, and guns.

"One of the most unfair things is that their property, businesses or farms the families have owned for generations, is confiscated and sold for pennies. The U.S. concentration camps are called *internment camps*. Same difference."

I frown. "I'm trying to reconcile what you're *telling* me with my vision of what the United States stands for."

Daniel grins and begins a familiar song: "*While the storm clouds gather far across the sea, Let us swear allegiance to a land that's free . . .*"

"Very funny!"

"*God Bless America*," he continues sarcastically with his hand over his heart. "*Land that I love! Stand beside her, and guide her, through the night with the light from above!*"

I can't help but laugh, but there's a part of me that hates him, hates him as he makes fun of our country. Men are dying for his right to be free.

21

May 2, 1942

A Tasty Treat

$\mathcal{E}$very spring, Dan and I go up to our high pasture on the side of Spruce Mountain to clear out the saplings that grow in each year. This spring, he's been so busy with lambing, he hasn't gotten around to it, so today, while he's in Liberty making a call, I'm going alone.

By midmorning, the children are off to school and my farm chores and housework are done, so I pull on my rubber boots and my old wool jacket and go out to the barn. When I lived at the end of Wild Rose Road by myself, before Bitsy came, I used to do things like this alone all the time. I don't need him, I remind myself.

First I get an ax from the tool room in the barn, then, since all the other horses are in the lower meadow grazing, I put a bridle and harness on old Mack, who is gentle and lazy. A workhorse isn't trained to wear a saddle, thus I plan to ride bareback. Also, Mack is a Berkshire and about a foot higher than a riding horse so I have to stand on a stool to get up.

"Come on, Mack," I say, making a clicking sound with my mouth. "Let's go clean up the pasture!"

It's a cloudless, brisk day with a wind from the south, and I pull my beret down over my ears. As we plod along (there is no galloping with a workhorse), I look up at the mountain. Along the edge of the forest, pink mountain laurel bloom amongst the spruce, and on the lower shelf yellow mustard. It's the young maples and oaks, sprouting here and there that will soon destroy the grazing land.

Within an hour, I've chopped down fifteen young trees with trunks the size of my wrist and am feeling rather proud of myself. It's a small job, but important. Since we don't want the dead trees lying around, I drag them to the edge of the barbed-wire fence. That's when I see him . . . not forty feet away.

The bear is standing at the tree line, partially hidden by a young spruce, and I freeze, trying to recall whether I'm supposed to look him in the eye or look away. Since our eyes are already locked, I hold my pose.

Next I can't remember whether I'm supposed to appear intimidating or try to look meek. I decide to look fierce, but this is not easy. I'm only five-foot-five and even wearing my bulky red-and-black farm jacket I'm not very scary.

The bear goes back to scratching under a fallen tree for spring mushrooms and I take a step back, but my movement is noticed. "Sorry," I whisper. "Sorry to interrupt your meal. I'm just going to *ease* over to my horse and go home now."

The animal looks me up and down, probably thinking . . . *I've been hibernating all winter and am mighty hungry. She could be a tasty treat.*

I take another step back. The bear shakes his head and moves toward me. Ax still in hand, I wonder if I'm strong enough to fight off a two-hundred-pound creature. *Probably not.* The bear makes a low huff.

I try to make the sound back. "Huffff!" The bear's ears twitch and he scrapes the leaves, ready to charge. This isn't a grizzly, just a common black bear, but still I doubt I can outrun him.

There's no way to yell for help. Daniel's in town spaying Mrs. Stenger's cat. Becky and Dr. Blum are on the other side of Spruce Mountain. I take another step back and whistle for the horse. I try again, but my mouth is so dry I can't pucker up.

"Mack!" I whisper. "Come!" The horse is fifty feet behind me and I can hear him munching grass. I'd sprint for him, but I'm afraid if I turn, the bear will be on me in a flash.

I take two more steps backward and the distance between us grows, but the bear now ambles up to the barbed-wire fence. Each time I move, I become more interesting, but I can't just stand here. I raise my ax, unsure the animal will even recognize it as a weapon.

The old horse has not smelled the bear yet and I fear if he does, he'll trot down the mountainside and into the barn without me. Slowly I rotate to the side, trying to keep both the horse and the bear in view. "*Mack!* Come!"

The bear walks the barbed-wire fence looking for a way to get under. This is my chance! I decide to break for the Berkshire, but now another obstacle occurs to me. There's no stool to stand on, not even a tree stump. How am I going to get up? I decide to go for it anyway. If I can make it to the horse, I may be able to grab his mane and pull myself up. Indians do this in the cowboy movies all the time.

The creature wags his head and scratches the grass again. It's time to go. Weapon in hand, I run for the horse, but just as I reach for his mane Mack spots the bear and shies away. It's then that I fall. I fall on the ax.

Resurrection

So tell me again; what you were doing?" Daniel asks when he returns from town.

I'm lying on the sofa with my leg on a pile of towels. I found some gauze in the Baby Cabin and wound it around my calf to slow the bleeding and then I called Mrs. Stenger to see if Daniel was still there, but he'd already gone.

Now my husband sits on the sofa staring at the same leg he stitched up ten years ago when I cut myself while sledding, only this time he's not sympathetic.

"How did this happen exactly?" he asks again.

"Well, I went up the mountain to clear the pasture. You know, cut down the saplings."

"I *said* I'd do it," my husband snaps.

"I know, but you've been so busy with lambing you're hardly ever home and I thought you'd be glad. Anyway, I rode Mack up Spruce Mountain and cut down a few dozen trees, but it wasn't until I was dragging them to the fence line that I saw the black bear."

"Oh, for Christ's sake, Patience. You shouldn't be doing things like that when no one's around."

"Aren't you going to look at my cut to see if we need to call Dr. Blum?"

"Yeah, but I want to hear about this bear."

"It was just a big black bear."

"So how did you get away?"

"I didn't. I fell when trying to mount Mack, but then Mack ran away, so I just lay on the ground and played dead."

"Oh, Jesus!"

"You really shouldn't swear so much, Daniel. The children will pick it up."

"You just lay there and played dead!" he says, ignoring my reprimand.

"Yeah. He snuffed me up a little and then walked away. I must have stayed there an hour and got really cold, but finally I lifted my head and he was gone, so I resurrected myself and limped home."

After that, Daniel says nothing while he cleans and dresses my wound. I can tell he's mad. This time I don't need stitches, but I'll have another scar, right above the old one.

"The kids will be home soon. I need to figure out what to have for dinner," I say.

"No you just rest. I'll clean and sterilize my instrument tray, then I'll take care of dinner."

"Is that *doctor's orders?*"

"Yep, but don't do any more stupid stuff, okay, Patience? This family needs you. The bear could have torn you to pieces." He kisses the top of my head. "I need you too."

22

May 8, 1942

Draft Board Blues

There's something I probably should tell you, Patience . . ." Daniel clears his throat. "I've received a letter requiring me to register for the draft." We're driving through Liberty on our way to the feed store to get a roll of barbed wire.

I glance over at the Selective Service Office located at the old dress shop across from the movie house. UNCLE SAM WANTS YOU, DON'T WAIT FOR THE DRAFT, VOLUNTEER NOW! a poster says. Another exhorts the reader to LET 'EM HAVE IT! JOIN NOW.

"I thought everyone had to register during the peacetime draft last fall. Didn't you send the form back?"

"No, I ignored it."

"Daniel!" I scold. "What were you thinking? If you're male and age eighteen to forty-five, you were supposed to register. You were still forty-three."

"Well, we weren't at war yet and I was hoping we never would be. Anyway, I already did my duty in the first world war."

I let out my air in exasperation. "So what are you going to do?"

"I don't know. So long as nobody on the local draft board notices, I'll be okay. If they do, I can pretend I never got the letter."

"You'd lie?"

He grins his funny grin. "Probably not."

"Who's on the draft board anyway?" I ask.

"Well, Judge Wade, Mayor Ott, Louis Tinkshell, and wouldn't you know it, Aran Bishop . . . I know Aran doesn't seem like the patriotic type, but he and his brothers fought in the Great War."

"There's a parking spot," I announce, pointing to a small space between a pickup truck and a shiny green Ford on a street behind the feed store.

"Someone's doing well in this war economy," Daniel snorts, indicating the green auto. "Whoever he is, he must have purchased the car just before the Ford plant switched to making tanks and fighter planes. No one can get a new car now. Not for love or money."

Inside, the red-haired kid, Patrick, is sweeping the floor while Sadie, the owner, takes care of a customer at the counter. Sadie, a stocky woman with thinning short blond hair, looks up from the cash register, then snaps the drawer closed. "What can I do you for, Dr. Hester? I ordered that new Sulfa medicine, but it hasn't come in yet."

"That's fine, Sadie. Just call me when it arrives. . . . All we need today is barbed wire to repair fence in the back pasture." He tells her how much while I look at the colorful fabric seed sacks arranged along the floor in back.

Some contain cornmeal, some chicken feed, some flour. A pink pattern with blue flowers catches my attention and I try to estimate how many twenty-pound bags of cornmeal it would take to make a dress for one girl.

Meanwhile, I catch a snatch of conversation from the front of the store. Two men have come in and one of them sniggers when they approach Daniel.

"Well, if it isn't *Dr. Hester*," the older one says with scorn. "Kill any good horses lately?"

"Howdy, Aran. Nice to see you, Mr. Blaze," my husband addresses them, ignoring the dig that stems from an event that happened over ten years ago in which Dan was called too late to save the Bishops' prize stallion, Devil. The brothers have never gotten over it and still blame him.

"Haven't seen you in town lately," Aran Bishop complains. "Too busy avoiding civic duty and hanging out with your German friends?"

Dan stands up tall. "What's that supposed to mean?"

"Everyone knows you refused to be on the civil defense board and the draft board. I figure you just don't give a damn . . . or maybe you're on the Axis side."

"Give the man a break, Aran!" Sadie comes in. "It's lambing season, for God's sake. He ain't got time to play soldier with a little tin hat."

Bill Blaze says nothing but watches it all, wondering, I suppose, if there's a story here.

"I have your order out on the loading dock, Mr. Bishop," Patrick says. "Want to pull your truck around?" I give him a smile, thanking him for defusing the situation.

Sadie brings the roll of barbed wire out from the back and Dan forks over five dollars. "This stuff is getting expensive," he says.

"It's the war," Sadie says. "Soon we won't be able to get anything made of steel."

"It's the war. It's the war!" Dan grumbles as we leave, and I wave to Sadie.

May 10, 1942

Sweat and Fear

*Y*ou seem tense," I say to Dan as we walk out to the barn. There's not a cloud in the sky and the clean sheets and quilts that I washed this morning flap gaily on the line.

"Yeah," Dan says. "I'm worried. If a foal isn't born in an hour after the mare's water breaks, you'll likely have trouble. That's why I wanted you with me. It's been two hours, now. I probably should have done an internal exam sooner, but Meadow's never had trouble before and this is her fifteenth delivery."

"Mrs. Kelly always said, 'Never let the sun set twice on a woman in labor.'"

Dan shakes his head and smiles. He's heard all of my Mrs. Kelly stories more than once.

Years ago, in fact, on the day we met, I assisted Dan at a difficult foaling—not a romantic first date, but an interesting one. Now here we are, ten years later, bumping across the barnyard with a bucket of hot water and all his gear, on our way to another delivery.

As we push back the double doors and step into the dark interior of the big wooden building, I'm proud to note all Dan's modern renovations. Last year, he and Isaac Blum put in ten new wooden stalls, with short walls between so that the horses and cows can socialize. There's a ten-foot-wide corridor down the middle and a work area at each end.

As we approach the foaling cell, which, unlike the other stalls, has high sides to give the mare a sense of safety and privacy, I smell amniotic fluid—a sweet, earthy odor that I actually like, but there's something else . . . sour and sharp, the smell of sweat and fear.

Dan opens the gate and I'm surprised to see our black-and-white mare rolling on the floor. I've seen horses roll in the dirt and the grass outside, but never in a barn. She gets up and stamps her feet in the straw. She whinnies and snorts, paces around the small space, and then lies on her side and rolls again.

Dan looks her over and then when she stops for a minute, he pushes her against the barn wall and takes her vital signs. "Write this down," he says to me as I open the small black leather journal that he keeps in the side pocket of his vet bag.

Meadow, Twenty-year-old Mare, Pulse 55, Respirations 58, Temperature 102.

"Is that too high?" I whisper, and Dan nods that it is.

"The pulse is especially worrisome. It should be thirty to forty. Let's wash up." He strips down to his undershirt and scrubs up to his elbows with strong lye soap, then dries on a rough, clean towel. I roll up the sleeves of my red plaid flannel shirt and copy his motions.

"Is the foal still alive?" I ask.

"I'll tell you in a minute," he says, lubricating his hand and reaching into the mare's vagina. "Notice her flanks. See how she sweats. Never a good sign."

"Almost all women sweat in labor, at least at the end."

A smile breaks out on my husband's face.

"The foal is breech," Dan explains. "I felt its tail move, so it's still alive. . . . Sure hope I can save them both. Meadow is normally a good breeder. Never had a problem in all these years."

I watch as my husband attempts to break up the breech. He gets one hind leg out, but the mare pulls away, pushing Dan down. She rears up on her hind legs and almost rolls on him as he scoots away through the straw.

"Damn," he says. "The hoof has retreated. I think the second leg is stuck under its body. It's a good-size foal too. I'll wait until Meadow settles down, then we'll have to tie her to the wall."

Thirty minutes later the foal is still not delivered. Daniel's strong arm is working back and forth inside the mare. The first hoof is out again, but the second one won't come and Daniel is sweating worse than the mare. Every time she strains he bites his upper lip and I know that it's painful.

"Want me to try?" I ask.

Dan stands and stretches his back, his face gray with worry. "Sure, I'll take a break. Maybe your small lady hands can get in a little farther. Remember, the hoof isn't where you think it will be. It's under the foal's belly."

I wash again, this time removing my shirt and standing behind the mother in my brassiere. *Once a midwife*, I think to myself. *Now I'm a horse midwife.*

"Okay, Meadow," I say in my most soothing midwife voice. She turns her head to see who's talking. "We have to work together to get your baby out. . . . I've got it," I whisper to Daniel. "I've got the hoof."

"Keep pulling; only put your whole hand around the sharp hoof. You don't want to lacerate the birth canal as you draw it out."

Slowly, I bring the hoof into the light and Dan takes over, working the baby out as the mother strains. I watch for the first breath, but no effort is made. The all-white colt lies there as still as a stone.

Dan feels for a pulse, but there's no heartbeat. He bends over and shuts one of the foal's nostrils and puffs into the other one, trying to stimulate breathing. I take a handful of straw and rub the little animal, hoping it will bring him around, but it's no good and we both know it. Sometime in the last hour, the cord must have been pinched and his oxygen supply cut off.

"Too bad," Dan says. "He would have been a beauty."

Meadow stands, legs spread over the colt, sniffing him and nudging her baby's body. She whickers and whinnies for the colt to get up, but after another hour, Dan ties a rope to the foal's back legs and drags him out of the barn.

"I'll pull him out to the back field with the tractor," he says. "And bury him there. Can you tend to Meadow? Give her water and fresh hay and wipe off the sweat?"

The whole time I'm brushing Meadow, she keeps looking at the barn door for her colt and I don't think she understands that her baby is dead. All animals have an instinct to protect their young. When the baby's gone, they don't know what to do. I have seen it with patients who've had stillborn babies. They're not just heartbroken; their bodies cave in around them.

LATER, WHEN OUR children and Willie come home from school, I set out glasses of milk and oatmeal cookies in the kitchen and tell the kids what's happened.

Death is not new to any of them. Willie lost his mother. The twins lost both mother and father, and their baby brother too. Our own kids have seen dead hogs when we butcher in the fall and dead deer when Dan hunts for our winter food, but Meadow's foal is different. We'd all looked forward to having the little colt frolicking around the barnyard, leaping and hopping and licking our hands.

"Can we see him?" Will wants to know.

"Where did Pa put him?" Danny asks.

"Well, your pa is out in the field burying him now. He may not be done. Let's go."

In a line we march out to the back pasture, Danny and Mira leading the way. Willie trails behind with me.

"Have you seen dead animals before?" I ask him, thinking because he's a city boy, he may not have had that experience.

"I've seen lots of roadkill when Bitsy and I travel on the motorcycle—rabbits, fox, snakes—but nothing big."

"You used to limp a little when I first met you, Willie," I observe. "Mine is worse."

"It's okay for a woman."

"What do you mean?"

"Limping's okay for a woman. You don't have to be strong."

"Willie! I'm surprised at you. I have to work as hard as anyone." The boy looks down.

"You know what I mean," he says. "You might work long and hard, but you don't have to be tough."

I let out a long sigh. Once I told Sheriff Hardman that midwives were warriors. What I meant is that we have to be brave, that we have to be able to call on the life force when there's danger, that we have to summon strength in ourselves when all strength is spent. Maybe that's not the same as *tough*.

"Come on, Mom!" yells Danny. "We're going to have a ceremony." I take Willie's hand and, laughing, we run together. Limpity-limp. Limpity-limp.

When we get to the gravesite we find that Daniel has already lowered the white colt into the ground. "We need a name," Susie says.

Will squats down and touches the little foal's mane, still matted and damp.

"You name him Will," I whisper.

"Me?"

"Yeah," Daniel agrees.

"Snow," says Willie, patting the little horse's white head. "Let's call him Snow."

"Hold hands," orders Mira as we circle the grave.

"*Hush-a-bye, don't you cry. Go to sleep, little baby,*" I sing, an old lullaby that the kids know. "*When you wake, you will have all the pretty little horses.*"

"*Blacks and bays,*" Daniel and the children come in. "*Dapples and grays. All the pretty little horses.*"

No one cries. We haven't known Snow long enough to mourn deeply. I look around the circle at my beautiful children. They will meet sorrow soon enough. There's no way to be in this life without it. Across the barnyard we can hear the mare. She whinnies and neighs, whinnies and neighs, calling for Snow, but Snow cannot answer.

May 9, 1942

Grief

All night, Meadow's braying keeps me awake. I put the pillow over my head to mute the sound, but it's no good. Then, at first light, Dan gets up and goes out to her, but by the time he comes back she's calling again.

Breakfast is a solemn affair, with the sounds of spoons scraping and little conversation. Susie's face is white with dark circles under her eyes and I think she's glad to get on the school bus to get away from the sound of the horse's sorrow.

"I'll go out to Meadow as soon as the chickens are fed and the cows milked," I tell Dan as I wipe off the table. "What should I do for her? Just keep her company?"

"Yes, take her outside of the foaling stall and put her in with the other horses. I have to make a visit to Mrs. Stone's farm to see her prize Nubian goat, and then I'll be back. Hope it's nothing more serious than parasites." He comes up behind me to give me a hug. Ordinarily Daniel Hester is not an outwardly emotional guy, but the loss of Meadow's colt has cracked him open.

"You did your best," I console him.

"No," he says. "No, I didn't."

Dan doesn't return for our noontime meal, so I just pick at leftovers and then hurry out to the barn again. I bring Meadow some carrots from the root cellar. I take the currycomb with the red wooden handle and brush her over and over, starting at her head and working back toward her flank. When I reach the itchy spot on her neck she rolls back her lip and tries to kiss me.

"I know you like it, Meadow," I say, leaning away from her mouth. "But a tender nip to my thin skin wouldn't be pleasant." Later I ride her around the meadow, but she plods without spirit.

Toward afternoon, I run into the house to soak some dried peas and cut up some vegetables for our evening meal. While I stayed with Meadow, her crying had stopped, but now it's started again and I try to think what to do. When I return to the barn, I try to imagine what I would do for a grieving human mother and decide I'll sing and try to get Meadow to sleep.

"*Somewhere, over the rainbow,*" I begin the popular Judy Garland song. "*Way up high. There's a land that I heard of once in a lullaby.*" The black-and-white horse reaches over and licks my face. Finally I get her to lie down and I lie down in the new straw with her, my head on her shoulder.

"*Somewhere over the rainbow, skies are blue. And the dreams that you dare to dream really do come true. . . .*"

It isn't until almost dark that Daniel returns and it's not just him in his Model T, but old Mr. Roote, driving a big Chevy truck with high wooden sides. The children and I are listening to the news when we hear the vehicles come into the yard. The last U.S. troops in the Philippines have surrendered. Japanese forces have captured the remainder of Burma and reached India. Things are not going well for us.

"Who's here?" the kids cry, and before I can stop them, they run out on the porch and I follow after them.

The truck bed of the Chevy is filled with straw, and the elderly Mrs. Stone is sitting in the back with a small brown colt. "We brought Meadow a new baby," she says, standing up and leaning over the wooden slats. "Our neighbor, Mr. Hummingbird, recently lost a mare after she had a retained placenta."

"It doesn't take long with horses. They're more sensitive than cattle. You have to get the afterbirth out in a few hours or they'll get infected," Dan explains as he and Mr. Roote open the gate at the back of the truck and assist Mrs. Stone down.

"Did you do okay riding back there, sweetheart?" Mr. Roote asks.

"Fine and dandy!" the old lady responds, brushing the straw off of her behind and laughing. "When Mr. Hester came over to see our goat and told us what happened to Meadow, we knew just the cure. Mrs. Hummingbird was trying to bottle feed their colt, but it wasn't going well. It's a big job, feeding a baby horse every two hours. They were happy to give him away."

"I promised the Hummingbirds three free vet visits in exchange for Brownie, and they were more than grateful," Dan adds as he pulls a ramp out of the truck and leads the little colt down. "He's just a few days old. How did Meadow do today, Patience?"

"Well, she stopped crying for a while, but you can hear she's starting up again. Okay, kids, enough excitement. You can see Brownie in the morning. Pa has work to do. Can I get you a cup of coffee or some nourishment, Mrs. Stone and Mr. Roote?"

"No, it's late," Mr. Roote says. "We better get on." He assists the old lady into the cab of the truck and turns the ignition. "Good luck with everything," he says.

"God bless you!" the old lady calls, and then they're gone.

An hour later, the children are tucked in bed and I make a hot mug of soup to take out to Dan. "Have you eaten today?" I ask him as I lean over the gate of Meadow's stall and hold out the cup.

"Mrs. Stone fed me after I purged her goat. I think she and Mr. Roote are an *item*." He grins.

"You mean as in *sweet on each other*?"

"I mean as in *shacking up*."

"Oh, Daniel! Don't be so crude. How's Meadow doing? Will she let the new colt suckle?"

"Her bag is pretty full and tight, and so far, she's kicking him away. Poor little guy. He can smell her milk and he's persistent. Trouble is, she can smell *him* and it's an unfamiliar odor. I just tried something new. I took some of her milk and rubbed it all over him. That might fool her."

He exits the stall and leans with me on the gate, drinking the soup. For thirty minutes we watch as Brownie circles the mare. If Meadow rejects the new colt, we'll be in the same position as the Hummingbird family and I'll be bottle-feeding every two hours day and night.

"Come on." I interrupt the bonding and open the gate. "I think I can help."

"*Patience, be patient!*" Daniel whispers.

"No, this is what midwives do, help mothers breastfeed. You stand by the mare and soothe her while I see if I can get the little one to latch on."

Dan gives a big sigh and does what I say. "Watch out she doesn't kick you in the head," he warns.

"Here, Brownie!" I squeeze some of Meadow's milk on my fingers and hold them out to the colt. Brownie steps forward and sucks on them hard. I pull back and dabble more milk on my fingers, over and over drawing him forward, little by little, until he's only a few inches from the mare's teat. "One more time. Don't let Meadow pull away," I instruct my husband.

"Here, Brownie . . . Here, Brownie." Now his mouth is right where I want it and I slip the teat in. Meadow tosses her head. "Don't let her get away!" Dan leans on her hard, holding the mare against the barn wall. A few minutes later we let go and stand in a corner watching. It's not Meadow's first time nursing. She's had fourteen healthy foals before, and the feeling of the rhythmic sucking must be as familiar to her as breathing.

The long-legged colt sucks and sucks. He must be half-starved. Finally, he steps away and looks up at his new mom. Meadow turns and sniffs him from head to toe. She nuzzles his head. "*Neeeeeigh!*" she knickers softly. Then the little colt returns to her teat, and this time he doesn't need coaxing and she doesn't pull away.

23

May 10, 1942

Mother's Day

Dan and I stand leaning on the deer fence inspecting the garden while the kids prepare a Mother's Day surprise. There's not much coming up, only a few pea plants sprouting through the soil and the tops of the onion sets that he put in last week. It's the satisfaction of *imagining* our potential harvest that attracts us.

The early crops, which won't mind a frost, are already pulsing with life under the surface. A sprout reaches for the sun and the root stretches down seeking water and nourishment. I've had a garden every year since I moved to Union County, on the run from Pittsburgh, with Mrs. Kelly . . . This was back when I was sought for murder, several years after the Blair Mountain incident. . . .

"Patience?" Dan interrupts my thoughts, touching my arm. "A bald eagle! I think it's nesting on the top of Spruce Mountain. This is the second time I've seen it today . . . you seem far away. What are you thinking about, hon?"

I take a big breath and let it out slowly. "Blair Mountain. I don't even know how I got from enjoying the garden to something that happened two decades ago. . . . I'll never forget the feel of my husband's skull cracking like an eggshell. I shiver just thinking about it."

"I know," he says, putting an arm around me. "I've killed people too. Combat makes you crazy. I wish I could banish those memories." Then he surprises me by lifting me up and swinging me around. Around and around and around . . . until, laughing, we fall in the grass.

"Mom!" Mira yells from the kitchen door. "Mom! Quit fooling around and get in here!"

"*Happy Mother's Day, dear Mom. Happy Mother's Day to you*," the children bellow when we come in the back door to see our noon meal on the table, along with a bouquet of daffodils and tulips

"Remember last Mother's Day?" Dan says. "You had two women in labor."

I smile thinking about it, one in the Baby Cabin and one in the house. "That was fun. Thank goodness I had Becky to help me. . . . It's a lot harder to be a midwife with four kids than I thought it would be."

"Do you have anyone due?" Dan asks as we clean up the dishes.

"Somehow I don't feel as busy as before and I've wondered if it's getting around to . . . you know . . . politics. Word may be out about your position on the war," I say under my breath. "And some women might not want to come here."

"I hardly think that could be true." Dan gives me an irritated look. "Anyway, I wish we could afford more help."

"Har-har," I mock. "Like a maid or a cook?"

"If you could have one thing for Mother's Day, Mom, what would it be?" Danny asks.

"One thing? There are so many . . . but you just want one? How about a new electric broom, Hoovers they're called, or an indoor toilet or an electric butter churn? No, that's three!"

"Come in the living room, we have something to show you." Our son takes my hand and leads me out of the kitchen.

"Surprise!" the children yell, jumping up and down. They push a large box out from behind the sofa.

"What's this?" I ask, sinking into a chair.

"Open it! Open it!" Mira insists.

Inside the box I see a familiar dark-red symbol. HOOVER, it says and I can't believe what's inside. It's the miracle machine that the radio announcer says "*Beats . . . as it sweeps . . . as it cleans. The ultimate electric broom with revolving brush and suction!*"

"It's not brand-new," Dan tells me. "But it might as well be. I got it from a client over near Delmont, a miner, making good money, and he just bought the newest model for his wife."

"I love it," I whisper with tears in my eyes. "Thank you, everyone. Let me give you all hugs."

"Let's try it!" Danny says, taking the long electric cord and plugging it in. "Here's the On button, Ma." He points to a little red switch.

"It's kind of like learning to drive," Dan says. "Here you go. Sprinkle some salt on the kitchen floor, Susie."

I click the red button. *Vroooom!* the machine roars into operation. "Just push it across the linoleum," Dan instructs me. "The lady that owned it before gave me a demonstration."

Timidly, I begin. "You're doing great," Dan says.

"Yay, Mom!" the kids cheer. Then we all try it.

May 15, 1942

Blackout

There's an air-raid drill tonight, Mom," Danny tells me. "Can we make popcorn and listen to the radio in the dark?"

"Yes, if the chores are done. Remember, we can't walk outside with lanterns or have a light in the barn. The civil defense people are getting really strict about it. Also we need blankets over the front windows and the front door. Can you girls take care of that?"

"What will happen if we mess up and a little light gets out?" Susie worries. I take her in my lap. "Will they take us to jail?"

"No, honey. That's not going to happen. Anyway, we plan to follow the rules."

By dusk we have the chores finished and begin preparations for the drill. The children and I actually enjoy this excitement, but as usual, Daniel refuses to participate, saying that it's all government propaganda, an attempt to heighten civilian fear.

If we lived in town we would have to take the drills more seriously. Air-raid wardens actually patrol the streets wearing uniforms and tin helmets. Once a month, on random nights and at random times, the drills are announced in the paper and everyone must turn out their lights, pull the curtains, and stay off the roads for two to four hours.

The movie marquee will be extinguished. The neon lights on the tavern are turned off, even the streetlights go dark. If a person is already on the road, he must pull over and turn off his headlights until he hears the "all-clear" siren. The purpose of the blackout drills is to prevent enemy planes from spotting our towns and bombing us.

This evening, the children and I begin by going room-to-room, starting with Danny's bedroom, pulling down blinds and closing the curtains. According to the public announcements, not a speck of light must show.

While we work we sing a new song we heard on the radio, "Obey Your Air Raid Warden": *"Don't get in a huff. Our aim today is to call their bluff!"* Even Daniel, the grump, sings along.

Finally, when all is secure, I light a kerosene lamp, make a big pot of popcorn, and we all settle down in the living room.

My knee is sore tonight and my husband lets me prop it up in his lap. "I think we're pretty well set." He laughs. "Now, turn on the radio. . . . No, wait. I hear a motor." He steps to the front window and pulls back the curtain.

"Papa!" Susie squeals. "Be careful; the light!" Her father complies and drops the opening to a slit.

"See anything?" I ask.

"No, but someone's coming." The noise gets louder and now everyone hears it.

"Aren't they supposed to stay home during a blackout?" Sunny wants to know.

"Obey your air-raid warden!" Mira sings.

A few minutes later Bitsy's Indian motorcycle without headlights turns into the drive and Daniel goes out.

"Bitsy! Willie!" I hear him say. "Are you okay?"

"Stay here, kids," I order, and join him in the drive.

"Can't we come out?" the children all cry. This is as exciting as Christmas, maybe more so, because there's the element of vague danger. An air-raid warden might get us!

"What's up?" Dan asks.

"We need a midwife," Bitsy says. "We heard one lives here!"

"Very funny," I say, then I see a second dark vehicle creep across the wooden bridge.

By the time the woman, the one with the two boys that we once saw at the Texaco station with the camper, is in the Baby Cabin, she has to push, and we've opened and closed the doors five times.

May 15, 1942

Birth of baby girl to Oriole and Bull Jackson, new neighbors from Hazel Patch, at 8:22 P.M. in the Baby Cabin. Attending the mother were myself and Bitsy Proudfoot. Mr. Jackson was a great help in soothing his wife, who said she felt she was being pushed by a runaway train and couldn't slow down. Daniel Hester was also present, because in the rush to get Oriole comfortable, he got stuck in the corner when I moved my rolling table over to the bed.

He apologized mightily to Oriole for invading her privacy and said that he'd kept his eyes closed the whole time, but I doubted it. I bet he took a peek or two. Who could help it . . . hearing the sounds of one life giving birth to another.

The baby weighed 6 pounds 7 ounces and cried right away. No excessive bleeding. No tears. Placenta intact. The Jacksons didn't have any money until the mister gets his first paycheck at the woolen mill, but I said that was fine. Actually, it was a joy.

24

May 30, 1942

Decoration Day

*T*he Decoration Day parade, or Memorial Day, as some now call it, was created as a time to celebrate those who've fallen in battle to defend our freedom, and this year it seems to have more meaning.

The parade, though not as big as the Fourth of July parade, is still exciting for the children. We find seats on the courthouse steps. Far down the street and around the corner we hear the rat-a-tat-tat of a drum, then music, and the crowd stirs. It's the Liberty High School Band, proudly wearing new dark-blue uniforms, with tall red hats with white feathers; followed by a color guard from the American Legion; then the snappy All-Negro Drum Corps from Delmont.

The drum corps also has new uniforms, but not so fancy—brown pants, with sharp white military shirts and brown-and-red military-style hats in the army tradition. Trailing behind them are the old vets in their old uniforms.

The elderly Mr. Roote winks as they pass. A few years ago there were Civil War vets in both blue and gray, but they've passed on now.

There's even a CCC truck decked out with American flags and a jazz band playing "Boogie Woogie Bugle Boy." As the crowd cheers, it saddens me to think that these boys will soon be sent to the battlefield; *cannon fodder*, Dan would call them. The generals who plan the wars put the young men on the front lines while the old guys stay out of harm's way.

A yellow-haired young man sings the lyrics through a megaphone. *"They made him blow a bugle for his Uncle Sam. It really brought him down because he couldn't jam. . . ."*

Everyone under thirty starts to dance, including my children—especially Mira, who really shakes it, and Daniel has to grab the back of her dress before she can dash into the streets and put on a show. A trumpet player in the truck stands up with his horn and improvises a few bars and then the singer comes in again . . . *"He's the boogie woogie bugle boy of Company B!"*

After the jolly interlude, the Army National Guard marches by with a clipped cadence. The crowd roars with approval, but there's not one smile on the men's faces. These are serious soldiers, and they know that they will soon be fighting for our freedom and for their lives.

"Sound-off; one, two!" the drill sergeant calls.

"Sound-off; three, four!" the soldiers respond. Then all together they bark in their strong male voices, *"One, two, three, four. One, two. Three, four!"*

When the parade ends, we get in the Olds and head for the cemetery at the end of Third Street. Memorial Day in West Virginia is an important ritual. Nearly everyone has relatives who've died in some war . . . soon they will have more.

At the cemetery, old oaks and maples shade the graves and the lawn has been freshly cut. The strange part is the division between the Catholic and the Protestant cemeteries. A wrought-iron fence with sharp points at the top divides the two graveyards, as if after death the dead might jump the fence and intermarry. No worry about the colored. Negroes are buried behind the AME Methodist Church downtown.

Other years, I've let the children run among the tombstones, laughing and playing, while Daniel and I decorated the grave of some soldier who seems to have no kin, but this year people greet us with a solemn nod rather than a hearty hello. *It must be the war*, I think. Decorating the graves of soldiers who died in the past reminds us of the grief that is coming.

As we wander through the graveyard, we look for a suitable vet to honor. "How about this one?" Dan asks, pointing to a plain gravestone with an American flag carved into it and no flowers. "Private Jefferson Long," he reads. "Wounded in the Battle of Philippi. Died in his mother's arms in Liberty, WV, one year later. 1841–1862."

"That's the Civil War. He was just twenty-one," I say. "Not much more than a kid. . . ."

"He was lucky to make it home. Most men died on the battlefield or from disease in a prison camp. . . . Come on, kids. You can help put flowers on the soldier's grave. We'll pretend that Private Jefferson was your cousin from long ago."

Later, as we chug up Wild Rose Road on our way to the small graveyard we established behind the house with the blue door, the first thing I notice, when we park and get out, is that Becky and Isaac have whitewashed the picket fence.

The beautiful enclosure around the front yard was handmade by Dr. Blum as a present for Becky before they married, and each stave has a flower carved at the top. There are also new poles and wires. After all these years, the Blums finally have telephone and electricity coming into the house.

"Come on, kids," Daniel says as we get out of the Olds and troop past the barn. "Keep up. Dr. Blum, Nurse Becky, and Sally aren't home. They went to the parade in Torrington. Get off their porch, Danny!"

A large limestone marker at the entrance to the cemetery says HONORING THE HEROES OF THE HOPE RIVER WILDFIRE, 1935. There are eight people buried here; all died in the fire, including Willa and Alfred Hucknell, Susie and Sunny's parents and their baby brother, Alfred Jr.

No one would notice the three small wooden crosses in the corner. Two are for the babies I lost and one is for a premature baby someone left in a cardboard carton at Becky's Mother and Baby Clinic during the Great Depression.

After we scatter flowers on the graves, the children can run and play. Dan and I pull a few weeds around the gravestones then sit in the grass looking down toward the Hope.

"I like it up here," I say. "The soil isn't as good as our farm, but the view is better."

Dan takes my hand and we lie down on the warm earth. I imagine our two bodies buried next to each other. "I want to be with you always," I say, rolling over to rest my head on his chest. He touches my hair, brushing it away from my face. "Will you promise to find me in heaven?" I ask. "Whoever gets there first has to wait and watch for the other. Promise?"

I'm serious, but he makes a joke. "Are you sure we'll both get there? I curse quite a bit." I can see his grin without looking.

Summer

25

June 3, 1942

To Bind the Wounds

Today Dan went to a meeting with Judge Wade to discuss his refusal to register for the draft. I was hoping to be there, but he said it wasn't my business. This hurt a little, but I decided to go to the Red Cross meeting instead.

At the Methodist church our project again was to roll bandages, a simple, tedious task that's apparently helpful to medics. While we worked, the women discussed something that happened in town two days ago.

Ida May, the town hairdresser, begins the story. "A young man from Berkeley Springs, who'd just been drafted and received orders to be sent to the front, went home to say goodbye to his ma and pa.

"I got this straight from Jim at Jim's Tavern. The fellow snuck off the train when it stopped to unload at Liberty and came into the bar. Jim said the soldier tossed back three drinks and kept saying over and over to himself, 'I won't go. They can't force me.'

"Finally, he asked the barkeep where the john was. . . . I swear this is the truth. . . . He walked down the back hall, went straight to the latrine, and everyone in the tavern heard a crash.

"Jim was the first to get to the door. The soldier had shoved both his hands through the window glass.

"One-Arm Wetsel ran for the sheriff. Hardman bandaged the soldier up, threw him in the squad car, and went roaring out of town for the hospital in Torrington, siren wailing. Word is that the fellow nearly bled to death. By the time they got there, he was unconscious. The doctors saved him, but he'll never use his hands again."

"What a coward!" Mrs. Wade declares.

"Disgusting," Mrs. Goody snaps. "What *some people* will do to get out of their duty!"

"I think it's just sad," I interject. "We don't know the fellow's whole story. We don't know what he's seen or heard about war. We don't know what made him so desperate."

The women all look at me as if I had just thrown the American flag on the ground and stomped on it.

To escape their cold stares, I push up my glasses and begin to furiously cut my first piece of gauze, but stop short when Mrs. Goody, the chairman and preacher's wife starts the Red Cross prayer.

"Lord, we give this gift of bandages to bind the wounds of our *loyal* soldiers. Protect them in battle. Bless them for their *courage*." She emphasizes that word, *courage*, as commentary on the young man they see as a gutless coward. "Keep them safe as they fight for our freedom," she goes on. "In Our Savior's name, Amen."

"Amen," we all say.

To lighten the mood, Lilly Bittman begins to sing a popular tune by Glenn Miller and His Orchestra, "*On the old assembly line. On the old assembly line. Everything is hum-hum-hummin'? On the old assembly line.*"

Ida and Mrs. Wade spread more fabric and get out their scissors. Everyone rolls the bandages as fast as they can. We may differ in our opinion of the young soldier, but we are united in our will to bandage the wounds of those who fall in battle. "*On the old assembly line,*" Ida and I come in, singing harmony like the Andrews Sisters. "*On the old assembly line . . .*"

"SO WHAT HAPPENED at your meeting with Judge Wade?" I ask when Dan picks me up.

"It was okay," he says, twisting his mouth.

"Okay as in you aren't in any trouble?"

"No. Okay as in, I explained my position and the judge listened. He's going to do some research. I'm the only objector to military service in Union County so far."

"Will you fill out the registration form?"

"No," he says firmly without looking at me.

"I don't understand, Dan. What's the big deal? Just fill out the stupid form! It's not likely you'll be called."

"That's what Judge Wade said. He feels I'm putting him in a spot. Other people on the draft board are pushing him to report me."

We cross the stone bridge over the Hope and Daniel stops in the middle. Below, two men fish in the rapids. One man catches a golden trout and shouts with joy, "Hot-diggity!"

"I'm sorry, Patience . . . I never wanted to cause you pain." He turns in his seat to face me. "If I'd known I was a pacifist when we decided to marry, I would have told you. If I'd known there was a war looming, bigger than the Great War, I wouldn't have had kids."

We look in each other's eyes for a long time, then I sigh. "The Creator puts people in your path for a reason. It couldn't have been any other way and I can't imagine the world without our beautiful children."

"You're right," Dan says. "It *is* what it is. We'll be okay. We may bleed a little, but we won't die."

June 8, 1942

Double Trouble

This morning while I was trying to get the hang of using our new Hoover vacuum, I heard a car bump across the wooden bridge over Salt Lick, coming fast. Soon after, there was a knock at the door and when I answered, a short, very plump auburn-haired woman and a thin man wearing coveralls were standing on our porch. "Are you the midwife of Hope River?" the woman asked as she closed her eyes and rubbed her belly.

I didn't wait around for introductions. It was clear what was happening. "Let's go back to the Baby Cabin," I said as I took her arm. "I'm the midwife."

Thirty minutes later a small, lively female baby was born without difficulty. *That was easy*, I thought. *I'm getting to like these fast deliveries.* But when I palpated the woman's abdomen to see if the placenta had separated, I was in for a surprise.

"Oh!" I exclaimed, in a most unprofessional way. "There's another one!"

I have delivered twins before, but never without an assistant, and I considered calling Dan or one of the girls for help, but there wasn't time. The bottom of the second baby was already coming.

"Here," I said to the father, handing him a swaddling blanket. "Hold your baby. Another one is coming bottom first, and I order you not to faint."

The man plunks down in the rocking chair, embracing his first baby.

Thirty minutes later, a second female infant is born in a whoosh. I don't even have time to perform the breech hand movements; she just squirts out. After I deliver the two separate placentas and make sure both mother and babies are stable, the father finally speaks.

"Thank you. My name is Howard Wilson, and this is my wife, May. It's her third delivery. Sorry we didn't have time to properly introduce ourselves. We were visiting her cousin in Liberty and he's the one that told us about you. Tell you the truth, I thought this was false labor. My wife received care from a doctor in Mountain Ridge. How come he didn't know she was carrying twins?"

I shrug, looking at the two beautiful infants resting on their mother's chest. "Sometimes one is lying on top of the other, so you can only hear one heartbeat. I imagine the doc just thought you had one very large baby. It happens. I have adopted twin girls myself and their mother, before she died, told me they were a surprise too."

There's a knock at the door of the Baby Cabin. "Patience," Dan calls. "Everything okay? Do you need hot water or anything?"

"No, we're good," I yell back, laughing.

June 8, 1942

At 4:30 P.M. and 5:00 P.M. twin girls were born precipitously in the Baby Cabin, to May and Howard Wilson of Mountain Ridge. The first infant weighed 5 pounds 15 ounces. The second, 5 pounds. Both babies appeared to be a few weeks early, but breathed right away. Two placentas delivered spontaneously ten minutes later and bleeding was brisk until I gave May a spoonful of Mrs. Pott's tincture. Estimated blood loss, three cups. The babies are not identical because they each had their own sacs and placentas, though they look very much alike. Present for the delivery, other than me, was the father, Howard, whose face was as white as chalk.

Later that evening, after our children and Dan crowded into the Baby Cabin to see the new babies, the mother named her new girls Sunny and Sue, a great honor. Mr. Wilson gave us thirty dollars, the most I've ever been paid. The doctor in Mountain Ridge, he informed me, would have charged a lot more.

26

June 11, 1942

Fall from Grace

"Have you heard about this?" I toss the newspaper across the table to my husband. The children are off at school and this is our hour of time together.

"Japs Slay and Torture Prisoners on the Long March to Bataan," I read the headlines of the *Liberty Times* out loud, hissing out each word like mustard gas. "Did you see the photos?" Two American men look out at us from skull-like faces. Both are naked except for khaki shorts and every rib shows in their chests, literally skin and bones. "You telling me this is just propaganda?"

"No, that's real," Dan says.

"And do you still feel this war isn't worth fighting? It says here that American men were butchered; heads were chopped off. The Japanese forced the prisoners to sit for hours in the hot sun without water," I run on like a racecar out of control. "If a soldier was too weak to march, they just shot him. You want men like that ruling the world? I wouldn't even call them men."

"That's the trouble, Patience. They don't think we're human either. Seventy-six thousand U.S. soldiers surrendered in the Philippines after months of fighting and the Japanese believe *no true man* would ever surrender; therefore we're subhuman and deserve to die. That's just how they think.

"When the white man came to America he treated red men like they were subhuman. America was built on the backs of black slaves . . . Of course, what's happening in this war makes me sick," Dan goes on. "But killing each other only makes more hatred. God said, '*Thou shalt not kill.*' He didn't give us any exceptions."

I didn't mean it to happen, I really didn't, but when I stood up my coffee spilled and it seemed like I'd thrown it. "Well, *you* make me sick, Dr. Hester, with your pious platitudes. How would you feel if that were Danny or the girls being force-marched through the hot sun? Look at those men! Have you no outrage?" And then I ran upstairs.

Now here I sit, my jaw stiff with fury, flipping the pages in my journal, almost ripping them as I continue to write . . .

Downstairs, the kitchen door slams and when I stand and look through the window, I observe my husband slump across the farmyard and get in his Model T. *Just as well*, I think. I don't want to talk to him anyway.

When Dan and I don't agree, it leaves a sinkhole between us, and I've slipped over the side and fallen in. We've never before diverged on something so fundamental, so important. I pace the creaking wooden floor, then finally go out for some air.

Above me, three blue jays call to one another and the little creek laughs at my side. How can a person be this sad on such a brilliant summer day? No one in our family is ill or injured. We have plenty to eat. We have good friends. Bombs aren't dropping on us, but I don't have Daniel. Europe's war has become our war.

Carefully, I cross the creek on flat rocks and enter the forest. Then, I plop down. White trillium bloom among the dead leaves and it's the trillium that break me. Lying on my back on the forest floor, I let the tears come. I can't stop them.

I've often retreated to nature for solace, but never with such sorrow and a sad song comes out of me, minor in key, but solid and round. *I have been lost before and come into these woods to lay my body down.* Above me, a golden finch hops on a branch.

I have been lost before and come into these woods to lay my body down. And You have taken me in arms of light and sang to me. Rocked me gentle in the limbs of trees. You have taken me in arms of light and sang to me. And wiped away my tears with bits of leaves.

June 12, 1942

Mutiny

Hester has been gone for twenty-four hours. If he was off doing vet work and ran into an emergency, I'm sure he would call. (Note: I have reverted to calling him *Hester* as I did before our marriage, a sign that our bond is weakening.) While he's been gone, I've covered for him with the children, saying he's traveling from farm to farm helping with lambing, but Danny is on to me. He knows enough about vet work to realize that by June most of the lambs have already been born.

In truth, I'm worried and can't imagine what's become of Dan. Once, years ago, Isaac Blum disappeared in the night. It was during his silent phase when he refused to speak or even take care of himself. Daniel knew Isaac could drive a tractor, but no one realized he could drive a car all the way to West Penn Hospital in Pittsburgh to re-trieve a specialist's report that Becky badly needed for one of the sick CCC boys.

"Mama?" Mira wants to know. "When will Papa be home?"

"Pretty soon, honey. I wouldn't be surprised if he made it for supper."

But Daniel doesn't make it for supper. He doesn't make it for bedtime. When I put away my journal, he's still not home.

At four in the morning, I hear Sasha bark and the Model T pulls into the drive, but I pretend to be asleep when Dan enters our bedroom.

"Patience? You awake?" I keep my eyes shut. "Were there any vet calls? I went to Philadelphia to talk to some Quakers about refusing to register for the draft."

Here I pop up like a jack-in-the-box. "What the hell, Daniel! You went all the way to Philly? *I was worried!* The whole time you were gone, I lied to the kids and said you were out lambing. For all I knew you'd had an auto accident or maybe were just sleeping off a bender in a ditch. If you weren't home by this morning, I'd made up my mind to go the sheriff."

"Well, I'm back." He strips to his underwear, doesn't even put on pajamas, and slides under the covers. I close my eyes again and back away from his warmth even though there's nothing I want more than to lie next to him.

"I shouldn't have blown up at you yesterday. I was very sad afterward," I say, looking up at the ceiling. "I just hate it when we aren't in harmony."

"I'm sorry too, Patience. I'm not trying to be stubborn. You know what the Great War was like for me. The slaughter of horses, the slaughter of men. And I killed too, many times. I've told you I would never do it again."

"Not if Danny and the girls were threatened?" I whisper. "Not if *I* were threatened? You wouldn't defend me?"

Dan rests on his back, his hands behind his head. "The Quakers asked me that same question. Would I use violence to defend my family?"

"And what did you say?"

"I said I didn't know, but that I *intended* to never kill a human again."

"Some would say you aren't much of a man if you won't defend your family or country." I take a deep breath, feeling anger boil up again. "I'm sorry I said that . . . Let's go to sleep before we get in another fight. I'm just disappointed. It's the first time I've ever been disappointed in you."

"I am who I am, Patience. That's what I told Mr. Ross

in Philadelphia. I might not be Amish, or a Mennonite or a Quaker, but I'm Daniel Hester, once a soldier, now a pacifist."

"*Pacifist*. That's a dirty word to some. People around here will have a hard time buying it, since they've seen you in a few fights."

Dan doesn't respond and I take his hand under the covers. Our fingers find their familiar place, curling around each other; they can't help it. Finally he speaks. "Fists are different, Patience. Unless you're a raging lunatic, you don't kill someone with your fists. . . .

"I told you I've shot men who were supposed to be my enemy. I didn't tell you everything. One day, in the last war, we got orders to storm a German platoon that was hiding in a bombed-out school. This would have been toward the end of the war.

"We charged through an open field and my fellow soldiers were falling to the left and to the right of me, but I just kept running forward, sure if I stopped I'd be killed. I jumped over a stone wall and was confronted by a German man crouching there—not the stereotyped blue-eyed Nordic the Nazis now idolize, just a regular stocky young brown-eyed guy.

"He looked at me with his eyes wide, pleading with me in German not to kill him, but my bayonet was already moving. He put his hand over his gut where I'd stabbed him, but I thrust again and again. Blood came out of his mouth and he died.

"I nearly vomited. My knees were shaking and I was, quite frankly, ashamed. When I told my fellow GIs about it, they were undisturbed. One of them boasted that he'd killed a German officer with the butt of his rifle. Another one had strangled an enemy with his bare hands. A third had shot someone in the head point-blank and then bashed his brains out.

"How did it happen that they were so coldhearted? We'd been told in boot camp that the good soldier kills without thinking. The moment he sees the enemy as a fellow man he's useless on the battlefield, but I couldn't forget the young German's eyes. They burn my soul still.

"If I had met the fellow somewhere on his farm or in the feed store, we could have been friends. I had nothing against him. . . ." Dan is becoming more worked up as he speaks, and finally I cut him off.

"Honey, I'm tired. I've been lying here awake worrying about you. . . . Let's put the discussion under the pillow. We both need some sleep. I'm just glad you're home."

My husband pulls me toward him and my longing for the comfort of his body defeats my anger and confusion. "This is where I belong," he says.

"Me too," I whisper. "I missed you. I never want to be apart from you again. Promise."

"Joined at the hip? Every minute?" I imagine him smiling into the dark.

"You know what I mean . . . joined at the heart . . . as long as they beat . . . and after."

27

June 21, 1942

Picnic

*I*t's Father's Day and the children went in together and bought their pa a new tie, but for the first time, with the worry about the draft and our uncertain future, I forgot to give him anything. Instead, I made his favorite breakfast—popovers and wild strawberries that I picked out in the pasture—and later we're going to a picnic at the river.

"Did you see this?" Dan asks, spreading the *Liberty Times* out on the table. "It's official. . . . White Rock Camp Civilian Conservation Corps is closing in a few weeks, along with all the other CCC camps in the nation."

"Lou Cross told us they might not be here much longer," I answer. "But I didn't realize it would be so soon. The army will be happy that all the CCC fellows can now enlist, but a lot of people in Union County will lose their jobs, including Becky and Isaac. Is there enough vet business nowadays for Dr. Blum to work as your assistant?"

Dan shrugs, apparently unconcerned. "We'll make do. We always have."

When we get to the Hope, I'm surprised to see, among the other familiar vehicles, Lou Cross's green Plymouth. Daniel pulls over on the side of the gravel road and the kids tumble out and start to run for their friends. "Hold on, there!" Dan yells. "Everyone has to carry something. Here, you, Danny, take the fishing poles. Girls, help Mommy with the baskets and blankets."

It's a beautiful clear blue day without a cloud in the sky, and Lou, Willie, and Bitsy are already fishing on the bank, where the river runs swift and clean.

"Here, hold it this way," Lou says to Willie. "That-a-boy!" Willie has a big smile on his face and I realize he may never have been fishing before.

"Hello, everyone!" we greet our neighbors. This is the first such outing we've had since last summer. The twins run off to see their sister Sonya. Mira and Danny go down to see Willie.

"Lou Cross again," I murmur to Dan.

"So what?" says Dan. "I'm surprised at you, Patience. Did you expect your pal Bitsy to stay single forever?"

"I just don't want her to get hurt. Lou Cross seems overly friendly."

Becky and Mildred Miller have already spread blankets on the grass and are sitting together talking earnestly. Mrs. Maddock's in her wheelchair today. Sometimes she uses the walker and braces that her husband, an ex-engineer turned farmer, made for her, but when her legs hurt she reverts to the chair. I spread my blanket near her feet. Sarah is over fifty and almost died from polio when she was young, but her silver-and-gold hair frames her nearly unlined face like a halo.

"Did you hear that Sally Blum is going into the WACs?" she asks in a soft, low voice like the film star Lauren Bacall. "Congress just passed a law establishing the Women's Army Corps a few weeks ago. They're looking for fifty thousand female recruits to work office- and mechanic-type jobs. If they get that many, it will free up fifty thousand men for combat."

"I thought Sally liked working at the munitions plant."

"She quit. Told her parents it's too boring and she wants to serve the war effort more directly."

"Holy cow! Becky must be crushed. They are so close. Where is Sally anyway?" I ask, looking around the meadow for the pretty eighteen-year-old.

"In Liberty, with her boyfriend, Patrick McKenzie. He enlisted in the army and is shipping out next week. That's part of the reason she wants to leave too."

"Boyfriend! That red-haired young man, Patrick, who works at the feed store? He's a cutie and seems ambitious, but he must be twenty-five. Is it serious?"

"He's twenty-two, Becky told me . . . and Sally's eighteen," says Sarah Rose with a laugh.

"They're talking about getting married."

"Sadie, at Farmers' Supply, must be fit to be tied! All the young fellows are going to war. Who's going to carry the feed sacks and lumber?"

I watch Becky as she talks to Mrs. Miller. The kind pastor's wife takes my friend's white hand in her smooth brown one. I can't be sure, but it looks like my friend is crying and when I realize I've never seen her cry before, a lump comes in my throat. Sally is the Blums' only child. They adopted her when we adopted the twins, and she's been with Becky and Isaac for almost seven years. On top of that, the two have lost their income at the CCC camp.

"Oh, my!" I say to myself, but it comes out of my mouth. "Becky's had so much loss in her life and she's always waiting for the other shoe to drop. Her mother died of cancer when she was young. Two brothers died in the Great War. Her father had a stroke not long after his boys died, and then her husband, another veteran who came home shell-shocked, killed himself." I let out my air in a sad whoosh.

"My problem is," I go on, "I want to protect everyone from suffering. If someone threw a grenade and I could get there fast enough I would jump on it, but it's not possible is it, Sarah?"

"No. Suffering comes to us all. The best we can do is survive the wounds in one piece and pray we aren't blown apart and swept down the river . . . Becky will be okay."

A Change in the Weather

I notice Sarah's attention is now on Bitsy and Lou Cross down on the riverbank.

"It looks like Bitsy has a boyfriend too," Sarah says, and I can't tell if she disapproves because of the racial difference or if she's just commenting.

"I'm not sure. Lou is Bitsy's foreman at the woolen mill and I've seen them together quite a bit, but they might just be friends. Willie seems to enjoy the man's company. He never knew his father."

"Ma! Ma!" I hear Danny call. "Come play."

Some of the men have driven two stakes in the ground and are setting up a game of horseshoes. This is a simple competition that doesn't involve much strength or practice. For some reason, I'm surprisingly good at it, so I join Daniel's team and the three of us play against Isaac Blum, Milt Maddock, and Reverend Miller.

A half hour later, my team is one point ahead, and when a cloud passes over the sun I look up and see a mountain of billowy white, with gray underneath, sailing this way. When a wind comes up, I realize I haven't looked for my girls in a while. Then I see them.

Sunny, Sue, and their sister Sonya are sitting on the rocks near the rapids and Mira is still with Willie, near the fishing hole. Bitsy and Lou are spreading out their blanket in the grass and I note that he's brought one of those new-fangled folding card tables I've seen in the Sears catalogue, so we don't have to serve our food from the ground—a nice addition to our feast.

"It must be time for dinner," I comment to Dan, looking up at the clouds again. "I'd better help set up. You guys go on and play without me. Take my turn, Danny. I'll call you when it's time to eat."

Becky and I meet at the tables, each putting out our offerings. "You okay?" I ask my friend.

"Oh, you know . . . It never rains but it pours. You heard that White Rock CCC camp is closing. Then Sally announces she's going to join the WACs. Life as I know it has been blown apart."

"There's nothing you can count on but change, Mrs. Kelly used to say. But that doesn't mean you have to like it."

Becky chews on her lower lip. "It's this damned war!"

"You're right. Dan and I are even having trouble . . ." Just then there's a scream. It's Mira! Daniel races across the clearing toward the river, but Mira and Willie are no longer on the bank.

"Mira!" I yell. "Where are you?" The scream comes again. Sunny and Sue stand on the rocks and point downstream.

All the men, along with Bitsy and I, run that way, but with my leg, even in an emergency I can't run very fast. "Mira!" Dan calls.

"Willie!" Lou calls.

Then we see them both climbing up the embankment, about thirty yards downriver, looking like drowned rats. Mira is crying and her face is so white her freckles stick out like polka dots. Willie holds her hand. They both plop down in the grass, panting.

By the time I get to them, Mira's color is better and Will is smiling. "I saved her," he says. "I don't know how I did it. I was always afraid of the water before and never learned to swim, but when Mira slipped on the bank and fell in, it was like my body suddenly knew what to do."

"Willie rescued me!" Mira agrees. "I was way down the river calling for help, and no one could hear me. Half the time my head was under the water, but then my feet would hit bottom and I would push up and was able to breathe. Willie swam up to me and grabbed the back of my shirt."

"Sorry, Mrs. Hester. I think I tore the collar."

"Oh, Willie. I don't care. Thank you. Thank you for saving our baby." Dan picks Mira up and carries her back to the picnic area.

"Come on, kids." he calls. "From now on, no one near the river, unless a grown-up is there for a lifeguard. Who here is a strong swimmer?" Willie raises his hand, now full of confidence. Lou, Daniel, Danny, Milt Maddock, Isaac Blum, and I raise our hands too.

"Damn!" says Lou, looking at the rest of the group. "I'm gonna start a swimming school."

June 22, 1942

To Dance

Today I expected five patients for the Pregnant Ladies Society and only three showed up. The first two were Martha Wallace and Ada Mullins. Both are expecting their first babies. Then Hannah Dyer arrived in her late-model DeSoto, a half hour late, her long, dark hair flying.

Hannah and John Dyer live on rich bottom land on the banks of the Hope about five miles south, and she's pregnant again with her third. I took care of Hannah when she had their other two children. She has easy labors and was a delight.

When I'd finished everyone's prenatal exam, we sat down on the wooden benches in the gazebo for peppermint tea and biscuits with honey.

"Today we're going to talk about labor," I explain after everyone has been served. "Hannah has had babies before, and I thought maybe she'd tell you about it. What would you like to ask, ladies?"

This is one of the things I enjoy about the group. I've found that the women are eager to listen to one another and they seem to learn more than if I give them a lecture or a Health Department pamphlet.

"Well, does it hurt as bad as they say it does?" Martha asks. She's a tall girl, with a square jaw and thick, short, sandy hair pinned back on the sides like the Andrews Sisters.

"I didn't know what to expect," Hannah answers. "My ma had passed and I had no sisters to talk to, but my sister-in-law from Kentucky had her baby at home with a midwife and she told me I could do it."

"So did it hurt like the bejeezus?" Martha persists.

"No, actually. I'm sure everyone's different, but at the beginning the pains were just like menstrual cramps that came and went. When it got hard and the cramps were closer I had to keep moving. John, my husband, put some music on to soothe me, but dancing is what helped."

"You danced through labor?" Martha squints her eyes.

"She did," I come in. "I'd never seen it before. The harder the contractions got, the faster she danced. I couldn't keep up with her."

"You danced too, Mrs. Hester?" asks Ada in her Minnie Mouse voice. She's wiry and small, has a blond bob with bangs, a sweet country girl. "It sounds like you were having a party."

"If you think of it, having a baby is a party—*a birthday party.*"

"What about you, Mrs. Hester? You have four kids. Except for dancing, is there any other way to make the pains easier?" Martha chimes in again, tucking her tawny mane behind her ear.

This is an awkward question. I've had very difficult births and don't want to scare my patients, so I answer indirectly. "Here's my advice, ladies. Labor is less painful if you stay out of bed. Stay out as long as you can."

"You aren't going to make us dance, are you?" Ada squeaks out a laugh.

"Definitely not. But I will walk with you. You can lean against the end of the bed and sway back and forth." Here I demonstrate by bending over the gazebo rail, wiggling my butt, and they all laugh to see me doing the hoochie coochie.

"I would like Ollie to be there if it's okay," says Ada. "He's been called up for service, but because I'm due anytime now the Red Cross arranged for him to have a two-weeks' delay. Do you think I'll have the baby by then, Mrs. Hester?"

"There's a good chance. The man helps make the baby," I say as I end our meeting. "And if he is willing, he can help it be born."

28

July 1, 1942

False Labor

*I*t's been ten days since the last meeting of the Pregnant Ladies Society and Ada has called me three times thinking she might be in labor.

Today she was crying because Ollie must report in three days for induction. "Please," she begged. "I know exactly when I got pregnant and I'm two weeks late. I want my husband to see his baby. I *need* him to be with me. We're making love every night and I'm eating sour pickles from Bittman's, but there must be something you can do!"

I told her I would get back to her, that I would think about it. The truth is, I've never interfered with labor before, and I don't think it's right. I asked Daniel what he would do if he had a prize horse or a pedigreed dog that was overdue.

"Vets use Piturin, an artificial hormone, but I wouldn't advise trying it on a woman. Blum says that in the hospital, when the patient has toxemia and they need to get the baby born, they use something similar, an injection of Methergine, but that's definitely beyond the scope of a midwife."

Finally, I ask Bitsy. "What do you think? Ollie is about to be inducted into the army and sent off to the front. Ada is two weeks overdue and she desperately wants him to be with her in labor and get to see their baby before he goes."

"Is she contracting at all?"

"Yes. She's called me every evening, thinking it's the real thing, but it stops in a few hours. One time she even showed up at the house and I did an exam in the Baby Cabin. Her cervix was thin, but she was only one fingertip dilated. I know she's been having marital relations and I've told her to walk a lot . . ."

"What about castor oil?"

"The laxative?"

"Most every family has some. A gypsy midwife I met in France told me it stimulates contractions."

"Do you just rub it on the abdomen or drink it or what?"

"The woman drinks it and then the man rubs some on her belly and breasts. I know it takes a while, probably a few hours, to see if it's going to work. Tell them three hours of the rubbing and to take three teaspoons of the oil every three hours."

I wrinkle my nose. "That stuff is nasty. Three times? She has to drink it three times and the massage goes on for three hours?"

"Yes, three hours. Three's the magic number. She can mix the castor oil with milk and honey."

"You aren't putting me on, are you?"

"Maybe a little," says Bitsy. "But tell her *three*. That's the magic number . . . Tonight's Saturday, and Willie and I are going into Delmont for dinner with Mr. Cross at a fellow mill worker's house, but if the baby comes on Sunday, call me, we can do the birth together."

Ada is as excited as a kid on Christmas when I tell her the plan. I use expressions like *magic* and *old gypsy recipe* to encourage positive thinking. The worst that can happen is she'll get diarrhea and won't go into labor, but it's worth a try.

"Oh, thank you! Thank you," she says. "I just know it's going to work."

The kids are tucked in and I'm just crawling into bed in my summer cotton gown when the telephone finally jangles. My husband is still downstairs listening to the news. "It's now official," the announcer declares. "The U.S. has recently defeated Japan in the Battle of Midway, halting their advance across the Pacific, a major victory."

When the phone rings, he turns the radio down and picks up the phone. "Daniel Hester," I hear him say. "Just a minute, I'll get her."

Ada

*D*an doesn't even have to come get me. I think I know who it is and in a minute I'm in the kitchen holding the phone. "Hello!"

"It's Ada," she says, her voice even higher than usual. "I took the castor oil three times and finally I think I'm in labor."

"Great!" I respond. "I'll leave the light on in the Baby Cabin."

Thinking I can still catch a few winks before she arrives, I'm deep into a dream about wooly little lambs when Daniel shakes me. "Patience, Sasha's barking and a vehicle just pulled in the drive." He rolls over and goes back to sleep, while I dress quickly, put on my specs, and before anyone can knock, I'm downstairs at the door.

"Hello. Miss Patience, this is my husband, Ollie," Ada announces. "We did exactly as you said and the magic worked. I'm sorry if I smell bad, I had a little accident and pooped myself on the way over."

"She sure did!" says the grinning young man standing beside her. "That castor oil is strong stuff and I been working it into her breasts and belly for hours. Makes me feel like I'm helping." He sets Ada's suitcase on the porch floor.

"I'm sure you *are* helping. Come on. Let's go back to the Baby Cabin." I step into my shoes and lead them around to the little log house that Daniel and Isaac Blum built for me. "Are the contractions harder now?" I ask over my shoulder.

There's no response. And when I turn I see that Ada is leaning on Ollie, her fingers digging into his muscular arm. That answers my question. The contractions *are* strong. Three minutes later, just as I get the young woman cleaned up, she has another hard one.

This time Ollie kneels on the floor behind his wife, pressing his big hands into her sacrum. He's a short, stocky guy, with longish dark hair and a clean-shaven face. "Higher!" she says. "Rub harder!"

"Take a big breath at the end of the next contraction, Ada. Then I want you to lie down just for a minute and be as quiet as possible while I listen to the baby's heartbeat. I also need to examine your belly to make sure the baby's head is still presenting. Breathe with her, Ollie."

The slender blond woman does what I say and stretches out on the bed. "Your baby's heartbeat is fine," I announce, after counting one hundred and fifty beats a minute with my metal fetoscope. "Now let me examine your belly and see what his or her position is . . ."

I feel first just above the pubic bone and find a large hard, round object. Good! The head is down, but inspecting the abdomen I see something's not right. Instead of the smooth outline of the back along the right or left side, there are bumps and lumps everywhere and a depression around the belly button. This baby is lying *sunny-side up*, meaning it's facing the mother's belly button, instead of her spine. The bumps and lumps are the baby's little arms and legs.

"Ow! Ow! Ow!" Ada squeaks as another contraction comes on. "My back. It's killing me. I can't lie like this. Ow! Ow!"

"Oh, honey babe, don't cry like that," Ollie says. "You're paining me so!"

"I'm paining *you*? You have no idea, mister!" Ada snaps.

Ollie looks confused. "If you want me to leave . . ."

"No you don't, buddy." That's Ada rolling over on her hands and knees and grabbing his arm. "Rub!"

I can't help smiling. Clearly, the young woman is nearing the last stages of labor and her angry energy is normal.

"It's okay," I whisper to Ollie. "Your sweet Ada is not possessed by the devil. She just doesn't have the energy to be polite. She'll be herself again as soon as she has the baby in her arms." It's then that I hear another vehicle in the drive and cracking the door, discover a green Plymouth just outside.

Bitsy jumps out of Lou Cross's Plymouth and runs to the door of the Baby Cabin. "I saw the lights. Is it Ada?" she asks. "Did the castor oil work?"

"It did, and how!" Ollie says, looking over his shoulder, and Ada manages a smile.

Back Labor

Shall I stay for the birth?" Bitsy whispers. "Mr. Cross was bringing us home. Maybe Willie could crawl into bed with Little Dan."

"Sure, I'd like that. . . . Ada and Ollie, this is my assistant midwife, Bitsy Proudfoot. If it's okay, I'd like her to be here. She's the one that gave me the castor oil recipe."

"Fine with me," Ada says between contractions. "I can use all the help I can get."

Bitsy runs out to the car to thank Lou for the ride home and in the shadows of the willow tree I see them embrace. She leads Will into the farmhouse and a few minutes later she's back in the Baby Cabin, taking off her cute little red sailor hat. She's dressed to the nines in a red short-sleeved dress and red heels with white trim and looks more like Minnie Mouse herself than a homebirth midwife.

"Mmmph. Mmmph. Mmmph," Ada moans.

"The contractions are getting closer," Bitsy observes.

Suddenly, Ada's voice drops into the normal range for an adult woman and she rises up on her knees and growls the birth song. She grips Ollie's arm and I notice he already has a tattoo of an American flag on it, with *Victory* in fancy letters, no doubt in preparation for the war.

"But oh, my back! Is it supposed to hurt this bad, Miss Patience? I feel like a knife is stabbing me. The only thing that helps is when Ollie rubs hard."

"It's normal," Bitsy reassures her. "Not every woman has back pain, probably only one in four, but you're doing great and it won't be much longer. Maybe an hour of pushing, that's all. If you can endure this, you can do anything."

"An hour!" Ada yelps. (*Quite likely more*, I think, but I keep that to myself.)

"Oh, my baby doll, you can do it," Ollie says. "God made us a baby. God will give you strength."

"Pray for me, husband! Pray for our son."

I raise my eyebrows at Bitsy. *How does Ada know it's a son?*

Three hours of pushing on her hands and knees on the cabin's pine floor and dark hair is beginning to show at the perineum. "Come now, Ada, can you get back in bed?"

"No. No. I can't move. It's coming!" She pulls on the mattress edge, but she won't get off her hands and knees.

"Push a little. Blow a little. Do it with her Ollie. Push a little. Blow a little," Bitsy instructs.

"Oil," I request, nodding toward the little brown bottle, and Bitsy swabs some around the opening. Then suddenly the whole head is out. I check for a cord around the neck, but there isn't one.

"Get your hands down here, Ollie!" Bitsy orders.

What is she doing? The man's big bare hands are shaking, but he does what she says.

"With the next big contraction the baby is going to turn and come out," my assistant instructs. "All you have to do is support him, but hold on. He'll be slippery!"

Ollie looks at me and I nod as if this is routine, but in fact I have never seen a husband help deliver his own child before, never even dreamed of it. Perhaps this is another one of those French things.

As predicted, with the next contraction, Ada gives it all she's got and the baby rotates and falls into the father's hands. I watch as Bitsy wraps her in a cotton blanket and hands her back to her pa, who holds his infant daughter in the crook of his arm with the American flag and the *Victory* tattoo. This would make a good poster, I think. "The soldier goes to war for our freedom, leaving his newborn baby at home."

Then Ollie holds the wailing infant out to his wife. "It's a girl!" he says, tears streaming down his face.

Tomorrow this GI will take the troop train to Torrington. He'll march with the other inductees down the cobbled streets to the courthouse, where a barber will shave his head. He'll be given a uniform and sworn in to the U.S. Army. In a month he'll be on a ship to Europe or Asia, where he will carry a rifle with a bayonet and kill or be killed.

July 1, 1942

Baby girl, Olivia Jean Mullins, 6 pounds 5 ounces, born to Ada and Ollie Mullins of Liberty, West Virginia, at 11:05 P.M. The father was to be inducted into the army the next day so the patient's labor was stimulated with castor oil, an old French recipe that Bitsy came up with.

Ada experienced severe back labor with the baby in posterior position, but the infant delivered nicely into the father's hands. Bleeding minimal. There was only one small tear that I had to suture. Present for the delivery were Bitsy Proudfoot and myself, proud sister midwives. We were paid one crisp five-dollar bill and promised another one when the soldier gets his first paycheck.

29

July 4, 1942

Independence Day

The Fourth of July has always been a big celebration in my family. Even when I was a kid and lived in Deerfield, Michigan, there would be a parade, and then my father and mother and I would picnic at the park on the banks of the Des Plaines River. In those days, there was a bandstand, where a small brass band, complete with tuba, played polkas, and people would dance. Sometimes there'd be a political speech.

Since I was a union activist and a socialist in my twenties and thirties, I always thought of myself as a citizen of the world, but this year I'm as patriotic as Danny. That's why I was as disappointed as the kids were when we heard that the parade and festivities in Liberty have been canceled.

According to President Roosevelt, the military and the government will not take a break for the Fourth of July, nor will the Post Office, nor any war-related industry. That means the coal miners will be deep in the ground and even

Bitsy will have to work cranking out wool blankets for soldiers.

INDEPENDENCE DAY DAWNED warm and clear, the sort of sparkling day that makes you want to do something special. "We could still have a picnic down at the river," I said to Dan. "Maybe Becky and Isaac would come and the Maddocks and the folks from Hazel Patch."

"Whatever you say . . ." Dan answers, a newspaper in front of his face.

"Okay, you might as well tell me. What's the latest horror story?"

"The American Liberty ship *Alexander Macomb* was sunk on her maiden voyage east of Cape Cod by a German submarine."

"There are German submarines right off Cape Cod?"

"Billy Blaze, the editor of the *Times*, reports there have been other attacks along the East Coast, clear down to Virginia."

"Do you think most people know the war is so close? New England! Cape Cod! Virginia, for God's sake! There could be German submarines anywhere."

"Spies too!" Daniel gives me a sarcastic grin as if he doesn't believe it, or maybe he just doesn't care.

A few phone calls later and our Fourth of July picnic is arranged on the banks of the Hope. Willie is with us today because Bitsy has to work, but I make a short drive over to Hazel Patch to spread the word. Then the preparations begin.

Just for fun, the girls and I make a red, white, and blue Liberty cake and plan to load on whipped cream from our cow, wild strawberries, and a few blueberries from our one bush near the porch. We also make deviled eggs with homemade mayonnaise and I cook up a mess of fresh-picked green beans.

Around three we load everyone up, dressed in patched play clothes, and drive around Salt Lick Road to the other side of Spruce Mountain. "Looks like Mr. Maddock mowed the path down to the river," Dan says. "Must have brought his tractor down. The grass on the bank is cut short too. It's almost like a park . . .

"Okay, here's the rule, kids!" He announces to all the children, including the Jackson boys, who have come with their parents and new baby from Hazel Patch. "*No one* can get in the water until a grown-up, who can swim, is with you. Got that?"

"Yes, sir," they all say.

"Does that include us bigger kids? You know, the ones who already can swim?" Willie asks.

"You bet it does. And if anyone disobeys, I'll bust your chops!" answers Daniel.

"Can we swim *now*? Will you supervise?" Danny asks.

My husband looks at me, since I'm the organizer of this event. "Patience?"

I glance at the timepiece around my neck. "Sure. See you in about an hour. Be careful, everyone." Dan and the boys run for the water as I yell one more time. "*Be careful!*"

I have no worries about the girls. Since her near drowning, Mira is afraid of the river as much as the twins. It's the overconfident young males I'm concerned about.

This time, since Lou and Bitsy are working at the woolen mill, we have no fancy folding tables, so Becky Blum and I spread the quilts on the grass. Becky is unusually quiet. "You okay?" I ask.

She looks around and sees that Mrs. Miller, Sarah Rose Maddock, and Oriole Jackson, with her baby, are over by the vehicles laughing. "Did you hear that the CCC camp is closing?" Becky asks me.

"What are you and Isaac going to do?"

"Well, our last day is next week. We've talked about opening an office and going back into private practice. People have enough money to pay for visits now, only, it means being on call night and day. You know how that is. . . ."

"I do. We do. Dan and I both."

"Or I could try to get a job with the State of West Virginia in public-health nursing. I don't know if there *are* any such jobs, but maybe . . . Then Isaac and Daniel could continue working together."

"Sounds good," I say, laying out plates and silverware. "So, why the long face?"

"It's Sally. She's joined the WACs and she's going to be sent to Washington, D.C., to work in the army's secretarial pool."

"I heard," I say, stopping what I'm doing.

"I just miss her so . . ." Becky says, swallowing hard and looking off toward the river.

When our Fourth of July feast is spread out, and the men and children come up from the river, Reverend Miller says grace.

"Dear Father, we thank thee for the opportunity for fun and fellowship on this Fourth of July. We know that we are blessed . . ."

I look around the group and find the boys imitating the men, standing tall, their hands at their sides, their eyes closed . . . except Dan. His eyes are open and he looks into mine. The little girls all have their hands folded under their chins, just as Mrs. Miller, Oriole Jackson, Becky, and Sarah Rose do.

"All over the world people are suffering," Reverend Miller goes on, "and dying for our right to be free. Protect them. Give them courage. Give them hope. Help us to do our part, collecting scrap metal, working for the Red Cross, or supporting servicemen and -women however we can. In the name of the Father, the Son, and the Holy Ghost. Amen."

After our picnic, we are surprised when Mr. Maddock gets out a packet of firecrackers. *Now it feels like the Fourth of July!* One by one he lights them, throws them into the field, and the kids go wild feigning they're wounded soldiers and doing dramatic death scenes.

Around four, just as we're loading up the Model T to go home, we see in the distance a line of vehicles approaching along the dusty road and hear the voices of men. "*Over hill, over dale,*" they sing. "*We will hit the dusty trail as those Caissons go rolling along.*"

What's this?

Seven brown army trucks full of soldiers follow a jeep with two officers and stop at the intersection of Wild Rose and Salt Lick. The troops get out and form lines. They're all dressed in camouflage, complete with heavy backpacks, rifles, and metal helmets. There must be more than a hundred and they march along the edge of the road. "Harch! One, two, three. Harch! One, two, three."

"Parade rest!" a sergeant yells, and the men stop smartly at attention with their legs spread apart.

A senior officer steps forward. "At ease," he says. "Men, this is your first opportunity to ford a river in full battle gear. There may be times when you'll have to cross waterways in Europe . . ."

We all stand at the side of the road watching. "Sir," the man giving orders speaks to Daniel, possibly because he's the tallest. "We're from the National Guard out of Torrington. I've been told this stretch along the river is open land and we intend to do maneuvers here. Have I been misinformed? Is the property yours or one of your friends'?"

Daniel is silent, just staring at him, and I feel the military man harden. It's a simple enough question; why doesn't Dan answer?

Finally, Isaac Blum speaks up. "Officer, you're correct. This is open land. People camp here sometimes and picnic and swim, but no one claims it. We know what you're doing is important and we wish you well. Happy Independence Day."

"Happy Independence Day!" Daniel says under his breath as he stalks toward the car. "I can't even have a goddamn day with my family and friends without thinking of the war. Now the war has come home."

30

Lost

*F*or the last few weeks, Daniel is like a pressure cooker about to go off. The littlest things seem to offend him, like when he went to the Farmers' Lumber and Feed Store and Sadie told him they were out of chicken feed. He got all bent out of shape and seemed to take it personally. He hides behind the newspaper so no one will talk to him. And he's drinking again.

"Have you heard from Judge Wade about the draft registration?" I ask him one night when the kids are tucked in and we're getting ready for bed.

"Yes, I got a letter."

"You didn't tell me. When was this?"

He lets out his air like a steam locomotive. "Couple of days ago."

"Can I read it?"

"I threw it in the fire."

"*Dan!*" He leans over and takes off his socks. There's a hole in toe that needs darning. "I take it there was no good news." He shakes his head, not looking at me. "Well, summarize, at least. What did it say?"

"It was just another official order to come into the draft board and register, same as the first, along with a note from Judge Wade that said he'd done what he could. He'd traveled all the way into Torrington to discuss my case with the officials there. He tried to make a point that I'm a veteran of the previous war and wouldn't be required to serve anyway, but they won't make an exception. I still have to register like every other loyal American man. It's what I expected."

I chew on my lower lip, holding in what I'm thinking. *Well,* are *you loyal?* I want to yell. *Do you care about this country or just your precious ideals?*

Dan pulls back the covers. "Come to bed, honey," he says in his quiet way.

I stand, shaking my head no. I would cry, but instead I get out my journal, sit in the rocker, and begin to scribble. For over ten years we have been best friends, lovers, husband and wife. We have had conflicts, but they were always minor.

Now our differing points of view about the war and registering for the draft seem fundamental. It's about duty and loyalty, family and home. It's about stopping Hitler.

Once Daniel Hester was my rock; now he's the slime under the rock. I've been knocked off my feet, pulled underwater, and I'm lost in the rapids of the Hope River.

July 17, 1942

Win One for the Gipper

*J*uly has not been good for the crops. It's stormed in the afternoon every day for two weeks, and the tomatoes and peppers are blighted. I can't get into the garden to weed because of the mud and I'm afraid by the time the soil dries out, the carrots, beans, winter squash, and potatoes will be choked out by plantain, sheep's sorrel, and ragwort.

July has not been good for the Allies either. Edward R. Murrow tells us on the radio that so far this month, German U-boats have sunk ninety-six of our ships and Billy Blaze reports in the *Liberty Times* that German troops are marching toward Stalingrad, a major industrial city on the Volga River. Control of Stalingrad would effectively cut off most of Russia from ports on the Caspian Sea and enable the Nazis to control the oil fields of the Caucasus.

"Look at this," Daniel says one morning as he pores over the paper. "Mr. Flanders at the Eagle Theater is offering another free movie today. This time it's *Knute Rockne: All American* with Pat O'Brien and Ronald Reagan. It was a big hit a couple of years ago."

"Can we go, Pa? Can we? Can we?" all the children want to know. I lean over to get a look at the ad and put my hand on Dan's shoulder, noticing his warmth. There hasn't been much touching lately. "What's the movie about, anyway? Is it suitable for children?"

"Oh, Mom. Everyone knows about Knute Rockne and the Fighting Irish," Danny says. "Knute's a football coach from Notre Dame. He won a lot of games and invented some great plays."

"He *was* a football coach," Dan adds. "He died in a plane crash about ten years ago. The movie's supposed to be inspiring."

"Do you girls want to see a movie about football?" I ask doubtfully.

"Will there be cartoons?" Susie wants to know.

"I'm sure there will be," Dan says.

According to the newspaper, the free movie starts at three P.M., but we aren't sure if that's the feature film or the shorts, so we get to the Eagle at 2:30 and the uniformed usher finds us seven seats together with ease. Will is with us and he sits between Danny and me.

"Did you see the soldiers at the train depot?" Danny asks Will. "Boy, do they look sharp! I'd love to be going off to war right now. I want to be a pilot."

"Me too," says Willie.

"Some of them were even *colored* soldiers," Danny whispers.

"Yeah. So what?" Will asks.

"I just never saw a brown-skinned soldier before."

"You think they can't fight? Bitsy's a fighter!" Willie slashes back. "Negroes are probably the best fighters! Ever hear of the Harlem Hellcats in the Great War? Ever hear of Jack Johnson, the heavyweight champion? Ever hear of Jessie Owens? He won four gold medals at the 1936 Olympics right in front of Hitler's stupid face. All colored men."

"Negro men are drafted and volunteer just like white men, Danny," his father whispers. "There's even a school for colored pilots at West Virginia State University, in the southern part of the state."

Suddenly, without warning, the lights in the small theater dim, the blue velvet curtains open, and a serial short, *Flash Gordon*, comes on. All the children are on the edge of their seats. Mira is so excited she's standing in the aisle and I have to pull her into my lap. The twenty-minute segment ends with a cliffhanger. *Will the Wicked Queen kill Princess Aura? Or will Flash Gordon save her life?*

Next there's the cartoon *Goofy's Glider*, where the gangly dog of unknown breed tries to build his own warplane using an instruction book. I look over and notice that Daniel is laughing out loud and I almost get tears in my eyes. I haven't heard that laugh for days.

Finally, just before the feature film, the newsreel comes on. "The British Sink the *Bismarck*!" the announcer shouts with glee, and the audience erupts in cheers. The film shows rough ocean waves splashing up on the bow of a German warship while a military band plays in the soundtrack.

"With the help of an American seaplane," the narrator crows, "the Brits locate the pride of the German fleet, the *Bismarck*, and torpedo it!"

In the short film, British sailors are cheering on the deck of their ship and half the moviegoers are too, including my children. "Killer Diller! Sink the Nazis!" Danny yells, and I roll my eyes.

What's interesting *to me* is that when the German prisoners of war are marched across the plank from the wounded *Bismarck* onto the British ship they all look the same as our sailors. They could be young men from West Virginia, Pennsylvania, New York, or anywhere in the U.S.A. Not one has a little mustache like Hitler. Not one has fanatical eyes.

Finally, with fanfare, the main feature comes on. As Dan told us, it's the life story of All-American Knute Rockne of Notre Dame. I don't remember much of the plot except when the star football player, George Gip (played by heartthrob Ronald Reagan) dies. I'll tell you, I couldn't see Dan's face, but the rest of us were wiping our eyes.

And then there's the scene, near the end, when Coach Rockne gives his team a pep talk in the locker room. "None of you ever knew George Gip . . . It was before your time. But you know what a tradition he is at Notre Dame . . ." There's a faraway look in Coach Rockne's eyes as he remembers the Gip's deathbed words . . . and then he looks in the faces of his team and says, "Sometime, when the team is up against it, and the breaks are beating the boys, tell them to go out there with all they got and win just one for the Gipper. . . ."

Of course, at the end of the movie, the Notre Dame team wins and the whole audience stands and applauds! The funny thing is, we were cheering for something far more important than the Notre Dame football team.

I imagine the coach saying to our soldiers, *When the U.S.A. is up against it, and the breaks are beating the boys, tell them to go out there with all they got . . . and win one for our old Uncle Sam!*

31

July 20, 1942

We Interrupt This Program

We felt the blast just after breakfast while the children were playing out in the yard and though the chickens had not been fed, I herded the kids back into the house and began to barricade the windows. *Bombs*, I thought. *It's finally happened. The war has come to West Virginia!*

"Is it the Nazis?" Mira wanted to know. "Is it the Japs?"

"Sit down and be quiet, all of you. Your pa is out on a call. He will know what to do. Just sit down and be quiet."

"Can we turn on the radio?" asks Willie, who stays with us most summer days when his mother is at work.

"At a time like this, you want to listen to *The Lone Ranger*? No! We have to listen for bombers and maybe go down in the root cellar. I can't tell how far away the blast was."

"No. I meant *the news*, Mrs. Hester. Maybe there'll be an alert or something from the air-raid warden."

"Oh," I say, realizing the boy's more level-headed than I am. "Okay, then, but turn down the volume so I hear if there are any more bombs." I go to the front door imagining low-flying planes with swastika signs painted on the undersides, but there's only the sound of wind in the maples and a honeybee in the blue chicory growing next to the porch.

"Anything?" I turn back to the living room to see Susie and Sunny hiding under the quilt with the flying goose pattern, and Mira, Danny, and Willie kneeling on the floor next to the radio.

"I can't find the station out of Torrington," Danny says. "There's nothing but static." *This is not good*, I think. *Maybe Torrington was bombed*. Maybe the enemy has taken over the radio station and cut off communication.

"Try the one out of Wheeling," I suggest. Danny does what I say and as the Andrews Sisters sing "I'll Be with You in Apple Blossom Time," an announcer breaks in.

"We interrupt this program with news just in from Torrington, West Virginia. An explosion at Stewart Munitions Plant rocked the city and surrounding countryside at nine this morning, destroying the factory, the adjoining railway yard, the nearby radio station, and much of the south end of town. Hundreds are feared dead and windows were broken as far away as Liberty, West Virginia.

"The mayor of Torrington has ordered all roads into the area guarded so that military personnel and medical workers can get to the scene. Stay tuned. We will update you on further developments. And now back to the Andrews Sisters."

"Do we know anyone who works at the munitions plant?" Danny wonders.

"Sally *did* work there, but thank God she joined the Women's Army Corps instead. She had a friend from high school who worked there, though . . . I hope she's okay." Then the phone rings and I run to answer it.

"Honey! It's Dan. Is everyone okay?"

"Dan! Not even a broken window here, but what's going on? Where *are* you?"

"Isaac and I were on our way back from a vet call, but we stopped at a phone booth in Oneida. I called because they need help in Torrington, doctors and nurses. Becky is joining us in her auto."

"Oh, Dan. It must be the Japanese or the Germans. Do you have to go? The radio out of Wheeling said there might be more explosions. Shouldn't you wait until everything's stable?"

"When will that be, Patience? If I wait, more people will die."

"You're right. Just don't get killed or hurt. Okay? I love you."

"I'll do my best."

I picture the crooked smile of the man I've been so angry with. He may not be patriotic enough to fight for his country, but no one can say he's a coward.

"Stay close to the phone," he continues. "Don't go out, except when you and Danny milk the cows, and then have the girls sit in the kitchen in case I call. I'll be home as soon as I can. I love you too." Then the line goes as silent as a root cellar in winter.

"Are the Nazis coming?" Sunny asks.

"I'm scared!" says Mira.

Susie just stands there in a puddle of her own pee.

"Oh, honey! Sunny, get me a towel."

As soon as I have the mess cleaned up and Susie in clean panties, I call the kids back into the living room. There have been no recent updates on the radio, so I turn it down to a whisper.

"Pa won't be home for a while," I tell them. "He's going to Torrington with Dr. Blum and Becky to help the injured at the munitions factory. They don't know what caused the explosion yet, so it could be enemy sabotage. He says we're to stay in the house and he'll call us again when he can. Meanwhile, I'll read you a story and we can take turns listening to the radio to see if there's any more news."

"Could the enemy already be in West Virginia?" Will asks.

"I don't know. The explosion could just be an accident. Mira, can you get my copy of Hans Christian Andersen? Let's read to keep our minds off our troubles." I open my worn book to "The Tinderbox." That seems appropriate.

Waiting

*T*wenty minutes later, Danny whispers, "Quiet! More news about the explosion." Then he turns up the volume.

"We interrupt this program again to report on the ongoing story about the attack at the Stewart Munitions Plant in Torrington, West Virginia. William Blaze, from the *Liberty*

Times, is at the factory now, and he tells us by phone that the explosion rocked Torrington early this morning, shattering windows for miles and destroying the facility that has been running three shifts a day since the attack on Pearl Harbor.

"So far thirty-nine bodies of workers, some as young as sixteen, have been recovered from the warehouse, but another twenty are missing under the rubble and presumed dead. Hundreds of others have been injured in other buildings.

"Mr. Blaze was able to interview the owner of the factory. According to Mr. Stewart, the cause of the explosion is still unknown, but sabotage by German operatives is suspected. Military personnel are still searching for any suspicious timing devices that could indicate enemy involvement.

"Meanwhile, the mayor of Torrington has closed the city except to medical personnel and the National Guard. And now back to our regular programming . . ."

"So is Pa safe?" Mira wants to know.

"Yes, I think so. He's a very brave man to go and help. *Remember that*, no matter what anyone says. Your father is risking his life to save people he doesn't even know."

War Zone

*I*t was awful " are Dan's first words as he collapses into a chair at the kitchen table after midnight. "Like a war zone. Bodies torn apart, some almost unrecognizable. I haven't seen anything like it since the Great War. They're estimating fifty-three dead now, but there will be more."

"The news out of Wheeling said hundreds dead," I tell him, standing there in my red silk kimono.

"That was an early estimate, and you know how journalists sensationalize. Not that they needed to in this situation," Dan says.

"Did they find out what happened, whether it was the work of German spies or if the explosion was from something else?" I pour us both a cup of valerian tea to soothe our nerves.

"The owner of the plant, Mr. Stewart, wants us to believe it was sabotage, but there's no evidence. It's to his advantage to blame it on the enemy." He lowers his head in his hands. "Better than taking responsibility for some manufacturing malfunction."

"You want some food. Did you eat at all?"

"I'm not hungry now. Okay if I take my clothes off here and you put them right in the washer? I don't want the kids to see all the blood. It looks like I've been butchering hogs."

When Dan is clean and dressed we go out on the porch. It's a warm night and there's only the sound of the creek gurgling over the stones and tree frogs singing. He stares out across the moonlit lawn at the sunflowers along the rail fence and sighs.

"What are you thinking about?" I ask the man who tonight seems like a hero.

"Well, there was this one woman whose arm was blown off. I worked as Blum's surgical assistant while he sutured the main artery to stop the bleeding, and then the ambulance took her to Boone Memorial. I hope she made it. We had to do it without anesthesia, but thank God she fainted so it wasn't too bad.

"Another kid, maybe nineteen or twenty, had burns over two-thirds of his body. I had morphine in my vet bag, so Becky gave him an injection and sent him on. By this time the National Guard had mobilized, so we were basically just doing triage.

"The dead were laid to one side in a row and the soldiers came and hauled them away. It was just like the war, Patience. Finally, doctors and nurses were sent over from the hospital, whoever could be spared, and we got down to minor injuries, cuts, and concussions. One fellow couldn't remember his own name."

Daniel yawns and stretches his strong, tanned arms up toward the three-quarter moon hidden by the black lace of maple leaves. "I swear, Patience. The world has gone mad."

In the morning, Dan sits down at the piano. "*Fairest Lord Jesus, ruler of all nature . . .*" I sit down on the bench beside him. This is a song I know.

"*Fair are the meadows*," we harmonize. "*Fairer still the woodlands. Robed in the blooming garb of spring, Jesus is fairer, Jesus is purer, who makes the woeful heart to sing.*"

"Is your heart *woeful*, Daniel Hester?" I ask, putting my head on his shoulder.

He takes a deep breath and lets it out slowly. "You know that it is, Patience."

"*Schönster Herr Jesu*," he continues the song in his grandparents' tongue. "*Herrscher aller Herren, Gottes und Marien Sohn!*"

"Daniel!" I exclaim. "For heaven's sake . . . singing in German! Someone might hear you. Have a little sense!"

"Okay, okay, Nervous Nelly. How come I've sung German songs all these years and now it's *verboten*?"

"You know why! Because I don't want people to think you're sympathetic to the enemy, that's why. In the last war people got tarred and feathered for that."

"How about I just speak German to you in private, in bed. I've done it before. . . ."

"Not funny. I'd feel like I'm sleeping with a spy."

"Do you love me, Patience?"

"You know I do . . ."

The teakettle whistles and I run to the kitchen. When I come back, I want to ask him what will become of us if he continues to oppose the draft, but Daniel is on to a different hymn.

"*This is my song, O God of all the nations. A song of peace for lands afar and mine.*" The words of the tune are copied on a sheet of lined paper in Dan's handwriting.

"A new one? Who wrote it? You?"

"No, I heard it when I went to Philadelphia to visit the Quakers . . . *My country's skies are bluer than the ocean,*" he continues. "*And sunlight beams on cloverleaf and pine. But other lands have sunlight too, and clover, and skies are everywhere as blue as mine . . .*"

32

August 5, 1942

The Red Cross Quilt

Today, I prepare to go to town for the Red Cross meeting. Though the last one I went to was uncomfortable when I spoke up for the soldier who shoved his hands through the window, I'm determined to stick with it and not let women like Mrs. Wade and Mrs. Goody turn me away.

Before leaving, I open our little yellow sugar-rationing book to count the remaining stamps. The kids brought our first sugar book home from school in May. I'd been expecting it. U.S. imports from the Philippines have stopped and cargo ships that used to bring it from Hawaii have been taken over by the navy. The nation's supply of sugar has been reduced by more than a third and military personnel get first dibs. To prevent hoarding and skyrocketing prices, the government issued "War Ration Book One."

It looks like I have only one stamp left, and that means only six pounds of sugar this month. Each person—man, woman, and child—gets one pound, which doesn't go far if you want to preserve fruits and berries. Still, we have some crystallized honey Mr. Dietz gave me for delivering their baby a year ago and some maple syrup that Mr. Mattock made from his stand of maple trees this spring.

At 1:00 P.M. sharp, I pick Mildred Miller up in Hazel Patch. Dan is home mucking out the barn and he'll watch the children, so Mrs. Miller and I will have time to do our shopping and then report to the Liberty First Methodist Church for bandage wrapping. It will be Mildred's first Red Cross meeting. When I pull up to her neat log home, she waves me inside.

Stepping into the large living room with oak bookshelves against the log walls and the gently worn velvet sofa and high-backed easy chair they got at the flea market along the road in Delmont, I see that the Millers have restored their home to its former comfort and warmth.

Ten years ago, I first met Grace Potts, the old colored midwife, in this very room, when Mildred's daughter, Cassie, was having her first baby. I'd been called to assist with a hand presentation and with a little reflection and a lot of help we were able to get a healthy baby out.

Across from the front door is a newly painted bright-yellow kitchen with a pale-green enameled high-backed gas stove, and on the round oak table is a finished quilt, in a red, white, and blue pattern, wrapped up with twine.

"Do you think the ladies will like it?" Mildred asks, running her brown hand over the white background.

"You're bringing it to the Red Cross **meeting**? It's so pretty."

"Yes, I read about a woman in Texas who donated one to the Red Cross because she didn't have money and they raffled it off for fifty dollars. Fifty dollars would buy a lot of bandages. The lady has three sons in the army and wanted to do something helpful. I don't have any sons in the war, but all God's young men are my sons. . . . I finished it last night."

"I'm sure it will be greatly appreciated. The local chapter is always having fund-raisers."

It isn't until we enter the community room in the basement of the Methodist Church that I realize that since I've been coming to the Red Cross meetings I've never seen a colored woman there. *What was I thinking? This is a potential disaster.*

"Who's the chairman?" Mildred whispers to me, smiling.

There's no way out of this now, and I lead her to a table in front. "Mrs. Goody, this is my friend Mrs. Mildred Miller. She's here to volunteer for the Red Cross." Mrs. Goody stands up and the silence is broken only by Ida May's smoker's cough.

"I think we have something in common besides concern for the soldiers," Mildred Miller says. "We're both pastors' wives. You may have heard of my husband, Reverend Miller."

"I heard you moved away," Mrs. Goody responds coolly. "You've returned?"

"Yes. We're back in our own home in Hazel Patch. There was quite a bit to do, but we had help and now my husband is working part-time at the woolen mill." Mildred smiles my way. All the other women watch like owls in a tree, waiting to see what will happen next.

"I brought something I thought the Red Cross could raffle off at a fund-raiser for the war effort," my friend says, opening her canvas satchel. The women lean forward as she pulls out the quilt.

"Ohhhh!" they all say.

"What is it?" Lilly Bittman whispers.

"A beautiful handmade quilt. Do you want to see?" I ask her.

Mrs. Miller places the elegant blanket in Lilly's lap. Since the redhead is blind, she runs her fingers over the material, feeling the stitches.

"It's made of red, white, and blue diamonds in a star pattern," I explain.

"Beautiful," Lilly agrees. "And such workmanship. You're very talented, Mrs. Miller. Here, sit next to me. We welcome you." The blind woman pulls out a chair beside her and everyone relaxes—everyone but Mrs. Goody, who frowns and tightens her mouth.

Soon we are all making bandages, gossiping, and laughing. This time I work slowly, so I can show Mildred what we do.

"First, using the white adhesive tape on the tables for a guide, we cut the long pieces of gauze into four-inch-wide strips," I explain. "Then we roll the strips tightly. At the end, we fold the gauze into a point, so it won't unravel, then tie it with one of these pieces of string. Forty-eight rolls should fit in a box."

"Yes, the Army Medical Corps is very particular about their bandages," Mrs. Wade warns. "Each soldier is supplied a roll to keep in a special pocket of his haversack so that if he's wounded and a fellow soldier comes to his rescue, he'll know right where to find it."

The image of the wounded soldier sobers the ladies, and Ida, from Ida's House of Beauty, reminds us that we forgot to say a prayer about our work. "Would you like to say the blessing, Mrs. Miller?" Mrs. Wade asks. "Since you're a pastor's wife."

It doesn't seem gracious to put Mildred on the spot at her first meeting. No one has ever asked me to pray, but Mildred doesn't miss a beat.

"Surely," she says. "What a nice idea . . . Our blessed Lord," she begins, just like she'd prepared for the occasion. "We ask you to accept this small Red Cross effort, knowing that we live comfortable lives while others around the world exist under a rain of bombs and bullets. We are not soldiers or nurses, we are mothers and wives and working women who keep the home fires burning. Bless our fingers as we roll tight bandages. If we can save one life we will have done your work. In the name of the Father, the Son, and the Holy Ghost. Amen."

"Amen," the women whisper, and I see Mrs. Goody raise her eyebrows at Mrs. Wade, apparently impressed by how calm and eloquent Mildred was.

Two hours later, the bandages are packaged and rolled, the coffee cups and spoons are washed, and plans have begun for a harvest celebration. Ida May knows a country band that will play for free and a square-dance caller who will come. Mrs. Miller's quilt will be auctioned, as well as cakes and pies and any other items people donate.

Bold as anything, Mildred asks, "Will colored folk be welcomed and allowed to eat with the group?"

My heart does a thump. Everyone stops and waits. Who is to answer this question?

"Yes, of course!" Ida May replies.

"Sure thing," Lilly follows. "We're all trying to help the war effort. Why not?"

"The more the merrier." I laugh, trying to make light of the moment, a significant one in Union County. Though black and white miners have worked underground together for years, have trusted one another and relied on one another, there hasn't been much socializing between families . . . except on back porches in the dark.

33

August 10, 1942

The War to End All War

*D*aniel is leaving us for two days. He *promises* it will only be two. He's taking a trip to Aurora, Ohio, near Cleveland, a ten-hour drive in the Olds, which is our best vehicle. The purpose of the trip is to visit a small intentional community called Ahimsa, which he explains means nonviolence to all living things.

According to Dan's Quaker friend in Philadelphia, Ahimsa Farm is home to a number of pacifists, and he wants to discuss with them what they're going to do about military service. Some, he's heard, like him, are refusing to register for the draft. While he's gone, I will have to tend the gardens, the animals, the kids, and myself.

Last night, at bedtime, Dan told the children where he was going and why. "Kids," he said, "tomorrow I have to go to Ohio to visit some men who I hope will give me some advice."

"Is it about a sick animal, Pa?" Danny wants to know. "You could just telephone."

"No, it's something else, and I need to see them in person. It's about the war."

"Are you going to be a soldier?" Susie asks. "Please don't go. Soldiers get killed. Our teacher reads the names of the dead heroes from West Virginia out of the newspaper every Friday and we have to say a prayer for them and sing 'America.'"

Mira stands, puts her little hand over her heart, and belts out the first few lines of the song. "*My country, 'tis of thee, sweet land of liberty. Of thee I sing!*"

"Don't worry. I'm not going to be a soldier," her father says. "I did that once before and I'm not going to do it again."

"I don't understand," Sunny says, looking concerned. "What if you get drafted like the men at the feed store?"

"Well, I'm not going to get drafted, because I don't plan to sign up for the draft."

"You can do that?" Danny asks. "I thought there was a law that you had to register."

"There is a law," his father answers him. "And I'm breaking it."

Susie starts to cry and Daniel takes her in his lap. "It's okay, honey," he says.

"No, it isn't!" Danny yells. "You can't do that, Pa! I don't want to be *the son of a draft dodger!*"

"Danny! Stop it. You can't talk to your father like that," I scold him. "Just sit down and listen; your pa will tell you a story about the last war." I nod to my husband as if to say, *You've started this, now finish it, before our family explodes like a bomb dropped by the Japanese over Pearl Harbor.*

He takes a long breath and lets it out slowly. "When I was young, the Great War started. I didn't really understand what it was all about, except that England, France, and Belgium were in a scrap with Germany, Austria, and Hungary. Then I heard that America was going to jump in too. I was all excited about it, like you and Willie are excited about this war, Danny.

"I knew nothing about killing or death. I just figured it was a good chance to fight for freedom, so I enlisted right out of high school and was sent to Europe as part of the infantry. All my friends and neighbors congratulated me, made me feel like a big guy, a hero.

"The reality was another thing." He goes on to tell about the first battle and how he had to shoot a German kid about his age who looked almost like his best friend, Tom, from high school. Then he tells about the thousands of dead horses and how after a while he couldn't see the point of the war anymore.

"In the end, the smell of death was everywhere and the enemy wasn't some evil man, like in the cartoons, with a turned-up mustache, bushy eyebrows, and a black helmet with a silver point on the top. He looked just like me. So, the long and the short of it is, kids, they called the Great War *the war to end all war*, and I vowed I would never do it again. The Selective Service knows where I am, but if they come for me . . . well, they still can't make me fight. They can't make me kill."

BEDTIME IS A solemn affair. I ask each child if they want to pray about something. Sunny prays the usual, *Now I lay me down to sleep . . .*

Mira prays for Jesus to keep the soldiers and the horses safe. "On both sides," she says as an afterthought.

Susie asks, "Was Papa crying?"

"Yes, honey. I think he was. Your father is worried about these things. He says he won't go to war, but the government might not see it that way."

When I go into Danny's room, I find him lying on his bed, playing with his wooden bomber.

"You doing okay?"

"I hate him." Danny turns away from me.

"Oh, Danny, you don't mean that." No answer. "You're just disappointed. Everyone wants to believe that the war we're fighting is true and good. Everyone wants to believe that our soldiers and the Allied soldiers are going to save the world from evil. You want your father to be one of them, a hero."

"What will the other kids say if they find out?"

"Well, sticks and stones can break our bones, but names will never hurt us."

"Ma! I'm serious."

"So am I. When I was young, I marched in the streets so that women could have the right to vote. We were called suffragettes, and men who didn't want women to vote called us Bug-Eyed Betties, Fishwives, Fire-Eaters, and Battle Axes. Sometimes the men would throw rotten tomatoes at us or spit on us. But we held our heads high and marched anyway. Inside I would tell myself over and over, 'Sticks and stones can break my bones, but names can never hurt me . . .' Do you want to say a prayer?"

Danny rolls over with tears in his eyes. "No."

Outside his room, I lean against the cool plaster wall. Though I try to understand my husband's point of view, I'm angry with Daniel too. Why can't he just make this easy for us and sign the damn registration papers? The silver river we call the Hope is dark with trouble.

August 13, 1942

Ain't Gonna Study War No More

*L*ast night, when Dan got back late from his trip to Ohio, he asked how we'd fared in his absence.

"Okay," I said as he peeled his town clothes off and crawled into bed. "No big problems, except Danny Boy was a terror. He even back-talked me when I asked him to close the chickens in their coop after dark."

"That's not like him. I wonder what's up."

"Daniel!" I said, rising up on my elbow and facing him. "*You know what's up*. He's angry about your refusal to register. Is that still your plan after your visit to *that place*, the Ahimsa House?"

He takes a long breath and pulls me to him. "I missed you," he says. "You smell good."

I push him away. "So . . . ?"

"So what?"

"You know what. Any change in your thinking?"

"No, Patience, but I realize now . . . if I'm arrested . . . it's going to be hard on everyone." A cold chill runs through me.

"Arrested! Surely it won't come to that. Maybe the draft board will just make you do community service or something."

"One of the fellows at Ahimsa has already been sent to prison. He was apprehended in June. The usual procedure, it turns out, is they take you to a local jail before you go to court. Some men are released on bond if they can afford it, but if I'm going to serve time, I'd rather get it over with, not drag it out with a long legal battle. Other men plead guilty and read a statement about why they're resisting, then they go to a state facility and in a few weeks or a few months they're sent to a federal prison."

Listening to him, I feel the cold in my stomach grow from a snowball into a blizzard.

34

August 16, 1942

Viper

*I*n the five days since Becky and Isaac loaded up all they could carry in their Pontiac, locked up the little house with the blue door, and headed for Washington, D.C., I have secretly cried three times. They're on their way to work at Walter Reed Hospital, and all they left us (except tears) was their old dog, Three Legs, some furniture, and their address.

When I turn out the light and crawl into bed, I can hear Dan outside, sitting on the porch in the moonlight, playing his harmonica. *"I ain't gonna study war no more. Ain't gonna study war no more . . ."*

Maybe I shouldn't have been surprised. I knew our friends had both lost their jobs and also that Sally was going to be stationed in Washington, but it all happened so fast. Even now, thinking of it, a stone sticks in my throat. The next thing I know Bitsy will say that she and Willie are getting on their Indian motorcycle and heading out west to sell war bonds. It's as if someone has switched off the joy button. I lie in the dark listening to the mournful music through the open window and wet my pillow with tears. Becky and Isaac are gone.

SUNDAY MORNING I go over to Bitsy's. I haven't been there for a few weeks. We sit in her living room on the red flowered sofa that Mrs. Stone donated. A large American flag is tacked on the wall behind it. "This is so nice and homelike. . . ."

Just then we hear screams. "*Ma! Ma!*" It's Willie outside, running toward the house.

"What is it, Willie? What's wrong?" Bitsy yells from the front porch.

"Snake! A snake bit me."

"Stop where you are. Don't make another move. Sit on the ground," Bitsy commands. "Running will spread the poison." The two of us gather around the frightened boy, Bitsy kneeling.

"First we need a tourniquet. Where's the bite, Willie?" Bitsy asks

"Here's my belt," I offer.

"Ow! Ow! Ow! My ankle." Willie pulls up his pant leg as Bitsy tightens the tourniquet just below his calf. There are two purple puncture marks.

"Are you sure it was a snake? Not a briar or a piece of barbed wire or a nail?" I ask.

"I'm sure. Ow! Ow! I saw the snake slither away. Am I going to die like the outlaw on *The Lone Ranger*?"

"Not if I can help it," Bitsy growls.

By the time we make it back to the farm, we're fortunate to see Daniel strolling across the barnyard with two pails.

"Help!" I yell as I roll down the window. "Help us. Snakebite!" He sets the pails of warm milk on the porch and runs around back to throw open the door to the Baby Cabin.

I'm the first out of the Olds. "It's Willie! A snake bit him, probably a copperhead. We have a tourniquet on."

By now the poor child is delirious, whether from fear or the venomous poison, I can't tell. Bitsy steps aside to let Dan carry him into the cabin. First thing, Dan removes the belt from around Willie's calf. He checks the circulation, waits a few seconds and tightens it again. "The leg is still warm. That's good," he says. "You did the right thing. Do you have a rubber syringe, Patience?"

I hand him one of the ones I use to remove mucus from an infant's mouth and he takes a scalpel and makes a cut between the two fang marks. "Three drops of venom will kill a grown man. If we even get one drop out, it may save his life," Dan says, using the syringe to remove bloody fluid. I take the boy's vital signs. His blood pressure is low and his pulse is very fast.

"Get me my vet kit, Bitsy. It's in the Model T. If we relieve the fiery pain it will help him not go into shock."

"What else can we do," Bitsy wants to know. "Should we try to get him to the hospital in Torrington?"

"Let me think. They can't do much for him. I'm pretty sure there's no anti-venom medication, and the ride on the bumpy roads might just spread the poison. All they would do is keep him from going into shock. If we can do that, we may be better off staying here. Not everyone dies."

"Oh, Lord, help us!" Bitsy starts to fall apart. Just like any mother, she's as strong as a lioness if there's something she can do to save her child, but dissolves in a puddle if she's helpless.

"It's going to be okay," I say in my midwife voice. "Talk to him, Bitsy, talk to your boy."

Ten minutes later, after Dan has given him a shot of morphine to stop the pain, and so far the boy is still stable. Bitsy sits with her son's head in her lap, looking like a statue of Christ's mother holding the dying Jesus.

"Can you tell us what the course of a viper bite is, Dan?" I ask.

"Well, initially there will be swelling of the injured area, then it will turn purple or blue. That's the poison spreading. The venom affects the circulatory system. There will be massive edema. Blood volume falls when that happens, and this may result in shock or renal failure. In the worst cases renal failure is the cause of death. I'm going to go over to the house and use the phone. I'll call Boone Memorial. See what they advise."

"I'll go get the medicine, if you can find some anti-venom," Bitsy says. "The motorcycle is fast. Anywhere within four hours of here, I can be back in half a day. Anywhere."

"Don't get your hopes up," Dan says grimly, touching Bitsy's shoulder.

When he returns, the news isn't good. "The only place to get anti-venom," he tells us, "is in Australia, and it's just in the experimental stage, but I remembered an interesting story. A couple of years ago, Loonie Tinkshell's sheepdog got bit by a copperhead. Loonie told me that possum are immune to viper bites. I never had a way to look that up, but Tinkshell went hunting, killed him a possum, and made the dog eat the whole thing."

"Did the dog live?" Bitsy wants to know. We're taking turns spooning saline-sugar water into Willie's mouth to keep him from going into shock.

"Yeah, by golly the dog lived." Daniel chuckles. "But I doubt it was the possum."

Suddenly, Bitsy stands up. "Will you sit with Willie, Patience? I may be gone awhile."

"Sure, but where are you going?" She opens the door and a wind blows it back until it slams on the log wall.

"Possum hunting . . . Coming, Dan?"

The Heart of the Matter

Ma!" Willie moans, and his face begins to twitch. "She'll be back soon." I try to soothe the boy. "It's me, Patience, the midwife." I don't know why I say "midwife." It's hardly relevant, yet I'm doing what midwives do, supporting, comforting, and protecting him as best I can. "Be a brave soldier, Willie."

Thirty minutes later there are voices outside, and when the door opens, Bitsy stands there with a dead opossum held upside down by the pink hairless tail. Its white-and-gray fur gleams in the lamplight. "How's Willie?" she whispers.

"Ma?" Willie opens his eyes and reaches out for her.

"Stay awake, Willie. I want you to eat some of this critter's heart."

"We should cook it," Dan advises. "We need to cook it. It may have parasites."

"No," Bitsy disagrees. "Willie needs to eat some of it raw, *right now*, to get the full benefit. Cooking might ruin it. If he gets parasites, we'll deal with them later. Give me a scalpel or a knife," Bitsy demands, plunking the carcass on the counter.

I rummage through my bag until I come up with a pair of sharp scissors. My friend doesn't even go outside to skin the animal. In fact, she doesn't even skin it. She just cuts through the soft white fur, digs under the ribs, and pulls out a piece of dark shiny meat. Then she chops it into little pieces. I hold out a placenta bowl to keep the blood off the floor.

"Here, Willie. Wake up again. It's your Ma, Bitsy. I need you to eat this animal's heart. Dr. Hester and I just killed it, and it's still warm. After you finish this part, we'll cook the rest. Think of it as medicine." She puts the bowl down on the rolling table, picks up Willie's head, and feeds him with her fingers.

Slamming the door behind him, Daniel silently takes the small white animal with the pointed nose and pointy ears outside. It's clear he thinks giving the boy a piece of raw possum heart is like witch doctoring and probably unhealthy. He's had enough of this foolishness. But is it foolish? I take a clean cloth and wipe the boy's chin.

A short while later, Daniel reappears with the possum cleaned, chopped up, and cooked in a frying pan, and I give him a smile.

Bitsy again feeds the possum to her son, but this time with a fork. She didn't give birth to him, but conception and childbirth don't make a mother; the heart does.

Dan's so proud of his cooking, I have to take a bite. Not bad! A cross between raccoon and pig.

Sunflower

The recovery of Will Proudfoot was not without difficulties. We fed him saline and sugar water by the spoonful all the first twenty-four hours and he ate as much possum meat as he could stand. Finally he got stubborn and demanded cookies and milk. It was then I knew he was going to survive and now he just limps a little, like before.

This evening while the kids are taking swimming lessons with Mr. Cross down by the river, I take a walk by myself. Mr. Draft Resister shouldn't care. He's on his tractor cutting hay.

Again, I follow Salt Lick as it rushes over the water-worn rocks. Here and there little minnows flash in the shadows. There's an endless clear sky and a wind that rattles the willow leaves, but I hardly notice. Like an old horse, I have blinders on.

On a whim, I cut through the woods and begin to climb Spruce Mountain. Only when I'm halfway up do I remember the black bear. *Maybe this wasn't so smart.* I stop to look around.

Nothing seems amiss. No movement in the bushes. A chickadee sings from a red sumac bush, and a brown-and-white cottontail inspects me with big eyes. *Surely the bunny wouldn't be sitting out in the open if a bear were around.*

I decide that the risk is small and climb farther until I find the flat rock that looks out over the valley and lie down on it. Far below, the Hope River runs through the valley. There's the red barn, the Baby Cabin, and our stone farmhouse with the sunflowers growing on one side. I used to think of myself as a sunflower, beautiful and strong, but a wind has swept over the mountain and blown the sunflower down.

Daniel parks the old green tractor in the farmyard and stumps across the yard, head down in thought. Sasha and Three Legs come out to greet him and Dan leans down and gives both dogs a pat.

My feelings are so mixed. I still love him, but I'm full of sadness and shame too, afraid of what people will think when they hear of his resistance to the war. Then there's the anger. I once admired my husband; now he seems weak, even self-indulgent in his refusal to sign the draft registration forms.

Dan has his pacifist friends to talk to at Ahimsa House, but I have no one. I never even talked to Becky about it and I haven't told Bitsy. How would she react? What would she think of Daniel's position? I know he's not really a coward, but people will call him one or that other dreaded word from the Great War: *slacker.*

"*The Lord is my shepherd. I shall not want. He maketh me to lie down in green pastures: he leadeth me beside the still waters,*" I say out loud to myself, lying on the rock, staring out at the green meadows.

"*He restoreth my soul: he leadeth me in the paths of righteousness for his name's sake,*" a man answers. I hadn't even heard him coming up the mountain, but Dan lies down beside me taking my hand.

"*Yea, though I walk through the valley of the shadow of death, I will fear no evil,*" we say together. "*For thou art with me; thy rod and thy staff they comfort me.*"

"Is that true, Daniel? Can we walk through the valley of the shadow of death together? I'll tell you the truth, I'm afraid. If you go to prison, I'll be alone here with the kids. I don't know if I can do it. Take care of them. Take care of the farm. I've depended on you all these years. We were a team."

"We still are a team, Patience. Everything will be okay."

"It will?"

He holds me in his arms, my cheek over his heart, and I take comfort in the sound of its beating.

35

August 23, 1942

Square Dance

The last few days, since out prayer on the mountain, Dan and I have felt closer. I know he's taking a drink or two, but I've stopped nagging and he's stopped playing mournful songs on his harmonica. Even Danny seems to be coming around. He's quiet, but not so surly.

Yesterday, he and his father went on a long ride on the horses over the mountain. First they checked on the house on Wild Rose Road. It's technically still our house, but if the Blums come back after the war is over, Becky and Isaac can move back in.

"Danny and I stopped at Hazel Patch on our way home," Dan tells us at dinner. "Mrs. Miller asked if we're going to the Red Cross square dance at Arthurdale this week."

"I forgot about it. I suppose we should."

"Do us kids have to go?" Danny asks.

"No, buddy," Dan says. "It's for grown-ups. We'll call Mrs. Stone. Maybe she'll come to our house to babysit. Willie can stay the night if Bitsy wants to go."

Now HERE WE are driving down Salt Lick Road in the Olds, with Bitsy in the back, on our way to the dance. The Millers and the Jacksons from Hazel Patch are in the vehicle behind us. When we get to Arthurdale, we see that the parking lot in front of the inn is jammed. This is a good thing for the Red Cross, because in addition to the raffle of Mrs. Miller's patriotic quilt, they're charging fifty cents a head to get in.

The Arthurdale Rural Village is the New Deal experiment that Eleanor Roosevelt championed during the Great Depression. Each unemployed miner, from the poorest part of north-central West Virginia, was given a house and four acres of land to raise food and livestock. There are now some 165 cottages, a metal shop, pottery shop, woodworking shop, the beautiful inn where Eleanor had a room held for her, and a general store. Several small factories were planned but never took hold.

The idea was great, but well-meaning government do-gooders made so many mistakes that they eventually dropped the whole project. Now all the homes are privately owned and since the war started, the former miners are back digging coal.

"It's a good crowd," I comment as we enter the inn, which is decorated in red, white, and blue bunting. "There must be fifty people on the terrace and another fifty in the dining hall."

Tables are arranged around the edge of the large room and up front there's a small country band setting up. I'm surprised when I see Mr. Roote standing there, fooling with the microphone. He must be the square-dance caller.

Just then, the band starts up and Mr. Roote shouts into a microphone, "Welcome, ladies and gents, to the Union County Red Cross Social Hour and Benefit! We're going to start you off with a lively tune, 'Old Zip Coon,' and while the fellows limber up their fingers, y'all get into squares of four men and four women."

I do a quick count of our group. There are seven of us altogether, three couples and Bitsy. We need another man, and I look around for a willing subject, someone who doesn't mind dancing with a mixed colored and white group. I'm surprised when Loonie Tinkshell strolls over.

"Can I join this lively crew?" he asks, taking the spot across from Bitsy.

"Sure," Dan responds. "Ever done this before?"

"Never!" Loonie says over the music.

"Now, let's get started," Mr. Roote yells. "Just follow my commands and let her rip. If you're the couple nearest the podium, you're Head Lady and Head Gent. If you're toward the terrace you're the Foot Gal and the Foot Man."

Next to us is another group trying to get organized and I'm surprised to see Daisy Spraggs and her husband, Earl. "Daisy!" I yell over the noise. "How are you?" But I don't need to ask. She laughs and waves, flashing white teeth. Her blond hair is shiny and tied back with a ribbon. She appears lively and alert and has put on some weight. "Look,

Bitsy." I point to the woman who all but slept through her labor and delivered a baby who almost died from opium addiction.

"Howdy!" Bitsy calls back and waves, clearly as pleased as I am.

"Ready now!" Mr. Roote interrupts the socializing.

A few people who must know what they're doing shout, "Yes!"

"Okay! If you make a mistake, just keep on dancing! Here we go now!" The band starts up and everyone claps along.

"*Honor your partner,*" the caller shouts, and Dan and I bow and curtsy. Always one step behind, we follow the singsong instructions. We're like a herd of lambs crossing the road without a sheepdog, but we laugh and laugh.

Auction

An hour later, having learned how to do the Virginia Reel, the Red Wing Dip, and Oh Johnny, we break for refreshments. At a long table covered with a white tablecloth, Mrs. Wade and Mrs. Goody serve refreshments.

"Hello," I say. "The benefit seems to be going very well." None of them answers. *What's their problem? Were they offended by our group's loud, undignified laughter, the fact that Loonie danced with a Negro, or have they heard about Dan's refusal to register for the draft?*

At a separate table, Lilly Bittman, Ida May, and Ida's sister-in-law, Annie, serve lemonade out of a fancy Depression glass punch bowl for five cents a cup. Even though she's blind, Lilly uses a matching ladle and can dip and pour without spilling a drop.

"Don't forget to bid on Mrs. Miller's quilt!" Annie tells everyone. "We have a real auctioneer from Delmont."

"Where's Lou Cross tonight?" Reverend Miller asks as we stand enjoying our lemonade, waiting for the auction. Dan and Mr. Jackson have wandered out on the terrace to look out across the pleasant parklike grounds.

"Lou had to work. The second-shift foreman broke his arm cutting down a dead tree on his farm." Bitsy informs us.

On a table near the podium, in addition to Mrs. Miller's beautiful quilt, along with a dozen cakes and pies, there's a fancy silk shawl, donated by Ida May, a new family Bible still in the box from Gold's, and an electric butter churn donated by Sadie at the feed store.

"I wouldn't mind having that butter churn," I whisper to Bitsy. "But I'm sure it will be too dear."

A man wearing a white cowboy hat and a gray suit steps up to the microphone and pounds a wood gavel. "Ladies and gents. Quiet down, now! We're going to raise a little money for the Red Cross war effort. As you know, the organization provides comfort and aid to the armed forces and their families all over the world. In times of conflict, they produce emergency supplies for the medics and teach first aid. So folks, don't be shy. Get out your wallets and let's hear some bidding. I'm going to start with this electric metal-and-glass butter churn. It's been used, but there's a lot of life still in her. Isn't this a beauty?

"Do I hear three dollars? Three dollars now, now three, now three, will ya give me three?"

I'm surprised when the crowd stands silent and no one raises their hands, so I yell out, "One buck!"

"Okay now, folks! Loosen up. It's for the GIs, the men fighting for our freedom. Let's try two. Two-dollar bid, now two, now two, will ya give me two? Will ya give me two, just two greenback bills?"

"One twenty-five," says Judge Wade.

"*One fifty*," says Bitsy, giving me a grin.

After a few more minutes of trying his best, the auctioneer suddenly closes the bidding, probably realizing not many people still make their own butter. "Sold for one fifty!"

"What are you going to do with a butter churn, Bitsy?" I ask. "You don't even have a cow."

"I bought it for you!" she whispers.

"Oh, Bitsy!" I say, and hug her. "You are the best!"

The auctioneer goes on with the sale as Bitsy pays her money and puts her name on the churn.

"Next is this beautiful red, white, and blue freedom quilt!" He pounds his gavel again and holds the quilt high. "A brand-new coverlet, made by Mrs. Mildred Miller. Would you like to come up here, Mrs. Miller?"

Mildred steps up and the room goes quiet. I see a flicker of surprise in the auctioneer's eyes when he sees the color of her skin, but he continues without missing a beat. "Tell us, ma'am, how many hours did it take you to make this beauty?"

"I'd say about three months," Mildred says into the microphone. "This is just something I wanted to do to help raise funds for the Red Cross."

"Well, let's start the bidding then. Do I hear thirty dollars? Thirty dollars, now thirty, now thirty, will ya give me thirty for this beautiful freedom quilt?"

"Thirty bucks," calls a voice from the back. It's B.K. Bittman.

The high bids are way out of my league, so I look around for Dan. From a distance, I see that he's still on the patio and I wind my way toward him, but stop when I see Martha Wallace, the tall young woman who came to the last meeting of the Pregnant Ladies Society.

"Hi, Martha. You're getting bigger." I indicate her round belly with my eyes. She's standing with a gray-haired man with the same square jaw, who I take to be her pa. "Hi, I'm Patience Hester, the midwife," I introduce myself when the girl says nothing. "Martha's planning on coming to the Baby Cabin on our farm to have her baby."

"No, she's not," the gent responds, looking down at me and I'm taken aback.

Turning to Martha, I wait for clarification, but she just licks her lips and turns away, covering her belly with her hands as if protecting it from evil.

"I don't understand."

"My husband's in the navy," Martha finally says, lifting her chin. "He says he doesn't want his baby born into the hands of a slacker's wife."

My head swings back as if I've just been slapped, but

before I can respond, a disturbance arises on the terrace and Martha's father pulls her away.

Barnyard Brawl

Two men, dressed in light-colored slacks and dress shirts, no ties, pay their admission and swagger up the steps talking loudly.

"Hey, you old son of a gun," someone yells. "You missed the square dance, but there's still lemonade and cookies."

"Hell, we got our own lemonade," one of the newcomers says as he pulls out a silver flask and passes it around. Daniel, who's standing with Mr. Jackson, looks over and at first I think he's going to join the drunken fellows and have a swig too, but then I realize who the men are. It's Aran Bishop and his brother George. *Damn.* I should have known the Bishops would come.

The two men sidle over to my husband. "Howdy, Mr. Vet. Care for a drink?" George, the shorter of the two, snarls.

"No thanks, George. How you doing?" Dan responds, trying to be civil. I'm paralyzed, watching the action as though on a movie screen.

"Awww, come on," slurs Aran. "You aren't being very *friendly.*"

Most of the men and women on the terrace, sensing trouble, move away so that Dan and Bull Jackson are in the eye of the storm, but a new fellow joins the group: Bill Blaze from the *Liberty Times*, wearing his photographer's hat and carrying his camera.

Aran Bishop puts his finger on Mr. Jackson's chest, poking him hard. "Who's this? You another draft dodger like Hester? Yeah! We got us a couple of draft dodgers, folks! Hear that? Two lily-livered cowards, and one is a nigger."

Billy Blaze grins and takes a photo. I would expect such prejudice from the Bishops, but does the reporter feel that way too? Is he part of the action or just looking for a story? Before I can work my way through the crowd, Bitsy comes flying like a bat out of hell. She positions herself between Aran Bishop and Mr. Jackson, probably thinking he wouldn't dare hit a woman, but Aran shoves her aside and she falls on her knees on the stone floor.

What the hell? How dare he push Bitsy? I'm on my way to the rescue just as Lou Cross shows up. Seeing Bitsy on the patio floor, he rushes over and before he can assist her up, Aran whacks him in the face.

Lou does a head-butt in return and Aran goes down. Then Dan shoves Billy Blaze against the terrace wall and tears off a red, white, and blue bunting. George punches Bull Jackson in the gut, but Bull shoves him over. It's a barnyard brawl! More men jump in, swinging fists, until Sheriff Hardman strides through the crowd.

"Now, you stop this right now!" he roars like a father to a bunch of kids. No one pays any attention until he runs back to the dining hall, grabs Lilly's glass punch bowl, and pours the lemonade all over the fighting men.

They sputter and swear. Dan has a swollen eye, Mr. Jackson a cut lip, and Bill Blaze a bloody nose. Bitsy limps back toward the dining room holding on to Lou. Aran Bishop is still curled on his side holding his gut. The rest slink away with just bruises.

Sheriff Hardman is totally disgusted. "What kind of men are you?" he says, pulling Aran to his feet. "The Red Cross ladies went to a lot of trouble to stage this benefit and you act like you're having a scrap in Jim's Tavern. I have half a mind to arrest the lot of you, but I didn't bring a paddy wagon, so I'll let you go this time. Now, scatter."

"It was Hester that started it," George Bishop fibs like a fourth grader. "Yeah," says his brother. "We were just trying to be friendly and he and that nigger got hostile."

"I don't want to hear it," Hardman says. "*What I want* . . . is to see you gone! *Now. Pronto.* I'm going into the auction and return in five minutes. By that time you thugs better take a deep breath, get control of yourselves, and disappear. All of you!"

"SORRY," I SAY to the Jacksons and the Millers as we walk across the big well-tended lawn to our vehicles. "We had such fun when we were dancing."

Mr. Jackson's brown face is white with fury. Opal Jackson tries to smile.

"It wasn't your fault," says Reverend Miller.

Dan and I don't wait for Bitsy, knowing she'll get a ride back to Hazel Patch with Lou. We just take off in the Olds for home. It isn't until we're crossing the stone bridge over the Hope that either of us speaks. "Does your eye hurt?" I ask.

"Not as much as you'd think. I just feel choked with anger. It's a good thing Bill Hardman broke up the fight. If I'd gotten my hands around Aran's neck, I might have choked him to death. Don't say anything about this to the kids, will you?" he adds.

"I won't, but maybe *you* should. People will talk, you know . . . a big brawl like that. Bill Blaze was there. It might even get in the paper."

"Mmmmmmm," Daniel mumbles, shaking his head in a way that tells me nothing, then we bump along in silence.

We're already on Salt Lick when the wind, heavy with rain, blasts down the valley. A branch hits the side of the Olds. Thunder echoes off Spruce Mountain. The windshield wipers can barely keep up, but still we drive on.

36

August 28, 1942

Down by the Riverside

*I*t's been five days since we last saw our dog, Sasha, and we've searched everywhere. This morning we finally gave up. I knew he was getting on in years, but he didn't seem that infirm and he followed Dan everywhere. My husband says it sometimes happens like that, an old hound will just go out in the woods, lie down, and die.

This morning, the kids were crying and I felt like crying myself. Instead, we had a ceremony to celebrate our departed friend and all sat around saying nice things about Sasha.

"I liked the way he'd ride around in the Model T with me when I had to go out on vet calls at night," Dan said.

"I liked how he snuggled with me on the carpet when we listened to *The Lone Ranger*," Mira offered.

"I always felt safe when he was around," Susie whispered. It went on like this for ten minutes and then we all drew pictures of Sasha and I taped them up on the kitchen wall.

Three Legs, the dog we inherited from the Blums, groaned under the table. He missed his pal too.

Later, we went to church at Hazel Patch, the first time we've been there since Easter, and at times I was so touched by the scripture and hymns, I got tears in my eyes.

"I'M GOING TO *lay down my sword and shield. Down by the riverside, down by the riverside,*" we sing, my husband's deep voice the loudest, and it seems as if Reverend Miller's prayer is just for me: "Be strong and fear not, for God is here and he will not fail thee."

Afterward, Reverend Miller takes Dan and me over to one of the picnic tables in the churchyard. "Is it true, Dan," he asks, "that you plan to refuse military service if you're drafted?"

"It is," Dan answers proudly, but I hang my head.

When I look up, the pastor is staring not at Daniel but me. He takes a long breath. "And is there a conflict in the marriage about this?"

My husband turns, waiting for my answer. "I understand Dan's decision," I finally respond. "But it's hard for me. If I were a man, I would fight. I know the Bible says 'Thou shalt not kill,' but we *have to* stop Hitler. I'm also afraid of so many things. I'm afraid that eventually Dan will be arrested and I don't know how that will affect the children and me.

"It will be hard, to say the least. . . . I'm afraid about all the work on the farm and how I will cope. I'm afraid we won't have enough money. I'm afraid that Danny will start acting out and I won't be able to handle him. I'm afraid that people will shun us.

"Sometimes, to be honest, I'm at my breaking point, I'm so scared." Dan puts his arm around me and I'm about to go on when Mrs. Miller calls from their log house to say coffee and cake are on the table.

"I guess we have to go," the reverend says. "If you want to talk again, together or alone, I'm available. And Dan, if you'd consider applying for conscientious objector status, I'd write a letter of support as your pastor. There's a legitimate place for religious noncombatants now, doing community service or working as medics. It's not like the Great War, where the government put every objector in prison."

"Thank you," says Dan. "I'd better check on the kids." He squeezes my hand and lopes off to the field, where the boys, and also the girls this time, are playing army.

"Die!" says Mira, brandishing a stick that doubles as her sword (a little out of date for this war).

Be strong and fear not. I silently repeat the reverend's prayer.

"In a way, it feels good to have people know what we are going through," I tell Dan as we sit on the porch the next morning. "I haven't really talked to anyone, not even Bitsy or Becky, before she left. I guess I should. I just don't know what to say. It hurts that you and I don't feel the same about the war."

"I'm sorry," Dan says. Then the phone rings.

"Daniel Hester, veterinarian," he answers in his formal way. "Elroy! What's going on? . . . Oh . . ."

Listening to the one-sided conversation, I wonder who Elroy is; a farmer I've never met?

"So what happens now?" Dan continues his side of the conversation. "Okay, thanks. I guess all I can do is wait."

"What?" I ask when he hangs up.

"That was one of the men from Ahimsa. Ben and Martin were arrested by the feds this morning. . . . A couple of guys from Buffalo were picked up yesterday. Apparently the courts are starting to move." He stands and rolls up his shirt sleeves. "There may not be much time," he says with a jaw of steel. "I've got to harvest the corn. . . ."

August 31, 1942

Secrets

*F*or two days we harvest corn as if our lives depend upon it. Then, while Danny and Dan are outside digging potatoes, the girls help me shuck and preserve the yellow gold in glass mason jars. As we work we sing a satirical song by the comic Spike Jones.

"*When Der Fuehrer says we is de master race, we'll* Heil (*pbbbbttt*), Heil (*pbbbbttt*) *right in Der Fuehrer's face! Not to love Der Fuehrer is a great disgrace. So we* Heil (*pbbbbttt*), Heil (*pbbbbttt*) *right in Der Fuehrer's face!*" Mira thinks the fart noise is hilarious and wants to sing it over and over.

It's early for harvesting potatoes. They could stay in the ground for another month and grow bigger, but I understand Dan's urgency. If the draft board is coming for him, he wants to lighten my load and get as much stored up for winter as possible. Toward afternoon, I'm surprised when the Indian motorbike roars into the drive.

"What are you doing here?" I ask Bitsy as she takes off her leather motorcycle helmet. "I thought you had to work." Willie is dressed in a helmet just like hers and he puts his in the sidecar and limps off to find Danny.

"The mill is shut down again for a few days. They're bringing in some new equipment that will boost production."

"I'm just taking a break before cleaning the cellar. You want a cup of cold peppermint tea?"

"Sure." She throws an old copy of the *Liberty Times* on the table. "Did you see this?"

I glance at the headlines. MASSIVE BRAWL BREAKS UP RED CROSS AUCTION. Underneath is an action photo that shows Dan punching a man that I assume must be Aran Bishop.

"Oh, for heaven's sake! *Massive brawl?* Read it to me."

"A major fight erupted at the Arthurdale Inn Friday evening as men fought to defend their patriotic pride." Bitsy pauses to sip tea. "Local veterinarian and draft protester Daniel Hester threw the first punch and more followed as approximately fifty men fought to defend their right to free speech. Blood was spent and one victim was taken to the hospital in Torrington. Sheriff William Hardman arrested several combatants. Women and children were crying . . ."

I hold up my hand. "What a bunch of hooey! Let me look at that. Did you see anyone injured enough to go to the hospital? Maybe a few people were crying. . . . And really there weren't more than a dozen men in the fight."

Bitsy shakes her head in disgust. "It would be hilarious if it wasn't a bunch of lies. I'm going to throw it in the kindling box."

"Wait a minute. Did you see this?" Underneath the article about the Red Cross brawl is a smaller piece about wild dogs running throughout Union County. "One of the dogs, referred to as vicious beasts, is reported to have attacked a child in Burnt Town. Oh my God. It says she was the eight-year-old daughter of Earl and Daisy Spraggs, and she was taken to the hospital in Torrington. . . . The article warns residents that if they see a wild dog to shoot first and ask questions later."

"Poor Daisy Spraggs! I wonder if this happened during the square dance. Go ahead and burn the paper now. I don't want the kids to see Daniel's picture or read the story."

I stare across the table at my friend. It's either the country air or hard work at the woolen mill, but she looks so fit and strong. When she first came back to Union County she was a skinny little thing, but her face has filled out and she's got some muscles; even her breasts are bigger.

"We haven't had much time to talk lately, have we? I guess by now you've heard that Dan is refusing to register for the draft. He's not a draft dodger or anything like that; he says he's a *non-cooperator out of conscience*." Here I catch myself rolling my eyes and digging my fingernails into my palms. I'd promised myself to be more supportive.

"The Reverend Miller shared with the congregation that Dan is a principled man and that your family was facing hard times. He didn't say much else, but he urged us, regardless of our personal political beliefs, to be as supportive as possible. We prayed for your family."

Bitsy's matter-of-fact words give me comfort. It helps to talk about what's happening and to know that she doesn't think Dan's a coward.

I remember that even back in the Great War there were radicals who objected to the draft. Eugene Debs, the union organizer and my late husband's friend, gave an antiwar speech and got ten years in prison for sedition. Ten years, just for giving a speech!

After our iced tea and talk, I feel a little better. At least Bitsy didn't reject us and the Millers are being supportive. My friend asks what she can do to help with the harvest and we go down to the root cellar and begin the cleanup. Baskets of potatoes and squash are waiting on the back porch, all boxed up and ready to store.

"It's nice to work together again, Bitsy," I say as we sweep the old straw out of the lower wooden bins. "This is like when we lived on Wild Rose Road. . . . I know you make good money at the woolen mill, but sometimes don't you wish you could stay home like before?"

"That time may come," Bitsy says, looking away.

I turn my head sharply. "What do you mean?"

"I'm three months pregnant."

"Oh, Bitsy! What will you do?"

My friend smiles. "Have a baby, I guess. Lou and I are very happy."

"Will you try to marry?" I ask, sitting down on a bucket and pushing over a wooden box for my friend. In the dim cellar, I study her with a midwife's eyes. No wonder her face has filled out and her breasts have enlarged. How could I miss it?

"Well, that's the hard part. In West Virginia, interracial marriage is illegal. Those who violate the law are subject to a hundred-dollar fine and jail for up to a year. Those who perform an interracial marriage ceremony will be fined two hundred dollars."

"You could go to another state. We're not far from Pennsylvania. Segregation has been against the law there since the 1870s. No separate schools. No separate restaurants or movie theaters. I'm not sure about marriage. Does anyone else know you're pregnant?"

"Mrs. Miller and the reverend. We haven't told anyone else. It's not just white people that will be upset. Some coloreds don't like mixing either. Don't tell anyone, okay? Not until we decide what to do."

"Not even Dan?"

She shakes her head no. "Not even Dan."

Autumn

37

September 3, 1942

Winds of Change

"You smell good," I tell Dan, snuggling up to him. "Even though it'll be hard with the farm and the kids and helping women with childbirth, I'm just going to have to be brave. I've been through hard times before, haven't I? It's your smell and your warmth that I'll most miss."

He runs his hand down my back and when I look over, I see tears in his eyes. Dan's not a big crier. In fact, I've only heard him cry a handful of times. Once was when his mother in New York state died. He felt so bad, because he hadn't visited for a year. The other time was when I got pregnant with Mira and he thought I could die, and then recently when he told me about the German boy's brown eyes, how he can't forget them.

With the tip of my point finger, I wipe the tears down the side of his face and kiss him on the cheek. "Are you scared about going to jail?"

"No. In some ways it will be a relief. The waiting is the hard part, the waiting and not knowing. I told the kids what's coming when we were out in the barn."

Here I half rise on my elbow. "Without me? What did they say?"

"Danny was silent. Willie said he was proud of me for standing up for my beliefs, even though he doesn't agree. Mira tried to catch a butterfly. At seven, I don't think she understood. Susie cried and Sunny gave me a hug and told me she'd visit me every day if I go to jail. I don't think she understands I might not be locked up in Liberty."

"Where will you be?"

"I don't know. There's no federal prison in West Virginia, maybe somewhere in Maryland or Pennsylvania. Lots of the resisters get sent to Ashland, Kentucky."

"Oh, Dan. I wish I'd known. I'm like Sunny; I thought we could at least visit. When I worked with the unions, many of my friends were jailed, but they were always held somewhere local and usually for only a few days. Now, I *really* am scared. Everyone thinks I'm so strong, but I'm not."

"You're a midwife warrior, Patience. Remember that." He places one hand on my heart and one hand on his. "You'll protect our family. You'll do it alone or with friends, but you'll do it. And sooner than you know, we'll be together again." His hand cups my breast.

And then I hold on as our two bodies race through the winds of change. Holding on. Holding on.

September 6, 1942

When You Wish Upon a Star

Two more days of furious work and we almost have a full cellar. The shining canning jars of yellow corn line up like soldiers next to the green beans, tomatoes, and blackberries that we picked and canned this summer. Underneath the shelves of mason jars are the bins of potatoes, turnips, carrots, and beets. In the attic are the winter squash and the onions.

There are still more green beans and tomatoes to pick before the frost, but Saturday morning Dan says over breakfast, "It's time to celebrate the harvest. What do you think, kids? How about a movie?"

I check our cookie jar in the pantry. There are eighteen dollar bills inside, and another seventy dollars is buried in a tin box under the willow tree. Though we planned to build Dan a vet office where he could see small animals on the farm, we never got around to it, and now I'm glad because in the coming months, without his income, we'll need the money.

"What's playing?" Danny asks. "Not a girl movie or something with a lot of kissing."

Daniel and I look at each other remembering last night.

"It's a full-length Walt Disney cartoon called *Pinocchio* about a boy who lies."

"Okay," Danny says. "If it's about a boy . . ." His father ruffles his hair and whispers something in his ear.

Later I ask Dan what he said. "*That's my man*," Dan explained. "I told him out in the barn that he needs to help you and try to make your life better while I'm gone. That also means not arguing about every little thing."

"And if the draft board forgets to have you arrested, will the children still be nice and help me anyway?"

Dan smiles his crooked smile. "Probably not. Most likely they'd revert to hellions."

IN LIBERTY WE hurry through our shopping and meet under the marquee at the Eagle Theater. Mira is so excited she's dancing on the sidewalk. "Oh, I just love Pinocchio!" she says. "*I just love him!*" She throws a kiss to the poster of the boy puppet on the front of the theater.

"Settle down, honey," Daniel gently reproaches her.

Once in the theater, the cool dark closes around us and I feel more relaxed. The movie begins with the customary newsreel. A giant eagle flashes on the screen. Patriotic music fills the theater, and the audience cheers when bombs rain from a white U.S. fighter plane and smoke rises from a Japanese village below. This truly is a *world war*, and not one dead body in sight. I peer over at Daniel. I know he believes the newsreels are U.S. propaganda designed to stir up patriotic fervor.

At last the feature film opens with Jiminy Cricket singing in a beautiful tenor, "*When you wish upon a star, makes no difference who you are. Anything your heart desires will come to you . . .*" The green cricket, in a top hat, breaks into Gepetto's cottage and discovers the wooden boy puppet. The kids are all on the edge of their seats and even Daniel laughs out loud . . .

As the movie closes, Jiminy sings the theme song again. *"When you wish upon a star, makes no difference who you are. Anything your heart desires will come to you."*

I reach over for Dan's hand, thinking if I wished upon a star it would be that the war would end and things would go back to the way they were before Pearl Harbor. Unfortunately, Hitler still marches through Europe and he's not going away.

We leave the cool dark theater and enter the heat of early September. Willie, Bitsy, and Mr. Cross stand on the sidewalk. Now that I know she's pregnant, I see under Bitsy's sailor blouse the gentle curve of her abdomen.

"Hi," I greet them. "We just went to the movie."

"We saw you," says Willie. "We were upstairs in the colored section. It's great up there. You can see everyone. You can even drop popcorn on people's heads."

"Willie!" I say. "You didn't!"

"No, but I could have."

Lou and Dan stand aside in a separate conversation and I put my arm through Bitsy's. "That's nice you could all sit together. I didn't know they let white people up in the Negro balcony."

"They do now. Lou told Mr. Flanders that's the way it was going to be. . . ."

It's then that I see them . . . three strangers dressed in gray suits and gray hats leaning on a black car, and the hair on the back of my neck stands up.

The Long Arm of the Law

As the three approach, the hot air goes still.

"Daniel Hester?" one of the men says. Dan flashes his eyes at me and lifts his head, standing tall.

"Yes."

"Are you Daniel J. Hester of Salt Lick Road?" the man says again. He has big ears and eyes that turn down. The eyes are not kind.

"I am Daniel J. Hester of Salt Lick."

Bitsy takes my hand. Lou Cross moves closer to hear what's going on. Suddenly, the two other men put their hands on Dan as if he might run.

"What's going on?" demands Lou.

"This doesn't concern you, sir. This is a federal matter; please step back."

B.K. Bittman and Lilly Bittman come out of the theater with their children and stop to watch. I look for Willie and Danny. They're sitting on top of the Indian motorcycle, about a half block away, laughing about the movie and unaware of what's happening.

Mr. Linkous, the lawyer, who was also in the movie house with his family, stops and steps forward. "Excuse me, sir, I'm Dr. Hester's attorney. And you are who?"

For the first time, the lawman introduces himself. "I'm U.S. Federal Marshal Marvin Savage"—he flashes a gold badge—"and these are my deputies, Casey and Blackwell." He indicates the other men, who have identical Clark Gable mustaches.

"We're here to arrest Mr. Hester for draft evasion," Savage says loudly, as if announcing it to those who stand by. He pulls a sheaf of paper from his breast pocket.

Gasps run through the crowd, like water overflowing the banks of the Hope. In the background, I hear whispers, "Draft dodger!" "Traitor!"

Mrs. Stenger, the pharmacist's wife, leans down to our daughters, who cling to my skirt. "Come on, young ones," she says. "We're going to my house to have ice cream."

Sunny and Susie know the Stengers well because they stayed with them for a few weeks after their parents died back in '35. So away they go, skipping down the street, not realizing their father won't be coming home for dinner tonight . . . or anytime soon. A block away, Gertrude stops for the boys. The kind woman, like the Pied Piper, is taking them all.

"Now, if you'll just come peacefully, Mr. Hester," Big Ears says.

"Can I say goodbye to my wife?"

The marshal looks at the crowd. "No, that won't be possible." He pulls out a pair of handcuffs and grabs Dan's arm, but Dan pulls away. Then the other two marshals yank his arms behind his back.

"There's no call for that!" Lou Cross growls, and tries to push them away. "He just wants to say goodbye."

The head marshal at this point pulls a gun and points it up in the air. "Everyone, back off!" he yells, but I stand by Dan's side and I'm *not* going anywhere. "Mr. Hester, are you going to come quietly?"

The sound of a siren stops the action like a broken reel at

a picture show. It's Sheriff Hardman, who pulls the black-and-white squad car up with a screech. "What the hell's going on here?" he demands, jumping out. The lights are still flashing but the siren is off. "Put that gun back in your holster, man, before someone gets hurt. Who the hell are you anyway? If I have to draw *my* gun, I'm going to use it."

The marshal, moving very slowly, returns his gun to his shoulder holster and pulls out his badge again. "I'm Federal Marshal Marvin Savage, from Alexandria, Virginia, here to take Mr. Hester into custody for draft evasion. These are my deputies. The suspected felon was resisting arrest and his friends were threatening us." He hands a sheet of paper to Hardman, who looks it over. The crowd has grown larger now and people crowd in so they can hear.

Dan stands expressionless. He catches my eye and we hold each other. *I'm sorry*, he whispers.

The sheriff reads the document, scratches his head, and reads it again. "It isn't draft evasion, Sheriff Hardman," I boldly come in. "Dan is an American pacifist. He wrote the draft board a long letter. He knew he would have to pay a price, and he's ready. All he wanted was a chance to say goodbye to me."

"Isn't it customary to introduce yourself to local law enforcement when you ride into town like a cowboy, Savage?" the sheriff barks. "I would have appreciated a visit or a call, and this arrest could have been handled quietly. I know Dr. Hester well. . . . Now, stand back everyone and let the man say goodbye."

The crowd moves away, with a few teenage boys up near the curb chanting under their breath. "Draft dodger! Draft dodger!" Even Marshal Savage and his henchmen obey.

As if this is the last time we will see each other, maybe ever, Dan and I throw our arms around each other. "I love you," I say. "You are my heart."

A few minutes later . . . "Dr. Hester," Sheriff Hardman says quietly, "It's time."

38

September 10, 1942

No More Crying

The first night Daniel was gone it turned cold. By the feed store thermometer in the barn it went from 76 degrees in the day to 56 at night. Bitsy and Willie slept over and at dinner we prayed for Dan, Willie taking the lead.

"Our Father," he said, bowing his head and reaching out his hands so that we all made a circle. "Take care of Mr. Hester, wherever he is. Keep him safe and let your light surround him. Amen."

"WILL PAPA BE back tomorrow?" Mira asks on Sunday morning, sitting on the sofa and hugging Three Legs, the big yellow lump of a canine who has become her special pet. "He said I could ride with him up on Spruce Mountain."

"I don't think so, honey. Sheriff Hardman is going to telephone us when he finds out where the marshals took him."

"*I* could take you riding," offers Bitsy. "It's Sunday and I don't have to work today."

"On the motorcycle?" Mira wants to know.

"Well, I was thinking of a horse ride, but we could do a couple of loops in the cycle out to Hazel Patch and back. I could take two of you at a time in the sidecar. We can't play all day, though. We have to help your mom on the farm, okay?" The mood gets serious again.

"Do we have to go back to school in town?" Danny asks. "I don't want to. I might get in a fight if someone says something bad about Pa."

"Me too," says pipsqueak Mira. "I'll beat them up if they talk mean about him. He's a hero as much as a soldier, because he's trying to do what he thinks is right."

"Mrs. Miller is teaching Elroy and Marvin Jackson in the old schoolhouse at Hazel Patch," Willie interjects. "Maybe we could all go there."

I look at Bitsy. "What do you think? Our four kids, Willie, and the Jackson boys, that's quite a lot. . . . It would be nice, though. Mrs. Miller taught at least that many in years past. Maybe she could get funding for the school from the county like before."

"We can ask," Bitsy says. "What do you kids think? Would you like to go back to Hazel Patch for school?" The consensus is an overwhelming yes.

"Let's sing then," Bitsy says. "This is an old spiritual my ma, Big Mary, taught me. Let's sing for Daniel."

"*Oh freedom, oh freedom, oh freedom over me! And before I'd be a slave, I'll be buried in my grave, and go home to my Lord and be free!*"

"You think he's okay, Bitsy?" I break in when she takes a breath. "You think they're treating him okay? Prison is a hard place."

"Like Willie says, the Lord will protect him. Now another verse: *No more weepin', no more weepin', no more weepin' over me. And before I'd be a slave, I'll be buried in my grave, and go home to my Lord and be free.*"

Our voices get louder. My voice gets stronger, as if Dan could hear me. "*No more moaning . . . No more crying . . .*"

Bitsy stands up and waves her hands in the air as if we were in an old-time tent revival, and we all join her, almost dancing. "*There'll be singin', Lord, there'll be singin', there'll be singin' over me. And before I'd be a slave, I'll be buried in my grave, and go home to my Lord and be free!*"

September 12, 1942

Draft Dodger

*L*OCAL MAN ARRESTED FOR DRAFT EVASION the headline of the *Liberty Times* howls, and underneath is an article with a picture of Dan, taken two years ago when he was judging 4H sheep at the county fair.

"Dr. Daniel Hester, Union County veterinarian, was arrested in front of the Eagle Theater Saturday by federal marshals for refusing to register for the draft and other crimes

unknown. A crowd gathered, shouting 'Draft dodger! Draft
dodger!' and Sheriff Bill Hardman was called to the scene to
subdue violence.

"Are you sure you want me to read this to you?" Bitsy asks. "It's pretty awful."

"Yeah, go ahead. Thanks for bringing it over. I'd hate to go into town and see it for the first time on the newspaper rack at Stenger's Pharmacy."

Bitsy continues.

"According to Mr. Flanders, owner of the movie house,
two hooligans took advantage of the chaos to steal Hershey
Bars out of the glass case at the refreshment stand, but no
other damage was done.

"Mr. Hester, head down in shame, was taken away in
handcuffs after Sheriff Hardman broke up the crowd by
brandishing his gun.

"Marvin Savage, the lead federal marshal, was not avail-
able for comment, but an unidentified witness said she
overheard the lawman say he felt the draft dodger was a
danger to the community and wanted him locked up as
soon as possible."

"What a pack of lies. . . . Destroy it, will you? And anyway, Dan didn't hang his head in shame."

Bitsy does what I say and throws the paper in the stove. "Lou's sorry he can't come to Dan's sentencing tomorrow. He gave me the day off, but he's the foreman and has to stay at the woolen mill. Are you going to bring the kids?"

"I don't know. It might be too upsetting."

"I think you should," says Bitsy, stirring the flames to be sure that not a shred of the newspaper remains.

"Maybe you're right. They might not see their father for a long time."

September 13, 1942

Day in Court

*I*n the morning, we all dress in our Sunday best and head out the door. To get to the courthouse in Torrington by nine we have to leave at six and we go in two vehicles. I drive the Olds with my children. Bitsy and Willie come with the Millers and Mr. Maddock in the Millers' car.

I'm surprised when we enter the three-story brick court-house to see other people I know. Mr. and Mrs. Stenger are here, as well as B.K. Bittman. Mr. Dresher and his wife are sitting with Sheriff Hardman, who's dressed in full uniform, complete with a tie and his gold badge.

Judge Wade sits in the first row with a few other members of the Liberty draft board—Mayor Ott, Loonie Tinkshell, and Aran Bishop. Aran leans back on the wooden oak bench as if ready to enjoy a good show.

A man in a brown tweed suit stands. "All rise for the honorable Judge Milbank," he cries in a nasal twang.

"That's the bailiff," Bitsy whispers. She stands beside me, with Danny and Willie to her right, the girls on my left.

A very large man with a little mustache, heavy rimmed glasses, and a polka-dot tie enters the courtroom wearing a long black robe like a preacher. I study the forbidding individual, trying to read him, and decide that he's stern, but going by his tie, has a sense of humor.

The judge takes his place at the bench high above us. Behind him on the oak-paneled wall is a round brass seal. FEDERAL DISTRICT COURT it says over an eagle that holds an olive branch in one claw and arrows in the other.

Next, the bailiff calls for the prisoner and two guards bring in Dan. I'd anticipated seeing him in black-and-white stripes like a jailbird with a number stamped on his front, but he's dressed in the clothes he was arrested in: brown slacks, a white shirt, and no tie. He searches the courtroom, finds us, and grins, but quickly wipes the smile from his face. Despite the polka dots, I suspect Judge Milbank won't tolerate frivolity.

After that, things blur as Mr. Linkous, Dan's attorney, and the judge put their heads together. Twice I have to tell Susie and Mira to settle down. Finally, the judge turns to Daniel.

"I understand, Mr. Hester, that you do not wish to dispute the charges of draft evasion."

"That is correct, Judge Milbank. I have intentionally broken the law as an act of conscience and I know there will be a price to pay. I only ask that I be permitted to present a short statement to the courtroom about why I feel I must do this."

"I'll allow it."

Dan stands, turns toward the room full of spectators, and unfolds a piece of white paper. The flash of a camera goes off from the side, but there's a hush in the courtroom and all eyes are on Dan.

He clears his throat. "I'd like to read a simple statement about my pacifist beliefs so that Judge Milbank and my community can better understand why I'm willing to go to jail before I'll cooperate with the institution of the draft.

"I served in the Great War. In fact, I enlisted at eighteen and was a private in the Eighth Cavalry Division of the army. I fought and I killed, I'll admit it. It was kill or be killed, but like every man filled with fear and fury, I also killed unnecessarily. I could have taken a young German man, about my age, as a captive. He laid down his gun, but I shot him. Another time I could have only wounded a man, but I stabbed him three times with my bayonet . . . and there were other experiences that convinced me that combat only makes us barbarians. It doesn't solve problems.

"After that experience, I said to myself I would never participate in war again. Therefore, I feel compelled by my conscience and a vow I made to my Maker to resist war every way I can." Dan clears his throat and then goes on.

"Now, there are those who say, we *must* fight." He catches my eye. "We have been attacked by Japan at Pearl Harbor and Adolf Hitler is a lunatic trying to take over the world. This may be true, and I respect other men's and women's decision to go to war, but I cannot." Someone behind me whispers, "*Coward!*" but Dan goes on.

"I must resist conscription into the army, and have refused to sign up for the draft. I am a complete conscientious objector, and am obligated to protest even simple registration. The tragedy of war is that it never ends.

"In war there's always a winner and a loser, and sooner or later the loser will seek revenge, and so it goes generation after generation, an unending human chain of hate and slaughter." Here Dan puts down his script and looks across the gallery, taking in the faces of his friends and enemies.

"If going to prison for refusing to cooperate with the draft can save even one life, it will be worth the price. If over the years enough people all over the world refuse to serve, maybe war as a method of resolving international problems will end."

Someone coughs in the very quiet room and then a small voice says, "Tell them about the horses, Papa." It's Mira.

Daniel smiles his lopsided smile and looks up at the judge, who is frowning. "Okay, Dr. Hester. The young lady thinks you should finish your story, but make it short."

Dan shrugs and shakes his head, still smiling at Mira. "Sorry, Judge, my six-year-old is remembering what I told her about the first world war. . . . As a young man with farming experience, I was assigned to take care of the horses in my cavalry regiment. Most people don't know that when that war began, the British army possessed only twenty-five thousand horses.

"The War Office was given the urgent task of finding half a million more to go into battle. It was thought that the big animals were needed to pull heavy guns and supplies, to carry the wounded to the hospital, and to mount cavalry charges.

"Soon the U.S. began shipping horses across the Atlantic. One thousand beautiful horses were shipped to Europe for the military *every day*. I was one of the men assigned to take care of them.

"In the end, I watched the beautiful, intelligent animals die of exhaustion, broken bones, bloody wounds, and tetanus. There was nothing we could do. They should never have been there in the first place. Modern weapons made them sitting ducks. Eight million died in combat. . . . Eight million beautiful horses that we buried in mass graves." Dan sits down with a bowed head and I know there are tears in his eyes. The dead and wounded horses always get to him.

"Okay, Dr. Hester. That was quite a speech, and now it gives me no pleasure to hand down your sentence. Mr. Linkous. Mr. Hester. Please stand."

Without meaning to, I rise too, and then the children and Bitsy.

"The maximum sentence for refusing to register for the draft is five years in federal prison . . . the minimum is six months. I found your statement to the court an honest display of conscience and I understand that you are not a draft evader, nor a coward. Your lawyer, Mr. Linkous, has presented the court with twenty letters of support for your character written by citizens of Union County, and I have taken these into consideration. Therefore, I sentence you to two years in federal prison. Marshal, take the prisoner away."

Dan turns toward me, his hand over his heart sending me love. Bitsy feels my legs start to go and puts her arm through mine. The marshal and his men reach for handcuffs, but the judge stops them. "That won't be necessary," he barks, nodding toward the children. "They don't need to see their pa marched away in irons."

Though two years is a relatively short sentence, for the first time Daniel's imprisonment is real and I feel twenty-four months of boulders rolling down Spruce Mountain toward me. The girls burst into tears, suddenly understanding that their father isn't coming home, and Danny's eyes blaze with hate, but whether it's for the judge or his father, I can't say.

"It will be okay," Bitsy whispers and, with her arm firmly through mine, leads us out of the courtroom.

The Wake

Bitsy insisted on driving us home. It was clear I was upset and though I tried to comfort the children, I could barely talk.

Two hours after leaving Torrington, we pull across the wooden bridge over Salt Lick and into our drive and I'm surprised to see four other cars parked in the yard. "Who's here?" Danny asks, pressing his face against the window. Mira, who's fallen asleep on my lap, wakes up and asks, "Is Papa home?"

"No, honey. . . . What's going on?" I whisper to Bitsy.

"I guess people have already heard about the outcome of the trial and want to be supportive. Word travels fast."

The truth is, I was hoping to go to my room and let my tears fall, but that's not going to happen until the children are in bed, so I take a deep breath and march up on the porch and stare bleakly at the American flag on the door.

The first person to greet me is Oriole Jackson, who takes me in her strong, brown arms and holds me to her bosom. "I'm so sorry to hear about Mr. Hester, honey. The time will go fast and in a few years he'll be home. Women with men in the military have to face the same thing." She pats my back.

"Can I get you some coffee?" Mrs. Miller asks, wiping her hands on her flowered apron. "Mrs. Maddock sent over a peach pie, but she couldn't come because her legs hurt. . . . I made some sandwiches in the kitchen. I hope you don't mind."

"Come on, kids," comes a man's booming voice. It's Lou Cross. "Grab a sandwich. I want to see that colt of yours. Can I ride him?"

"No, silly. You're too big," Susie answers, taking his hand. "You can pet him though."

"We'll save you some pie and some of my sweet bread," Mrs. Jackson calls as they leave. Only Willie looks back.

Then Gertrude Miller takes me in the living room with a cup of coffee and sits me down on the sofa. "How are you holding up?" she asks.

I smile, but it's with half a heart. "Okay, I guess. As good as I can be. I'm just worried about the children and all the farm work. Dan was my rock."

"Well, don't be too concerned. Things have a way of getting done when friends are around. Mr. Roote and Bitsy are outside feeding the chickens and getting eggs and Milt Maddock will feed the stock. I can help milk the cows. I bet you didn't know I grew up on a farm, did you?"

I let my head fall back on the sofa, watching the fire, feeling these kind men and women around me. Though I fear the dark days ahead, for the moment we are safe. We are loved. We are cared for.

39

The Big House

Sheriff Hardman has kindly offered to drive me in his squad car to the West Virginia State Prison for my first visit to Dan. I am so apprehensive, partly because I cannot forget what I've heard about the conscientious objectors in the last war, especially the news stories about the three Hutterite brothers who were tortured by guards, chained to the wall, and eventually starved to death.

When we get to Moundsville, I smile. It's a pleasant place with wide, tree-lined boulevards and Victorian houses along the Ohio River, but the prison is nothing like the town. It's more forbidding than anything I'd imagined—a dark sandstone castle on a hill with guard towers and a ten-foot wall topped with rolled barbed wire.

"Oh, Sheriff," I exclaim when he parks the squad car out front. "I don't know if I can go in. This place is scary. I'm so glad you came with me. I'm sure if I was alone, I'd turn right around and head back to the Hope River." There are tears in my eyes and I don't care that he sees them.

"Now, Miss Patience, we came all this way, don't fall apart on me. Daniel is expecting you. Remember, years ago you told me midwives were warriors?" I nod weakly and wipe my eyes. "You just put on those white gloves and walk in there proud and proper. I'm going to go with you as far as I can, but there's only one visitor at a time."

I smooth my red flowered dress and pull my navy blazer closer. When you've been a radical, lived with radicals, marched in the streets and spent time in jail, you are always wary of guards and coppers.

Sheriff Hardman holds the heavy steel door open as we enter the fortress. The door slams behind us. A small man sits at a barred window, looking like a teller at a bank, except for the gray uniform and the silver badge.

"I'm Sheriff Hardman of Liberty, and this is Mrs. Patience Hester to see Dr. Daniel Hester, her husband," he announces in a deep voice, as if I'm being introduced to Eleanor Roosevelt in the receiving line at the White House.

The official looks me over and deduces, probably by the dainty white gloves, that I'm not a regular visitor at prisons. "You'll have to sign in, ma'am, and I'll need some ID." He pushes a form under the window bars. "Also, I have to confirm you're on his visiting list. Then you give me your handbag and anything else you're toting . . ." He indicates the paper sack I've brought with me.

"Do I have to? I just have some clean underwear for my husband, pictures drawn by our children, and two novels, *The Farm* by Louis Bromfield, and *My Life and Hard*

Times by James Thurber. Can't I bring the bag to him? I thought the presents would cheer him." Here my voice trembles.

"No, ma'am. The sack has to be searched for contraband. I'll give it to him later. Now, can you just sign? Visiting hours start in five minutes and you'll be late." I quickly give him the paper bag and my purse, sign his form, and then look at Hardman.

"I'll wait here," he says, taking a seat across from the door and pulling out a worn pocketbook western.

The admitting officer presses a buzzer, and a woman guard comes through a second metal door, one that slides shut behind me with a clunk, and we're in a tiny room about the size of a closet. There's only the one window in the room, and it looks back to the waiting room, where the sheriff already sits reading.

"Hello. How are you today?" I say politely, but the matron in gray uniform is having none of my pleasantries. She motions for me to raise my hands high and then she pats me up and down, both my arms and legs and then my front and back.

Finally, she nods that she's satisfied and says in a low smoker's voice, "When the door opens, you'll be in a large visitors' room. There are ten tables. You should see your inmate sitting at one. You can sit across from him, but you must not touch. If you do, a guard will terminate your visit."

"But I brought him some clean underwear and some drawings from our children . . . will someone bring them in?" I try again.

"No, the inmate will get them when he's back in his cell." A buzzer rings, the steel door slides open, and the matron almost pushes me out. "Now, move. You're taking up valuable time. Other visitors are waiting."

I step through the door and scan the large gray room with high ceilings. There are bars on the small high windows that let in dim light, and there's an observation deck where sentries with shotguns sit watching over the scene. Daniel is at a table against the far wall in a gray uniform with 14077 stenciled on the front. He's staring down and away, and for a minute I don't recognize him. His skin has lost color and he hasn't shaved for three days.

"Oh, Daniel!" I exclaim as I run to him. A loudspeaker squeaks and then a guard's voice orders, "Walking only! No sudden movements."

Whoops!

I sit down across from my husband. "Hi."

Dan smiles. "You're a sight for sore eyes. You even wore my favorite red dress."

"I brought you some clean underwear, some books, and some presents from the kids. I hope they don't get lost or stolen. The admission officer had to search them to make sure I didn't bring in a knife or a file." I think this is humorous, but Dan shakes his head.

"Don't even joke about it," he says. "The walls have ears. And by the way, watch what you say in letters. They are censored and read."

I make a bad face, like I've been caught by a teacher chewing gum.

"How are you getting along with the other prisoners? Are they mean?"

"Some hard-core patriots give me a bad time whenever I pass, and no one will sit by me in the dining room, but a man of conscience has to suffer a little for his beliefs."

"Are there really many flag wavers here?"

"You'd be surprised. This is a hot bed of loyal Americans ready to fight if they weren't in prison. They'd probably make good soldiers too . . . if they could read the oath of allegiance and if they could follow orders. That might be the problem. One thing though, it makes you wonder if they took to a life of crime just because they were illiterate and couldn't find work."

"No touching, Bill!" barks the voice from above and when I whirl around I see a big bald man kissing his bleach-blond woman on the lips. "I've told you that before." The guard laughs.

"How come they're not making *her* leave? The female guard warned me that if *we* touched I'd be sent away."

"That's Big Bill Boggs, from Huntington, part of the West Virginia gambling mob. He runs this place."

"Are you kidding? It sounds rough."

"It's safer than a battlefield, if you look at it that way."

Before we drop into the canyon of our difference about the war I ask him to tell me about his days in the fortress. A clock on the wall indicates we have thirty more minutes.

"Not much to tell. There are three meals a day, hardly worth eating, and one hour in the outdoor area called the yard, weather permitting. It's sort of like recess at school.

"I live in a cell that's five by seven, white concrete walls, and an open toilet. You'd like that. *Indoor plumbing*," he jokes. "I have a hard mattress—no sheets, just a blanket. I also have no cellmate, because the steel bunk above me is broken. This place is not in the best repair. I do have two friends, though."

"That's nice," I respond, wondering what kind of man in this hellhole could be his friend.

"The first is a murderer called Bones. Sometimes we sing together after lights-out. I'm teaching him how to read. The second is a rat named Ronald."

"A rat as in a snitch, a thief, or . . ."

"No, an *actual rat*."

"Not really!"

"Yep. I've got him so he will eat out of my hand and he sleeps in a little box under my bed."

"You better not mess with him, Daniel. He could have fleas. Didn't rats spread the bubonic plague?"

"I'm going to get a pet cockroach next," he jokes.

"How did you tame Ronald anyway?"

"I think the fellow before me already had him tamed. He just came and sat by my bed when I was eating. I dropped a few crumbs and little by little, over the days, I got him to eat out of my hand. I'm a vet, you know, good with animals, and I think he looks quite healthy. Bright eyes and smooth fur, probably a little overweight though."

"Well, if you bring even one cockroach into our house when you get home, I'm going to throw such a fit you'll wish you were back in the Big House." It's here that my tears come, because I realize that Dan's not likely to be home for another two years. Mira will be almost nine when he gets out. I wipe my eyes and force a brave smile.

Dan reaches for me but decides against it, and then under the table I feel his foot against my pump. He slips off his shoe. I slip off mine, and just for a moment we find comfort.

"HOW DID THE visit go?" Bitsy wants to know when she stops by after work the next day. The kids are all playing Candy Land in front of the fire.

I'm still very tired and emotionally spent, but I describe the stone prison, getting searched, and sitting at the table with Dan. I tell about the faces of the other prisoners, some innocent as babes, some as hardened as the cliffs at the White Rock CCC camp.

Eventually, Danny and Willie join us and we laugh as I tell them about the rules, *no touching, no running, no sudden movements.* I even mention that Daniel has a rat for a pet and that he's teaching the murderer, Mr. Bones, how to read.

What I don't reveal is the two sock feet under the table and that I've never loved Daniel more, Dan in his prison uniform with the number 14077 stamped on his chest.

September 28, 1942

Public Disturbance

A stiff wind blows out of the west, but the low sun is still shining when Bitsy and I leave the House of Beauty at 6:30 P.M. It's half-price day and Ida May stays late, so Bitsy said she'd pay for the hairstyles and matinee movie tickets for the kids. In her "strong opinion," I had to start taking care of myself.

I'm wearing a loose silk scarf over my hair so as not to flatten my smooth pageboy, and Bitsy has a new hairdo that makes her look like a young Lena Horne. "The movie should be over soon," I say. "I wonder if Mr. Flanders will let us wait in the lobby until the kids come out."

"Hope so," says Bitsy, protecting her hair with both hands.

We don't have far to go and soon I can see Sheriff Hardman's black-and-white squad car parked in front of the theater with the flashing red light on. "Wonder what's happening," I say.

When we get to the theater, we see that the sheriff is sitting in his car and so are our children, all five of them. Susie's parked in Hardman's lap, crying. Sunny and Mira are both in the passenger seat playing with the buttons and dials on the dash, and Willie and Danny are sulking in the backseat. Danny has a black eye.

"What in holy hell!" Bitsy swears.

I tap on the squad car's window. "Did something happen, Sheriff? Is everyone okay? Bitsy and I were just down at Ida May's."

"Well, there has been some trouble," the lawman answers. "I was called about a disturbance in the theater lobby, a fight. I don't know who started it or who's to blame, but I took your boys into custody for their own protection. If you don't mind, Mrs. Hester, I'd like to get to the bottom of this. Okay if I drive them out to your house on Salt Lick Road? Otherwise we'll have to go up to the cooler."

"Sure. We'll follow you."

As if this is a real treat, to be driven home in a squad car, Mira asks innocently, "Can we have sirens?"

An hour later we're sitting in my living room with Will and Danny. "So, young men, can you tell me what happened?" the sheriff asks, balancing a little notebook on his knee, ready to take notes. The boys look at each other, and then Will, being older, takes the lead.

"Well, sir. Dan and I were sitting down front with the older kids in the Eagle Theater. His sisters were halfway back. This was the first time we'd been to the movies without our parents.

"The newsreel wasn't even over before some girls in the row behind us started whispering things about Danny and his pa, like . . . 'There he is, the son of the draft dodger!' and 'Jailbird, jailbird, sitting in a tree' and 'Yellow-bellied sap sucker!'

"I could tell Danny was getting mad," Willie continues, "so before he jumped over the seat and throttled them, I tried to shut them up. 'Hush, you vixens!' I said." He turns to Bitsy. "Is vixen a bad word, Ma?"

Sheriff Hardman wipes a smile off his face with the back of his hand.

"I don't think so," says Bitsy.

"It means an ill-tempered female," I offer.

"Well, that's what they were," my son finally comes in. "If the usher hadn't come down the aisle and shone his flashlight in their faces, I probably *would* have punched them, though I know it's not right to hit a girl."

"Anyway, all was quiet through the cartoon and half-way into the main feature," Willie goes on, watching the sheriff's face. "Until about the time the Cisco Kid breaks Miss Ann out of jail, and then the jeering started again, only this time it was the big boys. When intermission came, Danny and I took his sisters out front to get some popcorn and find new seats somewhere in back, and that's when all heck broke loose."

"I was drinking from the fountain when a big thug shoved me," Danny says. "That's how I got the shiner. I hit my face on the faucet. 'Son of a coward' the boy called me, and I punched him hard right in the belly."

The sheriff's mouth turns down. He has still not written anything in his book.

"And when another boy jumped in, I walloped him," Willie says, proud of himself.

"Do you know these boys' names?" Hardman wants to know.

Danny and Willie look at each other, but don't answer the lawman.

"I know who they are," says Sunny. "They're eighth graders from over near Burnt Town. Troublemakers. They only come to school when they feel like it. Mrs. Archer says she wishes they would just drop out and give her some peace. The Baker boys, Addison and Haywood." Now the sheriff's pencil moves.

"Tattletale," Will grumbles.

"No, Willie," I say. "Sunny is right to answer the sheriff.

He wants to know the facts. You didn't start the scrap, and I don't exactly know what you were supposed to do when the boy pushed you into the faucet, but I guess fighting in the lobby wasn't the best idea."

"They called Pa a *coward*. He's no coward!" Danny argues.

"Calm down, son," Hardman orders.

"Our pa is brave!" Mira shouts.

"Okay, settle down, *everyone*!" says the sheriff. "I understand you were threatened and mad, but your pa isn't going to be home for two years. People have strong opinions about the war, and this isn't the last time you're going to hear such things.

"You have two choices: figure out how to deal with it, or stay out of town. Now, I'm going to talk to Mr. Flanders at the movie house and I'm going to talk to the Baker brothers and their parents, but Mrs. Hester, can I see you in the kitchen?"

"I'm sorry, Sheriff," I say, sitting down at the table. "Danny and Willie are good boys. They're never in trouble at school. They help me at home . . . I'm sorry," I say again.

"Now, don't get all weepy on me, Mrs. Hester. No real harm was done. I don't know those Baker kids, but I think they're probably bullies and I want them to know they can't get away with it in my town."

"Thank you, Sheriff. I know Dr. Hester will appreciate your help. It's going to be a hard few years without him."

"I know, Patience," Sheriff Hardman says, putting his big hand on my shoulder. It's the first time he's ever called me by my first name.

40

Boone Memorial

I stare out my bedroom window at the bare trees, whipped by the wind. Almost all the crimson and yellow leaves are gone now and it's forlorn and gray. The only touch of color is our red barn.

Mr. Roote has had a stroke. I learned about it from Lou Cross, and I must go to see the old man at Boone Memorial in Torrington tomorrow morning. My plan is to stop at the hospital on the way up to visit Dan at the Moundsville Prison.

Though we've been corresponding, this will be the first time I've seen my husband since I visited him with Sheriff Hardman, the first time I'll visit alone. His letters sit in my top bureau drawer and I read them over again each night before bed.

At the admission desk of the new three-story brick hospital in Torrington, built just two years ago, after the old wooden one burned down, I ask if I can visit Mr. Roote.

"Mr. Charles Roote of Liberty, West Virginia?" the woman in a blue uniform with white collar and cuffs asks me.

"Yes," I answer slowly, realizing I've never heard the old man's first name before.

"Room 304," she says. "You can take the stairs or wait for the elevator."

I decide to take the stairs. Elevators have always scared me, and I've rarely been in one, certainly not since coming to West Virginia. By the time I hobble up to the third floor my knee is killing me. "Room 304?" I ask another nurse. She wears a white uniform and white stockings. She has a little white hat with a dark-blue stripe across the top, and I wonder if Becky dresses like that at Walter Reed. It would suit her well, with her short dark bob.

"You're headed the right way," the nurse says pleasantly. "Mr. Roote is in a four-bed ward and he's my patient. Are you family?"

I'm not sure if you must be family to visit, so I answer cautiously. "Yes . . . I'm his niece. How's he doing?"

"Well, it was a mild stroke, but he's bedridden now. It's affected his left leg, but not his hands or speech, thank goodness."

"How's his companion, Mrs. Stone?"

"The older woman with him? I assumed it was his wife. She cares for him so tenderly, even helps with the bedpan. The lady is there now and seems to be holding up okay." Then the nurse bustles down the hall.

"Mrs. Stone?" I whisper, standing at the open door to Room 304.

"Mr. Roote?" I ask a little louder. I've tended the ill at home, have even sat at the bedside of the dying a few times, but I'm not used to hospitals, and the smell of medicine and cleaning solution almost makes me sick. A curtain moves, a white head appears, and the face wrinkles into a smile.

"Oh, hi, honey. I thought I heard someone. It's so nice of you to stop by," says Mrs. Stone, poking her head out of a curtain.

"How's Mr. Roote?"

"He's a sassy old coot, but he'll live. Come on in. He's decent. Just finished his breakfast tray and had his bath. The doc says he'll be here about a week and then I'm not sure what we'll do. He can't live alone. I'm thinking of taking him back to my house." She pulls me into one of four cubicles. Mr. Roote sits up in bed, looking bright-eyed and clean-shaven.

"Got my own private nurse," he says, giving me a wink. "And she ain't bad-looking, either."

"Now, Charley, behave yourself," Mrs. Stone scolds. Then, to the patient on the other side of the curtain she says, "Can I borrow your chair, Mr. Phillips? We have a guest." There's only a grunt, but she takes the chair anyway.

"I was so sorry to hear about your stroke," I address Mr. Roote. "Is there anything I can do for you? I'm on the way to Moundsville today to visit Daniel, so I can't stay long."

"Going to see the jailbird, huh?" the old man jokes.

"Charley, can't you see it's hard for her?" Mrs. Stone reprimands as she fluffs his pillow.

"Sorry. I just don't get why the darn fool didn't register," says Mr. Roote. "They would have let him alone if he'd signed the papers."

I take a deep breath. "I'm his wife, Mr. Roote, but I'll be honest, I begged him to sign. Still I love him and will forgive him." I swallow hard, trying to make it so. "Danny, our son, is having a hard time with it. He got in a fight at the Eagle Theater when some boys called him the son of a coward."

"Hell!" says the old guy. "Daniel Hester's no coward, maybe a fool, but not a coward. I hope the little fellow gave those bullies a pounding."

"He and Willie tried, but the sheriff was called and broke it up. I can't decide whether to tell Dan about it or not. What would you do?"

Mr. Roote stares at the ceiling, thinking. "I never had children," he says, "but I guess I would be proud if my boy defended me, even in the Eagle Theater."

My visit is short and Mrs. Stone walks me down the hall as I prepare to leave. On the way, we pass a young man in a wheelchair. He's wearing a uniform and has no legs. Another victim of this awful war, I think, and I give him a small smile.

"Is Mr. Roote going to recover?" I ask the elderly lady.

"Oh, I think so. He's too stubborn to just fade away." We're standing in front of the elevator when the door opens with a ding.

"Here you are, honey," Mrs. Stone says, putting her hand inside the sliding panel to hold it open as if she's done this all her life. Then I remember that before the Great

Depression, she and her husband lived in New York City, so she probably used these mechanical contraptions all the time. She nods toward the opening, waiting for me to get in.

There's nothing else for it, so I step over the threshold. The door closes behind me and I hold my breath, bracing myself for the thump and whir as I hurtle down. I wait one minute. Nothing. I wait two minutes, still nothing, and unlike the elevator I rode with my father when I was eight, in Chicago, there's no operator in uniform to drive the thing.

I notice a row of buttons to the right of the door: 3—2—LOBBY—BASEMENT. *Maybe you're supposed to press one? This takes more courage than delivering a breech baby.* I punch the button for Lobby and feel my stomach jump into my throat.

41

Prisoner

I rode in an elevator today," I tell Dan, sitting again at the back table in the visitors' room of the Moundsville Prison. "It was an automatic contraption and I had to drive it myself. Can you imagine! Funny how you can get used to anything," I go on. "Even something fearsome like visiting a state penitentiary.

"It's only my second time here, but I was able to assist another woman who stood in the parking lot staring up at the big stone citadel with tears in her eyes. 'Come with me,' I told her. 'I'll show you what to do.'"

Across the room, my new woman friend is sitting with a prisoner who looks about fifteen. I know that's not true. He has to be at least eighteen to be here, but his very blond hair and smooth pink cheeks make him seem so young and vulnerable. "Do you know that guy?" I whisper, my hand hiding my mouth. "What's he in for?"

"There are a thousand men here, Patience. I can't know them all, but I do happen to know *about* him. A few days ago, I was given a new job. I've been sent to work with Dr. Greeley in the infirmary. I'm just there to file charts and clean up after he does a procedure, but I saw the white-haired kid's name. It's Peter Kaminski. He was just transferred in from Parkersburg and he's here for murder."

"Murder? He looks so innocent. *You* look tougher than he does and you're here for your pacifist beliefs."

"According to his record he hears voices," Dan says in a whisper.

"Well, then shouldn't he be in the state asylum at Weston?"

"Yes, but they don't have a ward for the criminally insane. Doc Greeley, the prison physician, says it's probably schizophrenia. Kaminski killed a hired hand, in cold blood, on his father's farm for no reason that anyone has been able to learn."

"Look at him over there," I say, turning my head in the youth's direction. "He looks like he couldn't hurt a fly."

"Don't do that, hon."

"What?"

"Stare. You learn in the pen to keep eyes and ears closed. Men have been killed just for being too nosy."

"Oh, Dan! I hate it that you're here. Do you know how long it will be or when you'll be transferred to a federal prison? Maybe it will be more civilized."

"Don't know. One of the other pacifists from Ahimsa House was in a county jail for two months before they moved him." He reaches across the table for my hand. "No physical touching!" a loudspeaker blares, and a guard saunters our way, but my husband snatches his hand back, smiles and says, "Sorry, Norm."

"You know the guards' names?"

"There's only about fifty of them on rotating shifts. I don't know them all, but Norm's on my cellblock and he's been bringing me stale bread for Ronald. . . ."

"So how are you doing?" I ask my husband. "Are you still okay?"

"I'm fine. I'm teaching Bones, that guy in for murder, to read . . . How are the kids? Behaving okay? I miss them."

"I brought some more drawings, but you know how it is, the guards have to search through them first. Danny sent a special letter of apology . . ." Here my husband goes on alert.

"Is he getting sassy again? God, I hope not! There's nothing I can do about it in here."

"No, it's not that." I fake a cough to give myself time. "I guess I might as well tell you. He and Willie were in a fight at the Eagle Theater."

Dan raises his eyebrows waiting. "Was it about me?"

"Yes. Some bullies were teasing Danny in the picture show. We took all the kids to *Cisco Kid* at the Eagle Theater and let them watch the movies alone while Bitsy and I had our hair done at Ida May's House of Beauty. Bitsy said I was 'letting myself go' and she'd pay for it on half-price day. I blame myself. I shouldn't have done it."

"What were the bullies saying?"

"You know, the usual stuff. 'Your dad's a draft dodger. . . .'" Here I get tears in my eyes. "And other stuff, like 'coward' and 'yellow-bellied sap sucker.'"

"Yellow-bellied sap sucker! That's a bird." Daniel laughs. "A small woodpecker that drills holes in trees and sucks sap. It has a red head and a pale yellow belly. I'm surprised the kid had even heard of it."

"You think this is funny?" I can't help but smile when I see Dan laugh. "The sheriff was called and he had all five of the kids in the squad car when we got out of Ida May's. I'm surprised it didn't get in the local paper. You know how Mr. Blaze is. Hardman brought them home and made the boys tell him the whole story."

Dan rubs the smile off his face. "I'm sorry, Patience. You shouldn't have to deal with these things." Under the table I feel his sock foot caressing my ankle and I slip off my pump.

"You aren't as upset about the fight as I thought you would be. . . ."

"Shhhh," he says. "Just listen." And he begins to sing, low and sweet. "*You are my sunshine, my only sunshine. You make me happy when skies are gray. You'll never know, dear, how much I love you . . .* "

Our eyes lock and the gray prison walls fade away. Dan and I are on the top of Spruce Mountain, sitting on the flat rock, looking down at valley still green, still alive, forever.

42

October 20, 1942

My Dear Patience,

How long have we been married? Eleven years? Twelve?

What an interesting life we've led and what great friends we have. I got a letter from Reverend Miller yesterday telling me to be of good cheer that the Lord is with me even in dark places. He asked if I was going to chapel and reminded me that even in prison there's church on Sunday.

I asked Bones about it and learned there is a service at nine, right after breakfast. You don't even have to wear a tie. Hahaha. I think I will go.

I heard the other prisoners talking about an execution coming up next week. It's that young blond fellow you noticed in the visiting area. His lawyers were appealing and now his time's up.

At night, I lay my hand on my heart and I think of you and imagine your sweet face, your eyes, your smell. Every day that goes by is one day closer to when we will be together again.

Your loving husband,
Dan

October 21, 1942

Dear Daniel,

I'll start with the big news. Mr. Roote and Mrs. Stone have tied the knot. Can you believe it, at their age?

Yesterday, I went to town for the first time since the boys were in the fight at the theater. Finally, I just had to face it. We were out of sugar, coffee, lard, kerosene, chicken feed, salt-pork, and soap. I took the girls with me, but not Danny. He had to stay and chop wood.

The first stop we made was Bittman's Grocery and we had to use our ration cards for the sugar and coffee. Lilly Bittman was cheerful and nice, indicating that your imprisonment for pacifism has not affected our friendship. The same wasn't true for Prudy Ott. She passed me coming out of the store with her nose in the air. Didn't even say hello.

And to think of the trouble I went to to deliver her baby when she was crying and carrying on!

Our next stop was their old elementary school, in town. The twins and Mira had collected a box of tin cans for the scrap drive and they wanted to see their old friends again. Luckily, we arrived just as recess began and they scampered off with half a dozen girls.

Mrs. Archer and I stood shivering at the edge of the playground and as usual she was full of chatter. "Did you hear the news about the White Rock Civilian Conservation Camp?"

It turns out they are making it into a German prisoner-of-war camp. Apparently such camps are popping up all over the U.S. The Brits have captured so many German and Italian soldiers, they have no place to keep them on their small island. On the other hand, the U.S. has a shortage of farm and factory workers, so they're already shipping the POWs here.

The idea is that they'll be rented out to farmers and factories around us. Apparently the town is all up in arms about it and I don't blame them. Think of it, Nazis right in our own backyard!

We miss you and pray for you every night. Even Three Legs.

Your hardworking, loving wife,
Patience

October 22

My Dearest Patience,

I was happy to hear that Mr. and Mrs. Roote got married. I guess if they were going to live together, they wanted everything to be proper. Hope Charley is getting back on his feet.

Except for missing you and the kids, things are going well here. Teaching Bones how to read has opened up new doors for me. The bald-headed guard you saw last time in the visiting area, Norm, has arranged with the warden for me to have daily reading classes, and I now have twelve students.

The men are touching in their appreciation and give me extra food and treats. I don't think many of them went beyond the third grade. You'd think maybe everyone in the big house would be a vicious criminal, but the longer I'm here, the more I realize that's not true.

One young fellow with a patch over his right eye was convicted of manslaughter when, in self-defense, he killed a man who accosted him in an alley in Martinsburg. He lost his eye, but still got fifteen years in prison. If I ever get out of here . . . (Sorry! I mean, WHEN I get out of here) I'm going to ask Mr. Linkous to look into it. It doesn't seem right.

But that's something you learn in prison. Life isn't fair. I don't know why I ever thought it was.

Some of these fellows are just regular fellows who didn't have the advantages I had. The Great Depression came, and just to survive they fought and they robbed.

It's odd to be locked up for protesting a war you hardly remember. The only news we get is when guards tell us what's happening overseas or if we're allowed to listen to the radio on Sundays.

Invasions in Guadalcanal, German attacks on Russia, counterattacks, victories and losses. It all seems so futile as the world turns red with blood.

On a lighter side, here's something that will amuse you. Ronald will now ride around in my shirt pocket and he's become sort of a mascot for my cellblock. There are twenty inmates in my section, but I still have a cell to myself. At night sometimes I get the men to sing the old songs we all know.

"I'll fly away, oh glory. I'll fly away!" That's something to hear echoing in harmony down these lonely concrete halls. "I'll fly away . . ." If only we could.

My love to you,
Daniel

43

October 23, 1942

Molly

*Y*esterday, I was called to the home of Molly Klopenstein, who lives on Buck's Run on the other side of Union County. The kids were still in school with Mrs. Miller and she kindly agreed to watch them if I didn't get home by dark.

I hadn't been up Buck's Run for ten years and was surprised when I got there to see that the small community, a variation of Old Order Amish, had grown to eight log houses. There used to be only four, scattered along the creek in the narrow hollow that runs back toward the mountains.

WHEN I KNOCK on the door, Levi Klopenstein greets me. He was just a young fellow when I met him years ago, but now he has a dark beard down to his chest, threaded with gray, and he wears the regulation black pants, white shirt, and dark suspenders of the rest of the religious order.

"Hello, Levi," I say as I enter the log house. It's simply furnished with handmade wooden furniture and illuminated with kerosene lamps. "Can you tell me what's happening? I didn't get much of a report when your neighbor phoned me. Is it Molly?"

"Yes. She delivered her fourth baby boy about six hours ago, but the afterbirth won't come and she's bleeding. Granny pulled on it and the cord broke. We don't know what to do."

I take a deep breath. "Okay. Well, you did the right thing by calling me. Where is she?"

Levi silently leads me down a short hall into a small room with a big wooden bed. Just like the last time I was here, the women of the community, all dressed in black, sit in a row on a long bench like six black crows. Three I know: Granny, Molly's mother, and Molly's sister, Ruth. A very pink newborn sleeps in a homemade wooden cradle.

I repeat what Levi told me, to be sure I have the story right. Then I turn to the patient. The first thing I note is she's very pale and her pulse is weak. A pile of red rags has been dropped in a bucket.

Time to get to work. This is what the medical books call the third stage of labor, and it's the most dangerous part for the mother. I wipe away the blood from Molly's vagina and put a clean folded towel under her bottom to better keep track of the bleeding.

The safest thing to do is get Molly in the Olds and head for Boone Memorial in Torrington, but I know from my previous encounter with the family that they won't even consider it. Hospitals, they believe, are hellholes, places people go to be tortured or to die.

"Ruth," I ask, "has Molly been nursing? Breastfeeding stimulates the uterus to contract and that might bring the placenta."

"Yes. She put the baby to the breast right away, and she's been feeding him every two hours, but nothing is working."

"Well," I say, to give myself time to think, "go get Molly some warm chicken broth. If you don't have any soup, bring me some tea with honey. And Mrs. Klopenstein, boil some water." I think the ladies might balk, but they both go off briskly.

"She won't drink, Midwife," says the old grandmother. "We already tried. She says she wants to sleep and that the Lord will take care of her."

"She'll drink if we make her. *God needs her to drink.* I can tell by looking that Molly's lost too much blood. If the placenta doesn't deliver, the uterus can't contract to stop the bleeding and her life force will drain out of her."

Hoping to find the afterbirth just inside the vagina, I put on my sterile gloves and separate the opening. If I can see the shiny organ, I'll get my fingers around it and drag it out, but I'm not that lucky. There's nothing there. Not even a blood clot or a piece of the severed cord.

Next I do a vaginal exam with two fingers and more blood and clots shoot out, but there's no placenta. This is going to require a whole-hand exam.

"Molly, wake up and look at me," I call. "I have to go in and see why your placenta isn't coming. This is going to hurt, but it has to be done. It will take only twenty seconds, maybe less. Ladies"—I turn to the crows still sitting in a row behind me—"can you count out loud to twenty slowly? And someone come hold Molly's hand."

"One, two, three . . ." I start off. Molly opens her eyes and groans but she doesn't squirm or fight me. She knows that getting the placenta out is critical if she wants to live.

"Twenty. Twenty-one . . ."

I slowly remove my fingers and let out my air.

"I'm sorry I hurt you, Molly, and I thank you for co-operating. Now, here's the good news." I turn to my female audience. "I'm pretty sure the afterbirth has separated. I was worried it might be embedded in the muscle of the womb, which would require surgery. But there's bad news too. Molly has a large fibroid just inside the cervix and I think it's holding the placenta back."

"Well, what can we do? Can you help her?" one of the women asks.

"I'll try," I say, looking straight at them.

When Ruth returns with the chicken broth, I explain the problem again and we take a few minutes to sit Molly up. "Honey, you have to drink this! I know you don't feel like it, but *we're talking life or death here*, and you don't want to leave Levi alone with four little boys. He needs you."

Finally, Molly opens her blue eyes and comes out of the dark hole she's been hiding in. She's a pretty woman, in her thirties now, with long blond hair braided down her back, but she's as limp as a tomato plant during a drought.

I hold the mug up and she sips a little, but I don't give up until it's all gone. Next Ruth and I scoot her to the side of the bed and get her to squat over a chamber pot. We wait five minutes.

Damn! I was hoping she'd urinate and the whole thing would plop out. Now what? More broth. While Ruth holds the mug, I try to think what to do. I was so convinced that getting her to void would solve the problem, but now my insides turn cold.

This is becoming a real mess. If the woman dies, I may be blamed. The times are not favorable for midwives, especially one whose husband is a draft protester, and I could be accused of manslaughter. Then *both* Dan and I might be locked in the big house. I look again at the circle of red on the clean towel under Molly; it's now the size of a sunflower.

When the second cup of broth is gone, Molly's color begins to improve, so we switch to tea with honey to give her some energy. "Can you push, Molly? Can you grunt and push like you're having another baby?" I ask.

"I can try," she answers, "but I feel so weak. I have to do it though, don't I? I have to try." Molly pushes with all her strength for ten minutes and then I tell her to stop. It's not working.

"Can you get a pan of hot water, Granny?" I request. The old lady shakes her head in disgust. She's never approved of me. "What now?" she grumbles, but she stomps to the kitchen.

When she returns, I indicate she should set it on the floor by the bed. Then I ask everyone to leave but the sister, Ruth. I'm not sure why I do this. Maybe it's because with the spectators sitting there, it feels like they're watching a movie. As they all shuffle out, Molly whispers. "Thank you for sending them away," she says. "I felt like I was letting everyone down."

"No, these things happen," I reassure her, though in the hundreds of births I've attended, I've never pulled off a cord. "Okay, up you go again. Ruth and I will support you, but I want you to feel the warmth from the water and try to relax your pelvis. Just think about something pleasant, soft, and loose. This time don't try to push. Just let it come."

"Can I have my specs?" Molly asks, and Ruth reaches over to the bedside table and helps her put them on. "Oh, thanks," she says. "I'm blind as a bat without them."

For another ten minutes she squats, but still nothing comes. Finally, exhausted, she begs to get back in bed. "I'm sorry," she says. "I'm so sorry."

When I look at the warm water in the pot, it's now colored red.

The Male Vigor

No, you can't come back in!" I almost shout to the ladies in black as they crowd around the bedroom door. "We're working here. What you *can* do is get Levi. I want Levi!"

"This is not a man's place! You have too many strange ideas," Granny grumbles, but she nods to the youngest woman, who puts her black coat on and trots out the door.

I'm running on empty here, but the first time I helped Molly, her labor had stalled and I had Levi come into the birth room to help her walk. I called his power to help "the male vigor," and somehow he brought the contractions back. Maybe it will work again this time.

Soon, Levi is at the bedroom door. "You okay, wife?" he asks. Molly, exhausted, reaches out her hand. "Can you walk again with me, Levi? Can you hold me and sing?"

The man looks at me as if he thinks his wife is delirious.

"Please?"

"Midwife?" he asks. "She shouldn't be out of bed this soon, should she? She's lost too much blood."

"Sometimes in labor the woman knows what she needs, Levi. It might help," I say as he and I assist her to her feet again. "Come on, Ruth, let's make some more tea."

In the kitchen, I get nothing but horrified looks. "You left her in there, by herself," the old lady hisses. "She could die!"

"No, she's with Levi. Just like before she needs the male vigor." Across the hall we hear singing, and when I peek in the bedroom, I see Levi holding Molly in his arms, swaying back and forth . . . just as in their first birth.

"*Oh, Shenandoah, I long to hear you. Away, you rolling river,*" he sings into Molly's ear, and she hums along with him. Her face has such peace as she rests on his shoulder . . . Then her eyes snap open. "*It's coming!*" she yells, and a ball, half the size of a loaf of bread, plops on the floor.

October 23, 1942

Called to the home of Molly and Levi Klopen-stein for a critical delay in the third stage of labor. A healthy eight-pound baby had been de-livered and six hours later the placenta was still inside. The grandmother of the clan, who serves as the community's midwife, had inadvertently pulled off the cord.

I had Molly drink two cups of broth and uri-nate in a chamber pot, but nothing helped until I called the husband to get her out of bed. As be-fore, he sang to her and they swayed in the kero-sene lamplight, and finally, a large afterbirth was delivered spontaneously, right on the floor. I must remember my concept of the male vigor. Again it has worked. There's something about male and female energy that when combined is more than the energy of either gender alone.

It was impossible to estimate blood loss be-cause most of it happened before I got there, but when I left, the patient appeared to be recovering. Her color was better and she was nursing the baby. I gave her a spoon of Mrs. Potts's medi-cine, just in case.

I was paid nothing, but Levi said he had heard about Dan's pacifism and protest and they were praying for him.

44

October 31, 1942

Haunted House

For Halloween, we went over to Hazel Patch because Bitsy, Willie, and Lou had fixed up one of the abandoned homes as a haunted house. They'd gone to quite an effort. There were dummies made of old clothes stuffed with straw sitting on the porch, and one such scarecrow made up to look like Adolf Hitler was even hanging by the neck from the rafters.

Cobwebs made of string were tangled everywhere, complete with spiders molded from papier-mâché. The only lighting was from flickering candles placed in pumpkins with leering faces. Lou had even carried in an old hand-cranked turntable that played spooky music.

The Millers were there, and the Jacksons and their boys. Milt and Sarah Maddock came with daughter, Sonya, and there was our brood. Susie clung to me as we went from room to room, but the rest of the children ran around scaring one another.

Afterward, everyone went over to Bitsy's for cider, two kinds of cake, and peach pie. We even bobbed for apples, and Mira was thrilled when she got one. While Bitsy and I were cleaning up the refreshments and everyone else was in the living room listening to Lou tell a ghost story, I noticed Bitsy was wearing a ring with a small red stone on her wedding finger.

"What's up?" I indicated the ring with my eyes.

She smiled slowly, gazing at her hand. "A present," she said. "From Lou . . . we haven't decided what to do about marriage, and I'm still hiding the pregnancy, but I can't keep that up much longer. Neither of us can afford to lose our jobs if old man Vipperman objects to our union, and of course we don't want to go to jail."

"Oh, Bitsy. No one around here would put you in jail, certainly not Sheriff Hardman."

"Don't be so innocent, Patience!" she shot out. "Plenty of interracial couples have been sent to prison, or worse. It doesn't take a lawman to ruin someone's life."

AT HOME LATER, missing Daniel and unable to sleep, I snuck downstairs for a piece of the cake that Bitsy sent home with us, wrapped in a piece of newspaper. As I unfolded it, I glanced at an article on the front page of the *Times*. It was a firsthand account by a laborer who witnessed the slaughter of thousands of Jews by the German SS in Ukraine.

According to the article, summarized from a translation in the *New York Times*, the man, a carpenter working on a new bridge, first saw a convoy of military trucks come by filled with men, women, and children.

"I knew at once that they must be Jews," the laborer reported. "Because they were all wearing stars on their sleeves and I'd heard a lot of talk about the Nazis rounding them up. Soon we heard rifle shots and we ran in that direction. The people who'd been forced off the trucks were being ordered to undress by an SS man who carried a whip and flogged them like dogs. They had to put their clothes in piles, shoes here, coats there, belts, shirts, and pants.

"Without weeping or trying to escape, the people stood in family groups. They kissed each other, said farewell, and waited for another SS man with a clipboard, who stood near the pit, to call their name.

"I watched as one family of eight were herded that way. An old grandma with thin white hair was holding a one-year-old child in her arms and singing to it. The child was cooing with delight and the parents were looking on with tears in their eyes. All were shot in the head and thrown into the pit within minutes.

"When I looked down, I saw there were hundreds of the naked dead and dying Jews in the hole. Some were still moving."

After rereading the article, I sat at the kitchen table, tears running down my face, and could no longer think of eating carrot cake. Holding the noise of my sobs back with the back of my hand, so as not to wake the children, I cried for the grandmother and the parents and the little child who didn't know what was happening. I cried for all of those families and I cried for our family too.

There are no Nazi SS men here with a whip ordering me to strip on the edge of a mass grave in a gloomy European forest, but I stand on the edge of my own darkness, and my black anger at Daniel returns.

I've tried to understand, tried to be sympathetic, but was I only lying to myself about my feelings? Tonight a bond between us rips loose . . . not because he left me, but because he can't see the enemy threatens all human decency. Hitler and the Nazis have got to be stopped, and where is my husband in this struggle against them? Self-indulgently sitting in jail with his pet Ronald, singing "I'll Fly Away" with his jailbird friends?

Before bed, I take off my wedding band.

November 7, 1942

Dearest Patience,

I haven't heard from you in weeks and this makes me sad. I also wonder if you're sick or something is wrong and curse myself if my choice to go to prison is harder on you than I imagined.

Please write to me and tell me you are okay. Or if you aren't okay, tell me what you need and I will try to get someone to come help you.

With love and concern,
Daniel

45

It's Just the War

I keep Dan's last letter in the top drawer with the others. I should write to him, but I don't know what to say. I tried to be the good, understanding wife, tried to be supportive, but my love has curdled like cow's milk left out on the counter.

When I try to recall our passion for each other, Hitler stands between us, shoving women and babies into a pit. It's a vision I can't get over, the insane megalomaniac, dressed in a brown uniform with a swastika embroidered on his red armband, his black hair slicked over his balding head, and his ridiculous little mustache. He's a clown, but an evil one.

Then the phone rings. "Hello," I answer.

"Patience, what the hell is going on? It's Daniel."

"I thought you couldn't use a telephone in prison."

"I never made the one call every inmate is allowed at the beginning of incarceration. Norm, the guard, set me up. What's going on?" he demands again.

"What do you mean?"

"Patience . . . come clean."

"It's just the war." I evade the question.

"Any particular aspect?" he asks with sarcasm . . . "Or just general destruction and death . . . Patience, you're hurting me," he says more softly.

"I'm hurting too."

"Well?"

"I can't talk about it."

"Patience! This isn't like you. Come see me. Please. I need you."

There's a voice in the background. "Time's up, Hester," a man shouts.

"Okay. Okay. I'll come on the next visiting day."

"That's tomorrow."

"I know. I'll come."

November 15, 1942

Butchers

Morning dawns clear and cold with a streak of red along the eastern sky, a good day for travel. I get up before light and, with Danny's help, feed and water the stock and chickens, then feed the kids, bundle them up, and take them to school in Hazel Patch an hour early. Mrs. Miller kindly agrees to feed them both their noon and evening meal.

As I drive through Uniontown, Pennsylvania, on Route 43 and then across the old National Highway and down the Ohio River to Moundsville, West Virginia, I rehearse what I might say to Dan.

"I'm not ready for a divorce, but I no longer love you"? *No, that won't do.*

How about "Our differences about the war are too divergent and I no longer respect you"? *Closer to the truth,* but so cold. Or the worst idea yet . . . "Sorry, I can't be lovers with a spineless pacifist."

Oh, hell! What am I going to do, just live with Dan as a roommate, no longer man and wife, until the children grow up?

By the time I get to Moundsville, clouds have swept in and my mood is just as black. I pass through security, toss a paper bag with some clean underwear and Daniel's harmonica to the guard, and enter the visitors' room, where Dan's sitting at the familiar back table. He must sense my presence because before I'm even halfway across the cold concrete room, he looks up.

"Visitor for Daniel Hester," says a voice from the loudspeaker. Dan smiles.

"I wasn't sure you'd come. How is everything?"

"Fine," I lie. "I brought you your harmonica. The kids are being good. The cows and horses are healthy," I rattle on, fearing the silence if I shut my trap.

"We've had a few vet calls, but for the most part, I refer them to Dr. Swanson in Torrington. I don't know if the farmers and pet owners ever actually go see him or if Dr. Swanson will drive out to attend the sick animals . . .

but so far no one's complained." The whole time I'm talking I don't meet Dan's gray eyes.

"Patience?"

"Yeah?"

"What's wrong?"

None of my rehearsed speeches seem worthy of this man
with whom I share so much, so I just start with the story
about the Jews. "You *know* I've tried to understand and accept your point of view about the war . . . but I just see things
so differently, and it hurts me. I recently read a firsthand
account in the *Liberty Times* about the Nazis killing one
thousand Jews in a day in Ukraine, and it touched me deeply.

"There was a baby in the story and a grandmother.
They were stripped naked and had to stand in the cold at
the edge of a pit where other dead Jews had already been
tossed like someone's garbage. Naked in the cold! Just so
the Nazis could have their clothes! They were waiting for
their names to be called, waiting for their turn to be shot in
the head. The grandmother was singing to the baby, who
laughed and giggled while everyone else, knowing his fate,
wept silently. . . . Can you picture it? The grandmother and
the baby? It was so human and touching and brought the
war home.

"These Germans are butchers, Dan. Someone has to
stop them, and I don't know why the man I love doesn't
see that. It's like you and I are trapped in quicksand, with
only our heads sticking out, each looking the other way." I
stop there, but his only answer is his foot pressing against
my ankle and I jerk my foot away.

We have come to a place where even touch cannot heal.

WHEN I RETURN to the Olds in the prison parking lot, the low gray clouds have started to cry, and I'm crying too. What's the point in these visits? I'm talking to a stranger.

To save time getting home, I decide to try a shortcut Lou Cross told me about, but as I drive up Hogback Mountain, the rain turns to sleet, a wind buffets the auto, and the roads turn to ice. I stop the Olds in the middle of the two-lane and take a deep breath. On my side the steep mountain drops off a cliff. This may be one of the dumbest things I've done, but there's nowhere to turn around and I can't stop now. I have to get home.

Putting the car in low gear, I start off again at ten miles an hour. At this rate, I'll get to the Hope River by midnight. The wind whirls around me and a branch hits the windshield. Twice I slip sideways and finally near the top of the ridge, fighting for control, I come to a stop in a water-filled ditch.

For a moment I lay my forehead on the steering wheel. I'm uninjured but shaking, and after I rest, I decide that I should check in the back for tire chains. It's unlikely, since Dan went to prison in sunny September and he usually takes care of such things, but I tie my scarf under my chin, pull on my gloves, and push open the door.

That's when I feel the strength of the wind and cold rain. It wraps my skirt around my legs and I almost fall over, but little by little, I work my way to the rear, where I fight open the trunk and find there are no chains, not even a shovel. I'm just about to burst into tears when I feel something useful in the back corner—an old blanket—and for that I am grateful.

Hoping someone will come along, I get back in the car and wrap the wool cover around me. I have only a quarter tank of gas, so to conserve it, I turn the engine and heater on and off again. For hours I wait. Outside, the sleet turns to snow and the wind howls.

Holding Mrs. Kelly's pocket watch up in the dim dashboard lights I see that it's now nine o'clock; the Millers in Hazel Patch must be worried. For a minute, I drop my head back on the car seat, close my eyes, and start to drift off. *No you don't, Patience!* I pat my cheeks and bite down on my lip. I must stay alert for any sound of an auto passing. With the Olds down in the ditch and covered by light snow, any passengers may not see me.

To keep awake, I begin to sing old church songs. "*I'm gonna lay down my sword and shield. Down by the riverside, down by the riverside, down by the riverside . . .*"

That makes me think of Dan again and I choke on my tears. I left him in prison without even a smile. What if I freeze to death on Hogback Mountain? What if that dreadful visit was the last time I see him?

When I look at my watch again, it's midnight. That's when I hear a growling sound, either a large bear or a vehicle struggling up the other side of the mountain. When I roll down the window the low growl seems louder.

The sound dies away and comes back again, clearer and closer. Not likely a bear; *it must be a vehicle!* Over and over the motor roars and then stops. It roars and then stops again, sounding like someone stuck in the mud. I hear a car door slam and then voices, urgent and excited, almost desperate. Finally, I tie my scarf tighter and get out.

"Hello! Help! Over here!" I yell, though it's unlikely anyone can hear me. Then I have an idea. I get back in the Olds and press down on the horn. *Toot. Toot. Toot. BEEEEEP. BEEEEEP. BEEEEEP. Toot. Toot. Toot.* Over and over, I repeat the signal for *save our ship.* SOS. SOS. SOS.

Lioness in Pain

For thirty minutes I wait, warming my hands over the heater. Will the driver or passengers of the other vehicle come over the ridge to reach me, or should I struggle through the sleet, wind, and ice toward them? Finally, I decide I can't risk them turning around and heading back down the mountain.

Holding my pocketbook under my coat, I set out, but it's hard going. In the pitch-black, I can't see my feet and the surface of the road is uneven. My hands and face are stiff with cold. Twice I slip on the ice, fall, and bang my sore knee.

"Hello!" I shout. "Hello!" Over and over, but there's no answer, so I change my tune.

"*Over hill, over dale, we will hit the dusty trail,*" I sing at the top of my lungs like the soldiers on the Fourth of July. "*As those Caissons go rolling along!*"

Just as I'm beginning to think I've hallucinated the whole thing, I'm relieved to see headlights through the trees and the outline of a big truck with one wheel buried to the axle and held up by a good-sized log. When I get closer I see the writing on the side of the truck: DELMONT COAL.

"Hello!" I call. "Can you help me?" I don't know why I ask this. It's clear these travelers are as stuck as I am, but maybe they have food or more blankets. Just as I'm about to tap on the window, a wail rips the night, a woman's voice, screaming, pleading, louder and fiercer than the wind.

"Hey!" I boldly rap on the frost-covered window. "Hello in there! Is someone in trouble?" *It sounds like a woman is being violated.* The scream comes again, a lioness in pain.

"What the hell's going on in there?!" I roar in a manly, gruff voice that I haven't used since the KKK tried to burn down my house on Wild Rose Road. "Open up. This is the law!"

"No! No!" the woman keeps screaming while I pound. Still no response, and I really don't know what to do. I find myself trembling, whether from fear or cold I'm not sure. *Maybe I should get out of here! Maybe they'll come after me next, but I can't do that, leave a fellow sister behind! I was once nearly raped myself.*

Then the cry comes again, but this time an octave lower and I recognize it at once for what it is . . . the sound of imminent birth.

"No. No. No," a woman's voice calls. "It's coming. Something's coming."

46

Felicia

I bang on the door again, this time using my own female voice. "Hello! Hello! I'm not the law, I'm a midwife. I can help!"

Finally the driver rolls down the window and a man says in a strong Italian accent, "Praise Mother Mary! Is it true, a midwife coming from heaven above? We thought we were just hearing the voices of the storm. It's my wife, Felicia. She's in terrible pain. We were trying to get to the hospital in Torrington. Go to the other door and I'll try to let you in. . . . Felicia," I hear the man implore, "please calm yourself. Let me reach over you. God has sent us a midwife."

"It's coming. Oh. Oh. Oh. Martino, I can't move!"

"You must, *mi amore*. You must. Think of the baby. The midwife will help you."

"Let me in. Felicia! *You know me*. I'm Patience Hester, the nurse at the coal-mine disaster. You helped me set up the clinic."

"Uhhhhhg," she groans. "I can't! It's coming. Uhhhhh-hhhhhhhg!"

"Felicia, don't push!" I yell into the wind. "Blow. You'll tear yourself if you push too hard when the head delivers. Get through this contraction, then before the next one, open the door and let me in."

I don't know what I think I'm going to do. I have no sterile gloves or oil to prevent tears. I don't even know if the couple has a blanket to wrap the baby in.

Finally, someone pulls on the handle from inside and the vehicle door cracks open. There's a high running board, but I manage to pull myself up and squeeze in. "My angel," Felicia says to me, tears streaming down her face. "My angel from heaven!"

She's lying crossways on the seat with her back pressed into her husband's chest and her long dark hair is draped over his shoulders. Martino turns the overhead light on and I see that Felicia's face is sweaty and flushed. Then a hard contraction hits her and she digs her feet into me, almost pushing me out the door again.

"Martino," I address the father, glancing at the gas gauge and observing that it's close to empty. "I know you have to conserve fuel, but, just for the next hour, can you really crank the heat? I'll help Felicia get out of her trousers, boots, and heavy wool jacket."

I've delivered a baby outside in a flower garden. I've delivered babies with the mothers squatting on the floor. I've even delivered a baby in a bathtub, but this is the first one in a car, and I try to think how to manage it.

Finally, I maneuver Felicia around to face forward with her heels on the dashboard and I force my bad leg to bend so I can kneel next to the door. I'm not surprised to see a small hairy scalp at the opening.

"Is it alive?" Martino whispers.

"I don't know.... Put your hand on her belly. Sometimes when I tickle the scalp it causes the infant to move." Pulling up Felicia's plaid shirt, I use two fingers to briskly stroke the little head and watch as her abdomen bumps and then rolls. Feeling it, Martino flashes his smile. "Praise God!" he says, lifting his hand, kissing his palm, and breaking into a grin. He's a handsome man with short black hair, large brown eyes, and a roundish face.

"Oh, no. Here it comes again!" Felicia cries. "Uhhhhh-hhhhhhhg!" I watch as the head moves another half inch into this world. "Oh, hold me. Hold me!" Felicia begs.

Her husband puts his arm around her, but I know what she really means. *Hold her bottom that feels like it's about to split open.* So I put my hands around the emerging head like a crown and apply gentle pressure as the head slides out.

I check for a cord. Martino makes the sign of the cross. Then I gently push the head down so the top shoulder comes out, then lift up and next thing you know, I'm holding a wailing baby boy in my arms.

"Sorry, no blanket," Martino says.

Felicia, who has collapsed back onto the seat, reaches out. "My sweet bambino! Come to Mama!" She takes the infant, as confident as an experienced mother, pulls up her shirt and brassiere, and lays the baby on her chest. Martino takes off his jacket and covers them both. He takes off his knit cap too and tenderly covers the infant's wet hair. I still kneel on the floor of the cab, as if praying. The prayer has two words: "Thank you."

A Shift in the Wind

After I'd delivered the placenta and wrapped it in my bandanna, still attached to the baby's cord, we gobbled up all the sandwiches and oranges that Felicia had packed for her husband's lunch at the hospital.

Then, sitting in the dark cab, Martino told me how hard it is working in the mines, being Italian. Some of the men are suspicious and see him as the enemy, since Italy fights with the Germans and Japanese. "I tell you, Miss Patience, with all my heart I am an American!" he declares, and points to a little American flag on the dashboard. Since then we've been sleeping.

A few hours later, Martino wakes me. "Do you hear?" he whispers.

"What?" I shake the net of dreams from my head and look at my pocket watch. You can tell dawn is coming and we've been asleep for hours.

"The wind has shifted. It's not blowing so hard." The new father cranks the steaming driver's-side window down and peeks out. "I hear a motor."

Now I'm awake! Could help really be on the way? When Martino rolls the driver's-side window back up, I roll mine down. Far in the distance I hear the sound of a motor coming up the Hope River side of the mountain. For a moment, I imagine it's Daniel come to the rescue and then I remember that he's locked away in the pokey.

"I'm getting out. If we miss this vehicle, we may be here another day. You stay with Felicia and the baby," I say to Martino, and carefully step onto the edge of what used to be the road and is now a trail of slick mud and ice.

From a mile away, I hear the motor getting louder as it climbs, then I smell the exhaust fumes. Finally, two big headlights shine through the trees. In the dim dawn light, I can even see colors and I recognize the vehicle at once.

It is Mr. Maddock's green John Deere tractor. He comes slowly, his black hat tied on with a blue scarf knit by his wife, Sarah. Standing on the tractor behind him is Lou Cross in a camouflage jumpsuit, and following them is the Liberty ambulance.

They stop when they see us. "Halt!" Lou yells turning back toward the van. "It's Patience!" I'm so flooded with relief I stagger toward them and fall on my face. Mr. Maddock turns off the engine. Then Bitsy hops out of the van with a thermos of hot tea and Sheriff Hardman gets out and bends over me.

"How the hell did you get here in a coal truck?" Hardman asks.

"My Olds is in a ditch on the other side of the ridge, but there's a baby," I point to the truck. "There's a newborn. Get the mother and infant into the ambulance. Everything's fine, but take them to my place. Take them to the Baby Cabin, Bitsy. The placenta is still attached. I didn't want to cut the cord without sterile scissors." After Bitsy takes charge of the mother and infant, she brings me a blanket and gets me into the warm front seat of the old ambulance van that doubles as a funeral wagon.

For a few minutes the men confer about whether to try to tow the two vehicles out, but finally decide to leave both where they are until they can get more help and the roads are clear. Then the tractor leads the way down Hogback Mountain toward the Hope River.

"How long have you been stuck here?" the sheriff asks as we slip and slide down the slick slope.

I hesitate, thinking about the long night. "It must have been about eleven hours."

"You were damn lucky you didn't run out of gas and freeze your butt! Pardon my French." Hardman shakes his head.

"But how did you know where to look for me?"

"Lou guessed," Bitsy answers. "He knew you'd be hurrying to get home and he remembered telling you about the shortcut.

"A baby born in a coal truck! Good thing you were here," Bitsy says.

November 27, 1942

(Delivery Note, written one week later, because I got a bad cold and was very sick.)

A healthy male infant was born to Felicia and Martino Ricci in a Delmont Coal truck on the top of Hogback Mountain. We were both stuck in the mud and ice in separate vehicles, but I walked through the sleet and arrived just as the poor woman was about to give birth.

Fortunately, everything went well. The infant cried right away and was of good size. The mother didn't tear and blood loss was average, about one cup.

At dawn we were rescued and taken to the Baby Cabin, where I used my hanging scale and learned that the infant weighed 6 pounds, 12 ounces. The family stayed for two days.

Present at the delivery, mother, father, and midwife, Patience Hester.

47

November 29, 1942

Prisoners of War

Saturday, for the first time in weeks, the children and I went to town. We were out of lard, and sugar, so I took our ration cards and we all crowded into the Olds. It was a clear day, not a cloud in the sky and on the way we sang, *"The bear went over the mountain. The bear went over the mountain. The bear went over the mountain to see what he could see. And all that he could see. And all that he could see was . . ."*

"What do think he saw, Mira?" I asked.

"Another bear!" she laughed.

"A carnival," Sunny offered.

"An army fighting the Germans," Danny proposed.

"God," Susie surprised us.

"How about you, Mom?" Mira wanted to know. "What do you think the bear saw?"

"I don't know . . . your pa coming home?"

Something changed in me when I ran off the road in the storm and was stuck on Hogback Mountain. I've been so confused, swinging from anger at Dan to fear of being alone, hating him for abandoning us to scorning him for his moral purity, to missing him. . . . Now I don't care if Daniel's a convict, a felon, a draft dodger or a pacifist. I just want Dan home; nothing else matters.

Our first stop is Bittman's Grocery, which is already decorated for Christmas with a wreath on the door. "Stay with me, kids, but don't cause a commotion. If you're good, I'll get you a candy cane."

Inside, my four little ghosts silently follow me. Not one says a peep. B.K. is working behind the counter today and he measures out my allotment of sugar and coffee.

"I'll take five red, white, and blue striped candy canes too." I indicate the patriotic sweets in the glass case. "Oh, and how much are oranges?" The children's eyes get big.

"Ten cents apiece. It's a good price. How about a dozen?" I nod my head. "Did you hear the German prisoners arrived yesterday?" B.K. asks as he bags my fruit and puts my purchases in my cloth satchel.

"Already? I thought the paper said they were coming in December." Danny's standing very close, listening. He's been worried about the POW camp since we first heard about it.

"Yeah, but they arrived early. You should have been here. Two trains pulled into the station and the German soldiers got off and formed into lines like they were in a parade. There must have been two hundred of them. They were wearing sharp wool uniforms too, complete with medals.

"Our fellows, the U.S. military police, all looked about sixteen and were wearing wrinkled camouflage and heavy khaki jackets. On the other hand, our boys had the weapons—carbines and even a Thompson submachine gun.

"The guards marched the Germans down the street to five waiting army trucks. It wasn't until the POWs got in the trucks that I saw a trace of fear in their eyes. They must not tell the captives where they're going or what will happen to them. Of course, the Nazi propaganda machine makes all Americans look like flesh-eating monsters."

"Do you think anyone around here will actually hire prisoners?" I ask. "I'd be afraid."

"Don't know about that. A lady from Elkins was in the store the other day and said some of the Italian POWs at the camp near her home are carpenters and stonemasons. Her father had them build a nice little barn on their farm. She knew the prisoners by name and the family ate their noon meal with them every day.

"I tell you, Patience, there's a need for manpower in Union County. So many fellows have gone to the war. If I had a farm, I'd use them." I raise my eyebrows and Danny turns away in disgust.

Just then the bell on the store door rings and Ida May from Ida May's House of Beauty enters. It's clear something is wrong. Her eyes are red and she wears no makeup. I tell the kids to wait outside and approach her when she's smoking a cigarette back by the pickle barrel.

"Ida May, what's wrong?" I whisper, putting my arm around her.

"It's Gerald, my brother from Beckley . . . His plane

went down. He's a flight engineer in the air force. Now he's missing in action. Annie, my sister-in-law who's staying with me, got a telegram from the head of his squadron."

"Missing in action? That doesn't mean he's dead. He could've just been captured or in hiding from the enemy."

"No . . . it's not definite, but Annie is beside herself. She won't eat. Cries all the time. We haven't told their children. Oh, Patience! What can I do to console her?"

I try to think. What I would do? Hold Annie. Hug her. Pray with them both.

"Here, take these oranges." I shove the sack into her hands. "Maybe Annie's children will like them."

Out in front, my kids wait in the thin winter sunshine. Danny has his hands in his pockets staring at the National Guard soldiers unloading boxcars across the street. The girls are playing hopscotch on the sidewalk squares. "Thank you for being good in there." I pull out the candy canes and pass them around.

"What happened to the oranges?" Danny asks gruffly.

"I gave them to Ida May."

"She could buy her own oranges," my boy snarls. "She has more money than we do."

"I know, but Ida May is so sad. *This is a secret.* I don't want you to tell anyone. Ida's sister-in-law got a telegram this week from Washington that her husband, Ida May's brother, went down with his airplane somewhere over Germany. They haven't told the two little girls about their Pa, and I don't want them to hear about it from some stranger you've told."

"Dead?" my son asks.

"No one knows. He's missing in action."

Danny swallows hard. "That's okay, Mom," he says, taking my hand as we walk back to the car. "Those kids need the oranges more than us."

November 30, 1942

Dear Daniel,

I know you must have heard through Reverend Miller about my adventure getting stuck on Hogback Mountain on my way home from the prison a few weeks ago. I'm sorry I couldn't write, but I've been ill. I doctored myself with lobelia to thin the mucus and kept the fever down with Bayer Aspirin, but I'm still coughing and am surprisingly weak. Mr. Maddock and Sheriff Hardman got the Olds back last week and it wasn't damaged much and still runs.

Being stuck on Hogback Mountain, I thought about you and our differences and I was ashamed of how I left you. Something changed in me that night. Life is too short to be unkind. We are in this together and despite our differences about the war, I want to be together. I need to be together.

I thought of you on Thanksgiving and wondered what you had for dinner. Do prisoners get any special food? Since I was sick, we didn't have much of a celebration. Mrs. Miller brought over a plate of ham and Mr. Maddock brought a mincemeat pie that Sarah made, but I felt so rotten I didn't eat much.

So that's all the news.

I lay my hand on my heart.

Patience

Winter Returns

48

December 1, 1942

Anniversary

ONE YEAR OF WAR! the *Liberty Times* announces above an editorial by Bill Blaze.

> On December 7, 1941, life, as we knew it in the U.S.A. changed. We did not seek war. Americans have never been so reluctant to enter a war, but the devious Japanese pretended to negotiate while they prepared a deadly raid on our people.
>
> Nearly twelve months later the war still stretches before us, a struggle of years, not of months, and we must steel ourselves for losses and sacrifices. Here on the home front we will endure shortages and deprivation, but in the end, we shall triumph. Today, let us remember, in a moment of silence, those who died December 7, 1941, those who have died in combat since then and those who will die in the future fighting to protect our freedom.

On the same page there's another article headlined GAS RATIONING ORDERED BY PRESIDENT ROOSEVELT and an ad for Gold's Dry Goods that says ONLY 21 MORE DAYS UNTIL CHRISTMAS. It features photos of a toy farmstead, a stuffed Donald Duck, and a punching bag on a stand complete with boxing gloves for only three dollars. Our son would love the punching bag and if it would help with his anger, I might consider it.

I go to the money jar in the pantry to assess our finances; $35 and some change. If I spend a total of $5 for Christmas, there won't be enough for the punching bag.

December 3, 1942

Dear Daniel,

As Christmas approaches, I realize this will be the first time we've been apart in twelve years.

I remember the first Christmas we shared before we were married and I'm sure you do too. You came to my house on Wild Rose Road. It was a cold, snowy night and when you knocked I was surprised because I hadn't heard you drive up.

I'm not sure why I let you in. I'd only met you one time, when you came to treat my cow's mastitis. It was the middle of Prohibition and you stood there on Christmas Eve in a trench coat and fedora holding a bottle of booze. Pretty wild of me to let you come in, don't you think? But I'd just been singing carols with my two beagles, Sasha and Emma, and I guess you seemed trust-worthy.

Now for the news. It's not Bitsy Proudfoot anymore. It's Bitsy Cross. She and Lou Cross married! They went to Uniontown yesterday and tied the knot at the courthouse. There are laws against interracial marriage in West Virginia, but not in Pennsylvania. Bitsy says they were repealed in P.A. in 1780. Can you believe that, just a few years after the Revolutionary War?

Anyway, Lou now declares he's one-eighth Negro and he argues that no one can say he isn't. How do they know he doesn't have a great-great-great grandmother who was a slave? So even in West Virginia their union is legal. I congratulated the two wholeheartedly, but still I fear for them. Some people can be so unkind. On Sunday they are having a big party at the schoolhouse in Hazel Patch. It's in the paper and everything.

Now, back to Christmas. I saw a punching bag I'd like to get for Danny, but it's rather dear, three dollars; probably paper dolls for the girls and maybe a few new hair ribbons. What do you need? I'll try to get back to the prison before the holidays and bring some current newspapers and a book. After my accident, Sheriff Hardman insists I not go alone again and I guess he's right, so I'll have to find someone who can spend a whole day accompanying me, maybe Reverend Miller, though he's working part-time at the woolen mill. Maybe Mr. Maddock. I'll see, but he might not want to leave Sarah.

I try not to be sad that you are away and accept my life as it is.

We say our prayers for you every night.

With love,
Patience

December 6, 1942

Celebration

*B*itsy and Lou are officially living together at Hazel Patch now and I guess that's a good thing. Despite Lou's popularity, I'm not sure a mixed couple will be accepted in town, and there are no dwellings left in the colored section on the other side of the tracks in Liberty.

By way of the newspaper, they've invited everyone they know to celebrate. It was a paid advertisement on the back of the *Liberty Times*, complete with a holly border, fancy print, and two turtledoves.

Mr. and Mrs. Lou and Bitsy Cross
Invite all their friends
To celebrate their recent marriage.
Festivities will be held at
The Hazel Patch Schoolhouse,
Salt Lick Road, Liberty, West Virginia.
2 P.M., Sunday, December 13, 1942.
Refreshments and Dancing.
Children welcome.

I am shocked at their boldness and yet also pleased. If there's going to be gossip or objection, might as well get it out in the open. The children are excited and can't wait for the party. I offered to bring three apple pies. Lou will get a case of Pabst Blue Ribbon beer and there will be cider and popcorn.

SUNDAY DAWNS GRAY and cold, not the best day for a get-together, but by noon the sky clears. I'd planned to get to Hazel Patch early to help Bitsy set up, but at the last minute, Susie had to go make a trip to the outhouse and then I lost my keys. Fortunately, after a major search, Sunny found them on the banister of the porch, where I'd left them.

The sun broke through the blanket of gray as we followed the creek toward Hazel Patch. Salt Lick, half frozen, sparkled with ice, and the children sang Christmas songs at the top of their lungs. *"You better watch out. You better not cry. You better not pout. I'm telling you why. Santa Claus is coming to town!"*

"How many more days?" Mira breaks in. At seven she's the youngest and probably the only one that really believes in Santa Claus. Danny is all past that, but he never lets on. Susie and Sunny and I discussed the old guy recently when Mira was outside.

"The girls in Liberty told us that Santa Claus isn't real, that our parents bring the presents. Is that true?" Susie asked.

"What do you think?" I deflected the question.

"I think they're right," Sunny put in. "But I like to pretend."

Susie puts her hand on her hip and gives me a look. "Just admit it. You and Pa buy the presents."

"Okay," I finally say, "Santa Claus is a story, a legend from the old days. I think there actually was a real man like him once who gave presents to children in Europe. Germany or Holland, I think."

"The Germans have Santa too?" Sunny exclaims. "I thought they were bad people."

"Not all of them." I frown, wishing Dan were here to explain.

"Your pa's grandparents were Germans. Mr. Dresher is German. The family that stayed in the Baby Cabin after my car accident on Hogback Mountain, Martino and Felicia, are Italian. They aren't our enemies in this war. I've never met a Japanese person, but I'm sure there are some good ones." By this time we're almost to Hazel Patch and I start the song again.

"*He sees you when you're sleeping. He knows when you're awake. He knows if you've been bad or good, so be good for goodness' sake!*"

Two Left Feet

As we pull up next to the one-room schoolhouse, I compliment the kids on the decorations. Brown and white faces of paper elves, wearing red pointed hats, cut out of construction paper, are taped in the windows, and the small bell tower on top of the white clapboard building is festooned with holly and spruce bows.

"Willie and I did that," my son tells me proudly, pointing to the roof.

"They had to climb ladders," Mira adds.

I'm surprised that there are already ten cars in the lot. Inside, the Reverend and Mrs. Miller, the Jacksons, and the Maddocks greet us, but the big shock is when Opal walks in carrying little Joey. It's like the two are celebrities, at least to Bitsy, Willie, and our brood.

Joey is now one year old, and what a beautiful child he is, with the same brown skin and curly hair as his mother, but eyes that are a startling light gray. And what a smile! Willie carries him around introducing him to everyone as his cousin, and I think some people believe him.

Because of the crowd, I wasn't able to spend as much time with Opal as I would have liked, but her mother, who drove down with her, told me that Opal's father, a porter on the B&O Railroad, got her a job as a teletype operator at the station in Connellsville. She gets fifty-six cents an hour, almost the same as a factory worker, and she's already saving up money to buy her own car.

Grandma Johnson takes care of Joey when Opal's at work, and I could tell she's proud of them both.

LOU CAREFULLY SELECTS a record and puts it on a beautiful new electric portable turntable that he bought Bitsy for a wedding present. He lowers the needle and a new popular song by Bing Crosby comes on: *"I'm dreaming of a white Christmas. Just like the ones I used to know. Where the treetops glisten, and children listen to hear sleigh bells in the snow."*

Bitsy's wearing a calf-length red dress with little pleats down the front and a white lace collar, which goes beautifully with her coffee-and-cream skin. Her new husband has on a white cowboy shirt and a green bolo tie.

Before I can set my pies down and strike up a conversation, the door opens again and I'm surprised to see Bill Blaze, the newsman, come in carrying a camera with a flash reflector on it the size of his head.

What's he doing here? Trying to stir up trouble? Write a big exposé about miscegenation? INTERRACIAL MARRIAGE COMES TO UNION COUNTY!

I try to think how to stop him, but before I have a chance to say anything, Lou heads his way. "Hey, Bill. Nice of you to come! I expect there'll be more people stopping by. You can get some nice photos later, but first how about a beer?" And the two go off as if they're great pals. That's one thing about Lou; he's smart and makes friends with everyone.

I approach Bitsy, who's laying plates and silverware on a long table, and give her a hug. "You look beautiful," I tell her.

"Thanks," Bitsy says, giving me a one-arm hug in return. All the children's desks are pushed up against the wall, sunshine streams through the windows, and the potbelly stove radiates warmth.

"You look nice too," she says, and I glance down at my dress. It's blue with little silver stars and a scoop neck, one of Dan's favorites.

Lou slides across the room and, just like Fred Astaire, swirls Bitsy into his arms. Soon almost everyone's dancing to the romantic music, everyone but Billy Blaze and Patience Hester. "Care to take a spin, ma'am?" Mr. Blaze asks.

I swallow hard. I really don't want to. He's the man who wrote the terrible article about Dan in the paper, but it would ruin the party if I got in a squabble with him.

"Why, thank you, Mr. Blaze, if you can put up with two left feet."

"That's fine. I have two right feet," he quips, as pleasant as anyone. He takes his hat off and carefully lays his camera on a child's wooden desk.

"*I'm dreaming of a white Christmas. With every Christmas card I write*," Bing Crosby sings in his smooth baritone, and Lou Cross and Bull Jackson sing along. "*May your days be merry and bright. And may all your Christmases be white.*"

As Mr. Blaze and I dance, trying not to crunch each other's toes, more cars drive up and people from Liberty spill into the room. Judge Wade and his wife arrive with Sheriff Hardman. Next come B.K. Bittman, Lilly, and their two youngsters, followed by the lawyer Mr. Linkous and his wife and five children.

"Can I talk to you, Mrs. Hester?" Billy says.

"It's hard to dance and talk." I excuse myself. This is a man I consider as poisonous as the copperhead that bit Willie.

"Could we sit in the corner then?" He takes my arm and leads me to some chairs away from the crowd. There's no getting out of it. I'll sit with him for a few minutes, but if he's scheming for an interview with the "draft dodger's widow," it's not going to happen.

"I want to apologize," he says, looking right at me.

"For what?" I ask, raising my chin and narrowing my eyes, a defensive posture.

"For everything. When I came to Liberty, I was just a cub reporter and when the editor enlisted in the air force, I became the editor-in-chief and the *only* reporter. I was so afraid I'd fail that I wrote stories I shouldn't have. Sometimes I even invented the details. . . .

"For some reason, your family kept popping up. There was that nasty little piece about your daughter at last year's school Christmas program."

"I'd forgotten about that," I say stiffly, but the corner of my mouth curls up. "Mira is a piece of work, isn't she?" But Billy Blaze doesn't smile. He's on a mission, and he wants to get something out.

"Then there was my report on the fight at the Red Cross auction and square dance. I was actually *in* the fight, but I didn't mention that. I made it seem like your husband started it, and I knew that wasn't true. Maybe I hated your family because you seemed so happy and I had no one. Never had. I grew up in an orphanage in Charleston.

"Anyway, the worst was the last article about Daniel's public arrest. When you see him, will you tell him I deeply regret every word I wrote? I was at his sentencing in Torrington. I don't know if you saw me. I sat in back copying down every word he said, and I'm going to publish his statement before Christmas." He stops, brushes his hair from his forehead, and I swear there are tears in his eyes.

I swallow hard and place my hand over his. "Thank you," I say. "It never entered my mind that you were trying so hard to write sensational headlines and stories because you were afraid you'd fail. I just thought you were trying to be a big shot . . . and for the record I liked a lot of your articles; the one about the Jews and the piece about saving the tin cans. We save all our cans now. And your article about the anniversary of the war . . .

"One more thing . . . My family isn't always happy. I don't agree with my husband about the war, and there's been great conflict between us. I have one angry son and a daughter with anxiety problems. We have hardly any money, and here's something else. I grew up in an orphanage too."

A Toast

Hello, Patience," a voice behind me says. It's Lilly Bittman, led by her husband. She's carrying a tin of fruitcake and wearing a long red-and-blue polka-dot dress.

B.K. drops her off and leaves to say hello to the hosts, and Lilly and I go to the refreshment table, where Lilly tips the tin over on a Christmas plate and peels off the wax paper with quick, nimble fingers.

"Is it true?" she whispers.

"What?"

"Is it true that Mr. Cross is a Negro?"

"Yes."

"I didn't know. Not that it matters to us; our store is open to everyone. B.K. says Lou doesn't look Negro. Being blind, I can't tell, of course. . . ."

Mrs. Wade steps forward and Lilly tightens her mouth. The older lady is all dressed up, as if going to church, in a pale gray suit with little stars and stripes on the lapel. Mrs. Wade is Lilly's mother and though they love each other, they don't always agree.

"Oh, you brought a fruitcake," the woman complains. "I did too. You should have told me. . . . Doesn't Bitsy look darling. What a surprise to see them married, though." She looks at me. "Did you know?"

"I knew they were sweethearts."

"But did you know Mr. Cross was a Negro?"

"I suspected, yes, but one doesn't ask." That should shut her up.

"Well, it will be nice for her ward to have a father. Mr. Cross is a manly man, and a boy needs that, don't you think?" Here I almost laugh. She's so obviously digging for gossip.

A new recording starts up. Sheriff Hardman stands over by the door alone, so I step over to talk to him.

"Mrs. Hester," the sheriff says formally, and nods without smiling. "How are you getting on? No more solo excursions over the mountains, I hope."

"No, Sheriff, but if the weather holds, I would like to see Daniel one more time before Christmas." We both look out the window at the clear sky and sunshine.

"I'd drive you, but I'm tied up with the POW camp. The town council wants me to escort the prisoners each time they come through Liberty, even though they have their own military guard."

"How's that going? Have they established a secure prison at White Rock?"

"The barbed wire is up, but I'll be honest, it wouldn't take a genius to get out of that place. The good news is that out of around three hundred thousand POWs in the whole U.S.A. there have been only a few escapees, and the prisoners were caught right away. The young Germans know they have it good here. They're off the battlefield, have a full belly, have a warm bed and clothes on their back. Let's face it, even if they could get away, where would they go? Unless a man could speak English he'd be hard pressed to find a job."

"Has anyone local hired the prisoners to work on their farms?"

"Only Mr. Dresher, so far, because he speaks German. . . . It's a real problem. They have no interpreters at the camp and only a couple of the POWs speak broken English. Dresher's getting a bargain though. Forty-five cents an hour to repair his sheds, clean out the cow barn, and re-roof his house. . . . There aren't any local laborers left in the county, and many of the Germans were skilled craftsmen or farmers before the war."

Just then, the music stops and Lou Cross taps on a glass to get our attention. He beckons Bitsy over and puts his arm around her. "I know most people in town thought I was a confirmed bachelor, but Bitsy changed all that. We were married in Uniontown a week ago and we want to thank you for coming to celebrate with us."

"Hear, hear!" a few fellows shout.

"Hold it!" Mr. Blaze orders, snapping a picture with his flash. A nice shot, I think, and I hope Bitsy gets a copy.

"I'd like to propose a toast," Mr. Linkous announces, holding up his beer. "Love is friendship set to music. May your love last forever." Some people clap.

Then Mr. Vipperman, owner of the woolen mill, steps forward and raises his paper cup of cider. "I'm an old man, almost eighty, and Lou Cross is my right-hand man at the woolen mill. When he came to me and announced he intended to marry Bitsy Proudfoot, I was surprised, she being colored and all.

"Lou wasn't concerned about that. He just wanted to be sure they'd both still have jobs. People like Lou and Bitsy don't come around every day, people you can count on. I told him of course they'd both have work at the mill as long as they wanted. We need good, committed employees in these times of war. It doesn't matter to me if they're red, yellow, white, or brown. Congratulations!" Blaze snaps more photos. He's here. He's there. He's everywhere.

Murmurs of approval run through the crowd, though I have to remember, this is a gathering of friends. There are still many people who will oppose a mixed marriage, even if Lou says he's *colored*. The sheriff gives me a nudge. "What?" I turn to him.

"Your turn."

Oh dear! A toast! I haven't prepared anything! Hardman pushes me out into the middle of the room and I almost trip forward in my pumps. "I'd like to speak," I say, sounding more confident than I feel.

"Bitsy has been my friend for many years, almost my sister. Though we lost touch for a while, when she was in Paris, I'm so glad she's returned. Daniel and I welcomed her and her adopted son, Willie, into our home and now we count Lou as one of our friends. I remember a proverb I read somewhere: *Keep your face always toward the sun, and shadows will fall behind you.* Congratulations Mr. and Mrs. Cross!"

More people clap and then the music begins again. Bitsy comes over and gives me a hug. "Good speech," she says. "But did you have to include the part about Paris?"

I grin and lift my cup of cider. "It added a touch of class, don't you think?"

49

December 6, 1942

White Hurricane

Suddenly the one-room schoolhouse darkens as if someone has blown out the sun, and a moment later a wind roars down the hollow and crashes against the west wall.

Mrs. Wade jumps out of her chair and Susie runs to me. "What is it, Ma?"

"It's only a storm, kids, but I think we should be going."

"Really?" says Bitsy, looking disappointed. "The party's just starting."

I look out the window again. Already, snow scours the side of the building, little hard flakes blowing in sideways. The wind squeals in the stovepipe and rattles the windows.

"You only have to go a few steps to your house. I have to go a few miles. Sorry, Bitsy. It was a lovely celebration, but I don't want to get stuck in a storm again, especially not with four children."

"It will probably blow over by the time you get home, but go if you have to," my friend says, giving me another hug.

When we shuffle out into the entryway, we're chilled before we even get our coats on. When we open the door, the storm has already dumped three inches of white.

"Now, hold on to my hand, Mira and Susie. Sunny, you hold on to Danny. This wind will really surprise you."

Thirty feet away from the schoolhouse we're alone in the whirling white. When I look back there's nothing to see, not even the lights from the windows. At first I can't find the Olds. Finally Danny calls, "Over here!"

We stagger that way and he pulls the passenger door open, but the wind blows it shut again. Twice he has to do this before he can slip in. Gathering the girls on the driver's side, where the wind's not so strong, I struggle them in.

AN HOUR LATER, it's as dark as night and we almost miss our farm. "The mailbox!" Danny shouts, and I'm still shaking as we pull in the drive.

The noise of the snow, blinding, smothering, scratching, seems to last forever, but finally we stagger up on the farmhouse porch, each grab an armload of wood, and make it into the kitchen.

"The fire is out in both stoves. I'll have to restart it," I say, gathering kindling from the wood box. "Girls, pull down the curtains and shades like we're having an air-raid drill. Danny, bring in some more wood. Then we can sit around the kitchen table and get warm. It's like an icebox in here."

Finally, I have both stoves roaring and we stand around waiting for the teapot to boil. "Can we have chamomile with honey in it?" Sunny wants to know.

"Yes, and I have a surprise. I didn't just make three apple pies for the party. I made four, and one is back in the oven getting warm. Pie and milk for dinner!"

Despite the roaring fires, the house is still so cold we don't want to take our coats off and I begin to think maybe we should close off the second floor and sleep in the living room. The trouble is, it means bringing down mattresses and bedding.

Finally, I decide it's the best thing to do, so I assign the girls to carry down everyone's quilts, sheets, and pajamas and then Danny and I push two double mattresses down the stairs. All in all, it takes less than ten minutes, and after I close the door to the upstairs, we begin to warm up.

"Can we listen to the radio?" Mira asks after we've eaten our supper.

"Sure, if you can get a station."

Danny fiddles with the dial. At first there's just static, but finally WWVA out of Wheeling comes in. "*Praise the Lord and pass the ammunition. Praise the Lord and pass the ammunition. Praise the Lord and pass the ammunition*," someone sings. "*And we'll all stay free!*"

Then a newscaster breaks in: "*We bring you this breaking news. . . . A major storm continues to sweep over the Allegheny mountain range. Roads are becoming impassible, with the National Highway already closed. The heaviest snow and worst blizzard conditions will stretch from*

Union County, West Virginia, as far as Garrett County, Maryland, and the Shenandoah Valley in Virginia. Citizens are urged to stay home until the roads are clear.

"*I repeat, this is a major, dangerous storm, a white hurricane. We haven't seen anything like this for years! All you out in the mountains, we're praying for you, and those servicemen overseas, we're praying for you too. God bless America.*"

Outside, the storm howls like a pack of wild dogs at the windows. Scratches at the doors. *Howl, damn you,* I think. *We're all safe in this sturdy stone farmhouse. You can go mad if you want to, but you can't get us. You can't get us!*

It isn't until morning that I discover half the barn roof is gone.

50

December 9, 1942

Dear Patience,

It was nice talking on the phone last night. I've been so worried, and it was kind of the warden to give all the men with families who live in the path of the white hurricane a chance to call home.

Even here in prison we felt the storm. The stone walls are stout, but the barred glass windows are old and let in the wind. Of course, there's no provision for extra blankets when snow covers the ground; that would be too expensive.

I have no way of knowing for sure what the temperature was in the cells, but there was ice on my water bucket in the morning. The infirmary has been busy. So many of the men caught colds that night.

It grieves me to hear of the big hole in the barn roof following the hurricane and of all your difficulties. If only there was some way I could get home for a few days, I could get the work done. I'm sure lumber and labor would wipe out what we have in the tin box. I wonder if there's something we could sell to get the money for the barn roof. Maybe a cow?

Again, I'm so sorry to cause you this trouble. You don't deserve it. You've always been the kindest, most loving, bravest partner a man could have.

Your husband,
Daniel

51

December 10, 1942

Another Kind of Hero

*B*itsy and Lou came over on Sunday to survey the damage to the barn. (Everyone at Hazel Patch escaped scot-free because the community is located in a wide hollow where the wind didn't get to them.) They were ready to climb on the roof right then, but I explained I didn't have the money for lumber and tin.

When they left, they gave me a copy of *Little House in the Big Woods* that Mrs. Miller sent over. She has closed the school for winter break and the kids and I plan to read a chapter each night. Lou also handed me a folded-up copy of the *Liberty Times*.

ANOTHER KIND OF HERO the headline reads, BY WILLIAM BLAZE.

> *Today, the whole world is locked in deadly struggle as the nations advance upon each other in a worldwide war. In the midst of this bloody conflict, raging and roaring over all*

the earth, men fight for our freedom and we hail them as heroes.

But miles from Union County, in the Moundsville State Penitentiary, there's another kind of hero, a man who, because he refuses to participate in war, has been locked in prison. Some have called him a draft dodger. Even this reporter has used those harsh words, but recently I stood in the courtroom as he was sentenced for two years of hard time, and I began to think differently.

Dr. Hester is a veteran of the first world war. He fought in the Great War that was to end all wars, yet here we are less than twenty years later, fighting and killing again. He is only one small voice, but it takes courage to speak out when everyone thinks differently.

I was so impressed by the pacifist's testimony to the court a few weeks ago that I vowed I would publish it. We may not agree with Daniel Hester, but we must admire his courage. . . .

Under a photo of my husband, standing tall and proud in the courtroom, Mr. Blaze has printed Dan's statement, word for word.

I wipe my eyes as I look at my husband's brave face, and this time I leave the newspaper on the table, for Danny and all to see.

The kitchen door opens, something is pulled across the floor, and then . . . "Mom!" Sunny yells. "Come down here, can you!" Then laughter.

I put my journal under the mattress and limp down the stairs.

"Surprise!" they all yell, pointing to a six-foot spruce in a bucket in the corner by the parlor window.

After supper, I get down the decorations and we put up the lights. I try to act cheery, I guess we all do, but finally Mira begins to cry and then we all sit down and admit how much we miss Daniel.

"I can't believe he won't be here for Christmas," Sunny says. "Papa is always here and he gets such fun presents, like the pony last year."

"The warden should let him out for one day!" Danny grumbles. "It's not like he's a murderer or anything. He just wants to make the world better."

Here I wipe away my own tears. It's the first positive thing I've heard Danny say about his father in a long time.

"Maybe if we all wrote the warden a letter and begged . . ." Susie thinks out loud. "Can we, Mama?"

"I guess so. What could it hurt?"

So that's what we did. The four kids wrote the letter, with Susie as scribe because she has the best penmanship, and I put it in the mailbox this morning.

December 10, 1942

Dear Warden,

We miss our pa. His name is Daniel Hester. Can you please let him come home for one day for Christmas? He didn't do anything bad, like rob or kill. He is a good man and only wants to make the world better. Also, our mother is having a hard time after the storm. Many things need to be fixed, like the roof on the barn that blew away in the white hurricane and we don't have much money. If you are a father maybe you can understand. We try to be cheerful but our hearts are sore.

Thank you and have a Merry Christmas.

Danny, Sunny, Susie, and Mira Hester

December 14, 1942

A Gift in Time

"Hello," I answer the phone in the kitchen.

"Is this Mrs. Hester?" a woman's voice says. "Mrs. Stone here. I mean Mrs. Roote; I can't get used to my new name."

"Mrs. Roote! Well, congratulations. I heard the news about your marriage. Is Mr. Roote better?"

"Yes, honey. He's doing right well, but I have a favor to ask you."

There's a pause . . . "You know we'd do anything we could . . ."

"Well, this is a big one. We want to rent your little house on Wild Rose Road. We'll pay whatever you need and I'll pay to have a bathroom put in by those POW boys. Sheriff Hardman says a few of them are pretty handy carpenters. Mr. Roote is improving, but he still drags his foot and I don't think he'd do well with only an outhouse."

"But I don't understand. You and Mr. Roote have big farms and nice homes on the other side of the county that already have indoor plumbing."

"We sold out last week, honey. It's just too hard to keep up with everything. Charley's stroke brought us up short, made us think about life. We won't be here too many more years and we don't want to spend our time mending fences and cutting hay.

"Also, where we live now we're so far out of town that during the white hurricane we realized if something happened we have no one to call on. We don't expect you to adopt us, but we'd like to live near people who are friends. What do you think? Would two hundred dollars a month be enough?"

Two hundred dollars a month! I almost choke. Since the Depression we'd been renting the house to Becky and Isaac for ten dollars a month.

"I wouldn't think of it . . . I mean, yes you can rent and yes you can have a bathroom put in, but not for two hundred dollars a month. That's way too much."

"We'd want to move in before Christmas and to use the barn and the pasture too and bring a few livestock. Charley thought two hundred was fair."

"How about one hundred a month." *I still can't believe it!*

"Certainly not. Houses in town are going for two hundred. I won't go any lower than one fifty."

And that's how it happened. I can now afford to buy Christmas presents!

"CHILDREN," I SAY the next morning, "I have a few errands to do in town and I want to go alone."

"Are you Christmas shopping?" Susie wants to know.

"I'm not telling." I smile. "But here's something you can do while I'm gone. I already told you that Mr. and Mrs. Roote are going to move into the house with the blue door. I asked them if they would like help getting settled and they said yes. Mr. Roote offered to pay you."

"Hot-diggity!" Danny shouts. "I mean, I would anyway, but money is nice."

"The thing is," I go on, "there are German prisoners already at the cottage, painting and making an indoor bathroom out on the back porch. Sheriff Hardman says they're harmless, but I don't want you talking to them. You stay by Mrs. Roote and carry her boxes. Willie is coming over too."

"Do we girls have to go?" asks Sunny. "It will be boring."

"No, you girls can stay here." I rethink my plan. *Do I really want my little princesses around the horrible Nazis?*

"But then we can't get any money!" Mira complains.

"I'll write down some jobs for you and pay you each a dime if you do them well."

Now everyone smiles.

AT GOLD'S DRY GOODS, I run into Ada Mullins with her baby, a dark-haired cherub bundled up for the winter in a green woolen snowsuit. "Can I hold him?" I ask. "I haven't seen you for months. How's Ollie?" I remember the handsome young man with the *Victory* tattoo who was inducted into the army the day after his child was born.

"I think he's fine," she says in her sweet childish falsetto. "He's not allowed to say where he is, but I get a letter about once a week. It's been two weeks this time." She shows me a photo of her husband, handsome in his uniform, proud and brave, and I tell her he's probably just too busy to write, then when she leaves I wander the aisles of the dry goods store until I locate the punching bag and gloves for Danny.

"How you doing out there, Mrs. Hester?" says Mr. Gold. "You fare okay in the storm? It's been a heck of a winter and people say it will get worse."

"We're holding on, but the wind blew the back half of the barn roof off. I've moved the cows and horses up front. We can make do until I can arrange a few men to come out."

"You mean the POWs?" he asks.

"No, I wouldn't do that. . . . Have you heard much about them?"

"Well . . ." He draws out the word. "I said before I wouldn't trust them, but several of my customers have used them for cleaning stables and constructing rock walls. Haven't heard of any problems."

"I know what you mean, about not trusting them. I've thought of the Germans as the enemy for so long, I wouldn't be comfortable around them. Are there any local men you'd recommend? Dan used to take care of this sort of thing."

Here he screws up his face and rolls his eyes to the ceiling. "Not really, so many fellows have gone to war."

In the end, in addition to the punching bag, I get the girls each a puzzle and a book of paper dolls and then a large set of Lincoln Logs for the whole family. I also pick up some Tootsie Roll Pops for their stockings and two used books for Dan to read in his lonely cell. *Brave New World* by Aldous Huxley and *The Good Earth* by Pearl S. Buck.

"Nice choices," Mr. Gold said. "Pearl Buck is from West Virginia, you know, down around Hillsboro, south of here. She was the first woman to win the Pulitzer Prize."

"Really! Maybe I better read her book myself before I take it to my husband."

"How *is* Mr. Hester, anyway? They treating him okay? Take the books for free; tell him they're a Christmas present from Mr. Gold."

"Well, thanks. At a dime apiece I should get a few more. They'd be nice gifts. Can I buy some red and green wrapping paper too?"

Now I'm getting carried away, but I can't help it. I will soon have money from Mr. and Mrs. Roote and the books are such a bargain. In the end I purchase one each for Lou, Bitsy, and Willie, and several for the kids, all different reading levels.

As I pay for my purchases I make note of a two-quart canning jar on the counter. It's decorated in red, white, and blue, and on the side there's a photo of a woman with two small children in her lap. "I gave a man!" the caption says. "What can you give to help win the war?"

Her eyes look right at me and I believe in her pain; it's not propaganda. When Mr. Gold gives me my change, I put the three quarters in the jar and then I open my pocketbook and put in three more.

Parade

My next stop is Bittman's, but as I enter the store Lilly pushes past me feeling for the door, "Here they come!" she cries, and Little B.K. follows. When I turn, I see in the distance a parade of men marching, four abreast, through the town. They're all dressed in heavy blue pants and jean jackets with "POW" stenciled on the front. Dark blue knit caps cover their heads. No shiny medals and polished boots now.

"*Eins, zwei, drei, vier! Eins, zwei, drei, vier!*" one of the soldiers calls in a clipped military style. "*Eins, zwei, drei, vier!*" which I take to mean "One, two, three, four!" Their eyes are fixed on the road ahead, and two U.S. soldiers guard them with guns.

"It's the Germans," Lilly whispers, as if I wouldn't guess. Behind the small battalion Sheriff Hardman follows in his squad car, lights flashing, siren off.

"Sometimes they sing."

"Sing what?"

"We don't know. No one speaks German," Lilly tells me. "It sounds like a marching song. They're real good."

"Where are they going?" I ask.

"To small farms on the edge of town that lack manpower because the father or sons have gone off to war. The Wallaces have them cutting and stacking firewood at their place because this time of year there isn't much farming. They're using them at Vipperman's Woolen Mill too. People who live in town are jealous. They'd like to get a hired hand for 45 cents an hour, but the program is just for agriculture or manufacturing."

"Mrs. Roote has two carpenters from the prison out on my farm on Wild Rose Road right now, building an indoor bathroom for her new husband, Charley. She and Mr. Roote sold their big places and rented my little house and ten acres. She said two soldiers in an army truck brought the men out early this morning. The guards only spoke about three words in German, but when Mr. Roote drew a picture of what they wanted done, the POWs got right to work."

We watch until the prisoners and Sheriff Hardman cross the stone bridge over the Hope, then all the German soldiers break into song.

The tune is familiar, something Dan bangs out on the piano, but I can only catch one word "Erika," which is repeated at the end of each stanza and that makes me wonder . . . could *Erika* represent the men's sweethearts at home? Funny, to think of these hardened Nazis having sweethearts just like regular Joes.

In the grocery store, I pick up some coffee with my ration stamps then stop at the newspaper rack. WV PILOT TAKES DOWN FOUR NAZI PLANES read the headlines. "I'll take one,"

I say, and plunk down a dime. Back in the Olds, I scan the pages for an article about Bitsy and Lou's celebration and find a whole page with photos.

The article is titled LOCAL COUPLE CELEBRATE MATRIMONY and it features pictures of people dancing and giving toasts. There's a cute one of Lilly serving cake and one of Lou kissing Bitsy. There's even a photo of me giving my short toast.

"Lou Cross, prominent local resident and manager of the Vipperman Woolen Mill, and Bitsy Proudfoot, hosted a lavish celebration of their recent marriage at the school-house in Hazel Patch," the story says. There is no mention of the racial issue.

"Present at the event were Judge Wade and Mrs. Wade, Mr. and Mrs. Linkous, Sheriff Bill Hardman, Mrs. Patience Hester, Louis Tinkshell, Marvin Zipperman, Mr. and Mrs. Stenger, Ida May Cross and her sister-in-law Annie, the Reverend Miller and Mrs. Miller, Mr. and Mrs. Jackson . . ." and on and on. As is typical of small-town newspapers, Billy drops every name he can think of, because each name in print means another few papers sold to the families.

Before I leave Liberty I make a last stop at the Farmers' Lumber and Supply Store, to get an estimate of what the materials will cost to repair the barn roof.

I'm happy that the place isn't busy. In the parking lot, there's only a lumber truck unloading timbers and a pickup that says Delmont Coal.

"Hi, Sadie," I call as I enter the store. The short, stocky woman in coveralls and a plaid flannel shirt looks up from the counter, where she's thumbing through a tractor catalogue.

"Howdy, Patience. We sure do miss having the vet around. I heard Junior Wilson lost a calf the other day. Dr. Hester could have saved it. . . . What can I do you for?"

"I just need to price some lumber. Part of our barn roof blew off in the white hurricane."

"Do you know what you'll need?" I hand her my lists of joists, one-by-eights, and tin roofing sheets and she adds up the numbers. "That would be about sixty-seven dollars. You pay cash on delivery but it may not be until after Christmas. The fellows that used to work in the lumber yard and do deliveries for me have all gone to war."

52

We Greet You as a Friend

The first thing I see when I go up Wild Rose Road is Willie and Danny on the front porch of the Rootes' new home drinking hot chocolate. They're sitting with the POWs laughing it up, as friendly as anything, with *the enemy.*

At first I am furious. I told Danny to stay away from those men, but when I approach, the POWs jump up and salute me. "Madame," they say in broken English. "We greet you as a friend."

Danny grins a lopsided grin just like his pa's. "We taught them some English, Mom. Isn't that a gas?"

Before I can reprimand him, Mr. Roote comes to the door. "Well, look who the cat drug in! Did you see our new auto? Traded our extra one in. No new cars are available since all the auto builders have switched to making jeeps and tanks." He indicates a shiny red auto parked on the side. "It's a 1940 Chevy, but doesn't have a scratch on it. Come on in and see what the German boys have done."

I am astounded. All the walls downstairs have been given a clean coat of white paint. Mrs. Roote has installed a wine-colored carpet, an almost-new blue sofa, and two matching chairs. There are shiny antique tables and pictures on the walls. In the kitchen the POWs have built a wall of shelves for Mrs. Stone's collection of white flowered cookie jars, and on the back porch is the almost finished new bathroom, complete with a claw-foot tub, a commode, and a small sink.

"They did this all in one day?"

"Well, two days," says Mrs. Roote, "Eckhart and Leopold are great workers. The two guards who brought them told me these Germans were employed as carpenters before they were drafted into the Kraut army."

Outside there is singing. The same song I heard before. The marching song about Erika.

"DANNY," I BEGIN on the way home. "Do you remember I told you not to talk to the German soldiers?"

"Yeah."

"Well, how come you disobeyed me?"

"I didn't."

"I saw you Danny! You were sitting next to them and listening to their songs. You taught them a few phrases of English."

"But you *also* told me *always be friendly and kind to people*, so I was going by the earlier rule."

"Don't try to be funny. These are Nazi soldiers. I don't want you to be friendly to them."

"Not all Germans are bad. Some are just regular guys who got drafted and had to fight or be executed. I wish I'd learned more German words from Pa."

"Well, I'm going to ask you again, please respect me and stay away from the POWs."

Danny is quiet for a minute, clearly sulking, and then he begins to hum the German marching song . . .

December 15, 1942

Martino

What's that?" Danny asks standing up from the table before we've finished our noon meal.

"Oh, probably just more airplanes from the new Air National Guard Airport in Delmont. They fly over here every day now, remember?"

He goes to look out the back door. "There's a Delmont Coal truck in the drive. Did you order coal, Mom? Pa left us with five cords of wood, enough for the whole winter."

"No, certainly not. It must be a mistake." I jerk on my jacket and hurry out to confront the coal man before he unloads.

"Sir," I call to the driver, who's backing toward the barn. "Hey, mister!" The man finally hears me, stops the truck, and looks out the side window. *It's Mr. Ricci!* He opens the door of the cab and climbs down.

"Good morning, Miss Patience."

"I think there's some mistake. I ordered lumber from Farmers' Supply, not coal."

"No mistake. I brought you your lumber." He points to the back of the truck bed.

"Oh . . . Sadie said it might be a week or more." I laugh. "We saw the sign on the side saying Delmont Coal. Do you work for Farmers' Supply now . . . and the coal company too?"

"No, just the coal company, but I was at the feed store yesterday when you were there. The manager told me your barn roof blew off and you needed some lumber, but they didn't have a deliveryman, so I thought I'd bring it."

By this time, all the children are out in the drive. "Do you remember Mr. Ricci, kids? He and his wife came here after Mrs. Ricci had her baby in a coal truck on the top of Hogback Mountain."

"Nice to meet you," the children respond.

"You have a nice place here," the man says as he gets in the truck after the lumber is unloaded and stacked inside the barn. "Felicia and I are saving for a little farm. Nothing big. Just a few acres."

"Wait, I have to pay for the lumber. Cash on delivery, Sadie said." Martino turns with a slow smile.

"It's already paid for. Felicia and I paid your bill."

"No, I can't let you do that. Why would you do that? You could save that money for a farm."

"You saved our baby. You saved my woman. If you hadn't

come walking out of the woods, she could have bled to death. I know nothing of childbirth. Anyway, your lumber only came to sixty dollars. Do you know how much we would have had to pay if we had the baby in the hospital? Eighty. We also stayed here for two days at the Baby Cabin. So we thank you. I gotta go now." The man salutes us like he's in the army and drives away.

"So all that lumber and tin roofing were free?" Danny asks, his eyes big.

"It was a gift. Sometimes, Danny, when you're down and out, gifts come to you in the strangest way."

December 16, 1942

Dear Patience,

I know this will be the first Christmas that I won't be home, but I'll think of you every day. Thank you so much for holding our family and home together. That's my one regret about being incarcerated, that I'm not there to help you. Truly, I think you suffer more than I do.

Please, Danny, Sunny, Susie, and Mira, be good.

Your loving father and husband

P.S. Do not open your presents until Christmas morning!

Inside the envelope are five little paper packages with our names written on the top.

"So, Pa's not coming home?" Danny says sadly when I show the children their gifts.

"Writing the letter to the warden was a long shot, kids. Maybe I shouldn't have encouraged you, but at the time I thought why not try."

"That's okay, Mom. In a way, it's good to quit hoping," Susie says philosophically. "At least we have presents." We all look at the little white packages and wonder what they could be. Then each of us places our gift from Dan on a branch of the Christmas tree.

53

December 17, 1942

Help on the Way

The days are warm again. It's *so* warm it makes me wonder if another storm's brewing, so I have each child bring in an extra armload of wood. During this noisy process the phone rings.

"Good morning, Mrs. Hester. This is Sheriff Hardman."

"Morning, Sheriff."

"I wanted to tell you that I'm sorry I can't go with you back to the Moundsville Prison until after New Year's. I'm sure you wanted to see Daniel."

"Thanks, Sheriff, but the truth is I've been too busy to think of it. The last storm caused some damage here and I've been trying to get a few presents made for the kids . . ."

"Well, there's something else . . ."

"Yes . . ." I say, wondering what the problem could be. Danny hasn't been to town, so he couldn't have gotten into another fight.

"I heard from Mr. Gold that you're interested in hiring some POWs to help on the farm."

"I was asking about it. Do you think that would be a mistake? I know they use them at the woolen mill now. I really need to get the roof back on the barn before another storm blows the rest off."

"No, it's okay. I just wanted to tell you the POWs don't come with an interpreter. Do you think you can handle that?"

I swallow hard, thinking of the two young German soldiers at the house with the blue door. "The Rootes drew pictures of what they wanted done; I could do that. Do you know how I sign up for the service?"

He gives me a number at the courthouse and then adds, "I think it's good you're doing this, Mrs. Hester. Just, please, if you can, have Mr. Maddock or some other man with you. You know what I mean? You being a woman and all."

The sheriff's paternal attitude about my being female vexes me so much I dial the number immediately. "United States Employment Agency," a woman with a voice like Minnie Mouse answers. "This is Ada Mullins speaking. How can I help you?"

"Ada? This is Patience Hester. What are you doing at the courthouse?"

"I forgot to tell you, I work here now while my sister takes care of the baby. I'm the *whole* United States Employment Agency in Union County. Mostly I just handle the POWs. Send them out to their jobs and arrange guards and transportation."

Abruptly she changes subject. "Ollie's coming home soon. He lost his arm at Guadalcanal." I feel sick as I remember the young man with the tattoo of the American flag on his biceps and wonder if that was the arm that was amputated.

"Oh, Ada. I'm so sorry. Did you just hear?"

"The Red Cross called two days ago. That's why I hadn't gotten a letter from him. Of course I feel terrible to think of his body being injured, but I'll tell you the truth, Patience. I'm just glad he didn't get killed and he will make it back to West Virginia. On some of the islands the casualties were twenty percent. At least he's safe now. He hasn't seen little Dorothy since she was born. . . . *So what can I do for you?*" She suddenly becomes quite professional.

The abrupt businesslike change catches me off guard. I'm still trying to digest what she's told me about poor Ollie . . . "Well, some of my friends are using the German POWs on their farms and I thought I would ask, if it's safe, could I get a crew to fix our barn? We lost half the roof during the white hurricane, and as you probably heard my husband was sent to prison for refusing to register for the draft."

"Sure, I can get a crew out there in a day or two. Some of the prisoners are carpenters by trade."

"The Rootes had a couple of fellows that did good work, Eckhart and Leopold, big blond fellows. Do those names ring a bell?"

"I know exactly who you mean. How many days will the job take? I'll try to get the two you mentioned and probably two more, but remember, they don't speak English and I have to find transportation and guards. The guards don't stay, you understand. They just bring the POWs out and pick them up."

"And I'm supposed to pay you forty-five cents an hour for each man . . . is that how it works?"

"The guards will leave you a paper form. The POWs fill out the number of hours, you sign, and you pay me at the courthouse. Also, you'll need to give them a good midday meal. They work eight A.M. to five P.M. There'll be a consent for you to sign, of course."

"Okay, that's fine. Can I ask you something else, Ada?"

"Ask away, honey."

"Does it bother you, working with the enemy and your husband being a soldier and all? Don't you feel angry toward the German men?"

Silence hangs on the telephone wire. "No," she finally says in almost a whisper. "My mother was a German. She immigrated after the first world war. I don't tell many people that."

"My husband's grandparents were Germans too," I say. "Dan even speaks German. I don't tell *anyone* that."

54

December 19, 1942

Work Crew

When the house is quiet and the children are in bed, I take out my journal. Since Dan left, I write less frequently, probably because I'm too tired. I've also stopped listening to the news on the radio. The details of the battles blur, and without Dan to put little pins in his map on the closet door, none of it makes much sense.

There are attacks and counterattacks, losses and victories from Europe to Africa to Asia. I *can* tell that there have been a few more Allied victories lately. At first things were going very bad for us. Even the kids have settled down and, except for the Air Force fighter planes flying over, the war is more background to our life than the reason for living.

This morning, bright and early, Bitsy brought Willie over in the motorcycle sidecar because the German POWs were coming to fix the barn roof and she thought maybe he could help carry boards. Mr. Roote promised he'd come over later to be our chaperone.

Promptly at eight, an army truck arrived, with the POWs riding in back. I recognized Eckhart and Leopold right off, and Danny and Willie ran over like they were old friends. The U.S. military policeman, got out, introduced Eckhart as head carpenter, had me sign a consent, and left.

The children and I stood in the yard as the German men saluted me. "Frau Chef!" they shouted in a military way, which I figure meant *woman chief* or possibly *woman cook*, I'm not sure. Then in English they intoned with a strong accent "We greet you as a friend."

Will and Danny saluted back with big smiles. "We greet you as a friend," they said, and though I'd warned my son about being sociable with the POWs it touched me. If only world peace could be achieved so easily. *We greet you as a friend.* But I am naïve. People have told me this all my life.

I point to the hole in the roof and the pile of lumber and tools in the barn, then hand Eckhart a box of nails that Sadie sent over with the wood. Finally, I show them a picture of the barn with little stick men sitting on the roof with hammers and saws. I'm not much of an artist, and we all laugh about that.

One of the POWs points at the farmhouse and I follow his gaze to the side porch, where the three girls sit on the steps. "*Schwester?*" the man called Leopold asks Danny.

"Sister. Yes!" Danny grins.

Leopold, clearly pleased he knows a few words in English,

bows to the girls and repeats his salutation. "I greet you as a friend."

He turns to his fellow POWs and they all bow and copy him with big smiles. "I greet you as a friend."

Mira gets it right away. "We greet you as a friend," she says with a curtsy.

"Enough pleasantries! On to work, men." I point to the roof and hand Leopold a hammer and big yellow tape measure that says Farmers' Lumber and Supply on it, then I head back toward the house.

"Let me know if there are any problems, Danny," I say over my shoulder.

"Right, Ma!"

"Ma. *Mutter!*" says Leopold with another big smile.

"Girls," I order briskly as I step up on the porch, "I need you in the house." This is not true, I just fear for my little ladies with these young enemy soldiers around. Probably, I'd feel the same if they were a bunch of young American GIs, and I realize that part of my not wanting to hire the POWs is because I'm not comfortable bossing men. My whole life's work has been with women, and I have always left handling tradesmen, mechanics, and carpenters to Dan. Now I'm the *Frau Chef!*

"Oh, please let us watch, Ma," Sunny begs.

"We'll be good. We won't move from this porch," promises Susie, who I'm surprised to notice has grown in confidence since her father was imprisoned. I'd imagined she'd get more anxious, but she's actually risen to the occasion and has become my main helper.

"We won't talk to them either," vows Mira.

"Okay," I agree. "It *is* fun to watch, but I'll check on you from the window and if you move an inch off the porch I'll see and you'll be in big trouble."

By ten, Mr. Roote arrives, gets out of his shiny red car, and limps over to the barn. I go out to meet him. His stroke has left him with a small disability, but he got off lucky. Watching him limp, I realize that my leg hasn't hurt since the weather improved. That's something to be thankful for anyway. With missing Dan, I've hurt more on the inside than out.

"Howdy, Leopold. Howdy, Eckhart," the old man yells up to the carpenters.

"Howdy!" all the men shout down, pleased to be using English. Then they point to me and salute again, "*Frau Chef!*"

"How they doin'?" Mr. Roote asks me.

I stare up at the hole in the roof. All the ragged boards have been removed and the men are beginning to replace them with fresh lumber. "Looks great so far."

"Well, what can I do to help?"

"Why don't you come in the house and have a cup of joe with me. Basically, I was just a little scared of the Germans and wanted someone around. I'm not sure there's really anything to do, but keep us company."

"That's fine," Mr. Roote says. "I was getting in the missus's hair anyway. She's doing some kind of Christmas thing." The girls are bored with watching the workers, so they busy themselves inside making cranberry chains for the tree.

"Do you have plans for Christmas Eve?" the old man

asks. "Mrs. Roote wants to go into Liberty to see the mayor light the courthouse tree and look at the Baptist nativity scene."

"We've never done that before." I consider the invitation. "But with Dan gone everything's different. Maybe the kids would like it."

Before I get to answer, there's a knock on the door.

Hannah

*H*annah!" I exclaim, stepping out on the porch. The very pregnant woman is crying. "What's wrong? Where's your husband, John?"

"Dead!" is all she can manage to say.

"*No!*" I call out. Mr. Roote stands abruptly, almost knocking over the kitchen chair, and joins us outside while the girls gather around.

"He was drafted last September. I was alone at the house this morning when the Western Union man came, and I almost collapsed as he handed me the envelope. I was so devastated, I couldn't even sign." She holds out a crumpled yellow paper and I scan the words, hoping she's misread and her husband's only missing, like Ida May's brother. Unfortunately, she's all too correct.

The Secretary of War desires me to express his deepest regret that your husband, Corporal John

F. Dyer, was killed in action on December 4, 1942, in France. A letter follows.
Homer Webb, Acting Adjutant General

I hand the telegram to Mr. Roote and fold Hannah into my arms. Outside, the German crew has stopped working and stare at the very pregnant sobbing woman. Danny comes over and turns off the ignition of Hannah's late model blue DeSoto.

"Where's your mom, Hannah? Where are the kids? Come in and sit down," I say. The young woman grips the white wooden porch rail, breathing heavily, and it's then that I realize . . . she's in labor.

"Susie, get Mrs. Dyer a cup of tea."

"I'll go talk to the POW boys. Do you want them to keep working?" Mr. Roote says.

"Yes, I guess they should. Their ride doesn't come until five o'clock and I was hoping they could finish the job."

Hannah rests her head in her arms and cries as if her heart is broken, and it is . . . as broken as the barn roof—shattered, destroyed. It's so easy to talk about war in the abstract . . . whether it's justified . . . who started it . . . who fights it . . . who dies a hero, but this is what war looks like sitting at my kitchen table.

"Your mother. Can I call your mother or John's mother? Where are your children?"

"They're at school in Liberty. My mother lives near Oneida, just this side of the Pennsylvania–West Virginia border. She's in Pittsburgh today at a big Red Cross meeting. I have no way to get hold of her. John's parents are in Huntington, visiting the old man's ailing sister. They probably didn't get their telegram yet. Now we'll have to change the blue star on our banners to gold. . . ."

"I'll pick up your children from school," Mr. Roote says. "I'll take them home to the missus and tell them you're at the Baby Cabin having your baby, but I won't tell them about their dad." Here Hannah starts crying again. I pull a chair close and put my arm around her shoulders. In the presence of true grief, words are useless, like pebbles dropped in a deep, dry well.

December 20, 1942

Baby boy, Lincoln Dyer, born to Hannah Dyer, at 7:15 P.M. in the Baby Cabin.

This was Hannah's third baby, and labor was intense and lasted four hours. The poor woman had just received a telegram from the war department that her husband, John, had been killed in action, and I'm sure the shock of it started her pains. Tears flowed the whole time.

In her other deliveries, she and John danced through every contraction, but this time she didn't ask for music and there was no joy. As her labor progressed, I held her and we swayed together. Sometimes I'd hum a tune and I kept coming back to "Goin' Home." Bitsy and Lou taught me the song when we listened to it on a recording by Paul Robeson, the famous American Negro singer.

I was worried that Hannah might hemorrhage or have some other complication after receiving the shocking news of her husband's death, but all went well with the delivery. No perineal tears. Placenta delivered intact. Estimated blood loss, one cup.

Afterwards, while Hannah was nursing the baby, she looked over. "What was that tune you kept humming?" she asked. "I never heard it before. Are there words?"

I sang the first verse for her. "Goin' home, goin' home, I'm a goin' home." She listened as she nursed her new baby. "It's not far, jes' close by. Through an open door. Work all done, cares laid by. Goin' to fear no more."

Hannah took a deep breath and let out the air. "John is home now, looking over us. I can feel him. The whole time I was in labor, I felt your arms around me, but they were his arms. Will you call my mom for me now?" she asked. "She should be home."

I quietly left her and the baby, and after I phoned her mother, I went to the gazebo near the willow trees. It was a warm night, with high clouds skimming past the half moon. I cried a long time, for Hannah, for John, for their kids, for all of us in this dark and troubled world.

December 22, 1942

Dear Dan,

There are only a few more days until Christmas and I hope you receive your parcel by then. I mailed you three books and more drawings from the kids. Thanks for the little white packages you sent each of us. They're sitting in the branches of the spruce tree, which is decorated in lights, our old ornaments, and cranberry chains made by the girls.

Getting the presents you sent considerably cheered us. The children were hoping you might come home for a few days, and I will admit I encouraged them to write the warden, but later I realized it was cruel to get their hopes up. Anyway, they're now reconciled to your not being here.

I finally got up my courage and signed up to have the POWs come repair the barn roof. In the middle of all this, Hannah Dyer showed up at our door sobbing. She'd just received a telegram that her husband, John, was killed in battle. Can you believe it? He was such an intelligent young man with his whole life in front of him. The shock of receiving the dreaded telegram had thrown her into labor.

Mr. Roote was here, at the sheriff's suggestion, serving as our chaperone while the POW men worked, and he and the girls made dinner for the Germans while I delivered the baby, another healthy boy. It makes you think about life and death and war. What are we doing, throwing away the best of our young men? It's stupid, isn't it? You told me it was, but still we can't let heartless tyrants take over the world.

My heart is with you. Can you feel it?

Patience

55

December 24, 1942

Christmas Lights

This evening was filled with events that kept our minds off the fact that Dan is not with us and that John Dyer is dead. At five, just before sundown, Mr. and Mrs. Roote picked us up in their red Chevy. Though it's a few years old, the children had never ridden in such a new car.

By the time we got to Liberty it was dark. Since the children never go to town at night, they didn't realize how beautiful it would be. Most of the stores had some kind of Christmas lights, and the train station was decorated too. It was as gay as a Saturday before the matinee, with families walking up and down Main, some doing last-minute shopping.

We stopped at Bittman's Grocery to say Merry Christmas. "I heard about John Dyer," Lilly whispered. "Such an awful shame. I'm so glad B.K. can't go to war. He has a bad back. . . . Here's a present; I saved the last half dozen candy canes for your brood." She handed me a wrapped parcel.

"We're closing up the store for the lighting ceremony," B.K. said. "You all going?"

"That's what we came for," Mr. Roote said. "How much for a dozen oranges?"

Back on the street we walk down Main admiring the pretty windows with their Christmas displays. Frequently, along with the decorations, I see a white banner bordered in red with a large blue star in the middle. The blue star, Mr. Roote informs me, represents someone's son or husband serving in the military. The gold star means a man has died in combat. Some of the banners have more than one star. These must be the flags Hannah mentioned.

At Ida May's House of Beauty, there's one blue star on the banner, indicating that Ida has not given up hope that her brother, Annie's husband, is still alive. At Farmers' Lumber and Feed, the flag has four stars, three blue and one gold, and that sobers me. Dan knew all the fellows who worked there. Now one is dead.

Finally, at the end of Main, in front of the Saved by Jesus Baptist Church, we come to the live nativity scene. Under a wooden framed roof sits Mary and Joseph, dressed in traditional garb, played by Ada Mullins and her husband, Ollie, the one-armed veteran. Baby Jesus is the Mullinses' six-month-old baby.

There are also wise men and shepherds in costume, some with pasted-on beards. A donkey eats hay, and two sheep rest in the grass. Above the whole scene is a wooden star, painted gold, hanging from a tree and illuminated with white Christmas lights. "Oooooh," Mira says. "It's so beautiful. When I grow up I want to be Mary."

The children all pet the animals, then we reverse course back to the courthouse, where a considerable crowd has gathered for the lighting ceremony. On the corner, the Liberty High School Band plays "Jingle Bells," and before Mira has a chance to get into her dance routine, I lead everyone up the steps, where we can get a good view.

All around me are familiar faces. Some look away, shunning the draft evader's wife. Some observe me with pity. Others offer a hesitant wave. Danny sees Willie a few steps above us and heads that way to sit with his friend, but I call him back, afraid he'll get in a fight with some bully who'll taunt him and call his father a coward.

When the band takes a break, we hear sleigh bells and see, coming around the corner from First Street, a horse pulling a buggy, with Santa inside. The jolly old fellow waves and shouts "Merry Christmas!" and then turns on Main and disappears in the distance.

Finally, as snowflakes begin to drift down, the mayor plugs in a cord and minutes later we're blinded by hundreds of colored lights. "Awwwww!" "Ohhhhh!" the crowd calls out.

"Well, that's the show!" Mr. Roote says as we wander back to the car. "Only one more stop." He has a big smile on his face. "Hop in, kids! It's a surprise."

Sing

Where are we going now?" asks Danny, clearly excited. Myself, I'm just tired. I still have a story to read to the children and presents to wrap and get under the tree.

I'm surprised when Mr. Roote turns south at the railway station and heads out of town, following a score of other vehicles, all going the same way, up Crocker Creek, which roars around boulders the size of small houses.

As we motor higher and higher, the mountainside falls away into darkness. It's snowing harder now, flakes like chicken feathers that stick to the spruce bows, but not the road. Fifteen minutes later, we pull off the gravel road with the other vehicles, and wait. Mr. Roote looks at his pocket watch and rolls down the windows.

"Here they come!" he says to his wife as he gets out. The kids and I join him, looking around, but there's nothing to see except other people, leaning on their cars, talking softly, and smoking cigarettes.

Then we hear tramping. We all strain our necks. Mr. Roote lifts the girls up on the hood of the red Chevy, where they can see. Men in denim uniforms and dark knit caps are marching six abreast, filling the road. "*Eins—zwei—drei—vier*," they chant in rhythm. "*Eins—zwei—drei—vier. Eins—zwei—drei—vier.*"

A chill runs through me. What are we doing here in the dark next to the POW camp? There must be a hundred Germans coming toward us, with only four U.S. military policemen carrying guns. "*Eins—zwei—drei—vier. Eins—zwei—drei—vier.*" They march, ramrod straight, as if parading in front of Adolf Hitler himself.

The soldiers reach the autos. "Halt," the leader commands. They turn with military precision and then, my heart springs open. "*Herbei, o ihr Gläubigen*," the soldiers begin to sing in three-part harmony. It's only by the tune that I make out the song. *O come all ye faithful, joyful and triumphant . . .* Leopold, who stands in the first row, gives me a wink. Eckhart, two rows behind him, nods and his eyes shine.

Then Lou Cross, from somewhere in one of the cars behind us, runs out in the road with a little stick and begins directing. "Sing the second verse!" he yells, and hesitantly we Americans join the Germans, following Lou's booming voice. *"Sing, choirs of angels—sing in exultation . . ."*

I put my arm around Danny as one of the army guards lays down his gun and pulls a coronet out of his knapsack. Two POWs get their trumpets out too, and as the trio begins to play, the golden notes rise, echoing from the white cliffs behind the camp. *"Sing, all you citizens of heaven above!"*

The smiling foreign men are no longer our enemies. They're no longer Nazis. They're farmers, shopkeepers, machinists, glass blowers, and carpenters, not so different from us. I know that now and when I look up, the clouds have opened and we can see stars.

December 25, 1942

Christmas

*I*t's the sound of the rain pounding on the side of the house that wakes me. I get up to look out, but the bedroom window is coated in ice and I can't see a thing. This is weird, but it's been a strange winter.

Since the house is getting cold and I'm up anyway, I go downstairs to throw another log in the fire and peek out the door. An inch of ice covers everything, the ground, the trees, the porch steps . . . and as the rain scrapes the house it instantly freezes.

When I return to the dark living room, I plug in the Christmas lights. That's when I see them. The small white packages on the spruce tree, and I find the one that says Patience.

My husband said not to open them until Christmas, *but it's already Christmas morning, isn't it?* Slowly, I unfold the paper and inside find a red star. The star appears to have been made from layers of tape, perhaps bandage tape found in the infirmary, then painted red with Mercurochrome. Braided red suture serves as a chain, and I drop the necklace over my head and press it close to my heart.

Outside, the wind and ice slash the house again. The fire flares. I think of my love in his stone prison cell and the soldiers in their cold foxholes, then more wind and *crash!* The whole house shakes. "Mama!" Susie cries. "Mama!"

"I'm down here, kids!"

The children rush down the stairs and tumble into my arms. Danny goes to the kitchen and opens the back door. "Don't go out, Danny! It's an ice storm."

"I'm just looking. The top of one of the willow trees just fell and crushed the whole porch." Now we all go to see.

I let out a long breath and touch the red star that hangs over my heart. *More trouble. I should have known it was coming.* First the auto accident on top of the mountain, then the white hurricane and the destruction of the barn roof, now an ice storm and a tree falls on my house.

The clock on the mantel chimes five o'clock. "Look, Santa came!" Mira shouts, running toward her stocking. "We don't have to go back to bed do we, Mama? It's already Christmas!"

"Please!" the other kids echo.

"Okay. Okay. Go put your slippers on and I'll build a fire in the fireplace." By the time they get back, I have warm milk and ginger snaps on the low table, and for the next hour we take turns opening our presents.

The girls are happy with their paper dolls. Danny finds his punching bag in the pantry and they all want to try it. My present, from the children, is a colorful yellow and red flowered scarf that I tie around my neck. Finally we get down to their father's small gifts.

"You know, kids, Papa doesn't have any money in prison, so don't expect much. Let's start with the youngest. What do you think your pa gave you, Mira?"

"I don't know! Can I open it now?"

"Be careful," Susie says. "It might blow up!" Everyone laughs.

Slowly, Mira unfolds the square parcel. She looks puzzled. "Is it just a letter?"

"I don't know. Let me see it. If it is, it's still special. A private letter from your pa." Mira scoots across the braided rug on her fanny and holds out her two sheets of paper.

"'*The Blue Fairy.*'" I raise my eyebrows dramatically as I read. "'*Once, in a far-off land, deep in the forest, there was a tiny castle. It was so small it was hidden under a large white mushroom that kept off the rain. In the castle lived a tiny blue fairy, but she was very powerful . . .'* What do you think of that? Your father wrote you a story for Christmas!"

"Can I see mine?" Danny asks.

"Me too."

"I can't wait!" the twins cry, and each child carefully opens their pa's gift.

In the end we have four stories: "The True Tale of Jack the Flying Horse," "The Ice-Cream Princess," "The Legend of the Talking Moon," and of course, "The Blue Fairy."

By midday, the rain stops, the sun comes out, and the world outside sparkles. Each twig and branch is covered with ice, and the ice-laden telephone wires droop. On the other side of the road, a broad-tailed hawk perches in an oak, looking surprised. Even the red bittersweet berries are coated in ice.

It's a glittering world, but treacherous, and when the kids are dressed, before I can tell Danny to stop, he jumps off the porch and slides halfway across the yard. It looks like so much fun the girls try it.

I am more cautious. Carefully, holding on to my long walking stick, I traverse the barnyard toward the chicken house, but still I fall. No one has noticed, so I lay there a moment, recovering. I wasn't always this way, but age and circumstances have changed me. I have to be careful; if I fell and broke something, with no Daniel to help us, we would be lost.

When the animals are fed we return to the house and I begin to prepare Christmas dinner. It was so nice of Sarah Maddock to give us a ham. I'd planned on chicken, but we have that so often.

Just as the girls are setting the table, the phone rings. I hope it's not a woman in labor, but it wouldn't be the first time I delivered a baby on Jesus's birthday.

"Hello?" I answer.

"Mrs. Hester?" a man's voice responds. "Mrs. Daniel Hester?"

"Yes. Who is this?"

"This is Dr. Greeley from the Moundsville State Prison."

Beating

*Y*es?" I say again, my heart pounding. *Why is the prison physician calling? This cannot be good.*

"First, let me reassure you, Daniel is resting peacefully in the infirmary. I've given him pain medication. There's been an accident, but I believe he will recover fully in a few weeks."

"What? What? Please explain."

"Well, it wasn't so much an accident as a beating. Daniel was the object of zealous patriotism. It happened in the shower, and the guards were not as attentive as they should have been. Dan has a broken arm and a few lacerations.

The leader was a fellow recently discharged from the army who was sentenced for robbing a store. I probably shouldn't be telling you this much.

"As luck would have it, another man, a really big fellow named Bones, broke it up. The warden was going to notify you, but I said I'd do it. Mrs. Hester . . . are you still there?"

"Yes . . . yes. When can I visit him? Can I come tomorrow?"

"I'm keeping Dan in the infirmary until he's well, and I'm sorry there are no visitors here. Then the warden plans to transfer him to a federal prison, where there are special units for draft resisters and he'll be safer. Don't worry."

"Where might that be? Where is the nearest such prison?"

"I'm not sure. The federal prison at Leavenworth is a big one. That's in Kansas, and Ashland in Kentucky has a lot pacifists." My heart sinks. *Leavenworth! That's where the Hutterite brothers died.*

"If he would only sign for a conscientious objector we could get him out of here. We'll do whatever we can . . ." There's static and then the phone goes dead.

He's Alive

*M*erry Christmas!" It's Bitsy, standing at the front door. "Boy, what a mess. Did you see the telephone wire across the road? The pole just crashed over from the weight of the ice. And look at your porch. The top of the tree almost crashed through the window. Lucky it wasn't worse . . . What's wrong?" She can tell I've been crying.

"I can't talk about it now," I whisper. "Wait until the kids go out to play." She gives me a sharp glance and heads for the kitchen to make tea. Then Lou Cross and Willie come in laughing. But that soon stops when Bitsy gives Lou a nod in my direction.

"Smells good in here," Willie says. "What's for dinner?"

"Willie," Lou says. "Watch your manners."

"The kids are upstairs playing, Willie," I tell him. "Danny got a punching bag and gloves for Christmas." Here I try to smile, but it's a poor imitation.

"Nifty! I got a football. Maybe we can go out and play."

As soon as he's out of the room, Bitsy settles us with tea. "What?" she says. "Is it just the back porch? We can get those POW carpenters out in a jiff. Can't we, Lou?"

"Sure thing."

"No, it's not the porch. I got a call from the prison this morning. Some patriotic thugs beat Daniel up in the shower. Must be pretty bad. He's in the infirmary with lacerations and a broken arm."

"Oh, no!" Bitsy exclaims. Lou is silent, but his jaw goes tight.

"Greeley, the prison doctor, says he'll keep Dan safe in the infirmary as long as he can. He and the warden are trying to get him transferred to one of the big federal prisons, where they have better security and a whole unit for draft resisters."

"They should have done it a long time ago. I have a feeling they just liked having Dan around because he was helpful in the clinic and taught his reading classes," Lou says.

"Getting him moved to a more secure place sounds good, right?" Bitsy tries to be optimistic.

"No, not really. The places they're contacting are in Kansas and Kentucky." Here the tears come for real "Now I won't be able to visit at all. . . ."

My friend sits down next to me on the sofa. Lou walks to the fireplace and throws another log on the blaze. He paces the room like a tiger in a zoo until the boys tumble down the stairs, and then he goes out to play football.

"Oh, Bitsy, I've had bad days before, but this is the worst."

"Let's think of the good things," Bitsy says. "Dan is alive. He's *safe* today and you have us. . . ." This only makes me cry more.

56

December 27, 1942

Goodwill to Men

*Y*esterday was Saturday and I called Farmers' Supply to see about getting the materials to fix the porch, but there was no answer; Sadie's apparently taking an extra day off for the holidays. Today is Sunday and I know they'll be closed.

I'm really in no mood for socializing, but I decide for the children's sake, we need to go to the Hazel Patch Chapel for service. I still haven't told the kids about their father being in the infirmary. What good would that do? Only make them worry.

When Daniel was taken away to Moundsville, I mourned for him. It was as if he had died. Never did I think he *really might die*, but this must be how women who have men in the war feel. They go to work at the factory or stay home and do the wash. They care for the children and all the time they're sending love and light to shield their man.

Every waking moment, now, I think of Dan, hoping he's safe, and my whole body feels like a prayer.

The trip over to Hazel Patch is harrowing. The roads are still covered with ice and even though Danny and I took the time to put chains on, we almost slide into a ditch. Also there's the problem of a fallen tree that we had to move and the drooping telephone wires to avoid.

The service begins with a short prayer by Reverend Miller that feels as if it was written for me. "Lord, in this Christmas season, when every heart should be full of joy, many of us carry heavy burdens . . . we pray to you, our savior, bring us peace, bring us hope. In Jesus's name, Amen."

The solo by Mrs. Miller also brought tears to my eyes. It was one of Dan's favorites.

"*It came upon the midnight clear. That glorious song of old. From angels bending near the earth to touch their harps of gold! Peace on the earth, goodwill to men . . .*"

There were more prayers and then the sermon. The collection plate was passed and finally the children went up front and sang the old favorite. "*Jesus loves the little children. All the children of the world. Red and yellow, brown and white, they are precious in his sight. Jesus loves the little children of the world.*"

As we pass out of the chapel and head toward the Millers' sturdy log home for coffee and fruitcake, the reverend puts his arm through mine to support me on the ice. "I noticed you're limping again," he said.

"Yes, I slipped on the ice the other morning and pulled the same muscle in my knee as a few years ago. It's always been weak since that cow kicked me."

"It's a nice day and the ice will soon melt," the preacher observes. "But it's been a rough winter."

"'Erratic,' Dan would say. 'Just weird with ice and rain and the white hurricane.'"

"Speaking of Daniel . . . Lou Cross told me about his trouble at the prison. Patriotism is noble, but there's no excuse for what those men did. I wonder if the guards were absent on purpose. Sheriff Hardman and I are going up to Moundsville sometime this week."

"Dr. Greeley told me I couldn't visit Dan in the infirmary," I warn.

"I'm sure they'll make an exception for his *pastor*," the reverend responds with confidence. "We need to know that he's being properly cared for. I talked to the prison chaplain and he's going to arrange it. Moundsville is known to be one of the roughest penitentiaries in the country."

As we slip and slosh toward the Millers' home I tighten my arm through his. "Thank you for the prayer at the beginning of the service. It spoke to me," I tell him.

The reverend laughs. "I wrote it for you."

December 29, 1942

Thaw

All night the water drips from the icicles on the eaves and the creek below the house roars. In the morning, though it's not yet January, it feels like spring. There's an unseasonable softness to the air, and when I look in the flower beds I see little shoots of green that shouldn't be there, early signs of daffodils sprouting.

First thing, after chores, I try again to call the lumber and feed store. This time someone answers. "Hi, Sadie," I say. "It's Patience Hester. I had a tree fall on the back porch during the ice storm and we can't get in and out of the house through the back door. Can I order some more lumber?"

"I heard about the tree. This has been a hell of a winter . . . I heard about your other trouble too. Is Daniel all right?"

I swallow hard wondering how word travels so fast. "Yes, I think he's going to be okay. You heard what happened?"

"Some flag-waving bastard beat him up, Mrs. Stenger told me."

"Not just one man. Several. Despite Dan's beliefs about war, you probably know that in a fair fight he can give as much as he takes."

"Well, our prayers are with him, honey. Now, what do you need?"

I give her a list of the lumber I'll require to rebuild the porch. "That'll be about fifty dollars," she says. "I can give you credit if you need it."

"Thanks, Sadie. You're a pal, but I have a little money coming in from rent on our house on Wild Rose Road now, so we'll be okay."

"I'll try to get the order out there day after tomorrow, but you know we're shorthanded."

"That's fine. And Sadie, I saw the red, white, and blue banner with four stars in your window. I understand they're for your workers who've gone to war, but there's one gold star now . . . I guess that means . . ."

"Yes, Pat McKenzie . . . You didn't hear? He was killed during the U.S. invasion of French Africa in November. Such a shame. His mother . . ." Here I stop listening. Patrick was Sally Blum's sweetheart!

All this time, I've been worried about *my* family; I haven't given a thought to Becky and her family. I assumed that they were all well, living the good life, on the government payroll in Washington, D.C.

I don't have any way to call Becky. Since she moved, she hasn't called me, but I do know her address, so I'll write her a letter today. And there's something else I need to do, tell the children about what happened to their father . . . before some stranger does.

December 29, 1942

Dear Becky and Isaac,

I heard recently about the death of Patrick McKenzie, the young man at the feed store, and I wanted to tell you and Sally how sorry I am. I feel bad about not writing in all this time. What has it been since you left, three months? Four? With all that's been going on, I've lost track.

I don't know if you heard that Dan refused to register for the draft and was arrested. He says he's a complete conscientious objector and can't cooperate with war in any way. Maybe he talked to you about it, Isaac. For a while, I was very angry. In these desperate times, with the stakes so high, it seemed, at first, a cowardly position to take.

Daniel is now in the Moundsville State Penitentiary. He's supposed to be going to a federal prison soon, but they've been dragging their feet. It's only recently that it's become an issue. On Christmas Day he was beat up by some patriotic thugs in the prison shower. It must have been a major fight, because his arm is broken and they're keeping him in the infirmary for his own safety.

As you can imagine, I am exhausted with all the worry, the farm work, taking care of the kids, and occasionally delivering a baby, but here's some good news . . . Charley Roote and Mrs. Roote (formerly Mrs. Stone) have rented the house with the blue door. It is still your house, if you ever come back, but for now it's a little income that I sorely need. Let's not lose touch. You are my good friends.

With sympathy,
Love, Patience

December 30, 1942

ℬones

"a. Ma!" Mira slams through the front door all out of breath. "We saw a bear!" Susie and Sunny follow, also out of breath.

"Probably it was a big dog, girls. Bears hibernate in the winter. Mr. Blaze the newspaper reporter said there's a pack of wild canines roaming Union County and before your pa went away, he told me Mr. Dresher found five of his sheep dead in a field. The pack seemed to kill for the sake of killing. They hardly touched the meat . . . Where's Danny?"

"He's playing Indian out in the woods. Said he was an Iroquois. That's a tribe that used to live around here," Sunny informs me.

"I'd better go get him. You girls stay inside for the rest of the day."

Just in case there are bears or wild dogs roaming the countryside, I take my oak walking stick, the one that Dr. Blum made for me when he was coming out of his silence. It has flowering vines, delicately carved from one end to the other.

"Danny!" I call, heading across the yard toward the creek. Here and there I see spots of yellow and, leaning down, realize they're dandelion flowers; strange the last week of December. This recent warm spell has caused them to bloom. From the creek, I cut into the woods.

"Danny!" That's when I see them, footprints of a large animal. "Danny!" I call louder, but I freeze when I hear a twig snap behind me.

"Ha! Surprised you!" My son jumps out from behind a big oak. "If I was a wild Indian, you'd be dead!"

"You scared me! I want you to come home now. The girls said they saw a bear, but it was probably one of the wild dogs we've been hearing about."

"It *could* be a bear, Ma. It's almost like spring," Danny contradicts, but I let it go.

"Also I have something to tell you."

"Are you and Pa getting a divorce?"

"What? No! Whatever gave you that idea?"

"I thought maybe you were so mad at him for going to prison that you might not want to be married anymore. Also, Willie heard Mr. Cross talking about Ida May. She's Mr. Cross's cousin and she's divorced."

"I know about that, honey. I know about her husband, too. He got mean when he drank. Come inside, I'm going to make some peppermint tea and we can eat a few of the Christmas cookies Mrs. Miller sent over."

TEN MINUTES LATER we're gathered around the kitchen table.

"Kiddos," I say. "I have something to tell you. I've kept it to myself, because I didn't want to worry you . . ." The girls' eyes are big and round, but Danny squints as if ready for battle. "There was a fight at the prison and your father got hurt. He's in the infirmary being taken care of by the doctor and he's safe." That's all I plan to say, but Danny wants more.

"Was it Bones? The murderer? Did he attack Pa?"

"No, Bones is the one that stopped the fight. Your Pa is in the prison hospital and when he gets out, he'll be transferred to somewhere safer, a different prison that has a lot of draft protesters. I just wanted to tell you, because people in town already know."

There's silence around the table as the children digest this information. No one asks where Dan will be sent. No one asks what injuries he's sustained.

Finally, Danny stands abruptly, knocks over his chair, and runs up the stairs with Three-Legs tagging behind him.

"Don't flip your wig, Danny!" Susie yells. "There's nothing you can do about it." But he's already gone.

57

January 4, 1943

Limping Along

New Year's Eve was uneventful. Other times, when Dan was here, we'd stay up late and listen to the celebration on the radio while we drank rum toddies, but this year, I just went to bed. This is a year I don't want to remember, but I'm sure I will. It exhausts me to think of the memories I'll carry for the rest of my life, rocks in a knapsack.

Yesterday, a truck, with Farmers' Lumber and Supply on the side, rumbled across the wooden bridge and into the yard. Sadie jumped out and was already unloading the lumber by the time I got there. She was wearing men's coveralls, with heavy leather gloves and a green knit cap pulled over her short hair.

"Where's your helper?" I asked.

"No helper. You farmers can get the POW men, but in town we only have ourselves to rely on."

"Kids!" I called. "Come out and help!"

Sadie looked over at the demolished porch. "You've had a hell of a winter!" she said, wiping her brow with a red bandanna. "One blow after another. First your husband is thrown in the pen, then you have a wreck on Hogback Mountain, followed by all the storms and destruction. You're a brave woman, Patience."

When we were done, I asked Sadie in for a cup of joe, but she had to get going. "I have two more loads to deliver and I left the store closed," she says, and then she's gone.

Upstairs, I lock my bedroom door and get out my journal. Today, I've hit another low and am desperate to express my feelings.

"I know I shouldn't feel this way," I scribble. "I have much to be thankful for. We're mostly healthy, with the exception of my hospitalized husband. We have a warm place to live and plenty of food, with the exception of sugar, coffee, and lard because of wartime rationing. We have money, though it won't last long if I have to keep purchasing lumber. Most importantly, no one is dropping bombs on us."

Still, despair rolls down on me like a mudslide after a two-week rain. I realized, after Sadie talked about me being brave, that it's all a front, a role that I'm playing. Where is the proud sunflower woman who once withstood the wind? Where is the fearless comrade who marched with the unions? Where is the warrior midwife? *Limping along, exhausted, holding on to her walking stick, waiting for the next blow to fall. That's where she is.*

January 5, 1943

Slaughter

*T*his morning, when we go out to do our chores, it's raining, and Danny and I discover the wire fence around the chicken yard has been torn down.

"*Gott verdammt!*" Danny curses in German, just like his pa. A few ruffled hens sit on the roof of the coop, but the rest are scattered like rags in the mud. Their beautiful red-brown bodies have been torn to pieces, ripped apart, ravaged. Here and there, a head is intact; its yellow beak shining and its red eyes still open.

One of the injured hens is alive, flapping around, spraying blood, and I almost collapse. Danny takes his pocketknife out, catches the dying chicken, and cuts her head off. "*Gott verdammt!*" he says again and I don't even bother to scold him for swearing.

Not only is this an economic loss, it's just plain sad. I loved our chickens, their soft clucking, the way they followed me when I came into the pen to feed them. They were a comfort and our friends.

"Who did this?" I cry to the mountain "Who did this? Was it a fox? Wild dogs? A bear?" Mira thought she saw a bear a few days ago, but I told her they would be hibernating. Now I wonder. The weather *is* unseasonably warm.

"It wasn't a fox or a coon," Danny says, looking at the carnage. "Either one could kill a few birds, but not so many."

"Let's get our chores done and get back inside," I say. "We'll try to catch the live chickens and put them in the barn when the rain slows. I don't have the heart for it now."

TWO HOURS LATER, Danny, Mira, Sunny, and I go out to clean up the mess. I let Susie stay in the house to fold laundry because she's too tenderhearted for a job like this.

The first thing I look for in the chicken yard is the killer's tracks, but the place is a mud pit. When Danny and I first discovered the bloodbath, we were too shocked to investigate; now the rain has washed away any evidence of the predator.

After we capture the live hens and put them in an empty stall in the barn, we take the five mostly intact dead chickens and hang them above the barn door to clean and pluck later. If nothing else we can make a big stew.

"What should we do with the rest of the remains?" Sunny asks, picking up some entrails on the end of her shovel.

"Burn them, I guess. I have no heart for digging a grave and we can't leave the carcasses lying around to attract more night killers. Let's bring the scrap lumber from the old barn roof and make a fire."

For almost an hour, we throw the remains of our birds— wings, yellow legs, and whole heads—on the blaze. The stench of burning feathers and flesh is a bad one, so I send the kids inside and tend the fire myself, pulling my scarf up over my nose. Three Legs is with me, and his neck bristles as he paces back and forth.

When I go in, I get Dan's rifle down from the highest shelf in the pantry and clean it. I've not used a gun since

Bitsy taught me to shoot, down on the banks of the Hope River, but if I see the predator, I'll use it.

Attack

*B*y afternoon the sun has come out and the girls are out playing in the yard, so I pick up the phone to call the courthouse.

"Hi, Ada," I say. "This is Patience Hester. I'm trying to arrange for a crew of POWs to come back to the farm to rebuild the porch. I don't know if you heard. A tree fell during the ice storm. I've got the money now."

"I'm sorry, Patience," Ada says. "You know how it is. At first everyone feared the Germans, thought they were all evil Nazis. Now *everyone* wants them. I have a list a mile long, but I'll put you on it. You want those same fellows? That went okay, right?"

"Yes, the barn looks good. My son, Danny, even taught them a few words of English."

"That's still a big problem. Only the simplest tasks can be done because no one speaks German, so the more complicated projects are sitting on hold."

"How's Ollie doing?" I ask. "We saw you at the live nativity scene on Christmas Eve."

"Well, he's adjusting, if that's what you mean, and his stump is mostly healed. He loves taking care of the baby and can even change a diaper with one hand. Sometimes, he wakes in the night crying, though, and I don't know what to do. . . ." She stops and I can hear a voice in the background.

"Hey, Patience," she says, "I gotta go, I have another customer. I'll call as soon as I can get you scheduled, but it won't be for a week, maybe longer."

I hang up and that's when I hear barking. Looking out, I see Three Legs crouched in the yard with his fur standing up. *What the hell?*

"Mom!" Mira yells.

The first thing I do, when I see the dogs out the window, is head for the back door, but I'm forced to reverse my path when I realize the fallen tree still blocks the way. By the time I get to the front door, Danny is right behind me.

"Sunny, Susie, and Mira!" The three girls crouch on the lawn, clinging to one another, and Three Legs, stiff with fury, is facing four growling beasts. These are dogs, but not normal dogs. They're rangy and matted, with white fangs that snap. The wild animals circle the children, getting closer, taking turns lunging at Three Legs, who growls back just as savagely.

"Danny, get my walking stick and bring some kind of weapon for yourself."

"The gun, Mom?"

"No, not the gun. The dogs are in too close, I don't want to hit Three Legs or the girls."

"Sunny, Sue, Mira! Stand up tall. The wild dogs will be more intimidated if you don't look so little . . . Back, you vicious varmints!" I yell, waving my hands, and when the girls rise, Mira puts her arms over her head and starts singing in the loudest voice she has.

"*I'll fly away, oh Lord. I'll fly away. When I die, halle-lujah by and by. I'll fly away!* Sing, everyone!" she orders.

I take off my apron and wave it at the animals. "Git! Git!" And for a moment the dogs slink off, but then the one that looks like a gray wolf lunges back.

Three Legs whirls and hits him with his shoulder, but with only three feet on the ground, he's unstable and falls. The wolf dog comes back again, but Danny, running from the kitchen, without even thinking, drops the broom, strikes the wolf dog with the pole, and puts himself in the center of the ambush with the girls. Now there are four children circled by raging beasts.

The broom, Danny's second weapon, is lying in the wet yellow grass and I pick it up and wave it around. A big black bearlike dog snarls at me and dives for the handle, but I swing it away. Then a dirty white terrier goes for my ankle. I kick him like a football and he wails, but he's soon back.

Finally, a dirty brown beagle gets Three Legs down and goes for the throat. Both dogs' eyes are wide with fear and anger. Their white teeth flash the air and then I see blood. The smell makes the dogs more ferocious. One of them catches the hem of Sunny's coat, but Danny clubs him with the heavy walking stick and he backs off.

Susie screams, "Make them stop, Mama. Make them stop!" Danny and Sunny are yelling in their loudest imitation of their father. "Git. Git, you son of a bitch! Git!"

I have to do something or this is going to end like last night's chicken slaughter.

"Here, Sunny, take the broom." I toss it over and she catches it in midair and starts wildly whacking whichever animal is closest. "I'll bring Pa's gun!"

Running for the house, I'm surprised at my speed, even with my bad knee. When I get back, Three Legs is lying on the ground, gurgling blood, but still he tries to defend his family. He growls and snaps at the terrier that's chewing on his hind leg and finally gets his teeth on the terrier's neck in a death grip.

I fire once into the air and the dogs all jump and stare at me, but when I fire again, nothing happens. *Now what?* The dogs and children are in such a tight bunch, I dare not shoot at them. My only chance is if I can draw the varmints away, but it's dangerous. Finally, I have no choice. The black dog leaps over Three Legs and is five feet from Mira. I back toward the barn door, where we've hung the five chickens we saved for stew birds.

"Here, doggies!" I call, swinging a bird by its neck so they can see. "Here, doggies! We know you love chicken." The canine that looks like a small black bear turns, sniffs the air, and leaves the pack. I throw the chicken on the ground and back away so the animal will think it's free food and when he pounces on it, I shoot. *Crack!*

"One down!" I yell like it's a game.

"Yay, Ma!" Danny hollers.

I pick up the chicken and dangle it out again. "Here, canines," I encourage, hoping another animal will fall for the ruse, and the brown beagle goes for it. *Crack!* Another dog falls.

"Hot-diggity!" Mira crows.

There are only two final monsters and one, the terrier, is almost gone, still held in the jaws of the dying Three Legs. "Wallop the wolf, Danny," I yell. "Hit him so hard he'll see stars."

"Stand back, sisters," Danny says, winding up like he's going to hit a baseball coming fast. *Whack!* he blasts the animal up in the air. The creature whines, lands on his side about twenty feet away, and *bam!* I shoot him in the head.

"Is everyone okay?" I ask in the sudden quiet, after laying my firearm on the lawn and running forward. Susie and Mira are crying. Sunny is white as a sheet, but Danny is wound tight with fury. He takes his pocketknife out and finishes the terrier.

Then we all look at Three Legs. The gash on his throat, inflicted by the fierce wolf dog, has drained him. I kneel down and take Three Legs's head in my lap. "Poor brave puppy," I say.

He wags his tail once and then he is dead.

At bedtime, we pray for our brave dog. "Dear God," Susie says. "Thank you for giving us Three Legs. He was a great friend. He protected us and he died in battle, just like a soldier. Please keep him at your side until we come to you."

"*Glory, glory, hallelujah,*" Mira sings, and we all join in. "*Glory, glory, hallelujah. Glory, glory, hallelujah. His truth goes marching on!*"

Upstairs, I open my journal and sit with the pillows piled behind me in the bed. The experience with the wild dogs has affected us all in different ways. The girls are nervous and won't go out alone. Sunny keeps asking if we can get rabies from their saliva, and Danny can't stop talking about the incident as if the dog fight were a battle in the war.

Me . . . when I look out the window at Spruce Mountain, despite the raging war in Europe, Asia, and Africa, I am surprised to feel peace. This winter, I have survived an auto accident, a blizzard, and an ice storm, but in battling the wild dogs I've found a part of myself that I thought was lost.

I'm a woman alone with four children, but I can endure. The warrior once lost has returned.

58

January 10, 1942

Frau Chef

Today dawned gray and windy, but it was the first day of school after winter break and I drove the children over to Hazel Patch. Everyone was excited to hear about the execution of the wild dogs, and I felt like Annie Oakley, female sharpshooter of the Old West.

Back home, I fed the half dozen chickens that are still alive, put a load in the Maytag, and carried all the Christmas things up to the attic. Just as I was coming down the stairs, I was surprised to hear a familiar cadence.

"*Eins—zwei—drei—vier. Eins—zwei—drei—vier.*" Then in English, even louder, "One—two—three—four. One—two—three—four."

Heavy boots marched across the wooden bridge. It's the POWs, but Ada was supposed to call me!

The hair on the back of my neck rises. This time I really *am* alone, no Mr. Roote for a chaperone, not even Danny and the girls . . . but I'm tired of being afraid . . . so I take a deep breath, grab a sweater, lift up my chin, and go out to greet them. I'm *the Woman Boss*, I remember!

Standing in the yard are six German men in denim uniforms, including Leopold and Eckhart.

"*Frau Chef!*" All the men salute me. "We greet you as a friend!"

"Where are your guards?" I ask them. "There are supposed to be two guards."

The men look confused and shrug their shoulders. Then Leopold sees the fallen tree on the porch and the pile of lumber. "We work?" he asks, and I observe he's picked up a few more words in English.

I have no drawings prepared this time, but I pantomime what I want them to do, cut up the tree, remove it and reconstruct the porch roof. Then I take the men to the barn and show them Dan's tools and the lumber that Sadie brought.

When Eckhart takes charge, I head outside to hang out the laundry. It's another unseasonably balmy day, but I'm getting used to it. Already the hills are greening and though I know winter is not over, maybe we're through the worst of it.

Not long ago, this situation would terrify me. The men now have access to potentially deadly weapons—hammers, saws, and crowbars. They could kill me and escape. Back in the kitchen I glance at the highest shelf, where I keep the gun, but I don't get it down.

Moments later, there's the sound of a motor. It must be the army guards that always transport the POWs, but when the brown military vehicle bumps across the bridge, there's only one sentry. He's a thin man with his helmet pulled low. He gets out slowly and salutes, then he smiles a familiar crooked smile.

Light

*D*an hugs me so hard his plaster cast digs into my back, and the young Germans laugh as they watch from the barn. "Hurrah!" they call. "Hurrah! Hurrah!"

"But how? How can you be here?"

He puts a finger to my lips. "Let me be sure the boys have everything they need and then I'll explain. Do you have food? They'll need a midday meal. I told Ada Mullins not to call because I wanted to surprise you."

Quickly, he explains in German where to put the branches and trunk of the willow tree and where to pile the scrap lumber from the porch, then he comes inside. "Tea?" I ask. "We're out of coffee and I didn't get a new ration card in the mail."

"Tea's fine." While I'm in the kitchen he builds up the fire, then we sit down on the sofa, shoulders touching.

"How did this happen? Is it just temporary, or are you free?"

"Not exactly free." He touches my neck, then smells my hair. "I've missed you . . ." Then he tells the story. "You knew Reverend Miller and the sheriff came to see me at the prison?"

"I knew they were planning on it, I didn't know when."

"Well, a few days ago, Hardman, the Reverend Miller, and Billy Blaze showed up at Moundsville. They had it all planned, a three-prong attack, performed with military precision. The pastor sat at my bedside in the infirmary and told me how the farm work, being a mother, and worry were seriously grinding you down.

"He described how your knee was hurting again and how another storm had damaged the house. He convinced me that the moral thing, in this case, was to compromise my beliefs and sign myself out as a conscientious objector willing to do public service. He even brought the registration forms required by the draft board.

"Meanwhile, Sheriff Hardman and Bill Blaze met with the warden and made a pitch that I be transferred back home to be assigned as a translator at the White Rock Prisoner of War Camp. Billy Blaze threatened that he'd write an exposé about the unsafe conditions at the Moundsville Prison if the warden refused."

"That's all it took?"

"Not quite. We didn't want to tell you anything until Mr. Linkous met with Judge Milbank to be sure he'd change my sentence. I now have *one year* of public service at the POW camp."

There's a crash as the men saw through the big branch and it falls the rest of the way through the porch. Dan runs outside to be sure everything's okay and I can hear him talk to the men in German again. They answer in German and go back to work.

"Except for the porch, the place looks fine," he says when he returns. "Kids at school with Mrs. Miller?"

"It's their first day back after winter break. They'll be so excited you're home. We prayed for you every day. How long can you be here?"

"Just eight hours this time, and then maybe tomorrow if the men don't finish by five . . . I prayed for you too and for the kids and for the men at war on both sides. I prayed for my fellow jailbirds. There is so much misery in the prison, Patience."

Another crash breaks our conversation. "Are you sure they're okay?" I ask.

"Yeah, they seem to know what they're doing, but I'll check on them again, then let's go up the mountain, where it's quieter."

"It's gray and cold out there."

"Not so bad . . . We can take a quilt and snuggle." He grins and raises his eyebrows like a comedian.

"Daniel! With German soldiers just yards away?"

"I can watch them at a distance and they'll call if they need anything." He looks at the clock on the mantel. "We have two hours before the noon meal."

While Dan goes outside to supervise again, I quickly check the pantry to see what sort of food I can rustle up. I have a few cans of pork and beans and some freshly baked bread that will go with the homemade butter and cheese. I can get canned pickles and canned peaches out of the cellar . . . but nothing for dessert. Then I remember the decorated Christmas cookies Mrs. Miller gave me. There are still a few dozen left in the tin.

"Ready?" Dan calls, standing out in the yard. I grab my old farm coat and the flying goose quilt and hurry out to him.

"You're too thin," I say, looking up at Dan. He's wearing a blue denim shirt and a denim jacket, the same as the prisoners, but he has two white armbands. The one on the left says TRANSLATOR. The one on the right says GUARD.

"Don't they feed you in prison?" We hold hands as we take the path to the upper pasture, and I only ask him to slow down one time.

"Yeah. Three meals a day, but sometimes they were so bad, I couldn't eat them. Ronald, my roommate, got the leftovers."

"Ronald the rat?" I repeat.

Daniel nods, takes my face in his hands, and kisses me. "Yeah, I gave him to Bones when I left. . . . I'm sorry I put you through so much, Patience. I didn't know how hard it would be." We kiss again.

"I like it out here," Dan says, spreading the quilt on the flat rock we sat on so many times before. Below, us the Germans work diligently. One fellow takes a break, wipes his face with a bandanna, and looks up at us. "Woman Boss!" he yells, and salutes.

"I greet you as a friend," I yell back. Then, sitting next to Dan, I say what I've been thinking ever since he told me how he was released. "I hope signing the CO form and the draft registration doesn't weigh on your conscience. . . ."

"No. Now that I'm out, I see that I can do more good here. I'm teaching the POWs English and trying to get their workforce organized. My goal is for the young Germans to see we're more alike than we're different; same with the locals. Getting to know each other might make it harder to kill each other. We have only one world and we're in this together."

"I'm so tired of hate," I confess. "Hating the Germans. Hating the Japanese. Sometimes even hating you. Carrying it around wears me out."

"Drop the hate, Patience . . . It's our job to be happy. I learned that in prison. Every stinking day I was there, I tried to remember . . . It's our job to be happy and to love."

The echo of the German men singing rings off the mountain and the earth smells like wet dirt and growing things. Suddenly the clouds part and a golden shaft illuminates the river, a ribbon of light that winds through the valley.

"It's strange," I say, taking Dan's hand. "The drums of war still roar, but even in these dark times, the Hope is still here."

About the author

2 Meet Patricia Harman

About the book

3 Q&A with Patricia Harman

7 Reading Group Discussion Guide

9 Historical Photographs

Insights,
Interviews
& More . . .

Meet Patricia Harman

PATRICIA HARMAN, CNM, got her start as a lay midwife on rural communes and went on to become a nurse-midwife on the faculties of Ohio State University, Case Western Reserve University, and West Virginia University. She lives near Morgantown, West Virginia, has three sons, and is the author of two acclaimed memoirs. Her first novel, *The Midwife of Hope River,* was successful around the world. ∽

Callie Lindsey Photography

Q&A with Patricia Harman

Q: It's been a while since we've visited Hope River. What drew you back to Patience, her town, and her friends? Were there any challenges specific to setting the book on the home front during World War II?

A: As the author of the Hope River novels, I have come to love and admire the characters in the books. I missed them and wanted to find out what they would be up to in a time of upheaval, conflict, and worldwide turmoil. In my stories, I like to look at big events and imagine how they'd affect ordinary people on the local level. The challenge, as always, in writing historical fiction is doing the extensive research that goes with it, but I don't mind because I learn so much. ▶

Q&A with Patricia Harman *(continued)*

Q: Daniel is a conscientious objector. We haven't gotten many stories of C.O.s during World War II. Perhaps we think of objectors as more of a Vietnam War phenomenon. Daniel is actually patriotic, in that he fought in World War I and he does believe in his country, but he just doesn't believe in fighting another war. Can you talk a bit about the situation with conscientious objectors during WWII and what they faced?

My husband and many of my men friends were conscientious objectors during the war in Vietnam. Some served time in prison for their beliefs; a few went to Canada. I was a pacifist in those days too and we had the honor of meeting many of the older men from the War Resisters League, the Committee for Non-Violent Action, and Peacemakers who, like Daniel Hester, refused to fight in WWII. Their courage and dedication were so profound it humbled me.

Q: Patience is still a midwife, but the role of the medical community in childbirth changes substantially after the Great Depression. Why do you think women were so quick to hand their care over to the primarily male doctors at that time?

A: There were a number of reasons that women in the 1940s began to give birth in the hospital with male physicians. First, during the postwar period, roads improved in rural areas and hospitals became more accessible.

Women were convinced that hospital births were safer. Prominent physicians, like Dr. Joseph DeLee, the author of the most important obstetric textbook at the time, described childbirth as a pathologic process that damaged both mothers and infants. Because of that view, he said, only physicians should be allowed to deliver babies and the midwife should be abolished.

Women wanted to seem modern and informed. They heard about twilight sleep and knew they could only get it at the hospital. Twilight sleep was an amnesiac that gave laboring women the illusion of short painless labors, but the truth was they just couldn't remember a thing. They suffered tremendously and were often strapped down because they were uncontrollable. They still had pain and were treated like wild animals.

Finally, the American Medical Association actually did a publicity campaign to discredit midwives, portraying them as dirty, out of date, and untrained. It wasn't until British obstetrician Dr. Grantly Dick-Read's book *Childbirth Without Fear* came out in 1942 that women began to question what they'd been told about the process of childbirth and began to take back control of the experience and look for providers who would support them. Sometimes they found a midwife, sometimes a doctor, but ▶

they demanded to be treated with respect.

Overall, 80 percent of babies are currently born into the hands of midwives, so Dr. DeLee's scorn for midwifery has not held the profession back as much as one might think. In the United States obstetrics is still dominated by physicians, but as the Cesarean section rate hovers at 30 percent, more pregnant women are looking for midwives who will support them in their hope to deliver naturally.

Q: Let's talk about Bitsy a bit. She comes back to the United States, and to the South, after what sounded like a pretty delightful life in Paris. The folks in Hope River seem mostly open to Bitsy, but do you think her experience was unique?

A: Bitsy had to get out of Europe. Hitler was approaching Paris. She returned to the only home she'd known. West Virginia is not the Deep South. People are mostly open-minded and judge their neighbors by how hard they work and what they contribute to the community. West Virginians are not color-blind, but race is a minor factor. Integrity, generosity, and a good sense of humor seem to matter more. Also, Bitsy, for a year or so, had helped many of the Hope River families have their babies and she was remembered, respected, and loved by many. ⮑

Reading Group
Discussion Guide

1. When Patience is reunited with Bitsy after nearly a decade she thinks, "Have you ever noticed that when you're reunited with an old friend, someone you've been through hard times with, it's like you've never been apart?" Discuss times in your life where this has been true, or not true.

2. How did you feel about Daniel and his refusal to fight? Do you think his feelings were justified? Why or why not? Our history books tend not to talk about the conscientious objectors in World War II; why do you think this is?

3. It's difficult for us today to face the suspicion and hatred citizens of the United States felt for the Japanese at the time. In what ways does the novel address this?

4. Daniel and Patience both try to live life as usual: Daniel with his vet practice and Patience with her midwifery practice. Is this realistic in a time of war, even on the home front? Why or why not?

5. Were you surprised at how the community for the most part accepts Bitsy's "adoption" of Willie and her marriage to Lou? ▶

6. We may think of opioid addiction as a modern-day issue, but it's clear that Daisy is a drug addict. Did this surprise you? What other situations in the novel strike a chord similar to modern-day events? Even though decades have passed, have people and their situations essentially changed from the 1940s to now?

7. Have you ever taken an unpopular position in a group? Maybe you felt strongly that something was unfair or wrong and though you were nervous or scared you had to speak up. What were the results? Can you share the story?

8. At the novel's end Daniel tells Patience it's their job to "be happy and to love." In what ways is this possible during a time of war? What do you think might be next for Patience, Daniel, and their children? ∾

Historical Photographs

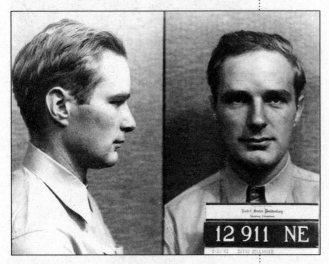

Dave Dellinger, who drove an ambulance in the Spanish Civil War and studied at Yale, Oxford, and the Union Theological Seminary, was born into a wealthy family. In 1940 when he told his father he was going to refuse to register for the draft, his father threatened to kill himself. Dellinger was sent to federal prison for his beliefs.

Historical Photographs *(continued)*

The U.S.S. *West Virginia* in flames after the attack on Pearl Harbor, December 7, 1941.

Japanese American family awaiting evacuation to an internment camp, World War II.
(Photo credit: Dorothea Lange)

Japanese Americans arriving at a concentration
camp in Tule Lake, California, 1943.
(Photo credit: Densho via courtesy of the National
Archives and Records Administration, Number G-575)

Posters recruiting both men and women
to serve in the war were everywhere.

Twenty thousand conscientious objectors served as medics in World War II.

Adolf Hitler takes Paris, June 1940.